LEGACY

LUCY ROY

Legacy

A Tessa Avery Spinoff

E-book ISBN: 978-1-955556-05-7

Paperback ISBN: 978-1-955556-03-3

Hardcover ISBN: 978-1-955556-04-0

Edited by: Autumn Reed

Cover design © Lucy Roy

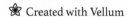 Created with Vellum

To my girls
When I question myself, you're there to keep me going

ALSO BY LUCY ROY

The Tessa Avery Series

Chaos

Paradox

Entropy

Catalyst

Halfblood Rising

The Valkyrie's Bond

The Valkyrie's Calling

Stay up to date!

Newsletter: https://bit.ly/lucyroynewsletter

TikTok: @lucyroyauthor

Instagram: @lucyroyauthor

Lucy Roy – A Reader Group: https://www.facebook.com/groups/
LucyRoyReaders/

Lucy Roy's Facebook Page: https://www.facebook.com/AuthorLucyRoy/

Twitter: @LucyRoyAuthor

MAJOR GREEK GODS

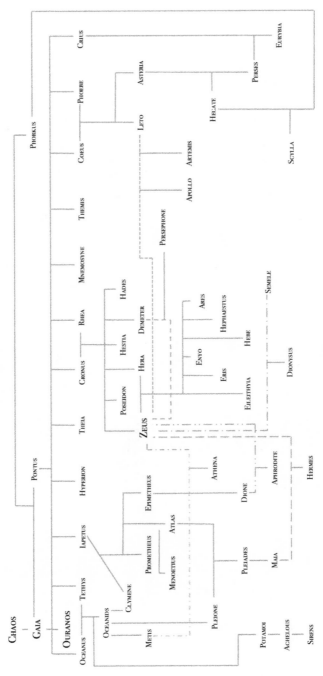

1

MARY

"Nock."

Fitting the small groove at the end of my arrow onto the string, I lifted my bow.

"Draw."

I took aim at my target one-hundred yards down the field and pulled back the string of my bow as far as it would stretch. My fingers itched to flex, the icy shaft of my arrow a numbing sting against the frigid Wyoming air.

Silence.

Flicking a glance at Susana, my trainer, I arched a brow.

"Hold..."

Gritting my teeth, I forced my hands to stay still. My fingers were starting to tingle with the cold, and I knew, immortal strength or not, numb fingers would make it almost impossible to maintain my grip on an arrow made of ice.

"Three more seconds."

Seriously?

"Loose!"

My bow string let loose with a soft *snap*, and I grinned in satisfaction when the arrow struck dead center. A moment later, the shaft crumbled, leaving the frozen head fully lodged in the target.

"Again."

I let the bow fall to my side and wiggled my fingers to regain some warmth, then looked at the skinny brunette who'd been making my life miserable the past three months. "My hands are numb. Can I switch to aluminum now?"

Susana folded her arms and shook her head. "You need to build up endurance, Mary. We've been over this."

"Yeah, that's great and all, but I also need to be able to feel my hands in order to shoot."

She pinched the bridge of her nose and huffed out a breath, which was a common occurrence with her. "Listen. I understand you were given carte blanche up on Olympus, but now that you've been assigned to my region, you need to play by my rules." She gave me a disparaging look. "And don't tell me your friends up there didn't expect you to bust your ass doing your best."

I snorted. "Have you met Chiron? Anything less than my best would've earned me extra track time." I shuddered as I thought about the massive stone track Ischyra recruits used to train on Olympus. It was great for both training and shredding your clothes and skin to bits if and when you fell.

Her lips twitched. "You shouldn't be surprised, then, when I push you as hard as he did."

Sigh. "What about gloves?"

"You've been in battle, Mary. Do you think gloves would've been appropriate?"

Shifting my bow to the other hand, I stared across the busy training field at the Ischyra headquarters just outside Jackson. I tried not to let her see the grimace brought on by her casual mention of one of the worst moments of my life. Other Ischyra, some recent arrivals and others who'd been in the field for centuries, were going about their daily exercise regimen. A fair number were doing weapons work, but most were, like me, working on honing their gods-given supernatural powers.

With a sigh, I looked back at Susana. "Yes, I've been in battle, but my part in that lasted all of two minutes. I shot like, six arrows. At the same target."

"You're talented enough that Artemis saw fit to gift you with a bow," she pointed out, gesturing toward the sleek piece of weaponry in my hand. "A high honor, one seldom bestowed upon an Ischyra. Certainly not one so recently transitioned."

"I didn't even see the main battlefield. I was clear across the world from where everyone else was fighting."

"Be that as it may, you've got a bit more experience with battle than most of the others here. You've taken on the biggest enemy we've ever had and won." She shrugged. "Expectations are higher for you, considering you haven't even been at this a year."

I held her stare for a moment, then turned and stepped up to my shooting line.

"Twenty rounds," she ordered. "Rapid succession. Then we'll discuss aluminum."

Gritting my teeth, I conjured up an ice arrow, freezing it to a rock-solid-and-nearly-unmeltable state, then lifted my bow.

My studio apartment at the Jackson headquarters was small but nice. A single room held a bedroom and small bathroom, both separated from the living area and a kitchenette by a half-wall. Two windows faced outward toward the training field, and one in the rear faced the mountains. There were no fancy decorations, just the basics. It was the opposite of me in pretty much every way, but I think that was why I liked it.

Technically, I was still finishing up my training year, one that had gotten cut short when the Ischyra on Olympus had been attacked by two Titans, slaughtering all twenty of my mentors and all but three of my fellow recruits. So, since there was barely a class left for me to train with, the other two survivors—my former roommates, Yana and Anette—were sent off to their own training facilities, while I was stationed on-compound in Jackson until Susana decided I was ready for real fieldwork. I had six months left in my training year, but she still hadn't even mentioned a move.

For now, though, the fact that I was working with real Ischyra and finally away from the lonely, depressing rock that Olympus had become for me was more than enough.

Even if it meant living alone. The jury was still out on whether that was a good thing or not.

I did have a TV, though, which was definitely a bonus. Despite its solar-powered Ischyra village, Olympus had exactly zilch in the way of digital entertainment.

As I walked across the compound to the housing area, I ran over the list of shows I'd added to my streaming watch list that had come out while I was training on Olympus. Of all the things that surprised me when I moved here, that surprised me the most. I'd missed out on a ton of good TV while I was on no-technology mountain, so I'd been spending my nights binging everything I could.

That plan was put aside when I stepped into my apartment and saw a familiar, green-eyed blonde waiting for me.

"Tessa!" Grinning, I launched myself at my best friend, throwing my arms around her in a hug as she caught me and squeezed. Stepping back, I held her at arms' length and gave her a questioning look. "What are you doing here? I thought you and Nate were globe-trotting or whatever."

Tessa shrugged. "He's waiting for me in Iceland. Athena needed to come by, and I haven't seen you in three months, Mare." She gave me a soft smile. "I miss you."

"I still don't get why you didn't wait till summer to go there," I told her, slipping out of my jacket and dropping it on one of the kitchen chairs before sitting down on the love seat in the living area. "January is definitely an equatorial time of year, and it's not like you don't have the time."

She laughed and sat down next to me. "We're going farther south next, but I wanted to see the Northern Lights first."

"You're a million years old. What's the rush?"

"I have a bucket list, Mare. A thousand things I want to see before I hit four thousand. Now, let's talk about you. How are things going here?"

I shrugged. "Okay, I guess. Susana is insisting on a shitload of endurance training." I wiggled my fingers. "After a hundred rounds with my ice arrows, my hands feel like they're going to fall off."

"Switch to something else?" she suggested. "Something you can wear gloves with?"

"Yeah, she mentioned switching to daggers next week. And full gloves will make it harder to interact with the arrow."

She gave me a crooked grin. "And here you thought having an affinity for water would be boring."

I rolled my eyes. Before going to Olympus, a water affinity—one of several powers elemental Ischyra could get—was the last thing I wanted. As it turned out, it wasn't only useful, but also pretty fun to play with.

Sometimes.

"Uh-huh. So, what did Athena need to come down here for?"

"Ischyra business," she replied airily. Casually, she flicked a curtain aside and looked out the small living room window. "Speaking of Nate . . . have you heard from Dionysus?"

I rolled my eyes. "Now and then. I haven't seen him since I left Olympus, though." Shifting in my seat, I stared at the door, not wanting her to see how much that fact irritated me. Dionysus and I had become pretty close in the aftermath of the attack on Olympus and my subsequent kidnapping. He'd been one of the main reasons I'd been able to dig myself out of the hole of shitty feelings I'd been confined to once I got back. And yes, I had feelings for him, no matter how vehemently I denied that to my friends. Tessa and our old roommate, Yana, saw straight through my bullshit, but they wisely didn't push the issue.

But regardless of his flirting, a fair few cuddle sessions, and spending nearly every day together for months, he never attempted so much as a kiss. I'd considered taking the reins and doing it myself, but the thought of ruining our friendship always stopped me. Once he got assigned to Germany by Zeus, he got so wrapped up in his work that I only talked to him a couple of times a month, at most.

"Huh." Tessa looked around the room, taking in my new living quarters. "Maybe he's waiting to find out where you get stationed before deciding where to settle down."

"He's a god, Tess. He can settle wherever and whenever he wants."

She smirked. "Uh-huh." Her eyes went distant for a second, then refocused. "Athena's on her way."

I frowned. "She's coming here? Why?"

Just then, the door opened and Athena, the petite, beautiful brunette and Nate's favorite sister, walked in.

I lifted my brows. "Come on in."

"Don't mind if I do," she said, then grinned and dropped down on the couch next to me. "How are you, Mary?"

"Dandy," I said. "You?"

"Happy to be off that damn mountain for a change," she muttered, then shot a glare at Tessa. "Not all of us get to go galivanting across the globe to celebrate our stellar victories."

"She's not wrong," I told Tessa.

"Having spent a few thousand years missing out on life, I won't apologize for taking advantage of my newfound ability to galivant," Tessa said primly.

"Anyway, on to why I'm here," Athena said, shifting to face me. "I've got an assignment for you, Mary."

My eyebrows shot up. "Seriously?"

"Seriously. I just wrapped up a meeting with Susana and her superior. I've informed them both you'll be leaving."

"That's . . . quick." I tried to wrap my head around leaving so suddenly, but my brain seemed to be shorting out a bit. "My training year isn't up yet."

"And I'm in charge of organizing Ischyra assignments." She gestured toward me with a long-fingered hand. "Like yours."

I bit my lip, not wanting her to see how excited that made me. "Where will I be going?"

"New York."

I wrinkled my nose. "City?"

"No, farther north. Have you heard of Lake Placid?"

"Lake Placid? Like where that hockey team did really well in the Olympics a million years ago?"

She paused, then frowned. "Setting aside my surprise that you even know that, yes, the very same. It's a lovely place."

"It was a great movie, too," I replied, grinning.

"Nate and I went to Lake Placid about a month ago to go skiing," Tessa said. "It's beautiful up there, Mare. You'll love it."

"You went skiing in New York? Why not the Alps or something?" I held up my hands before she could answer. "You know what, never mind." I looked back at Athena. "What will I be doing up there?"

"Well, one of my sisters has lost something. Two somethings, actually, and I thought you might be helpful in retrieving them."

I hesitated. "Which sister?" I didn't know any of her sisters all that well, but what I knew about them wasn't terribly nice.

"Aphrodite. I'll give you more details once we arrive, but we'd prefer to leave the gods out of direct engagement in this case. As an Ischyra, and a recently transitioned one, at that, it will be far simpler for you to infiltrate the life of the person we think stole it."

"Infiltrate?"

Across from me, Tessa grinned, and I realized she looked like she was about to burst.

"How'd you like to go to college, Mare?"

There was a heavy pause, then I squealed.

Yes, squealed.

Of all the things I felt I'd missed out on when I made my transition from human to Ischyra, going to college was the biggest. I'd always been quietly jealous of my human friends in high school as they met with guidance counselors, toured colleges, filled out applications, and picked majors. The whole process—picking a future instead of having it decided for me—was one I hadn't realized I'd wanted until it was really and truly an impossibility.

"I told you she'd be excited," Tessa said, grinning at Athena.

"I never should've doubted you."

"Are you guys serious right now? I get to go to college? Pick a major, pick classes, the whole nine?" I latched onto Athena's arm. "Athena, if you're messing with me . . ."

She laughed and patted my hand. "It came to my attention that you've always had an interest in that aspect of human life, so when Aphrodite asked for assistance, I immediately thought of you."

"Wait, what about the rest of my training?" I slumped back in my seat. "I still have almost six months to go."

"After a bit of deliberation and a very . . . emphatic recommendation from Chiron, the Elders and I feel you've more than demonstrated your abilities. You can continue to use the facilities at the compound in your region, if you'd like, but we're officially fast-tracking your training." She grinned. "Congratulations."

"You'll love it, Mare, really," Tessa said.

"Hang on." Narrowing my eyes, I looked back at Athena. "Whose life will I be inserting myself into?"

Tessa and Athena exchanged a quick look, Tessa's eyes widening almost imperceptibly.

"Spit it out, Avery."

Tessa sighed. "Her name is Calla Aiden, and she's the vice president of the South Lake University chapter of Iota Sigma Xi."

"Iota—you want me to join a sorority?" My eyes darted between the two of them. "You're joking, right?"

Athena winced. "Yes, Tessa mentioned that might be a bit of a . . . hang-up for you."

"Do you know how many rules those things have?" I cried. "Come on! They have *dress codes*, for fuck's sake!"

"To be fair, a good bit of rule-following could do you some good," Athena pointed out as she stood. "Anyhow, we should really get going. You're only a few days from the start of the spring semester, and you know nothing about the area."

"I—now?" I glanced around my small apartment at my belongings, meager as they were.

"Take what you need, of course, but trust me when I say your current wardrobe won't do where you're going."

I almost argued, then considered my collection of compression tights, joggers, and sports bras and figured she was probably right.

"Like you need an excuse to go shopping," Tessa said with an eye roll.

"I suppose conditions could be worse," I said primly. "All right, let me pack up a few things, and we can get on with it."

"Oh, and dress warm," Athena said. "It's frigid up there this time of year."

I sighed. "Lovely."

2

MARY

After packing up everything I owned and donning jeans and a down parka, Tessa and Athena teleported us to the small upstate New York town of Lake Placid. It was a beautiful town, small, with a shop-lined main thoroughfare that could only be described as quaint.

And it was cold. Like, really freaking cold.

"Uh, Tess? Does it ever warm up here?" I flicked a glance at the clock on a bank across the street. Ten degrees, and there was about a foot of snow on the ground.

"It'll warm up in the spring," Athena said.

"It's not too much different than the weather in Renville, really," Tessa said with a shrug, then surveyed our surroundings, considering. "A little colder, maybe. And they don't have to deal with the lake effect, so that's something."

Ignoring her shitty logic, I looked up at the building we stood in front of. It had a ski-lodge feel, with a high-pitched roof, dark exposed beams, and tall, angular windows. The first floor held a little café, and a wide balcony wrapped around the second floor. My mouth began to water as the smell of coffee and fresh-baked something hit my nostrils. "So, this'll be home?"

"There are two apartments upstairs," Tessa said. "We got you one overlooking the lake."

I nodded, then looked down the street at the quaint little village. It was easy to see why people would want to live here. "This place looks like a Hallmark movie."

Tessa laughed and Athena shook her head.

"Come on," Athena said. "Let's get you settled."

I followed her and Tessa up to the second-floor balcony, then around to the back of the building, where I stopped to stare over the rail at the large lake below that looked frozen solid.

"That's Mirror Lake," Tessa informed me. "Lake Placid is outside the main village."

I nodded, not caring a bit what the lake was called. It was the biggest body of water I'd been near in months, and all I wanted to do was pull out my magic and play. There were so many things I'd been wanting to try now that my work with weapons was coming along so well. Walking on water, making my own tidal waves, controlling the tides. I cast a glance at the mountains in the distance and wondered if it would be hard to make snow.

"It's perfect," I told her, smiling, suddenly not giving a single damn about the frigid temperature.

She grinned. "I knew you'd like it." Turning to the door, she inserted a key into the lock and pushed it open.

"We decided against getting you a roommate," Athena explained. "Unless you want one. There are Ischyra stationed in the area, so we could always reassign one, if you'd like."

"Nope." I stepped through the door and dropped my suitcase on the dark, hardwood floor. "I'd like to be able to walk around in my underwear without judgment, thank you."

She gave me an amused smile. "Well, what do you think?"

Tessa was practically bouncing with excitement, so I took in my new home. It had an open floor plan, so even though it wasn't the biggest, it felt roomy. The wall facing the lake was solid windows with blackout shades drawn all the way open to let in the afternoon light. The kitchen and dining area were separated from the living room by a cloud-like sofa. On the other side of the room, a gas fireplace was built into the wall with a TV mounted above it.

I grinned at both of them. "I love it."

"Perfect!" Tessa did a small clap. "Bedrooms and bathroom are back there," she said, pointing toward a hall that stretched away from the living room. "You've got the restaurant downstairs but no one next door. The owners are super sweet and think you're just a regular college student with rich parents who didn't want you rooming in the dorms."

Athena smoothed back her frizz-less brown hair and walked into the kitchen, where a stack of folders and a cell phone sat on the island.

"Your course schedule is here. As the spring semester starts in just a few days, I'd recommend making a run over to the campus tomorrow to get your texts and whatever else you might need." Reaching into the small brown pouch attached to her hip, she pulled out a credit card, a driver's license, and some kind of ID card. Holding up the credit card, she arched a brow. "This isn't unlimited, so don't get any ideas about buying out all the stores."

My eyebrows shot up. "The gods are giving me a credit card? And a cell phone? How very twenty-first century of you."

"You'll need both when you start making friends." Shaking her head, she held up the driver's license. "You do know how to drive, correct?"

"I—seriously?" I looked at Tessa, confused. "Yes, of course, I know how to drive." Sort of.

"Good. There's a car parked outside—"

My ears perked at that. "What kind?"

"A Volvo SUV. May I continue?"

I mimed zipping my lips, but I couldn't conceal my excited grin.

"Your family is supposedly very wealthy, and you live in an area that gets a good deal of snow. I'd recommend taking the shuttle to campus, though, because parking can be a disaster. "This—" Athena held up the ID card "—is your student ID. You are now twenty-one-year-old Mary Jameson of Reading, Pennsylvania, so get used to introducing yourself as such. You took a gap year, and your birthday is in December, which is why you're a twenty-one-year-old sophomore, in case anyone asks."

I tried not to be disappointed I hadn't gotten a more interesting name, but simpler was probably better.

"You'll need the ID on campus daily, so make sure you always have it. The credit card is for work-related expenses," she explained. "Use it for books, any additional clothes you might need now that you're back in society again, gas, and whatever you need to keep up appearances should you have guests, like food to stock the fridge."

"And here I thought you'd just leave me with a few gold bars to pawn if I needed money," I replied, smirking.

Ignoring me, Athena slid my schedule toward me. "Look this over; tell me if you have any questions. We chose courses we thought suited your interests but will also help make your assignment a bit simpler."

I picked up the paper, scanned the class list, and saw they'd registered me for biology, chemistry, physics, a sophomore writing course, and a literature class.

Curious, I skimmed the list of courses. "So, which major did you pick for me?"

"Bio. The girl you'll be following, Calla Aiden, is a political science major. She's picked up a biology minor this semester. You've been placed in two courses with her for now."

I cocked a brow at Tessa. "And that's why you chose me?"

"You would've picked a science major if you'd gotten the chance to go to college." Gesturing toward the schedule, she shrugged. "Now you can."

I bit my lip, then grinned. Tessa was one of only a few people who knew how much I liked science; chemistry, in particular. It had been my best subject in high school. I'd done so well that my teacher had recommended me for advanced placement organic chemistry my senior year. I'd been hesitant to take it, knowing it wouldn't lead to anything, but my guardians eventually talked me into it.

"Thanks," I said. "That really means a lot."

She slid her hands into her back pockets and smiled. "It's nothing more than you deserve, Mare. Enjoy being back out in the world."

"All right, now that that's settled," Athena said, "on to why you're here." She gestured toward the stools at the island and stood on the other side. Once we were settled, she slid another folder toward me.

"Two deific items have gone missing, both of which have recently been traced to this area. The first is Aphrodite's girdle, which Hera borrowed awhile back—"

"I'm sorry, what?" I stared at her, confused. "She borrowed her underwear?"

"You know, for such a smart girl, I'd think you'd be more well-versed in our history."

"Sorry. Continue."

"It's actually more of a sash," Athena continued. "A strap, if you will, that's worn around the lower torso and carries the power to induce love and desire. Hera often used it when she was helping married couples reconcile differences, but that ability is derived from the power of coercion that's interwoven in the fabric."

I nodded my understanding. "I can see why someone might want to get their hands on that."

"The last time Hera borrowed it was about ten years ago," Athena continued. "It's been missing since."

"Missing? Can't Aphrodite just . . . call it or something?"

"Normally, yes. That's the problem. Aphrodite's power ties her to it, yet she's lost all connection to it. The second item is a golden apple that also eventually found its way to Aphrodite. It originally belonged to Hera—"

"Oh!" I snapped my fingers. "I know that one! That's the one that started the Trojan War, right? Eris convinced what's his face to name Aphrodite as the prettiest, Aphrodite gave him Helen in return, and Helen's husband got pissy?"

Athena huffed. "His name was Paris, and yes, that's the one. My darling sister thought it would be amusing to imbue the apple with her discord and cause a fight between me, Aphrodite, and Hera just because she was insulted she hadn't been invited to a damn wedding." She reddened a bit at that, and I had to bite back a smirk because it was so rare for Athena to betray any significant emotion. "She didn't even *like* the humans whose wedding it was. My father could've just said Hera was the fairest, but no, he had to put a weak human to task—" Holding up a hand to stop herself, she took a deep breath. "Anyway. The apple went missing eons ago, but Aphrodite felt its pull right around the same time she felt that of her sash, so we're assuming they're together."

"So, what does the apple do? I know Eris used it to cause a fight, but I'm guessing that's not the only use?"

"No, it can be adapted to the user's whims. It can provide the user with immortality, love, health, wisdom, knowledge, power, anything you could wish for. Eris used it to start a war—"

"Well, she didn't, though," I amended. "Not really, anyway. She just wanted to start a fight between you three, right?"

Athena's jaw was so tight, I could've sworn I heard her teeth grind.

"Yes. And to be fair to Eris..." She inhaled slowly through her nose, as though those were the hardest words she'd ever uttered. "To be *fair*, my sister didn't intend for a war to happen. We had no idea just how quickly it could set a catastrophic chain of events in motion. But she did absolutely nothing to stop it once she realized Paris' intentions with Helen of Sparta, which, in my mind, was just as bad. Eris reveled in both it and the fact that she'd pulled one over on us."

"Sounds like Eris." Although it did seem as though she'd mellowed out some. Despite sucking up discord and conflict wherever she could, Athena's goddess-of-discord sister was actually kind of fun sometimes.

"The apple is technically Aphrodite's now because she was the winner of that contest," she continued, "but it went missing not long after. It's been sought after ever since, by gods and humans alike, and every time it makes an appearance, we either feel the call too late or the wielder manages to hide it before we can get to it."

"Where did Aphrodite last feel its presence?" I asked.

"Before now?" Athena frowned. "The last place was Mexico, but it's popped up in Ireland, Russia, China, Brazil, and I swear to the *gods,* Mary, if you say, 'Snow White's enchanted forest,' I will send you to Antarctica."

I forced my lips together to avoid laughing. "What I don't understand is, why do you want me to find these things?" I jerked my chin toward Tessa. "Sounds more like a job for a Mimic and her Coercer fiancé."

Tessa shook her head. "No, if the man we think took the sash was able to almost completely sever Aphrodite's magical ties to it, using deific power may not work."

"Who is he?" I asked. "And who severed her ties to the apple? I'm guessing that's why she only feels it now and then?"

"We're not sure who dealt with the apple, but it had to have been someone with deific power," Athena said. "As for the sash, the person who took it is named Stewart Aiden. And trust me, if Aphrodite could do it herself, she would. But even with a dampening charm on her power, Zeus didn't trust her to take on the job without letting her . . . emotions get in the way. So, we're going another route. When we discovered Stewart's daughter Calla was attending South Lake University, we saw an easy opening."

"For what?"

"To infiltrate Stewart's life and hopefully find and retrieve both items. Stewart is the president of South Lake University. Since Calla opted to attend SLU, getting close to her will be the best shot at getting close to *him*. We don't expect the sash or apple to be on campus, of course, but it's likely the girl knows where it is or how to find it. Or, at the very least, she can get you access to the Aidens' home to search for it."

"And I'm required to join her sorority? Doesn't that take time?" I held up a hand when annoyance flashed across her face. "I'm serious. I thought that was kind of a long process."

"Not really. Rush week is in two weeks. Pledging the same sorority as hers will make it easier for you to build the necessary friendships you need in order to gather the information we're looking for. You likely won't be a member long. At least, that's the hope."

Confused, I looked back and forth between them both as I tried to piece together what she was saying.

"Hang on, start over. So, Hera lost this bra—"

"Girdle."

"—sash thing of Aphrodite's a decade ago, and you want me to befriend the daughter of the person you think took it so I can spy on him in order to find both it and an apple that's been missing for nearly a thousand years?"

"Essentially, yes."

"It won't be as hard as you think," Tessa said. "Calla's pretty popular as it is, so it won't be difficult to get into her circle of friends. From there, you just have to move up, get as close to her as you can."

I nodded slowly. "Okay. So, what's this guy's deal, anyway? And how'd he get the drop on Hera? And why has it taken so long for you guys to start looking for them?"

"We've been looking," Athena said tiredly. "Aphrodite only recently felt the pull of both, stronger than she has in a long time, so we're assuming the objects were moved at that time, taken out from under whatever protections had been placed on them. It was brief, only a few hours, but she was able to trace the magic of both to the Aidens' home, although it wasn't quite strong enough for her to feel certain they were actually there. She returned to Olympus, told Zeus, but he forbid her from engaging directly."

"I bet that pissed her off," I murmured.

That drew a smile out of Athena. "As to your original question of how it was taken. Hera was drugged with a heavy dose of godsbane by the mistress of a man whose marriage she healed after he'd been unfaithful. We're not certain, but we now suspect the woman he cheated on his wife with was Missa Aiden, Stewart's wife."

"So, Hera got dosed by Calla's mom, who was cheating on Stewart with a married man who refused to leave his wife? I'm assuming Stewart put her up to it?"

"Yes, that's precisely what we think," Athena said with a nod. "The sash is incredibly valuable to a person who knows how to wield it. All he or she would need is a bit of godly power, and they'd be able to activate it."

"A bit of godly power?" My eyes widened. "Hang on. Are you telling me you're pitting me against a demigod?" There was no way they'd pit me against an *actual* god.

Tessa snorted, and Athena's mouth quirked in amusement. "'Pitting' is a bit of an exaggeration," Athena said. "We need you to gather information, that's all."

"Information that could help prevent another war," Tessa added. "Considering Stewart is a powerful demigod and in possession of both the gir-*sash* and apple, he'd be able to rally some pretty impressive forces if he wanted to."

"We need them in-hand," Athena said, "and that's going to require a long game, not a smash-and-grab like my sister would prefer. Newly minted Ischyra are perfectly suited for extended missions like this because it's easier for you to blend in as humans for long periods of time."

"It's unlikely he's much stronger than you," Tessa said. "But since his power is derived straight from Zeus—"

"Of course, it is," I muttered.

"—he'd have just enough power to activate and use the sash," Tessa said. She winced. "And . . . there's one other thing."

"What?" I asked.

"Missa Aiden is a witch," Athena said. "Not a very powerful one," she rushed to add when she saw the look on my face. "She's half human, so she can wield power over humans, but she won't be able to touch you." She pulled something from her back pocket and handed it to me. "Here, take this. It should make you feel a bit better."

Frowning, I opened my hand, and she dropped a necklace onto my palm.

"Whenever you wear that, your power and Ischyra mark will be concealed," she explained.

Picking it up, I examined it. It was gold, thin, and held a single charm—a golden apple.

I smirked. "That's a bit on the nose, don't you think?"

Athena's lips twitched. "You'll still be able to use your powers, but anyone who might be able to detect them won't be able to."

"Even gods?" I asked.

"Even gods."

"Put it on," Tessa said. "Let's see how it works."

Narrowing my eyes, I studied the inoffensive little chain, then slipped it over my head.

"Huh." Tessa frowned. "Weird."

"What?" I asked.

"Your essence . . . it's like you're just a human now. If I look hard enough, I can see it, but only because I know it's there."

"And I can't see a thing," Athena confirmed, squinting.

"Well, tell Hecate I said thank you," I said.

"You'd be fine no matter what," Tessa told me. Opening her arms, she pulled me into a hug. "I have to get going before Nate comes looking for me."

I rolled my eyes. "Tell him to hold his pretty horses. I haven't seen you in months."

"I'll check back soon, K?"

I patted her on the back and pulled away. "Sounds good." I sighed. "And tell your stupid fiancé I said hi."

She laughed. "Will do."

After a quick farewell to Athena, Tessa teleported away.

"I just have one question," I said once she was gone. "Obviously, these things need to be returned to Olympus. I get that. But what makes you so sure Stewart will just drop his desire to have them? If he can rally forces, wouldn't he do just that to get them back?"

Athena nodded. "Yes, if we allowed him to go back to his normal life. The objects will be returned, and he will be imprisoned. He's a demigod, and as such, is held to different laws and rules than humans. Once we have proof that he's in possession of the items, he'll be taken to Olympus to stand trial and be sentenced."

I grimaced. I didn't even know the guy, and I'd only spent a few minutes in a holding cell in the dungeons at the palace, but I could only imagine how awful the conditions would be for someone who'd actually committed a crime.

Flashes of the cell I'd been kept in for weeks flashed through my mind, but I quickly shoved them back and focused all my attention on Athena.

"One other question. What exactly do you think Stewart is going to do with the sash and apple if he has them?"

Athena shrugged. "We're not sure. There's been discussion of him running for some type of office, and the last thing we need is a demigod powered by objects meant for manipulation in any kind of elected position. He could start a feud between two countries just as easily as Eris did."

"Anything else I need to know?" I asked, forcing myself not to think about all of that.

She slid a stack of thick folders toward me, then fanned them out. "These contain all the information we have on the Aidens," she said, indicating the first three. "These last two are a crash course on sorority life and more detailed information on the girdle and apple." She looked at me, her gray eyes serious. "This is espionage, Mary, pure and simple. You need to know every aspect of this assignment, and that requires a good deal of studying. You'll also be expected to keep your grades up. Do you think you can handle that?"

"That depends. Can I put a ban on the word 'girdle' in my apartment?"

She huffed out a laugh. "Fine. Now, you'll get more information in the coming days. As it comes in, it will be delivered to you if we deem it necessary."

"K. I'll head to campus tomorrow so I can get a feel for the place, and I'll study up as much as I can between now and when classes start." I sighed when I saw her brows draw together. "I can handle this, Athena. Joking aside, I promise I won't let you down, okay?"

She flashed me a smile. "I know, Mary. I have the utmost faith in the decision to place you here. The biggest thing you need to remember on day one is that one of Calla's duties is to recruit girls to rush her sorority. You need to make yourself as presentable and appealing as possible so you can endear yourself to her. Oh!" She leaned down and picked up a sleek black messenger bag. "Here's a laptop. You'll be doing a lot of research, and you'll most definitely need it for school."

Grinning, I took the bag, then opened it up and pulled out the slim, gray computer. "So fancy," I said, opening the lid. Almost instantly, it flickered to life.

"Don't break it." She tapped her temple. "If you need anything, just call."

"Will do."

3

DIONYSUS

I scowled down at the yellow notepad on my desk. I didn't know why I bothered reviewing the notes from the department meeting I'd just come from, considering my memory was damn near perfect. It gave me something to do, though, which I guess was reason enough. In the past few months since my father had stationed me at a small university in Berlin, the days had been blurring together. More and more, I'd been finding myself searching for something to differentiate one day from the next, but I always came up empty.

I flipped through the pages of the notepad that listed the tactics the student health center was using to address the needs of those affected by the war that had been led by Cronus last summer. Olympus's war. *Our* war.

We'd decided on safe spaces, group and private therapy sessions, online chats where students who wanted to remain anonymous could address their fears and concerns, virtual therapy sessions for students who couldn't make sessions during office hours, and opening the center to outside students who felt they weren't getting the help they needed at their own schools. They were all great ideas, and I fully expected us to be able to help a lot of people. We were doing good work, better than a lot of other universities, and to be a part of that was something that made me proud.

Despite that, I couldn't stop thinking about Mary and how I felt like I was failing her, sitting here half a world away. I hadn't checked in on her in a couple of weeks, but it seemed every time I got a free moment, my head just wasn't there. The sadness of the students who came to visit me every day was so damn draining, and it made it hard to do anything but brood.

I didn't want to talk to anyone. And I didn't want to pass this shitty mood on to anyone else.

I knew damn well Mary didn't need to be checked on. I'd never known someone to bounce back, *truly* bounce back, after major trauma like she had. She'd been kidnapped, had her power siphoned, her friends had been killed, and she'd joined Tessa in striking the killing blows that had ended the war, all within the span of just a few weeks.

The fact that she'd been adamant that I stop using my power to help her after the war still took me by surprise. It had been an uphill struggle for her after that, but she did it. She still had nightmares, even if she didn't tell me, but from what I could feel, she'd learned some damn good coping techniques along the way to help work her way out of any hole she fell in.

I leaned back in my chair and tapped my pen on the desk, trying not to picture what had been done to her, the memories I'd seen in Nathaniel's head when he'd examined her mind as she lay unconscious on his couch. From that first day, I'd had this overwhelming need to make sure she was whole, to be near her. I would give anything to return to those days before the war, when we were carefree and she was practicing her powers on me, slapping me in the face with water ropes and drenching me with basketball-sized orbs of water.

The last thing I had expected was to fall for her.

Or, more accurately, to realize I'd *been* falling for her for a long time now.

Fuck, I missed her.

There was a knock at the door, dragging me from my ruminations.

"*Eintreten!*" I called, slipping into my best German.

The door opened and a student walked in. He was tall, lanky, with dark brown hair, and oozed sadness.

I bit back a sigh, then forced the brightest smile I could muster. "Hi! What can I do for you?"

He gave me a wary smile. "Hi, Dr. Ostrand. Do you have a few minutes?"

I smiled warmly. "Absolutely. Take a seat . . .?"

"Ben," he said, reaching out to shake my hand. He set his bag on the floor and sat down on the sofa across from my desk.

I reached out with my mind to feel him out and saw exactly what was bothering him. Bracing myself, I smiled again. "What can I do for you, Ben?"

He stared down at his hands clasped in his lap and hesitated. I waited patiently—this was always the hardest part. He'd tell me eventually, but I was the first person he was bringing his fears to, and vocalizing them for the first time was always a struggle.

"Last summer . . ." He let out a breath and clenched his hands into fists, then met my eyes. "Last summer, those things that came through Western Europe, the ones who were poisoning everything?"

I nodded. "The Telchines."

"The Telchines," he whispered. "Right. They came through my town and . . ." When he pressed his lips together, I sent a bit of calming magic toward him. "They killed my sister," he said quietly.

My heart clenched as his pain broke through my shields just a bit. "I'm so sorry to hear that, Ben."

"It wasn't just her," he continued, his words coming more freely now. "It was her entire school. They poisoned the well her school used. They didn't even have to *drink* the water, just get near it and—" His breath hitched. "It just . . . all of them were dead within hours. They managed to get a few to the hospital, but by then, it was too late."

He went quiet for a moment, then his eyes met mine. "My sister had asked to stay home from school that day, but our mother wouldn't let her. I walked her there, and when we were at the gates, she begged me to skip school with her, to keep it a secret, go off and have an adventure."

Guilt pressed toward me, wafting off of him in waves.

He wiped his eyes with the back of his hands. "I haven't told anyone and it's been eating at me for *months*. If I'd just done that one little thing she wanted, she'd be here and I—" His words broke off with a hitching breath, and I sat quietly, waiting for him to bring himself under control. It wasn't something I could do for him.

"Sometimes," I said after he settled down a bit, "it's easier to blame ourselves for these things when the perpetrators aren't immediately available. It's easier to punish ourselves than the ones who are truly deserving." I gave him a soft smile. "It's a perfectly normal reaction, Ben."

"So, what do I do?" he asked. "How do I stop this . . . feeling from consuming me?"

"We start by talking about it. For as long as you need."

"As long as you need" ended up being approximately three hours, but seeing Ben walk out of my office a bit lighter than when he came in made the emotional burden I'd taken on well worth it. It would take time for him to return to any semblance of normal, but he'd taken the first step today, which was the most important one.

That heaviness he'd left me with had just reaffirmed what I'd already figured out, though.

I needed to get the fuck out of this place.

The small, confining space of my office suddenly felt suffocating under the weight of all that grief. I had another meeting in an hour, but I knew I'd be useless. After sending my supervisor a quick email letting her know I'd be unavailable, I packed up my leather messenger bag with my laptop and the notes I'd taken earlier, then shut off the light and left my office. I loved helping people, I really did, but sometimes it got to be a bit much. Too much. Especially when helping them find happiness was pretty much impossible.

Once I made it to my car in the lot—teleportation wasn't an option, considering I was supposed to be fully human here—I leaned my head against the headrest and closed my eyes. A moment later, I felt the presence of my brothers in my mind.

'You're brooding,' Hermes said. 'I can feel you brooding, and I'm on the other side of the world. It's literally keeping me from concentrating on this very important conversation I'm having regarding the recruits' unhappiness with the quality of their dormitory food.'

I smiled. Last I'd heard, he was in New Zealand playing go-between for Zeus and the Ischyra there. Another stupid errand on my father's part, but his paranoia had kicked up a lot since last year, when he found out there was a rebellion launching against him. So, despite our squashing of said rebellion, we Elders had been assigned to do more menial tasks than we normally would, simply because Father thought the world was still out to get him.

'Leave him alone,' Nathaniel said tiredly. He always sounded tired when he dealt with us, like *he* was the big brother and not the other way around. 'D, if you're that unhappy there, leave. Zeus will get over it. Tell Athena or Apollo to work their magic and get you reassigned.'

'Apollo will do exactly fuck-all to help make my life easier, and Athena might have my balls if I ask.'

'I think you underestimate how much our sister likes when her brothers are happy,' Hermes said. 'And since when do you get this worked up over a woman?'

'I'm not worked up over a woman,' I muttered. 'This has nothing to do with Mary.'

'Liar,' he replied. 'I don't get it. You've had plenty of other lovers. Just go find another one, get your mind off the one you're too much of a bitch to actually talk to.'

'Asshole. I'm not telling Athena to get me reassigned just so I can be near Mary, and I'm not running out to find a distraction fuck.'

'So, you admit you'd want to be reassigned so you could be near her?

And that you need a distraction from her?' Hermes's tone was teasing now.

'Shut up.'

'Touchy.'

'Tell Athena you want to be reassigned—' Nathaniel suggested *'— because you're absolutely miserable, and your brothers would love to stop hearing about said misery for a while. Gods, you two are like children.'*

'I feel like you're being a dick,' I said. *'Are you being a dick?'*

'No, I'm being reasonable,' he said, speaking to me like I was exactly three years old. *'You can't do your job well if the job is the problem.'*

'It's great you like to help out the humans, but sometimes you need to know when to throw in the towel,' Hermes added. *'And maybe if you stopped and thought about it for more than two seconds, you'd see that now is that time.'* I felt him sigh. *'And going to hash things out with Mary might not be the worst idea. Get your head back in the game.'*

'Just don't be an idiot,' Nathaniel said. *'Do something nice. You know what she likes.'*

I thought about it for a few moments as the two of them continued to go back and forth about my love life. Hermes was right about one thing—having lovers had never been a question or an issue for me. I absorbed joy and pleasure and happiness; I needed them to exist. Things like sex or romantic relationships, in general, were the ideal ways of absorbing those emotions, but even simple friendships helped give me that happiness. So, when a job made me miserable, both due to its nature and the fact that I was separated from everyone I cared about, it was usually a simple thing to go out and find something to help alleviate that misery. Even a good party was enough to give me a boost. The collective happiness of drunken debauchery was always a good time and was usually enough to give me what I needed, but sexual encounters were the most enjoyable. Obviously.

Then, it came to me.

'I have an idea,' I said, cutting Hermes off from whatever he was about to say. Quickly, I told them my plan.

'You really thing Athena will go for it?' Hermes asked skeptically.

'No. But I'll make it work. And Nathaniel? You can't tell Tessa.'

'If she asks, I'm not lying to her.'

'I'd never ask you to besmirch your good name like that, brother. Wish me luck.'

I grinned, finally feeling a bit of happiness creep in. And for once, it was my own happiness, not someone else's.

4

MARY

Once I had my beautiful, empty apartment to myself, I dragged my suitcase back to the bedroom. The apartment was a little on the small side—about the size of my bedroom back in my hometown of Renville—but considering I had an entire apartment to hang out in, I didn't really mind. The bathroom was across the hall, a second, slightly smaller bedroom next to it.

I spent the next hour unpacking, putting things away, and going through the streaming services on TV. It was getting late, later than I wanted to be wandering out in the cold to explore town, so I put on my pajamas, turned on a supernatural teen drama for background noise, and plopped down on the couch with the files Athena had left me.

Calla Aiden seemed exactly like I would expect a person with her background to be. Beautiful, smart, spoiled, and popular. Her high school academic history revealed a social butterfly with stellar grades, no behavioral problems, and a load of extracurriculars that gave her college application a big boost.

Her social media really piqued my interest, though. Athena had given me login information for a handful of sites so I could comb through Calla's social history, which painted a much different picture than what was documented by schools and guidance counselors. Thousands of photos and videos were on her profiles, many showing the extravagant gifts she'd received from her parents, from red-bottom stilettos to a shiny black SUV, all captioned with things ranging from "Happy Birthday to me!" to "Daddy's little girl" and "#youwishyouwereanAiden." The last one was a picture of her dressed to the nines and sitting on the hood of her SUV, chugging a bottle of what I assumed was expensive champagne.

One of the more recent pictures was of her in a pretty floral dress and strappy sandals with her mother and an older woman, both of whom shared Calla's deep tan skin, bright blue eyes, curly dark hair, and slender build. They stood in front of a gorgeous Victorian mansion with gold Greek lettering above the door. The caption just read, "Legacies."

Frowning, I reached out to Athena.

'Athena, you there?'

'I am. Do you need something?'

'I'm looking over this girl's social media history. Is there any way you can get me legacy status at her sorority? If I had a grandmother or something who was a member, it might make it easier to get a foot in.'

'Consider it done.' There was a moment of silence, and then, *'Good thinking, Mary.'*

I smiled at that, allowing myself to feel a bit of pride. It was kind of nice to know I was starting off on the right foot, since I was pretty sure Athena thought I would screw this up on day one. Considering how, up until this morning, I thought I'd be sitting around the Jackson headquarters for months before getting an assignment, there was no way I was going to fail right out of the gate. As much as I loved working on my water affinity and honing my combat skills, the thought of focusing on something so humanly simple as college was a relief.

And hopefully, it would help keep my mind off the infuriating god who'd all but vanished in recent months.

Annoyed that I let Dionysus creep into my thoughts yet again, I went back to digging up dirt on Calla. I took notes on her interests—which seemed to consist of partying and spending her parents' money—and made a note to figure out the best way to dress to impress.

That thought made me gag a little, but I've known girls like her, and if I showed up in my preferred shades of neon, she'd probably turn her nose right up at me.

I picked up the credit card Athena left and ran my thumb over the shiny silver chip, contemplating how much was a reasonable amount to spend before the wrath of the Goddess of War came down on me.

Fitting in was a must with Calla Aiden, and if that meant expensive clothes, then who was I to argue?

So, setting Calla's info aside, I sent myself straight to Nordstrom's website. I spent about two hours poring over shoes, jeans, makeup, and everything under the sun until I had a shopping cart that totaled a sum even I was ashamed of. There were enough boots, jeans, sweaters, and shirts to last me a year, and, on a whim, I ordered an obscenely expensive down-filled puffer coat and matching cashmere scarf, because why the heck not? I needed winter gear and, well, there they were.

And considering there were only a few days until the semester started, next-day shipping was totally a must.

Gods, Athena was going to kill me.

'EIGHT *THOUSAND* DOLLARS?'

I was jolted out of bed the next morning by Athena screaming into my head. Based on the lack of sunlight coming through the window, I assumed it was barely the crack of dawn.

'What the—I was sleeping!'

'Goodie for you! What in all the realms did you need to spend eight thousand dollars on in one go?'

'Have you looked at this chick's social?'

Silence.

Then, seconds later, my bedroom door burst open and Athena stormed in.

"When I told you to use that card on clothes to fit in, I didn't mean for you to sample every high-end designer out there!"

I rubbed a hand over my face and scowled at her from where I sat on the bed.

"I spent several hours last night going over all of the information you gave me," I said, stifling a yawn. "That girl is rolling in money. If I show up in thirty-dollar dresses from Target, she won't give me a second glance." Which sucked, because I loved Target.

Athena huffed and put her hands on her hips. "Fine, but whatever you bought last night is it."

I arched a brow. "Did Olympus suddenly go bankrupt since I was last there?"

"No, it has not, but if word gets out that you're spending thousands of dollars on a new wardrobe, other Ischyra will expect the same. It sets a bad precedent."

"Oh." Logical. "Well, be more specific next time."

She pointed a finger at me and gave me a warning look. "You're lucky my brothers and Tessa like you, Mary, or you'd be scrubbing toilets in headquarters for the next twenty years."

I preened up at her. "Oh, you love me. Just admit it."

She narrowed her eyes but didn't argue.

I held up my hands in defeat. "All right. I promise I won't spend any more of your money unnecessarily. I sprang for overnight shipping—"

"Of course, you did."

"—so everything should be getting here later today. I'll head to campus and get my books and whatever else tomorrow. In the meantime, I'm going exploring."

She nodded. "Yes, it's a lovely town. If you'd asked yesterday, I would've told you there are plenty of shops right up the street where you could've found a lot of the outerwear you needed."

I bit my lip. I probably should've looked into that before ordering stuff sight unseen, but I suppose I couldn't un-ring that bell.

"Thanks. I'll remember that for next time."

Arching her brow, she smiled. "The cinnamon buns in the coffee shop downstairs are delicious."

"Okay, I'll check it out later." I glanced out the window at the snow that was falling. "Once the sun comes up. And my boots get here."

She huffed out a sigh. "Fair enough. Keep reading up on the Aidens in the meantime. Let me know if you have any questions."

"Any word yet on getting me legacy status?"

"Yes. I'm working on getting a few college records altered. Once I do, you'll be all set."

"K." I yawned again. "Can I go back to sleep now?"

"Fine. Let me know how things go at the college. Explore, let people see you, request information on pledging. If anyone asks, your grandmother was Suzette Jameson. She attended the University of Pennsylvania and was the recording secretary in Iota Sigma Xi. The records will be adjusted later today."

I gave her a thumbs up and smiled. "Got it. I'll check in when I get back."

MY CLOTHES and makeup arrived in the early afternoon, and I spent far longer than I'd like to admit gushing over it all before finally making my way outside. It was bitter cold, so my exploration of town lasted only long enough to make the quick walk downstairs to the coffee shop to introduce myself to the owners—Jane and Bill, two long-retired ski instructors—and get a cinnamon bun and latte. By the time I returned, I was pretty content to burrow on the couch with the Aiden files and not go out again until spring.

I spent the rest of the night reading, making notes, and poking around on the university website to get a better feel for the place where I'd be spending the next few months, before finally heading to bed around midnight.

The next morning, armed with my phone, my course schedule,

and my gods-given credit card, I hopped the shuttle to campus. I'd downloaded a campus map to my phone, so I wanted to explore that and possibly the surrounding area, where it seemed a lot of the sorority and fraternity housing was located.

The ride took about twenty minutes and gave me a good opportunity to see what my new home was like. The main road through town was full of stores, restaurants, and a couple of bars, but as soon as the shuttle crossed out of town, the scenery changed dramatically from a shop-lined street to a wooded residential road that slowly crept uphill. The houses gradually began to spread out, until we were traveling through the woods. We passed a few trailheads, and I thought briefly about how much fun it might be to hike around here before remembering the foot of snow on the ground that was getting increasingly higher. The mountains I'd seen from my living room loomed ahead, where I could just make out a handful of ski trails for the local ski resort and the revolving line of ski lifts making their way to the top. Angry gray clouds loomed over the mountaintop, threatening more snow, but I had a feeling a little blizzard wouldn't deter anyone up there.

Athena and Tessa had been right. This place was beautiful.

Ten minutes later, the shuttle stopped in front of the student center, so I didn't have far to walk to get to the bookstore just down the road. It was huge, bigger than I expected a college bookstore to be, and held a large section of non-academic books that I planned to make a point of digging through before I left.

A cashier, definitely a student by the look of her, stood behind the counter, an expectant look on her face. "Can I help you?"

I held up my schedule and flashed her a smile. "Just here for my books. Do you mind pointing me to where I need to go?"

She gestured toward the back of the store. "Head straight back there. One of the guys will be out to help in just a sec."

With a nod of thanks, I weaved through the maze of aisles toward the back of the store where a counter ran the entire width of the room. Behind it were shelves piled high with textbooks, with a door at the back leading to what looked to be a storeroom.

I approached the guy behind the desk. He was tall, a bit gangly, with brown hair and horn-rimmed glasses. The entire combination would've normally seemed completely nerdy, but he managed to make it look surprisingly hot.

"Books?" he asked. "Yup." I set my purse down on the counter.

He smiled, revealing two dimples in his cheeks that I imagined got him a fair amount of female attention, then tapped a small black scanner. "Scan your student ID, please."

I pulled my ID from my wallet and touched it to the scanner. A moment later, he pushed a few buttons, then the printer beside him started to whir. Pulling off the page, he handed it to me.

"Make sure this matches what you have. All sales are final."

Arching a brow, I skimmed the list and compared it to the schedule Athena had given me, then handed it back and smiled. "Looks good."

Tapping the list against his palm, he walked off, disappearing through the stockroom door. I waited, drumming my fingers against the Formica as I let my eyes drift around. The place was empty, except for a few students browsing.

"Here you go," Glasses said, drawing my attention back toward him. My eyebrows shot up when I saw the monstrosities he dropped in front of me.

"Those are . . . large."

"Science," he said, flashing those dimples again as he started to ring me up.

When he read me the total, I let out a low whistle.

He laughed. "I grabbed you used where I could, but chem and bio are both the most recent editions, so . . . next semester, price-match online."

I grimaced. "Probably should've thought of that myself."

After swiping my card, he loaded up my books into a box. "If you've got other things you need to do on campus, I can leave this here with your name on it and you can grab it later. Mary, right?"

Eyeing the pile that likely weighed a good forty pounds, I nodded. "Yeah, that'd be great. Thanks . . . ?"

"Shep," he said, holding out a hand to shake mine. "Good to meet you, Mary."

"Likewise," I said, smiling.

He slid the box under the counter. "You need directions anywhere? I can tell you're not from around here."

I laughed. "Is it that obvious?"

He grinned. "It's your Os. Northern Pennsylvania?"

I arched a brow. "Born and raised." Then, remembering I was supposed to be Mary Jameson from Reading, I amended, "I moved to south to Reading about ten years ago, though. You know accents?"

"It's a thing," he said with a shrug. "Always had a talent for guessing where someone's from."

I nodded, impressed. "Cool. Well, thanks, Shep. I'll stop back in a bit to grab my things."

"You sure you don't need directions anywhere?"

"Nope, just wandering. Thanks, though."

"No problem. See you around."

For the next few hours, I made my way around campus, committing the general layout to memory and observing the students that had already returned from winter break. Most of the girls had a snow bunny type of thing going on—fitted winter coats, skinny jeans or leggings tucked into winter boots, and cute yet functional glove-scarf-hat combos.

The campus was sprawling, so it took awhile to see the entire place. Despite the cold, it was a nice walk, and I enjoyed getting to see the outside world for a change. It had been months since I'd been surrounded by anything except weapons and training yards. Walking around here, surrounded by normal humans in normal human clothes doing normal human things, gave me a little bit of relief from stress I hadn't realized I'd been carrying. Even though the area was still unfamiliar and I didn't know a single person, being here was so . . . easy. Like breathing.

As eager as I was to dig into my assignment, part of me hoped it wasn't the type that would get wrapped up quickly. Or, at the very least, I hoped I would impress the Elders so thoroughly that being an undercover human became a typical assignment for me. The thought alone was enough to make me determined to kick ass at this job.

After finding all of my classrooms, as well as Calla's, and a few different routes to each, I pulled up sorority row on my phone. The road that held most of the sororities and a handful of the fraternities cut across the northern end of campus, which was about a mile from where I was right now.

As if on cue, snow started falling again.

With a sigh, I slid my phone in my back pocket.

"Street view, it is."

5

MARY

I won't lie. Taking a solid hour to get ready for my first day of classes was the most fun I'd had in months. The last time I'd spent any significant amount of time primping was back in June, when the other fledgling Ischyra and I had arrived on Olympus and were getting ready for the welcome feast for all new recruits. I wasn't getting as glammed-up this time as I had then, but after curling my hair for the first time in months and busting out my makeup bag, I was kind of flying high.

'I hear you're trying to bankrupt my mountain.'

I jumped at the sound of Dionysus's voice in my head, dropping the brand-new pot of plum-colored eyeshadow. I cursed when several small chunks flaked off into the sink.

'You made me drop my eyeshadow,' I grumbled. *'Warn a girl next time. And I'm not bankrupting anything. I bought clothes.'*

'Uh huh.' Amusement was clear in his tone. I could practically see his blue eyes sparkling with amusement.

'So, did you need something?' I asked.

'Just wanted to wish you good luck on your first day.'

I frowned, the brush in my hand inches from my eyelid. *'I haven't heard from you in a month, and now you want to be nice?'*

'*It hasn't been a month.*' He paused. '*Has it?*'

'*Yep.*'

'*Shit, Mary, I'm sorry. My father's been running me ragged. I never—*'

'*It's fine. I gotta go. Class starts in an hour, and I can't be late on my first day.*'

'*I'm sure your professor will understand.*'

Not the point, I wanted to say.

'*I heard that.*'

'*No, you didn't.*' I couldn't help but smirk, knowing how much knowing I was annoyed with him would drive him crazy. I felt a *little* bad, because I knew he was probably taking it to heart, but I wanted him to know how irritated I was.

I'd let him off the hook later, but I wanted him to stew a bit, first.

'*Okay.*' He paused. '*I'll, um, check in later, see how your first day went?*'

'*Yeah, that's fine. My last class is done at six.*' I tried not to let any excitement creep into my tone, because I really, really didn't want him to know how eager I was to talk to him for longer than just a few minutes.

'*I'll talk to you then,*' Dionysus said, sounding a bit morose.

'*K.*'

There was a soft push as he left my mind, and I instantly felt a flash of regret. It wasn't my job to keep him happy, but his knee-jerk reaction when people were unhappy was to try and fix whatever was wrong. Since he wasn't actually with me, he couldn't cheer me up, meaning he was stuck knowing I was probably moping.

Whatever. Not my problem.

Deep down, I knew distance between us had probably been a good thing for me, because I saw myself coming to rely on him to put my mind at ease far too much. We'd agreed that he'd stop using his power to help me only a few days after I'd been returned to Olympus, but his presence alone had gone miles to help ease me back into life. He'd done a lot to help me learn how to shut down my mind when it began to fall into the pit of depression it liked to visit now and then. Anytime I'd had a bad dream that dragged me back to the dungeon

I'd been held in, or when the memories of having my power pulled from my body put me on the verge of a panic attack, he had been there.

Until he wasn't. So, I figured out how to manage it on my own.

Zeus had been sending all his kids to different areas of the world, making sure all was well after the battle we'd had last summer. It'd been a hard fight to win, ending only when Tessa and I took down the guy we thought was one of our closest friends. But every now and then, some group popped up, causing trouble here and there. For the most part, though, it'd been quiet. Apollo and Athena had assigned me to the field, and that was that. Nate, golden boy that he wasn't, had all but thumbed his nose at Olympus and the duties his father wanted him to take on once the war was done, going right back to enjoying the human world.

I twisted my mascara closed and tossed it into my makeup bag, then packed up the sleek leather crossbody bag I'd ordered for my books. Double-checking my schedule, I packed my literature and biology texts, two notebooks, and a few pens, then headed out to catch the shuttle.

MY FIRST CLASS was biology with Doctor Trebauer. According to Calla's transcripts, she was scheduled for the same class, so I arrived a few minutes early and loitered outside the door, scrolling through my phone while I waited for her to show up. As the other students filed in and started to take their seats, I kept an eye on the time. When there were only two minutes left before class was set to start, I went in and looked around the room. Most of the tables were full, but there were two that still had two open seats. Taking a gamble, I headed toward the one closest to the window, where a mousy-looking brunette sat beside a blond guy who was absolutely a frat boy.

Not thirty seconds after I sat down, Calla Aiden walked in. She looked just as pretty as she had in her pictures, with long, curly black hair cascading down her back and piercing blue eyes. A ruby-red scarf wound around her neck, highlighting a modelesque jawline, and she wore a flowing, snow-white cashmere sweater over dark jeans tucked into thigh-high black boots. A black winter coat was slung over one arm.

I crossed my fingers, hoping she would take the seat next to me and make it easy.

Instead, she took a seat at the table beside me. Proximity-wise it was fine, I supposed, but for labs and group work, her sitting at the same table was kind of necessary if I wanted to get to know her.

I huffed.

Okay, then, I guess I'll have to do this the hard way.

Casually, I drummed my fingers on the black tabletop, focusing all of my power on the stool she'd just sat down on. Freezing steel to the point of breaking took more power than I was used to, but it was worth it when, seconds later, there was a loud snap as one of the bolts froze off, sending Calla tumbling to the floor with a screech.

"Oh, my goodness!" I leapt from my seat and rushed over to help, nearly taking out the guy who'd been sitting next to her who'd jumped up in alarm. "Are you okay?"

Scowling, she took my outstretched hand and let me help her to her feet, ignoring the stares of other students.

"This school can't even manage quality seating," she snapped, straightening her sweater and dusting off her jeans. "It's inexcusable."

"I know, right?" I murmured. Smiling, I gestured toward my table before she could look around for a new chair. "There's a seat open over there that seems pretty sturdy."

"Well, I certainly hope so," she said, tossing her hair over her shoulder. She sent a scathing look to our professor, who'd just walked in, then picked up her bag and followed me to her new seat. "You'd think he'd at least make sure his facilities were in order."

"Yeah, um, definitely." I shot a look at our table mates and saw that the girl was staring down at her notebook, clearly avoiding eye contact, and the guy was smirking.

"Hey, Calla," he drawled. "Who's your friend?"

"No clue." She arched a brow. "What's your name?"

I smiled brightly. "I'm Mary Jameson."

Her blue eyes narrowed slightly, and I had to force myself not to let my annoyance at her scrutiny show. Finally, she held out a hand. "I'm Calla Aiden. Thanks for the save." She jerked her chin toward the guy. "That's Jared. He seems to think going to high school together means he can talk to me."

She completely ignored the girl.

"Nice to meet you both," I said, putting on a friendly smile. I looked at the other girl curiously. "What's your name?"

The girl looked up at me, seeming surprised I'd spoken to her.

"Oh, I, um, I'm Brittany," she said quietly.

Calla hardly gave her time to respond before turning back to me. "Where are you from?"

"Reading. I just transferred from Lehigh, down in PA. You?"

Just then, our professor called class to order and started handing out the syllabus.

"I'm Doctor Trebauer," he began. "This course is restricted to science majors and minors only, so if you're not a science major, you need to go to student services and get placed in another course."

"Labs will be each Thursday," he continued. "On certain occasions, you may need to spend additional time in the lab, depending on the type of experiments we're conducting."

Eager to see what we'd be covering, I started flipping through the syllabus. It turned out to be a god-awful fifteen pages long and consisted of labs involving bacteria growth and onion skin and fetal pigs, among others that promised to be a shit ton of work.

I liked science and I was excited to learn about the various concentrations more in-depth.

That eagerness did not extend to formaldehyde-soaked pig fetuses.

I didn't realize how loud my facial expression was until Calla snickered.

"Gross, right? I might need a doctor to write me out of that one," she whispered.

I wrinkled my nose. "Can he write me one, too?"

"Aw, come on, a little bit of pig guts never hurt anyone," Jared whispered, smirking at me. "You can be my partner if Calla can't handle it."

Calla scoffed before I could answer. "As if, Larkin. Gross as it might be, I could do a dissection in my sleep. She's far better off with me." She sent me a look that all but dared me to dispute her claim. "Aren't you, Mary?"

"Totally," I agreed, casting a wary glance toward the professor, who was still talking. I seriously didn't want to get chastised on day one. "Girl power and all that."

"Exactly." Then, she paused, appraising me. "Assuming you've got half a brain, that is."

I choked back a laugh, biting my tongue before I threw the same insult back at her. "A full one, believe it or not."

"You're such a bitch, Calla," Jared muttered.

She shrugged. "At least I'm up-front about it."

I looked at Brittany, feeling bad that she was being completely excluded from the conversation, but she was writing furiously in her notebook, seemingly taking in every word the professor was saying.

Doctor Trebauer continued to prattle on for the next forty minutes, letting us go a half an hour before class was scheduled to finish. Once he dismissed us, I hesitated, unsure of how to talk to Calla now that we weren't stuck at the same table.

"Hey, so where's the best place to get coffee around here?" I asked. "My coffee maker went on the fritz this morning and I'm kind of desperate."

"Definitely the café in the student center." I could practically feel her scrutinizing me again. "I'm heading over there now, so I can show you."

"Oh, that'd be awesome!" I gushed. "Thank you *so* much."

"No problem," she replied with a wave of her hand as she tightened the strap of her bag across her chest. "Come on."

I gave Jared and Brittany a tight smile as Calla flicked her hair over her shoulder and brushed past them.

"Nice to meet you both," I said.

"Uh-huh," Jared said, shaking his head as he stared after Calla. "Good luck with that one."

With a sigh, I slung my bag onto my shoulder and followed her out.

"So, have you lived around here long?" I asked when I caught up with her.

"Only about six months," she said, smiling and waving at someone down the hall. "Do you know where the student center is?"

"Yeah, I think so."

"Good. Coffee shop is on the third floor, and it's the only thing resembling high-quality coffee anywhere in this godforsaken place."

Not seeing any sense in pointing out the half-dozen shops on Main Street, I smiled. "Where did you live before?"

"Manhattan," she told me. "Home of the best coffee, bagels, and pizza. And pretty much the complete opposite of here."

"That's cool. I've never been."

"Didn't you grow up near Philadelphia? That's surprising, then."

I shrugged. "Not really. Philly isn't as big as New York, but we've got pretty much everything."

She made a face as we exited the science building and began to make our way across the quad to the student center. "Cheesesteaks. You've got cheesesteaks."

I grinned. "And hoagies."

"I suppose if you're not used to the delis in New York, you would think that," she said airily.

Gods, it was getting so damn hard not to let my sass out. "Well, one of these days I'll try to expand my sandwich horizons, then."

"Oh! There's Kristy!" Grabbing my arm, she tugged me toward the large double doors of the brick student center.

Snagging the strap of my bag before it slipped off my shoulder, I let her lead me toward a girl standing outside the student center doors. She was tall, with long, red hair that fell around her shoulders in perfect curls. She had on a white puffer coat, with a matching cashmere hat and an emerald green scarf and gloves. The cold had turned the tip of her nose and cheeks pink.

"There you are," Kristy groaned as we approached. "It's freezing out here."

"Then you should've waited inside, dummy! Kristy Danielson, this is—" Calla frowned at me. "Mary, right?"

"Mary Jameson," I told Kristy with a smile.

"Oh, fun, a new friend!" She grinned and did a little clap. Pursing her lips, she looked me up and down. "Calla, do you think we can convert her? We still need a few more rushees if we're going to beat Kappa."

I looked between them, confused. "Convert me?"

Kristy pulled open the door and waved us inside. "To Greek life!"

I nearly laughed. There was no way they were going to make it *that* easy for me.

Calla looked over at me with that same appraising look again, only this time it was mixed with wariness. "Hmm. She's got the look, I guess. We'd have to talk to Willow, though. That is, if Mary even wants to rush. Do you?"

"Rush?" I played dumb. "A sorority?"

Calla rolled her eyes. "Yes, a sorority."

I opened my mouth, momentarily unsure of how to respond, then just went with the first thing that popped into my head.

"Well, my grandmother was in one, and I always really looked up to her." We stopped in front of the elevator and Kristy pushed the button for the third floor. "So yeah, I'm definitely interested."

Calla's eyes widened, and she put a hand on my arm to stop me. "Hang on. Which one?"

"Which one what?" I asked.

"Which sorority?"

"Oh! Um, Iota something? I forget."

"Iota Sigma Xi?" Kristy asked, the elevator forgotten.

I winced. "I think so?"

Calla's smile grew wider. "You're a legacy for Iota Sig? So am I! *And* I just happen to be the VP."

"You have to rush now!" Kristy exclaimed.

I gave them each a curious look. "A legacy?"

"Oh, boy," Kristy said, rolling her eyes. "Come on," she said, tugging me into the elevator. "We've got a lot to talk about."

6

MARY

Two cups of admittedly delicious coffee—that I'd paid for as a thank you for showing me where to find it—later, I'd let Kristy and Calla tell me all about Iota Sigma Xi, a national but very exclusive sorority.

"Willow—she's our president—is a real twat sometimes, but even she won't shoot down a legacy," Calla told me.

Her demeanor had completely shifted over the course of our conversation, going from aloof to bubbly in the span of a cup of coffee. Apparently, the idea of me being a guaranteed "in" erased any suspicions she had about whether or not she should continue being friendly. "I'm pretty sure she practically hated me when I transferred last year."

"So, you're a legacy, too?"

"My mother, grandmother, and great-grandmother were all in Iota Sig," she confirmed smugly. "It's a family tradition."

"You should totally join, Mary," Kristy said. "Deferred recruitment starts in a couple of weeks, so you're in luck. And since you're a legacy, you'll likely get an automatic bid."

"And that's when they decide they want to invite me to pledge, right?"

"Yup," Kristy said. "You seem super nice, too, so you'll be a shoo-in, don't worry."

"Especially with me backing you." Calla grinned.

"Well, it does sound pretty cool, and I've never had sisters." I chewed on my lip for a moment, then nodded. "Yeah, I'm in."

"Perfect!" Calla grinned at Kristy. "Oh, Willow is going to be so excited! Ever since those two pledges bailed last year, she's been dying for another good bid."

Kristy nodded somberly, then glanced at her phone. "Oh, shoot! Class starts in ten!"

"What do you have next?" Calla asked as Kristy took our cups to throw them out.

"Uh . . ." Setting my cup down, I pulled my schedule out of my pocket. "Lit with Professor Danson."

"Oh!" Kristy's eyes brightened as she came back over. "I heard he had a breakdown or something. I talked to Jolene—she's one of the other sisters—and she said the guy who replaced him is like, insanely hot. Godly, even."

Calla snorted. "As if she'd know how hot any of the gods are."

Kristy shrugged. "I'm sure she just meant it figuratively."

I widened my eyes at Calla in feigned surprise. "Have you seen one? A god, I mean?"

She sniffed and examined her lacquered nails. "My father always taught me not to brag."

"So, you guys are both in Danson's class next, then?" I asked, trying not to visibly gag at her attitude. "It's over in Stevenson, right?"

"Yes and yes," Kristy replied, smiling. She smirked at Calla. "Ten bucks says Calla will have him bagged by the end of the week."

"If he's as hot as Jolene says, then maybe I'll consider it," Calla said. She slung her bag over her shoulder. "We all know her taste in guys can be . . . questionable."

Kristy rolled her eyes at Calla's back, then her eyes widened when she saw that I'd noticed. When I mimed zipping my lips, she gave me a relieved grin.

"Oh, come on!" Calla snapped, stabbing the elevator button for the first floor. "These things take too long."

We rode the elevator down in silence then made our way out into the blustering cold with the throngs of other students. A light snow had started to fall, but it was so cold I couldn't even pretend to enjoy it. Not to mention what it would do to the hair I spent way too much time on this morning.

"Should we grab the shuttle?" Kristy asked, rubbing her hands together and blowing in them as we walked toward the sidewalk.

Calla tugged at her curly hair and pouted. "My hair's going to frizz if we don't. I forgot my stupid hat."

"Same," I said, then pointed down the street to where the campus shuttle was making its way toward us. "Perfect timing."

A five-minute ride later, and we were the last three to arrive to class, which I assumed meant we wouldn't get to sit together. However, it became immediately apparent that Calla's face was a familiar—and infamous—one. When she dropped her backpack at an empty chair in the front row and arched her brow at the two students on either side, both scurried off to find other seats.

Eyebrows raised, I sat down in one of the newly-vacated seats and watched as they took the last two remaining seats toward the back.

I felt bad for them and was torn between putting on a show of indifference for my present company or sending them both apologetic looks. Neither seemed like a good option, so I went with ignoring them all, pulling out my notebook and the three-inch thick monstrosity our professor called a textbook, then started to tap my pen impatiently as we waited.

Calla snapped her fingers, then inclined her head toward my phone, which was sitting on the table next to my notebook.

"What's your number? I'll text you mine."

I rattled off the number for her as her fingers dashed over the screen. A few seconds later, my phone buzzed with a new text. Opening the message, I tapped the number to save the contact.

"Rule number one! There will be no cell phone use in my class!"

I froze, then my eyes fell shut at the sound of what could only be our professor's voice.

"Oopsie," Calla whispered, wincing. "Good thing you're in good company."

Ignoring her, I rubbed a hand across my forehead as the familiarity of the voice sank in.

I scowled up at Dionysus as he strolled down the center aisle and hopped up to sit on his desk, looking far too fabulous in a crisp, blue button-down and slim-fitting jeans. I didn't know whether to be surprised he was there, irritated he hadn't told me he was coming, or happy to finally freaking see him again.

'You've got to be fucking kidding me right now.'

'I think you know me better than that, Mary.'

He flashed a bright, perfect smile at the class. "For those of you who haven't heard, Professor Danson had a bit of an emergency, so I'll be taking over for him this semester. My name is Professor Deon, but you can call me Joe."

'Deon? Seriously?'

"I'd say Jolene's assessment was pretty spot on, Cal," Kristy whispered. "Totally hot."

"Damn straight," Calla murmured. Smirking, she added, "I'll have him by midterms."

I bit my tongue so hard I tasted blood.

"I'm also not a fan of talking while I'm talking," Dionysus continued, glancing pointedly in our direction. A silver ring hung from a chain on his neck, presumably dampening his power. "And I'm not above rearranging seats."

Calla's jaw clamped shut, but I saw a flash of defiance in her eyes that all but screamed, *I'd love to see you try.*

As he began going over our reading assignments for the semester —a mix of literature from around the world—I tried very hard to focus on the fact that he was here and not that he hadn't bothered to tell me he was coming. But what the heck? I'd just talked to him a few hours ago, and he couldn't have just given me a head's up?

I narrowed my eyes at him.

'Asshole.'

His lips twitched in the middle of whatever he was saying, nearly causing him to stumble over his words.

I smirked as I jotted down a note about what he'd just said.

'Twatwaffle.'

Coughing, he turned his back to the class, then picked up the bottle of water he'd left on the desk and drowned half its contents.

"Apologies," he said, clearing his throat again as he set the bottle down. "Allergies."

'It's January.'

"Believe it or not, they can even pop up in winter," he said, giving the class another dazzling smile. "Now, let's start off by going around the room and introducing yourself. I want your name and something interesting that no one would ever guess."

'Ew, you're one of those?'

"Ugh, he's one of those," Calla muttered.

"This will count as your participation grade for today," he continued. "I'll start. My name is Joe, I'm from Maryland, and I sort my Skittles by color, then eat them one at a time in rainbow order to make them last." He pointed to a student in the back row. "Back row, far right, we'll start with you."

I arched a brow when he mentioned my, admittedly odd, candy habit.

Calla snorted. "Weirdo," she murmured.

"Right?" I whispered back. I leaned back in my seat and quietly started tapping my pen on my hand.

For the rest of class, each student talked a little about themselves, some only saying a few words while others engaged in actual conversation with our "professor."

When he got to me, I smiled sweetly and said, "My name's Mary, I'm a Virgo on the cusp of Libra, and I love a good California pinot with a side of truffle fries. My biggest peeve is people who make weird noises in their sleep and don't return phone calls."

Calla snorted next to me, then clamped a hand over her mouth to cover her laugh at the disparaging look Dionysus sent my way.

'*What?*' I asked innocently. '*You giggle in your sleep.*'

By the time class ended an hour later—he took us right until the last minute—all I wanted was to get back to my apartment and veg out. I rushed out right behind Calla and Kristy, unsure whether or not he would try to talk to me. It wasn't that I didn't want to talk to him, per se, but I sure as shit didn't want Calla to see me as any kind of competition.

'*Mary—*'

'*Later.*'

Calla and Kristy babbled the entire way back to the shuttle, Calla going on about what she would wear to class next week in her attempt to "bag" our professor. The thought had me grinding my teeth.

After climbing off the shuttle at the student parking lot, the three of us made plans to catch up for coffee again on Thursday after biology so they could give me a crash course on how to present myself to their president.

All in all, I'd say my first day was a success.

7

DIONYSUS

To say I was disappointed Mary didn't stick around after class would be an understatement.

I suppose it made sense. It looked like she'd already gotten in good with the girl she was supposed to attach herself to, and stopping to talk to me probably wouldn't have looked great, considering said girl was hoping to get me into bed.

Even still, the way she brushed me off rankled a bit.

But the fact that she'd buddied up with Calla Aiden on day one boded well for her, so I couldn't be too annoyed.

'How is she?'

I frowned when I heard Athena's voice in my head.

'Mary? She's fine. Why?'

'First day of classes, you're my eyes on the ground, so I'm curious.' There was a teasing lilt to her voice. *'Is she mad you showed up without telling her?'*

'Number one, I'm not your eyes on the ground. If you want to check up on Mary, talk to her. Number two . . . If the colorful array of names she called me when she saw me are any indication, yes, I would say she's mad at me for showing up unannounced.'

'Can't really blame her, can you? She never struck me as the type to love surprises.'

'She'll get over it. Anything else?'

'Yes. I won't ask you to be my eyes and ears there, but I just want to know ... Do you think she can handle this?'

I couldn't help but feel a little insulted on Mary's behalf. 'Obviously. That's why I recommended her. This job is perfect for her. And, before you question me, she's already in good with Calla Aiden, so you don't need to fret there.'

'Already?' I could practically feel my sister's surprise. 'Fast work.'

'She's a people person, believe it or not, and she's smart. Very smart.'

'Agreed. But Dionysus, do not distract her. She needs this for a multitude of reasons, but mainly because she has to demonstrate to Zeus that he didn't make a mistake in allowing her to graduate early. And selfishly, I don't care to be reamed out by him if she doesn't succeed.'

'Fret not, dear sister. I may not be the most serious of your siblings, but I'm not an idiot.'

She huffed. 'I suppose you're not wrong. All right. Let me know if anything happens I need to know about. I'll be checking in with Mary daily, but I'm assuming you two will be discussing things regularly, as well?'

'Most likely.'

'Good. And Dionysus—'

'For fuck's sake, Athena, will you relax?' I felt bad snapping at her, but Athena was wound tighter than a spring these days and it was getting tiresome.

'Fine. Sorry.'

Once we'd disconnected, I gathered up my things and set out to find my office. As I'd arrived only a few hours before classes started, I hadn't done much aside from meet with the department chair, go over Professor Danson's lesson plans, and get directions to my office. There hadn't been time to go to my office earlier, so I aimed there now to finish getting myself set up.

"Thank the gods," I muttered when I opened the door to the medium-sized office that had not one, but two large windows. It was like a godsdamned palace after the closet I'd had in Germany. Which, to be fair, wasn't the university's fault. The college was very small and very old, so large corner offices weren't exactly plentiful.

I breathed another sigh of relief when I saw the bookshelves behind the desk stocked not with psychology texts and manuals, but literature. Fiction. Made-up worlds that were a complete escape from reality.

Okay, maybe I was being a little overdramatic.

I'd just sat down to boot up the ancient laptop-slash-paperweight on my desk when I heard Hermes's voice in my head.

'So, how did it go?'

'Eh.'

'That well, huh?'

'I think she might be more pissed than I realized,' I admitted.

'She doesn't know how much you fall off the grid when you're on an assignment,' he said. *'Just do—what did Nathaniel say? Something nice.'*

'Helpful.'

The computer screen finally flickered to life, so I logged into the email account that I surprisingly already had access to. That kind of thing always took a few days, if I was lucky, when I ended up on a last-minute assignment.

'Work your charm, brother. You know how to handle a woman.'

Not this one, I thought.

'I've got a couple of ideas,' I said. I drummed my fingers impatiently on the desk as the icon on the screen spun. *'It just might take some trial and error.'*

'Good luck with that.'

I rolled my eyes.

We talked for a few more minutes as I skimmed over my email. There was nothing of any great importance, so once I cut off with Hermes and closed the computer, I tried to figure out what else I might be able to do to get back in Mary's good graces.

After a few minutes, I knew what to do.

8

MARY

I'd just closed my apartment door behind me a few hours later when the bell rang. Rolling my eyes, I dumped my bag on the counter and opened the door.

"Yes?" I asked when I saw Dionysus leaning against the frame.

Grinning, he held up a brown paper bag and a bottle of wine. "Peace offerings."

As he said it, the vinegary scent of white barbecue sauce hit my nostrils and my mouth began to water.

Suspiciously, I eyed the bag in his hand. "From where?"

"Barbecue from that place in Nashville you liked and wine, straight from Napa."

Stepping back, I held the door open and let him in, silently letting myself feel relief that he was here.

For the first couple of months after we'd defeated Chaos, we'd traveled around to a bunch of different places with Tessa, Nate, Yana, and a few others. Mostly, we just wanted to see things were back to normal, but it was also largely a diversion, a way to celebrate a victory but distract us from what it had cost us. I'd still been struggling to come back to the surface, fighting against nightmares and cold sweats and the occasional panic attack, so staying in any one place too long made me antsy. Traveling all around like we did was the main reason Zeus didn't start dishing out assignments right away. We'd been doing our part to make sure the status quo was slowly returning, and I'd been doing what I could to help myself heal. I was still a bit of a work in progress in that respect, but I was getting there.

While we bounced around and I did all I could to move past my kidnapping and the death of one of my closest friends, Dionysus and I quickly realized that we shared a love of food, especially when it came to trying new foods in new places. It became a thing of ours, a routine that we stuck to each time we went somewhere new. It was small, but it gave me something to look forward to when we traveled.

As he passed, he flicked my hair and smirked. "I like the curls."

"Thanks," I muttered as I shut the door behind him.

"So, how mad are you?" he asked, glancing over his shoulder as he started getting plates and glasses down from the cabinet.

Shamelessly, I took a second to check him out from behind before I began to pull the food out and open containers. The jeans he'd worn were basically a crime, so it was hard to drag my eyes away. That was, until the full force of Johnson's barbecue hit me. I practically drooled when I opened an aluminum tray of pulled pork. Johnson's was a place we'd gone on our first night in Tennessee after Nate's sister, Eris, swore it was to die for. Afterward, I'd dragged Dionysus back three times before we left, each time for the pulled pork, fried green tomatoes, and tater tots fried in duck fat.

"Quite," I told him, plucking a piece of shredded meat and popping it in my mouth. "For various reasons."

He lifted his eyebrows and started uncorking the bottle of pinot noir. "Being?"

I held up my hand and started counting off reasons on my fingers. "You barely said goodbye when we had to leave Olympus, you've been MIA constantly the last few months, and now you show up in my Lit class *as my professor* without even a head's up." Irritated, I stuffed a fried tomato in my mouth. "And you startled me this morning when I was doing my makeup and made me break my eyeshadow, which was very expensive."

Pouring me a glass of wine, he slid it across the island then reached for the containers of food. As he started portioning it out, he frowned.

"We were both sent off on assignments with almost no notice," he said. "My father sent me to college in Germany because he thought there was unrest there, rebels who were trying to dredge up old business." He opened a foil container of truffle fries. "There weren't, but he didn't believe me, so he insisted I stay the entire fall semester. Which sucked, in case you were wondering. I'm starting to see why Nathaniel stepped back from Olympus for as long as he did."

"We talk telepathically," I pointed out. Gods, I sounded needy. "It just hurt my feelings is all. I'd feel the same way if it had been Tessa."

"I've told you before that I enjoy working at universities, even if it's my father's paranoia that puts me there." He pushed my plate toward me, then set his aside and leaned on his forearms. "But I was the only counselor in the student health center, and it was surprisingly busy for such a small school. You'd be surprised at how much that clogs up one's brain, even a deity's, especially when you're dealing with students who lost a lot when Cronus returned. And if it's any consolation, I've hardly talked to anyone, not even my brothers."

"No, I get it, I just . . ." What? What could I possibly say that didn't sound whiny or insecure? And I *wasn't* whiny or insecure, a fact which made my current state of mind that much more aggravating. "I was worried, that's all. And it was weird. I went from seeing or talking to you every day to not at all, then Tessa and Nate left, and Yana got sent to finish her training year back in Romania, Anette went back to Norway, not that she cared to spend time with us, anyway, and Tessa's brothers went to wherever it is they live when they're not on the mountain." It had all happened within the span of a few days, but I was the last to leave because Athena was still making arrangements for me to finish my training year in the US. "I guess it all left me a little shell-shocked."

Smiling sympathetically, he came around the counter and pulled me into a hug. "I'm sorry," he murmured against my hair. "You know if you needed me, I would've been here in an instant, right?"

I nodded, then rested my forehead against his chest, letting his closeness relax me as he tightened his arms around me. I'd never been one to need physical contact with others to get by, but the last few months had been lonely. My friends, the ones I had left, anyway, were scattered around the globe doing their own things, and while the panic attacks and bad dreams I'd had in the few months after my kidnapping had finally dwindled to the occasional heart-pounding nightmare, spending so much time alone had filled me with an emptiness that sometimes just left me feeling helpless and damn near touch-starved. I'd always been an extrovert, but the fact that I'd essentially been forced into an introverted lifestyle was a lot harder to deal with than I thought it would be, considering.

Wrapping my arms around his waist, I sighed. "We're all dealing with stuff. I get it."

"True." He pulled back and sat down on a stool, then nudged me down onto the one beside him, so we were knee-to-knee, and took my hands. "But I still could've been a better friend, which brings me to why I'm here. I could tell you were furious with me when we spoke this morning, so I told Athena to pay off your literature professor so I could take his place." He wiggled his eyebrows. "Now you get to see me all the time."

A fact that was equal parts crazy and amazing. Not wanting him to see how excited that made me, I smirked. "Stalker much?"

"And if it were anyone else, I would've gone with a different method. *You* need grand gestures, Mary Miller." He grinned and stuffed a fry in my mouth, which was apparently hanging open.

I arched a brow and swallowed the fry. "I do?"

"If I'd just said, 'I'm sorry, I'll promise to check in more,' would you have believed me?"

"No."

"Well, there you go."

I huffed. "I guess grand gestures mean something different when you're dealing with a god, huh?"

"Oh, absolutely," he agreed. "Did Tessa tell you that in each town they visit, Nathaniel has an entire restaurant empty out so they can have it all to themselves?"

I rolled my eyes. "Yes, and I try very hard not to imagine *why*. She also told me they're small restaurants and he more than compensates the restaurant owners and workers. And taking over a restaurant for one night isn't the same as paying a professor to let you take his job while spreading the rumor that he had a mental breakdown."

Dionysus laughed. "I certainly didn't do *that,* but it's not surprising that's what people think. If a professor bails last minute for whatever reason, students *always* think it's because they had some kind of mental break. Regardless, we paid him four semesters' worth of wages and his bills for a year. He's now on his way to fulfill his life-long dream of backpacking through Europe."

"How nice for him," I deadpanned.

"It is," he agreed, ignoring my sarcasm. "We should do it some-time. Now, eat."

Scowling, I picked up a fork. "I'm still mad at you," I said stub-bornly as I started digging into the food. "This changes nothing."

Smirking, he tugged on a lock of my hair.

"Liar."

AFTER I'D SUFFICIENTLY GORGED myself on food and changed into a cami and pajama pants, Dionysus grabbed the bottle of wine and pulled me over to the couch.

"So, tell me about your new best friend," he said. "How did you manage to befriend her so quickly?"

"I froze the bolts on the stool she was sitting on, she fell on her ass, and I kindly pointed out the empty seat next to mine," I told him as I settled on the soft sofa, tucking me feet beneath me.

He gave me an appreciative smile. "Nice work. What's she like?"

"She seems okay sometimes. Other times, she seems like a raging bitch. It's only been one day, though."

"Do you think you'll be able to handle her?"

I lifted my eyebrows and took a sip of wine. "I've already got an invite to the sorority house this weekend."

His eyes widened. "How on earth did you manage that so fast?"

"Dumb luck. Seriously," I added when he gave me a dubious look. "We just happened to run into one of her sorority sisters outside the student center when we went for coffee and they started talking about rushing."

"Hang on." Turning mildly serious, he set his glass of wine down and put his hands on my knees. "Do *not* tell me you're going to pledge."

Blushing, I rolled my eyes and shoved his hands away. "How else am I supposed to get to know this chick? Athena faked some records at U Penn, so now I have legacy status. It's pretty much an automatic in."

Amusement flooded his face. "Mary Miller, a sorority girl. I never would've pegged you."

"I've heard some great things about sororities, so it might not be all bad," I told him, surprised at how defensive I sounded. It wasn't a lie, either. After I'd gone over Calla's records, I'd done a little digging on her sorority, then fell down a research rabbit hole. I planned to look into them in more detail over the next few days, but on the surface, it seemed like most really fostered a family lifestyle that lasted long after graduation.

"No, I agree," he said. "It's just going to end up taking up most of your time, that's all."

Teasingly, I poked his side. "You're not just trying to stop me from doing this so you don't have to live in this winter wonderland for the next five months, are you?"

"And miss out on teaching you how to ski? Not a chance."

"Teaching?" My eyes widened in annoyance. "What makes you think I don't already know? I might be able to wipe the mountain with you."

He snorted. "Unlikely."

I tapped the side of my head. "Go on, take a look. You'll see."

"Nope," he said, shaking his head. "I prefer to be pleasantly surprised."

"When you eat my dust?"

"I'm a god, Mary," he said seriously, as if that were enough of an explanation.

"Modest, too."

"One of my more endearing qualities." His eyes flicked to the television. "Now, I have to ask . . ."

I rolled my eyes. "The new season got added a few weeks ago, and no, I haven't watched." We'd realized not long after we became friends that we both shared a love of a certain reality TV dating show, the last season of which ended not long before I left for Olympus back in June. I just liked the trashy TV aspect of it, but he insisted he watched it and others like it to keep up with human pop culture.

It took about thirty seconds of tickling to get him to admit the truth.

He grinned. "You must not have been that mad at me, then. Give me five minutes to get changed."

I frowned as he stood. "Where are you living, anyway? You're not commuting from Olympus, right?" The constant time zone changes would've been annoying at best.

"I thought about it, but my adoring sister informed me that the apartment next door was empty, so I bought it."

My heart picked up a bit at that. "Um . . . why not just rent?"

Surprisingly, he looked almost wary. "I like it here. I might want to come back once this whole thing is over."

"To a one-bedroom apartment with octogenarian shop-owner neighbors?"

"Do I strike you as the type to need a lot of space?" He brushed a thumb across my chin and smiled. "I'll be right back."

The second he was gone, I reached out to Tessa.

Tell me you didn't know Dionysus was coming here.'

'Nate just told me, I swear!'

'Tell Nate he fucking sucks. I was blindsided in the middle of class, Tess! He's my godsdamn teacher!'

There was a pause, and I swore I could feel her amusement before she responded. *'Does that mean you're, um, hot for tea—'*

'Finish that sentence and I will end you.'

'I'm sorry. But hey, now that you have him there with you, maybe you'll get a chance to talk. Considering all he did to get there with you, it's clear he's got some pretty big feelings.'

'I guess. He's hardly lacking in confidence, though, so if he wanted to act on said feelings, he would've by now.'

I ran a hand through my hair, annoyed that any sense of confidence I had—which was a lot on a normal day—seemed to evaporate when it came to him. I routinely thanked every god in existence that Tessa, Nate, and Chiron had taken the time to help me build up some kick-ass mental walls, otherwise every single thought and feeling I had for him would be on full display.

'I was thinking more along the lines of you kissing him to see if he kisses you back.'

'I've definitely considered it.' Many, many times.

'So do it!'

'I don't know. I want to, but at the same time, we have such an amazing friendship. I'd hate to ruin that, especially considering he's Nate's brother. And now that I have this assignment, I absolutely cannot fuck this up, or Athena will literally send me to live with the penguins.'

She laughed. *'Listen, here's the thing about empathic gods like Dionysus. They don't take relationships lightly. The feelings are more . . . intense. Some avoid relationships entirely, others just dive right in. He's the type to do that latter once he finds the right person, and according to Nate, he definitely thinks that's you.'*

'I guess.' I sighed. *'Just give me some time. Now that we're in the same place and I'm finally back on my feet—'* I cut off with a grunt as Dionysus rolled over the back of the couch and pinned me down. "Jerk!" I pushed against him, but I might as well have been pushing against a brick wall.

"That's what you get for trying to distract me in class," he said, propping himself on his elbow. "Now, I require your full attention, so tell Tessa you'll talk to her later."

'Mare?'

'Gotta go.'

"What makes you think I was talking to Tessa?" I asked once I cut the connection with her.

"You get this weird vacant look of concentration when you're talking to someone telepathically," he said, shifting back and pulling me into a sitting position. "And last I checked, she's the only deity you talk to on a regular basis."

"You get the same look," I pointed out.

"Not like you." He picked up the remote and turned the television on. "I think it's harder for Ischyra than gods to hold the connection."

"Apologies for my sorely lacking telepathy skills," I said dryly.

"Shush, you know that's not what I meant." Wordlessly, he held out an arm.

With a sigh, I slid over and snuggled against him.

He got the show set up, then turned out the light on the end table.

We were quiet for a few minutes as the first episode recapped the previous season, then he kissed the top of my head and sighed contentedly.

"I missed you, doll," he murmured, his breath hot against my ear.

I smiled as he pulled me a little closer. "Ditto, loser."

9

DIONYSUS

Bright sunlight was coming through the living room windows when I opened my eyes the next morning. Not for the first time, Mary and I had fallen asleep on the couch wrapped up under a blanket together. I'd just clued in to my surroundings when I felt a small shake.

"It's eight o'clock," Mary mumbled against my chest, tightening her arm around my waist. She did things like that when she was still groggy in the morning—pressed herself closer, let me hold her a little longer.

"So?" I tightened the blanket around us and snuggled deeper into the couch, throwing one leg over hers. Then, realizing it was morning and I was fucking hard as a rock, I shifted so I wasn't pressed quite so close, but kept my face nuzzled into her neck. I took in her scent and couldn't help but think that waking up like this every day for the rest of eternity would literally be the perfect life.

"You have to teach in an hour," she murmured.

"Good thing I can teleport."

"How about you teleport yourself downstairs and get me some coffee, then?"

Sleepily, I laughed and squeezed her side, letting my hand linger a little longer than one might expect for a friendly gesture, then leaned back to look at her. "Is this still punishment for my absence?"

She angled my head to the side. "Yes, actually. I don't think you've groveled enough." With a sniff, she wrinkled her nose. "Brush your teeth first, though. You might kill someone with that morning breath."

I grinned, the only warning I gave before I pinned her underneath me and started tickling her. Which, considering my below-the-belt status, was probably a bad idea, but I couldn't help myself.

"You love my morning breath," I said, laughing as she tried to wriggle off the sofa. "Say it and I'll stop."

She squealed and tried to push me off, but it was no use because, well, godly strength and all that. "I—" She did a weird laugh-squeak as my fingers danced across her rib cage where her shirt had ridden up, revealing that golden-tan skin of hers. "Fine! Fine, I love your stupid morning breath!"

My hands stilled and she let out a relieved breath. She hated being tickled more than most things, so it was always a guaranteed way to get her to give in.

Smiling, I ran my eyes over her face, taking her in again. "That's better." I smacked a kiss to her forehead and stood up. "I'll be right back."

She rubbed her eyes and stretched. "K."

I teleported over to my apartment to dress and brush my teeth, then went downstairs to the coffee shop, hoping they opened early. Luckily, Bill, the owner, was just unlocking the door when I showed up.

"Hi, there!" he said, greeting me with a wide grin. "Here for coffee?"

I nodded and thanked him as he held the door open, then gestured at the case of cookies on the glass counter that held an assortment of pastries. "And cookies. The biggest you've got."

He chuckled. "Cookies and coffee for breakfast. My pa would've had my hide if I tried that."

"Morning!" Bill's wife, Jane, greeted me from behind the counter.

"Two coffees, hmm? I don't suppose one is for that pretty girl upstairs?"

"Sure is," I said. "Mary's the one with the sweet tooth."

'How's it going?'

I gritted my teeth when I heard Athena's voice, then ignored her while I waited for my order. Once I had coffee and cookies in hand, I thanked Bill and Jane and left.

'How's what going?' I asked.

'Mary. Does it seem like she's got this one handled?'

'How many times do I need to tell you I wouldn't have recommended her otherwise? And you're not going to start using me as a means to spy on her every move. You wouldn't have sent her here if you didn't think her capable.'

'True, but I also don't want you to be a distraction. It's fine if you want to get back in your friend's good graces, but she's not there to have fun.'

I winced and shook my head as I realized how clueless my otherwise intelligent sister was when it came to relationships. Anyone with half a brain knew I wasn't here to "make things up to my friend."

'She's doing fine.'

'Good, because Father is not happy I agreed to shift your assignment, and Apollo is being Apollo, so he's just dying to say he told me so. So, if you do anything to distract her from doing this job any less than perfectly, you'll be feeding Cerberus the next time Hades and Persephone take a vacation.'

'Actually feeding him, or I'll be the food?'

'That remains to be seen.'

'K. I have to go.'

I cut off the connection before she could question me any further, not really wanting her to know just how concerned I was about distracting Mary. I wanted a relationship with her; that was a given. An actual relationship, not a fling like Hermes might think. Which caused problems on a larger scale, because Zeus was very particular about the kind of people his children had serious relationships with. If I was going to have something with her, it would damn sure be serious.

Although, after Tessa and Nathaniel, it would probably be tough to disappoint him. Zeus hadn't been so crazy about her at first, considering her father and brothers had openly fought against him in the Titan war. But he warmed up to her once he saw just how cemented she was to our cause.

At the end of the day, though, he still had his issues with her, mainly because she intimidated him, which he would never admit. He also knew Nathaniel had no problem thumbing his nose at the entire mountain for the rest of eternity if Zeus so much as thought about giving him a hard time.

Even still, there were times I wasn't sure a relationship with Mary was as good an idea as I thought. For all I knew, she'd probably assume I was pursuing her because of my constant need to fix both things and people, which was completely false. Yet, it could explain why she hadn't attempted to tell me how she felt. I knew how she felt; I'd seen it in the way she'd look at me and could feel it in the obvious comfort she felt when we were snuggled in a way that was miles past appropriate for friends. And even though I knew she'd managed to bounce back from the attack on the Ischyra arena, her kidnapping, and her part in ending the war, when I thought about how traumatic all of those things had been for her, it was hard to believe anyone would really be able to move on in just six months.

But that was the thing about Mary. She could. I'd seen her mind when she'd returned and I'd felt her conviction when we decided I'd back off from helping her. Yes, she'd had more than a few panic attacks, and yes, her nightmares were pretty vicious, but as far as I knew, the only thing that rivaled her pain was her stubbornness, and that often seemed to win out.

And yet...

There was a nagging voice in the back of my head that wondered whether she'd tell me if she was still having a hard time.

Shoving that thought aside, I let myself back into Mary's apartment. When I stepped inside, I heard the sound of the sink running in the bathroom, so I set the coffee and cookies down on the counter and made my way back. I found her standing at the sink, her hair piled on top of her head in a messy bun, brushing her teeth.

She met my eyes in the mirror and grinned, flashing me a smile full of toothpaste that was beyond endearing.

"You're so gross," I said.

She rinsed, spit, then dried her mouth on a towel and faced me. "Did you remember cookies?"

I rolled my eyes. "I've met you before today. What do you think?"

She walked past me, tossing me a smirk as she made her way out to the kitchen.

"So, what are your plans for the day?" I asked when she picked up her coffee.

"I need to research the Aidens a little more and look into Willow, the sorority president." She unwrapped a cookie and broke off a piece, then dunked it in her coffee. "I have to figure out the best way to make a good impression with her. Legacy or not, I need to convince her I belong there."

I rested my forearms against the counter and picked up my own cookie. "Considering she's the face of the sorority, she's likely more restrictive about what she shares online. What are you thinking?"

"Not sure." She popped another piece of cookie in her mouth. "I'm guessing anything less-than-savory will show up in her friends' social media and not her own or any tied directly to the sorority."

"Probably." I gave her an appraising look. "You know, considering how much you dislike research, you seem pretty good at it."

She shrugged. "Just because I don't like it doesn't mean I don't know how to do it."

"True. So, dinner tonight? I'm only teaching until six."

She nodded. "Bring me pizza." She pursed her lips and thought for a moment. "That place in Rome Tessa told me about."

"So, this will be my penance, then? Fetching you food from around the world?"

"For at least another decade." She patted my cheek and gave me that fucking smirk again. "Now, go. I have work to do and you've got class."

I swallowed the last of my cookie, blew her a kiss, then disappeared.

10

MARY

Since I didn't have class until eleven that day, I dove into research the second Dionysus left, needing something to distract myself from the amount of close contact we'd had on the sofa.

Contact that told me *way* more about him than I'd realized. Sure, we'd fallen asleep together before. But the way he put his leg over mine... that was new. And telling.

So, I shifted my focus to other, more mundane things.

I read up a bit more on Calla's father, who was suspiciously lucky in life even by immortal standards. He had a privileged life with his upper-upper-class parents in Malibu, where he'd excelled in basketball, soccer, lacrosse, field hockey, baseball, and track. He'd finished first in his class at Harvard when he got his bachelor's in biology, then again at MIT and Yale for his post-graduate degrees in genetics and physics. From there, he'd landed a job as a biophysicist with a company that specialized in nanobiotechnology, which is, apparently, a thing. By the time he was thirty, he'd amassed so much wealth in stocks that he kept his hundred-thousand-dollar-a-year job in order to continue his research instead of taking the multi-million dollar executive position that had been offered. He'd met his wife, Missa, by chance when they both jumped into the same cab in New York City, and their daughter Calla had been born two years later.

All of that was available in his bio on his company's website, but I did a bit more digging on certain aspects and was a bit disturbed to find it was all true and then some.

Not only had he met his wife in the most rom-com way imaginable, he'd rented out the Eiffel Tower so he could propose to her on top of it without any onlookers present. He'd even had fireworks go off the moment she said yes. Their wedding was held in Central Park, which he'd also managed to have closed off to everyone but the wedding guests. I was incapable of comprehending how much money it would've cost to do *one* of those things, much less two.

Honestly, the only other person I would've expected that much extravagance from was Nate, but he'd been stupid and proposed to Tessa on a bench in Disney World.

Closing my computer, I reached out to Athena.

'You said this guy had mental manipulation powers, right?'

'Yes. Why?'

'I'm looking at all of his info and he's got Coercer written all over him.'

'Similar, but not quite as strong. If he were a full god, he'd likely rival Nathaniel, but since he's half human, his powers don't extend past manipulating humans and weak-willed demigods.'

'Got it. And there's been no evidence that Calla inherited anything?'

'It's incredibly unlikely for the child of a demigod to inherit his powers, but no, there's been no indication she's got powers. But don't—'

'Let my guard down, I know.' I sighed. I was going to have to work on the assumption that Calla *did* have powers because, rarity or not, if she were my kid, I'd do my damnedest to keep them hidden. *'By the way, do we know if Stewart knows his dad isn't his bio dad?'*

'Yes, he knows. Stewart was ten months old when his parents started dating. Mr. Aiden adopted Stewart just before his second birthday. Reportedly, his mother told him his biological father was killed in a car accident not long after he was born.'

Interesting, but not terribly damning. Zeus probably forced an interdiction on Stewart's mom.

'Was there anything else?'

'You mean, aside from not forewarning me that Dionysus was coming?'

'That was a last-minute adjustment.' Her annoyance at that fact was obvious. 'Just do me a favor? Try to refrain from any future guilt trips. I didn't appreciate having to take time out of my day to find a replacement for him at the university where he was working in Germany so he could beg your forgiveness. I also had to run interference with my father, which is something I like to avoid doing more than once a century.'

I rolled my eyes. 'No one's begging for anything, Athena. Rearranging his entire life was unnecessary.'

'Take it up with him,' she quipped. 'I've got to go. Check in later to give me your progress report on Calla.'

Progress report. Right.

'Sure thing, boss.'

Pause.

'Please go next door and ask my overly-accommodating brother to fill you in on how to properly prepare a progress report.'

'Will do.'

Deciding the basics of my job weren't something I needed to rely on Dionysus to help me with, I pulled my notebook over and started jotting down everything about my first impressions of Calla. My initial opinions based on her online presence seemed pretty spot-on: beautiful, entitled, a bit bitchy—a typical mean girl who was only willing to allow people into her social circle if she saw them as part of her class or beneficial in some way. In my case, bringing in a legacy would look good. After meeting her and seeing her responses to other students, the minor guilt I'd felt about spending so much money on clothes had evaporated. If I'd introduced myself to her in anything but designer *everything*, she likely would've turned up her pert little nose at me.

All of that considered, there was no way I was going to be able to truly befriend this girl without going crazy if I couldn't find some kind of common ground with her. Being sorority sisters seemed like the best bet, but cementing myself as a valid choice for a pledge might be a hard sell when it came to the other sisters.

Biting my lip, I pulled up the site for South Lake's library, hoping the online catalog would be helpful enough to save me from leaving for campus early.

After trying a few different search terms, I managed to pull up a history on each of the university's sororities. I immediately dove into the area for Iota Sigma Xi. I read up on the foundation of the sorority at the turn of the twentieth century to their more recent endeavors with charity work and other noble causes.

By all accounts, it was a stand-up organization that did a lot to help the community. Each semester, they held a university blood drive that always had a huge turnout. In the fall semesters, they would adopt a few families in need to help with winter clothing and food, and they held car washes in September and May to raise money for school supplies for local kids. It didn't seem like they went above and beyond any other organizations, but they certainly weren't atypical by any stretch.

Leaning back against the sofa, I tapped my pen on my notebook.

If the sorority wasn't on the up and up, there likely wouldn't be anything right there in black and white in their history.

Frowning, I picked up my laptop and started scrolling back through the information I'd found on Iota Sig and set about taking notes on their causes, goals, and past charity work. On the surface, those things all seemed perfectly benign, but shady people always hid behind things like that to do their business, especially when witches were involved.

As I wrote out the list of all the things Iota Sig had done in the past for the local community, I really hoped it was all legit. Even if they had ulterior motives, it would be nice to know they had at least done something right.

But I learned a long time ago not to get my hopes up.

11

MARY

I broke at ten to head to campus for my chem class before returning to my apartment around noon. Calla was in that class, too, but we'd already agreed ahead of time to sit together, so I didn't have to jump through the same hoops to get close to her. It was more or less uneventful and seemed like it was going to be a pretty good class.

After contemplating just being lazy for the rest of the afternoon until I had to leave for comp at three, I decided to spend the rest of the day researching Stewart Aiden. While his life story and background were interesting and provided a lot of insight into who he was, one of Athena's earlier suppositions had been right.

Aiden *was* running for office. And not just any office. Congress. He wanted to be the Representative of New York's twenty-first district, which encompassed a large swath of Upstate New York. He had no party affiliation, which was basically unheard of for that area, but something told me that wouldn't matter a single bit when election time came.

Which, coincidentally, was this year.

'Athena?'

'Yes?'

'You know how you said Aiden might be running for office?'

'Yes?'

'Well, consider that official. He's running for US Congress.'

She was quiet for a moment.

'Well, that's unfortunate.'

'No shit.' When she'd mentioned him running for office before, I'd assumed mayor or city council. Knowing him, he'd be crowned Speaker of the fucking House the second he got elected.

'Considering we've been doing extensive research on him, this must be a new development,' Athena said. *'How did you find out?'*

'I Googled him. Four times. This website absolutely wasn't there this morning.'

'All right, I'll look into it a bit more, and I'll see if Dionysus can find out anything through the university. He may be able to use his powers to get some information.' She sighed. *'I suppose it's not so bad he's there, after all.'*

I thought about waking up with him this morning in a far more compromising position than we had before and smiled.

No, it definitely wasn't a bad thing he was here at all.

My phone buzzed, dragging me away from my research. When I picked it up, I saw that Calla had texted me a picture. Opening the text, I saw that it was a selfie of her and Kristy, each holding a steaming cup of something while sitting on some kind of porch. The text just read, 'Come drink with us!'

Laughing, I shook my head.

'Calla's texting me. I have to go. Let me know if you find out any more.'

'Same to you.'

Closing the connection to Athena, I turned my attention to my phone.

Mary: *Can't. I have comp at 3.*

Calla: *Lame. Text me after.*

I sent her a thumbs-up emoji then set my phone back down, surprised at how easy it was to turn down her invite, but happy I'd gotten one all the same. That was progress.

A year ago, I would've been completely down to skip class and go hang out with friends, especially knowing this was just a job and not something that would make or break my college career. Right up until the day I left Renville, I was always a party girl, so much so that I showed up to my first day on Olympus hungover after a graduation party that had gone late into the night. Something had changed since June, though, and not only because of all the terrible things that had happened since. Sure, betrayals, kidnappings, and battles with former friends had a hand in changing my general outlook on life, but the responsibilities and expectations that had been placed on my shoulders made the things I once found enticing wholly unappealing.

But, considering my current assignment . . .

Yep, it was time to dive back in.

With a sigh, I picked up my phone and texted her back.

Mary: *I'll be done by six. What are you guys doing later?*

Her response came almost immediately.

Calla: *Kappa O is having a thing. Text me when you're done and I'll tell you where to meet us.* A giant smiley face immediately followed.

Rubbing a hand across my forehead, I reached out for Dionysus.

'So, what does one wear to a frat party these days?'

'Already getting invites?' he asked, sounding amused. *'Does this mean you're ditching me tonight?'*

'Looks like.' As bummed as I was at that fact, skipping out on an opportunity to get closer to Calla and her friends, because I'd rather gorge myself on pizza with Dionysus, would just be counterproductive.

'Is it a party-party or a smaller gathering?'

'I don't know. She said they were having a thing.'

'Nothing flashy, then. Find a balance between dressy and casual.'

Helpful.

'Which one, anyway?'

'Kappa O.'

There was a second of silence.

'That a problem?' I teased.

'Nope. Have fun. Let me know if you need me to come pick you up.'

'Will do.' I paused and bit my lip. *'I'm sorry I'll have to bail on dinner.'*

'*You've got a job to do. And you can make it up to me later.*'

'*Thanks,*' I said. I knew he'd understand, but I could still hear the disappointment in his tone, even if he'd tried to hide it.

I couldn't help but be a little happy at the fact that he was disappointed we wouldn't be spending time together tonight, because it meant he actually wanted to see me.

Which would be great, if a tiny voice in my brain wasn't wondering if he just wanted to see me because close proximity to my lingering brokenness would feed his need to fix broken things[

Immediately, I shut down that thought and went back to work.

CALLA OFFERED to pick me up after class so I wouldn't have to GPS it to the frat house, but I told her I could drive myself.

Which I could. Totally.

However, as I sat in the driver's seat of my shiny new Volvo, I began to second-guess such a rash decision. Despite the confidence I'd shown Athena, I'd driven a car exactly two times before this, not counting the heart-pounding practice I'd had with Chris and Alan in their ten-year-old Camry before my driver's test.

Mortified, I contemplated calling Dionysus, but I squashed that instantly because I absolutely did not need a guy to show me how to operate a car.

I picked up the key fob, then frowned when I saw no actual key attached to it.

"What the fuck, Athena," I muttered, turning the useless piece of plastic over in my hand. "Give me this fancy-ass car and don't even tell me how to start it."

I looked down, checking to see if maybe something had fallen off the ring, then caught sight of the great big "Engine" knob. I turned it, but nothing happened. Then, remembering Chris's number one rule of starting cars—always have your foot on the brake—I pressed down on the brake pedal, turned the knob, and the engine roared to life.

I grinned.

"See, Mary? You're no damsel."

With a quick glance into the street, I put the car in drive and slid my foot off the brake and pressed the gas. Immediately, I slammed my foot back on the brake when the damn thing shot forward.

I do not need help, I do not need help, I do not need help.

Gritting my teeth, I took a deep breath, then *slowly* pressed the gas and guided the car into the street from the side lot I'd been parked in. Traffic was light on Main, so I took my time driving the few blocks out of the busier area until I was on a quieter stretch of road. Thankfully, my Ischyra instincts and muscle memory kicked in pretty quick, so after about fifteen minutes of driving around aimlessly, I felt pretty confident in my newfound skills. Once I'd pulled over and put the address in my GPS, I made my way back toward campus.

The Kappa Omega house was an old Victorian just off campus that looked to be surprisingly well-kept. The bushes were neatly trimmed and the boards on the porch were smooth, the paint, chip-free. The shingles that made up the outside walls were either original or replicas, but the owners hadn't gone the "just slap on some siding" route I would've expected of someone who owned a frat house.

Calla and Kristy were crossing the street as I got out of my car, so I waited on the sidewalk for them, my gloved hands stuffed deep into the pockets of my coat. I'd gone with fleece-lined leggings that were shockingly warm, a green thigh-length cashmere sweater, fur-lined leather boots, and I'd darkened my eye makeup a little bit to bring out the hazel colors. I felt like I landed somewhere between dressy and casual, so hopefully, I made a good impression.

"Hey, you!" Calla said, looping her arm through mine. "I'm so glad you could come!"

I grinned at her and Kristy. "Yeah, pizza and homework sort of lost its appeal after we talked."

Kristy laughed. "She's a rotten influence, Mary, I'll warn you now." She glanced down at my feet. "I love your boots! They look so cozy."

I gave her a smile of thanks as Calla tugged me toward the house. "Come on, let's get inside. It's cold as fuck out here."

I wrinkled my nose as we made our way up the walk. "Is it always this cold? Or is this just an obscenely cold winter?"

Calla snorted and Kristy laughed. "It's thirty degrees out," Kristy said. "That's balmy for us."

I made a mental note to pour a bucket of ice over Tessa's head the next time I saw her.

Kristy rang the bell, then we waited. There were a bunch of loud thumps, some cursing, then a loud bang. A second later, the door opened. Shep, the guy from the bookstore stood there, grinning.

"Hey, girls!" Recognition flashed when he saw me. "Hey! We met, right?"

"Oh, um, yep." I smiled, giving him a half-wave. "Mary."

Calla hip-bumped me. "Already making friends?"

Shep stepped aside so we could come in. "We met when Mary bought her books the other day. Come on, Milo just got a fire going out back."

I could practically feel my bones warming at the mention of fire.

"So, it's just the six of us tonight," Calla whispered as we followed him through the massive, and surprisingly clean, house. "But some of the other brothers might be in and out. It's not like, a triple-date thing or whatever, so don't worry," she added when she saw the look of alarm on my face. "They're just our brother frat, and if you're going to become an Iota girl, it's important you get to know some of them."

"Why?" I frowned. "I'm brand new."

She bit her lip and exchanged a quick look with Kristy. "Well, that's the thing. You're super new. Like, boom, out of nowhere new, *and* you're a legacy. I talked to Willow, and she's all about slapping your colors on right now, but you have to mesh well with our brothers."

"It's all about harmony," Kristy explained when she saw the confused look on my face. "Our houses do a lot together."

"Most things, really," Calla added as we stepped onto the back porch. "Mixers, fundraisers, the whole nine."

Kristy nodded. "We can't accept someone who won't or can't get along with her sisters and brothers."

But no pressure.

"Don't let her scare you, Mary," Shep said as he opened the door to the backyard. "We don't bite, I promise."

"Well, that's good to hear," I said with a grin. "I'm really looking forward to meeting everyone."

The backyard was fairly small, but had a decent-sized patio fit with a propane firepit surrounded by some mismatched patio furniture and four tall, outdoor heaters. Two guys stood warming their hands by the fire.

"Oh, thank god," Calla groaned. "Last time, they couldn't get the stupid thing started because some dumbass freshman used all the gas and didn't fill up the tank." She jerked her chin toward one of the sofas. "Come on."

The two guys noticed our arrival and Shep made introductions. "Tristan, Milo, this is Mary."

Both stepped away from the fire. The first, tall and thin with deep brown skin and brown eyes, extended a hand. "Tristan," he said as we shook hands. He angled his head toward the second guy, who was more on the stocky side with a complexion that looked like he would fry to a crisp after a day in the sun. "This is Milo."

"Nice to meet you both," I told them as I shook Milo's hand.

Tristan waved us over toward the fire. "Come on, sit. We're always happy to meet new recruits."

I arched a brow at his choice of word, then smiled. "Yeah, I was really lucky to run into Calla."

"How did you guys meet, anyway?" Milo asked.

"We have some classes together and she seemed not-annoying," Calla said, taking a seat on one of the sofas.

Kristy smirked. "Calla fell on her ass and Mary helped her up."

"Bitch," Calla muttered, and I couldn't help but laugh.

"I don't know what that means, but okay," Tristan said. "So, you girls want dinner or drinks first?"

"Liquid appetizers, obviously," Calla said. "We can eat later." She sent me a sunny smile. "And it'll give us more time to get to know Miss Mary."

"On it," Tristan said.

He and Milo went in the house and came out a minute later with six beers. Once we'd all settled around the fire with drinks in our hands, conversation shifted toward school and the relationship between Iota Sig and Kappa O.

"So, what's your major, anyway?" Shep asked. "You bought all those science books, so I'm guessing something in that arena?"

"Bio," I said. "You?"

"English." He rolled his eyes, then shifted in his seat so he was facing me directly, one arm slung across the back. "Biggest mistake ever."

"Yeah? Why?"

"I'd planned to be a professor, but after the last conversation I had with my advisor, I'll be lucky if I get a job as an adjunct."

"That's good money, though, right? And you could get your foot in the door somewhere?"

"It's decent money for what it is, but not really enough to live on unless you're partial to ramen and condensed soup." He took a swig of his beer. "But yeah, I could get my foot in the door, which is my main goal right now."

"Hopefully you'll be better than our professor," Calla said, rolling her eyes. "I can already tell he's going to be a total pain in the ass."

I arched a brow, and Kristy laughed.

"Does that mean you're not going to try and get him into bed?" Kristy asked.

Calla shrugged. "He doesn't really seem like my type, after all."

"That's Calla speak for 'he has too much of a soul,'" Milo said with a laugh.

Calla threw a piece of bread at him. "Dick."

He deflected it and stood. "I'm gonna check on the lasagna."

We talked for a few more minutes before Milo called us in for dinner.

"Just a head's up, Mary," Tristan said as we made our way inside. "Be prepared for a shit ton of questions over the next couple of weeks.

Iota Sig are pretty particular about who they let in, even legacies, so they'll want to know every damn thing about you."

"Don't worry," Calla said, tossing me a grin over her shoulder. "We'll go easy on you tonight."

I grimaced. "Awesome."

Tristan wasn't wrong. As soon as we sat down, Calla and Kristy started firing off questions. They were simple at first. They wanted to know what it was like growing up in a small town (boring), why I moved from Reading to Lake Placid (aforementioned small town was boring and I loved to ski), what sports I played in high school (softball, archery, track), and so on. I barely had time to squeeze bites of food in between answers, which was super irritating.

At some point, Shep seemed to notice my annoyance and broke into the conversation.

"So, Calla, I talked to Willow earlier. She said your mom wants to do a meet-and-greet thing at your parents' house?"

"Ugh." Calla rolled her eyes. "Yeah. She's annoyed she couldn't do it last year. She and my dad, well, mainly her, want to 'meet the people their little girl is spending so much time with' or whatever. So yeah. Probably in a few weeks, once we have the pledges nailed down."

"That's nice that your parents want to be involved," I said. When she sent me a look, I laughed. "Or not."

She wrinkled her nose. "No, I guess it is. My mom is just so . . . mid-life-crisis-y. Her prime was two decades ago, so she keeps trying to live vicariously through me. She was an Iota Sig, too, so she likes to regale us with stories of her heyday."

"What about your dad? Is he like her with wanting to know all your friends?"

She flipped her dark curls over her shoulder. "He cares, but he gives me more space than she does. It's definitely preferable. He's so wrapped up in his campaign now, though, so it's hard for him to give much attention to these kinds of things."

I gave her a curious look, hoping my feigned ignorance was convincing. "Campaign?"

Her expression turned smug. "Didn't I tell you? My dad is running for Congress."

"Oh! I had no idea. That's kind of awesome."

She shrugged. "I guess. He just decided. Like, literally a week ago. I was kind of surprised he got a campaign up and running so fast, but that's my dad, I guess. I honestly think my mom wanted it more than him." She frowned at Tristan, who was pulling a roll from a bowl, then leaned over and snatched the one he'd just picked up out of his hands. "Don't hog the bread, Tris!"

He laughed, then lunged to take it back. "Don't be a bitch, Cal!"

And with that, the topic of her dad was closed.

I decided not to push her with any more questions on her dad, so I switched my focus to Kristy and let the conversation drift toward getting to know one another. It was sort of nice, spending time with people who were completely removed from my life as an Ischyra. It had been a long time since I'd had a casual conversation regarding anything that didn't have something to do with Olympus, so it was kind of relieving to talk about things like classes and celebrities and music.

It kind of sucked that it was all a ruse.

12

MARY

I spent all of Friday fleshing out my backstory before my meeting with Willow the next day. I'd realized during dinner with the Kappa boys that there were still a few holes in Mary Jameson's history that needed filling, and the last thing I wanted was to get caught forgetting something. I also had Athena get a few records faked, showing I'd done community service in a few places in Pennsylvania, which was, according to Calla, a huge part of being an Iota Sig. Dionysus came over with pizza and wine to quiz me on all of the details that night, which took several hours and led to us, once again, crashing on the couch together and waking up in a tangled mess of legs.

Sigh.

After agonizing over an outfit and my hair and makeup for two hours the following day, I left my apartment with plenty of time to get to the Iota Sig house promptly at six to meet with Willow Higgins, president of Iota Sigma Xi.

When I pulled up out front, I took a minute to take in the massive Victorian in front of me, which seemed to be the general theme of all the Greek houses at South Lake. It was directly across the street from Kappa O and was nearly double in size. Again, whoever kept up the property did a damn good job, because even in the dead of winter, it was manicured to perfection.

I had the horrifying thought that they might make the first-year sisters do it.

I'd gotten halfway up the steps to the front porch when the door swung open and a willowy girl with long black hair, dark, almond-shaped eyes, and an overall carefree look about her stepped out. She wore a white V-neck shirt with a red cardigan and jeans. A gold pin in the shape of a shield with red enamel lettering was pinned just below her collar.

"Hi!" she said. "You're Mary, right?"

"That's me," I said with a smile.

She held out her hand. "I'm Willow. Thanks so much for coming by!"

I shook her hand, then followed her into the house, shrugging out of my jacket as soon as I stepped inside, where the heat felt like it had been set to "fires of Mordor."

"Here, Rochelle will take that," Willow said, gesturing to a girl who was coming through an archway to the right.

Rochelle held out her hand for my coat and smiled. "I'll hang it up for you. Just let me know when you need it."

I thanked her, then turned back to Willow and smiled.

"Come on, let's sit and chat," she said.

She gestured toward the room Rochelle had just come from, a living room that looked like something out of a historical romance novel. It had wood-trimmed couches, a roaring fire, glass-topped tables, and even a chandelier. Pretty but odd, considering the occupants.

Willow settled on one of the brocade sofas, tucking her long legs beneath her, then patted the spot next to her. "Come, sit. Rochelle will bring us some water."

I set my purse down on the floor and sat down next to her. "Your house is beautiful."

"Thank you! We're diligent about upkeep around here, which

you'll see pretty quick." Letting out a quick breath, she gave me a sunny smile. "So, Mary Jameson, tell me about yourself."

"Oh. Um, what would you like to know?"

"What are your interests." She angled head a bit and gave me a small smile. "What do you like to do in your spare time?"

"It depends. Back home, I was into archery and I like to read now and then." I gave her an embarrassed smile. "And I'm a total sucker for really angsty reality TV."

Her eyes widened with excitement. "Oh my god, me too! Those married-in-a-week shows are my absolute favorite!"

"Mine too!" I put a little extra enthusiasm into my words. "I'm finally getting caught up on last season. It's so much fun!"

She grinned. "It really is. So, what else? What were your favorite classes in high school?"

I thought for a minute. "I did best in science, sometimes math. I guess my favorite was chemistry, though." Which wasn't a lie. It had actually become the one I was most thankful I did really well in because it came in super handy when it came to my water affinity.

"Why choose bio for your major, then?"

"A lot of the classes overlap, so I might pick up a chem minor or shift to premed next year. I just didn't want to mess with changing majors five times," I added sheepishly.

"That makes sense. I've changed my major three times now, much to my parents' chagrin," she said, rolling her eyes dramatically. "I finally settled on psych, though. It's so much fun, learning how people's brains work."

"I was thinking about minoring in psych, actually," I said, making up that tidbit on the spot. "I might have to pick your brain about it at some point."

She laughed. "Pun intended?"

"Of course!"

Her face turned a bit more serious, although traces of friendliness remained. "Now, I have to ask. Have you done any volunteer work or community service in the past? That's a big part of what we do here at Iota Sig."

"Well, I helped run a blood drive my junior and senior years, organized the joint car wash the softball team did with the cheerleaders, and always helped out at the food and clothing drives my town did in the fall and winter. I was captain of the track team, so my senior year, I worked with my coach to lay the groundwork for a program that would send school athletes to the local nursing homes to do small exercise programs with the residents there."

Willow's eyes widened, her approval obvious on her face. "Oh, wow! You were a busy girl, huh?"

I grinned. "I sure was."

"That's great, though. It sounds like you'll fit in with the Iotas really well." She smiled. "So, let's go over what will be expected of you as a sister." She picked up a glass of water from the coffee table and took a sip.

I picked up my own glass, mirroring Willow's movements, and took a sip. "Let's hear it."

"Well, like I said, community service is huge. You've got a great background there, so that shouldn't be a problem for you. We're still working out our programs for this year, but we normally run blood and clothing drives twice a year, and it's a requirement as a member to sign up for the campus cleanups the college runs each semester. We also require all members to do some sort of volunteer work on campus of their own choosing. It can be anything, as long as it's campus-related. As far as house responsibilities, everyone pitches in with chores, even the sisters who don't live here. The ones that do are responsible for keeping their own rooms clean, but the communal spaces and outside are on everyone."

"That makes sense." I frowned and looked around. "How many sisters live here, anyway?"

"Twenty-six. Three girls to a room, except in the loft on the top floor, which sleeps eight."

"That's . . . a lot." I couldn't imagine eight people in one room. I'd probably die. Or smother someone with a pillow. Or *get* smothered by a pillow.

She laughed. "The loft is for the testers. Not everyone gets offered a spot in the house, so those who do have to do their first year in the loft. Any who manage it get offered a permanent spot, then the next semester, more are brought in."

"Wow. How many usually make it the whole time?"

"Half. Sometimes a bit more. If you make it in, you'll probably get an invite to live in the loft next year."

"That sounds awesome." I bit my lip. "So, can you tell me a little more about rush week? All I really knew before coming here was that my grandma was a sister, but I didn't get to learn much from her before she died."

"Absolutely!" She tucked her hair behind her ear. "Basically, rush week is when you would normally bounce around to the different houses and see which ones you like best. Rushees will list their preferred houses, then at the end of the week, the sororities will offer bids to the ones they like. Once you accept the bid, you'll start the official pledge process."

"How long is the pledge process?" I asked.

"Six weeks," she replied. "Legacies like yourself usually receive an automatic bid, unless their family members were in poor standing with their house. Once you become a pledge, you'll take the time to get to know the house, the sisters, our history, and complete certain tasks. After the pledge period is initiation, where you become a full-fledged sister."

I arched a brow. "Tasks?" Horror stories involving streaking and TPing classrooms flashed through my head.

Her eyes widened. "Oh, we don't do hazing here, Mary. No way. The tasks you'll be asked to complete will be difficult, but not degrading or dangerous in any way, I promise."

I breathed a sigh of relief. "That's good to hear."

"Now, of course you're welcome to visit the other sororities during rush week," she continued, "but I don't think you'll find a better fit that Iota Sig. You seem like a sweet girl and your background is impressive, so you'll fit right in."

I beamed. "That's great! I've only known Calla and Kristy for a few days, but they seem pretty awesome, and I met some of the guys at Kappa O. They were super welcoming."

"Oh, that's so good to hear! The Kappas are just wonderful, and we have such a blast when we do events with them."

"That sounds amazing." I glanced around the room. "Hey, do you mind if I use the bathroom really quick?"

"Not at all!" She pointed to a door at the back of the room that led into a wallpapered hall. "It's straight through that door, down the hall, take two rights and a left."

Standing, I nodded. "Two rights and a left. Got it."

I made my way out of the room, then once I was through the door and out of sight, I slipped my phone from my pocket and opened the running app I'd downloaded that tracked routes. Setting it to record, I started walking down the hall, taking two lefts and a right, then turning around, retracing my steps, and taking the correct route to the bathroom. It didn't give me much—maybe half of the first floor— but I was hoping I could get a tour out of Willow before I left. My goal was to map out all of the houses or places of interest I would visit, including the Aidens', which I knew was about as likely as Stewart offering up the sash and apple without a fight. But it was worth a shot, and any info was worth having.

"Sorry," I said when I walked back to the living room. "I accidentally went left when I should've gone right."

She laughed. "No worries. This house is a bit maze-like to newbs."

"I could tell," I replied with a laugh. "I'd love to see the rest of it, though."

"You will, don't worry. At the end of rush week, we take all the rushees through for a full tour, but as I'm sure you can understand, we don't do that until we know girls are serious. Which it seems like you are!" she rushed to add. "But you know how it is."

"Absolutely, I totally get it." It was a struggle not to let my disappointment show.

"So, did Calla tell you about the meet-and-greet Missa wants to have at their house?"

"It was mentioned briefly at dinner the other night, but she didn't really get into detail."

"Missa absolutely loves to be involved in sorority life. She's been a great source of information since they moved here, and she likes to get to know the girls who are carrying on what she considers 'her' legacy." Willow rolled her eyes and smiled. "She's super sweet, though. And with Stewart so busy now. running for office, I think she looks forward to these things more than she normally would."

"I would *love* to meet her," I gushed. "It's so great that she wants to be involved like that."

"It really is."

We talked a little while longer, mainly going over the rush and pledge processes a bit more and touching a little on the history of the house. Before I realized it, three hours had passed and I was itching to be back in the comfort of my apartment. So, I said my goodbyes and promised to check back during rush week, then made my way home, my mind running a mile a minute as I catalogued our conversation.

13

DIONYSUS

I was halfway through studying Professor Danson's lesson plans for the semester, tweaking them to my own specifications, when I heard Mary's door open and close. I flicked my eyes toward the wall that separated our apartments, then took a sip of my wine. Glancing down at the bottle, I smirked.

'I have wine.'

'Sounds good. Bring it over,' she said absently.

I grabbed the bottle and my laptop, figuring I could work over there just as easily as here, and went next door.

When I walked inside, I found her sitting in front of her own laptop, typing furiously, her phone and an open notebook next to her. Smirking at the cute little furrow that had formed on her brow, I got a glass down from the cabinet and poured her one.

"You know," I said, setting the glass on the table next to her, along with my own computer. "You're going to get wrinkles with all that frowning you do when you concentrate," I said, touching her brow.

She smacked my hand away. "I'm immortal, dumbass. We don't get wrinkles." She picked up the glass and took a long sip, then let out a heavy sigh. "Thank you. Gods, that girl can talk."

"It went well with Willow, then?"

"Yeah, it just took a lot out of me. So many damn questions." She leaned back, then looked down at her outfit and stood up. "I need to get changed. These jeans are too damn tight."

"K. I'll be here."

I leaned back against the arm of the sofa and shamelessly watched as she walked back to her bedroom, admiring every inch of her too-tight jeans.

Once she was out of sight, I looked down at her notebook to see what notes she'd gathered so far, but all I found was a sketch of something that looked like a map.

"What's this?" I called, glancing back toward the hall.

She stuck her head out of the door. "Map of the sorority house, or as much as I could get, anyway." Tugging a tank top over her head, she stepped back into the hall, giving me a glimpse of the bottom of her black lace bra.

Gods, this girl was going to be the death of me.

When I saw the smirk on her face, I could tell she knew it, too.

I couldn't help but feel a little frustrated. She never struck me as the type of person to let a guy come to her. Her confidence was through the roof when it came to her looks and personality, so I really believed if it were any other guy, she would've made a move long ago. Normally, I'd take care of it for her, but I knew she had her reasons for being hesitant. Her best friend was engaged to my brother, for one. And maybe a part of her just wasn't quite ready to open herself up yet, not after what she'd been through last year.

So, I would wait. As much as it fucking sucked, I would wait.

"How'd you manage mapping the place out?" I asked.

"I used a running app and recorded myself when I walked around." She sat down and slid her phone toward me to show me the screen. "I only got about half of the first floor, though. I won't get to see the full house until rush week."

"Huh." I looked at the phone, impressed at her forethought. "That's good work, Mare."

"Obviously." She tightened the bun she'd knotted on top of her head and turned her screen toward me. "I'm just typing up the notes from my conversation with Willow now. There wasn't much, honestly, but I figure everything's worth noting, right?"

"Definitely," I agreed. "Don't take offense to this, but I honestly thought it would take you longer to dive in here, considering how abruptly you were thrown in."

"I'm nothing if not adaptive." She smiled. "But thanks, though."

I didn't realize I was staring until I saw her smile falter a little.

"What is it?" she asked quietly.

"Nothing, I just . . ." I slid a little closer and took her hand. "You seem to be enjoying yourself here. I'm happy for you."

She shrugged and wrapped her hand around mine. "It helps to have a friend here. I know I'm supposed to be making friends, and I guess I kind of am, but it's not real, you know? Sometimes, when I'm talking to them, like when I was at the Kappa house the other night, it just seemed so normal? But then I come home and type up my notes on why this one or that one seems suspicious." She wrinkled her nose. "It's just . . . something."

The feelings of disappointment that rolled off her were impossible to miss.

She sighed, then leaned against me when I held out my arm. "I don't know. None of these girls are the type I would normally hang out with, but at the same time, it's been so nice to just be normal for a change. Even when I was still in Renville, I was always training with Chris or Alan or preparing to go through my transition. I actually feel human here, which is nice."

I smiled and touched my lips to her temple. "Why do you think I spend so much time in the human world? The simplicity of it compared to what we deal with on the mountain is kind of freeing."

She leaned back and looked at me. "You think I'll get assigned to do more things like this?"

"Prove to Athena you can do it, which I don't see you having a problem with at all, then absolutely. She's already impressed with how you've been doing, and it's only been a couple of days."

She frowned. "You've talked to her?"

I rolled my eyes. "She attempted to check in on you through me.

And before you get mad, I shut that down immediately. But yes, she's told me she's happy with the job you've done so far."

She scowled. "Well, thank you for shutting it down. It's bad enough she wanted me to ask you how to write up a progress report."

I snorted. "I bullshit my way through every progress report I write. I'm the last one you should ask. Hit up Apollo for something like that."

"Apollo is literally the last person I would ask for anything. He's so grumpy, and I'd never hear the end of it."

"Unless Athena tells you otherwise, I don't see you needing much help at all."

She smiled. "Thanks. That means a lot."

"I wouldn't say it if it wasn't true."

I didn't realize how close our faces were until the scent of her perfume registered. The smile faded from her face as she met my eyes, and I felt myself leaning closer.

Then her fucking phone dinged with a godsdamned text message, breaking whatever focus we'd had on each other.

While she picked up her phone, I cleared my throat. "So, I've actually been doing some research, too. Since I'm here, I figured I'd make myself useful."

"Yeah?" She finished tapping out her message and set her phone down. "What kind of research?"

"Just gathering more information on the sash and apple, my own memories of stories I've heard, that kind of thing. I wasn't born yet when Eris used the apple, but I heard it was quite the fight between my sisters and Hera."

"Gods, I would've paid to see that. Athena's always so reserved and Aphrodite is so pretty and sweet-looking and Hera is so . . . Hera."

I laughed. "You'd be surprised how different they all were back then. Even years later, once I was born, they were still bouncing back from the Trojan war, especially Athena. Their emotions were still a bit raw. Hermes and I tried to get the three of them to reenact it once, and I almost lost a hand."

"Somehow, that doesn't surprise me." She picked up her glass. "So, tell me what you found."

"It's more what I've been told over the years, although it's been awhile. The sash was used by Hera and Aphrodite a lot throughout the centuries. Hera was particular about the marriages she helped heal, but she often used the sash as a means of reviving intimacy, calling back emotions that had started to fade over time." I snorted and shook my head. "She used it on her and my father's marriage more than once."

Her eyes widened in feigned surprise. "Shocking. It seems like the sash is more straightforward than the apple, right?"

I nodded. "The apple's powers reflect the user, so it can do anything from save a life to start a war."

"So, the sash is more coercive, and the apple is basically the Swiss Army knife of deific objects?"

I laughed at her comparison. "Pretty much, although it's a bit more complicated because you have to know how to wield it in order to use it."

She arched a brow. "So . . . it's basically the Swiss Army knife of deific objects?"

I grinned. "You're such a jerk."

"And yet here you are, fetching me wine and doing part of my job for me."

"Anything for you, doll." I touched my thumb to her chin, considering whether or not to revisit whatever moment we'd had before we'd been interrupted by her phone. When she leaned back against the opposite arm of the sofa, though, I took that as a sign that I should let it be and switch my focus to something safer than the dirty things I very much wished to be doing with her.

We stayed up for a few more hours, going over my memories of the sash and apple and brainstorming other ways to tackle her mission. Based on everything she'd said and done so far, I could tell she was a natural at this. Diving into a new life, switching from one persona to the next, and knowing what to say and when to say it were skills it took some immortals centuries to perfect, if they ever did.

Whatever skills and traits she'd brought with her into the immortal world would serve her well, I had no doubts.

Hopefully, in time, she'd let me stay by her side as they did.

THE NEXT MORNING, Mary dug into the research she'd abandoned the night before and I set up at the counter to focus on my own work. I got through the plans Danson had left, so I was set with those for the semester. Once I closed out those files, I switched over to working with Mary.

"What are your thoughts on me getting some satellite images to map the sorority and frat houses? And the Aidens'?" she asked.

I glanced up from my screen and looked over at her. "It can't hurt, at least for the houses. I'm not sure how accurate a map for the Aidens' house will be, though. If they have the sash and apple, they'll likely be hidden, and maps won't show hidden areas in the house."

"Yeah, you're right." She wrinkled her nose. "Hmm. I wonder if I can get blueprints . . ." Her voice trailed off as she clicked the mouse a few times and became reabsorbed in her work.

I shook my head, smiling at the way her mind worked.

We'd been at it for a good two hours when the door opened and Athena walked in, followed by Aphrodite, who looked like she'd rather be anywhere but here.

Mary jumped up when she saw Aphrodite, and I realized this was probably the first time she'd been in such close proximity to my big sister, who could be intimidating on a good day.

"Athena!" Mary said. She gave a sort of half-wave to Aphrodite. "Hi, Aphrodite."

Aphrodite's dark eyes flicked from Mary, to me, then back again with that infuriatingly knowing look of hers. To Mary's credit, she held Aphrodite's stare, but I hoped I was the only one who caught the slight wince when my sister eyed her.

Aphrodite smirked at Mary, her mask of haughtiness slipping

entirely when she scented whatever it was that seemed to linger between Mary and me.

"Mary." She arched a brow at me. "Baby brother."

I sent her a stern look. "Why are you here?"

"What's going on?" Mary asked at the same time.

"We're just here for an update," Athena said, "and I thought you should actually meet Aphrodite, considering you're being forced to do her dirty work. Sit."

I had to stop myself from going to sit next to Mary on the couch to act as a buffer between her and my sisters. She and Athena got along great, for the most part, but Aphrodite could go either way when it came to new people, especially when there was any potential for a romantic relationship. *Especially* when her younger siblings were involved. She was territorial, to put it mildly, and to someone who didn't know her, that could and did often come off as a bit terrifying.

"What are you working on?" Aphrodite asked me, frowning.

"Lesson plans." I shut my computer, not wanting her to see that I'd been doing my own information-gathering.

"Seriously?"

"Just because I'm pretending to be a teacher doesn't mean I don't actually have to teach, Aphrodite."

She gave me a look that told me she thought the exact opposite, then smiled at Mary.

"So, Mary." With a smooth smile, she walked over and sat down on the sofa, then patted the cushion next to her. "Tell me how things are going."

Athena took a place in front of the fireplace, arms folded, her expression focused. I stood, then went over and leaned against the wall by the door, putting myself in closer proximity to the conversation without seeming like I was hovering.

Not batting an eye, Mary sat next to Aphrodite. "Good, so far. I've managed to become friends with Calla Aiden, and I met with Willow, the sorority president, yesterday. I'm not sure if I've endeared myself to them yet," she said with a smile at Athena, "but Willow all but offered me a bid when we talked, so I think I'm on the right track there."

I bit back a grin at how flummoxed Athena looked at Mary's simple slip into professionalism with Aphrodite.

'The girl can read a room,' I said to her.

'Clearly,' she murmured.

Aphrodite nodded, her expression shifting into something more neutral. "That's great. Anything else?"

"I'm working on mapping out the houses, both Iota Sig and Kappa O. I'm not sure it'll lead to anything, but if nothing else, I can compare those to aerial shots or blueprints to see if there's anything not visible structurally from the inside. I'd love to get into the president's mansion on campus, but I'm not holding my breath. I doubt anything important would be kept there, anyway, because it's not permanent housing, but I still want to check it out."

"Yes, that's unlikely," Aphrodite agreed. "Have you met Stewart yet?"

Mary shook her head. "His wife is having a meet-and-greet for Iota Sig soon so she can meet the new pledges, but I'm hoping I'll get to meet him sooner."

I raised my hand. "I actually may be able to help with that."

Mary frowned. "How?"

"I've only been around staff for a couple of days, but it's a known fact Stewart Aiden has an obsession with the coffee from the café on campus. I overheard a couple of professors saying how great it was that he'd upgraded from a coffee cart to a full café, and that he's there at least twice daily."

"Do they take volunteers?" Mary asked, instantly picking up on my thought process.

"If not, I'm sure they can be persuaded to."

She nodded slowly. "Okay, I might be able to work with that. Let me think on it a bit."

I flicked a glance at Aphrodite, then back at Mary. "You should also request Calla as your big sister."

"Agreed," Aphrodite said. "There's no guarantee you'll get her, of course, but it's certainly worth a try."

"Yep, I already have that on my to-do list," Mary said. "So, Aphrodite, would you be able to give me a bit more information on the sash and apple? I've talked with Athena and Dionysus, and I've done my own research, but it might help to have a bit more straight from you."

As the two of them dove into conversation about the connection of deific objects to their owners, Athena inclined her head toward the door.

"I spoke with Father," she said once we were in my apartment. "He wants updates from you about what you're doing here, and he wants to know when you plan to return to Germany."

A mix of anger and annoyance flickered inside me. "Father can fuck off with his updates," I snapped. "I'm here because I'd like to have a break from a job that was making me miserable. If he wants to get up-to-the-minute details, he can slap on a glamour and come do it himself."

Her eyebrows winged up at one of my rare shows of aggravation. "Okay, then. Tell me how you really feel."

I sat down on the sofa and rubbed a hand across my brow. "I'm so over him snapping his fingers and expecting us to just *go*. I get it; we just wrapped up a war, a lot of insane shit went down, we had spies on the mountain, but we're not his damn servants." I gestured vaguely toward her. "You may not mind the orders and instructions, but it's getting old pretty quick."

She frowned and sat down on the chair across from me. "It's not that I don't mind them, Dionysus. I merely see the need for them. The last thing we want is dissension within our own ranks."

"Ranks," I scoffed. "You and I both know I'm an Elder in name only. Nathaniel was smart when he skipped out on that duty."

Surprise flashed across her face. "So, you want to follow in Nathaniel's footsteps now? Leave Olympus?"

"If it means I can go where I want and not be forced into perpetual misery? Yeah."

She leaned back in her chair. "I never knew you felt that way.

You're always so . . . you."

"You've got your boxes to check, Athena. You're built for war and following orders. That's not me."

"You're a god of Olympus, though. We're all built for war."

"That's your perfectionist bullshit, and you know it."

"I'm sorry, but why are you angry with me? I'm only the messenger."

I sighed and closed my eyes. "You're right." I looked over at her. "I'm sorry."

Concern was written on her face, mixed with confusion. "It's all right. I understand why this is harder for you than the rest of us, but we have to tread lightly. Now isn't the time for rebelling."

I thought about how Zeus would react if and when I told him I planned to have a true, honest relationship with one of his Ischyra and felt irritation wash through me. "Father's a dick, and you'll never convince me otherwise."

"And you sound like a spoiled brat who's never had to deal with the aftermath of a war," she snapped. "I love you, Dionysus, but don't you dare pretend to know what he's going through right now."

"I'm not. I never could. But I'm also not going to pretend to like being shuffled off here and there for the next five hundred years just to quell his suspicion about another uprising that isn't going to happen."

"We don't know that," she countered. "Which is why you were sent to Germany."

"Where I dealt with one PTSD victim after another. You're so worried about what he's going through, but you're a goddess of war. Do you ever consider what these duties do to the rest of us? To the rest of your 'soldiers'?"

She frowned but ignored my dig. "I thought you liked that part of your job?"

"I do! I love working to help students. But fuck, Athena. Do you know how fucking hard it is to bring a PTSD sufferer back from the brink, even for a god? *Especially* when that person is suffering because of the actions of our own kind? Multiply that by a few

hundred and maybe you can get an idea of what I'm dealing with."
Averting my eyes, I huffed out a breath. "None of you have any idea
what unraveling the collective pain of that many people alone is like.
I'm maxed out and need a damn break."

"I'm sorry," she said softly. "I just assumed . . . I thought that placement would be perfect for you. I didn't realize how bad it would be.
You could've told me."

"I didn't know how much of a problem it would be until I was too
far in. It just . . . lingers. Their pain and suffering, it's so much
different than dealing with even one person. I talk to them, help inch
them closer to happiness, which is normally all I need. That little
spark of happiness is usually easy for me to cultivate. But then they
slip back again and again, and there's nothing I can do to stop that
repeated backslide except go through the cycle again. With all of
them."

"And you end up in the dark too." She was quiet for a moment,
then she sighed. "I had no idea it affected you that much."

I shrugged. "We've never been in this position before. Yeah,
there've been wars that I've helped people work through, but never
like this. This is the first time it spilled off our own mountain and into
the human world."

"So, take a break," she said. "But you won't be able to avoid Father
forever. Sooner or later, you'll have to talk to him."

I thought about my intentions with Mary, how I hoped we could
take this time to move past friendship into something much, much
bigger. I thought about how I'd be perfectly content to rediscover the
world without the weight of my duties as a god on my shoulders, and
I couldn't help but smile.

"I'll talk to him eventually," I told her. "But I can't promise he'll
like what I have to say."

With a nod, she stood. "Fine. Just don't put me in the middle of it,
whatever you do. I've got enough to handle without running interference between our father and anyone who deigns to disagree with
him."

The bitterness in her own tone made me laugh.

14

MARY

Aphrodite wasted no time changing the subject once Athena and Dionysus disappeared to wherever it was they went.

"So," she said, leaning back in her seat. "We'll chat about the sash and all, but I'm curious . . ." Her dark eyes shifted toward the door. "What's going on with you and my brother?"

I gave her a surprised look. "With Dionysus? Nothing. Why?"

She tapped her nose and her red lips curved. "Goddess of *love,* honey. I smelled the tension the second I walked in."

"Oh." Shit. "There's nothing going on, though. Really."

"Yet. There's nothing going on *yet.*" She leaned forward, drawing in another breath, and I fought against the instinct to shrink back. "You seem sincere, so I suppose that works in your favor. I think you could be good for him." The sweetness that had been present just a moment before vanished as a predatory gleam filled her gaze. "My brother is very dear to me, Mary. Don't screw it up."

I gave her a tight smile and tried not to let her see how intimidated I was by her. "I'll do my best. But like I said . . . there's nothing going on."

Her expression turned skeptical, but she shook her head. "Fine. Now, let's talk. Based on what Athena's told you and what you said

Dionysus explained, it seems like you have a pretty good idea of what the sash and apple do. Have either of them explained the sort of . . . hum . . . deific objects tend to have?"

I frowned. "Sort of, but it was kind of hard to understand."

"Okay. So, basically, all objects have energy, from the dirt at your feet to the clouds in the sky. Deific objects have *more* because we imbue them with our power. Gods and titans can feel that energy strongly, but immortals can feel it, too, if they know what to look for."

"What does it feel like?"

She touched a long finger to her lips. "It's hard to describe. Sort of like a background noise you don't realize is there until it isn't anymore, if that makes sense?"

"Sort of. Where did you feel it here?"

"Near the Aidens' house." She tapped her finger on her chin. "You know what? It'll just be easier to show you. Do you have your necklace on?"

I touched a hand to the apple at my throat. "Yup. Got it."

"Great."

The next thing I knew, we were standing in front of a tall iron fence. In the distance sat a monstrosity of a house, so big, it rivaled some of the houses I'd seen on Olympus.

"That's a large house," was the only idiotic thing I could come up with.

"Mm-hmm. The Aidens have lived there for about six months now." She took my hand. "Now, I want you to concentrate. I can still feel the magic of the sash and apple here, so if you focus, you should be able to, as well."

I closed my eyes and tried to focus on the air around me, but all I heard was silence. Finally, I opened my eyes and looked at her.

"Can you do that thing where you show me a memory or what you're thinking so I can get a better idea?"

That skeptical look flashed across her face again. "I suppose . . ."

A moment later, I had her own memory of standing outside the Aidens' house in my head, and she was guiding me toward what she felt in that moment.

"Huh. It's like that few seconds after your ears pop. Weird."

"Yes, that's an apt description." She frowned. "You're a bit odd."

"So I've been told."

"Do you think you'd be able to recognize that feeling if you came across it again?"

Glancing back toward the house, I tried to focus on the sensation I'd felt in her memory and felt for it in the air around me. It was there, but not nearly as strong as it had been for her. I'd have to focus extra hard in order to catch it, which meant I'd need to be on the lookout nonstop.

I nodded. "Yeah, I think I'd be able to. It might be a little tricky, but I'll manage."

Her expression turned dubious. "Are you certain? These are important objects, Mary, and you've come highly recommend by a number of people on the mountain, which is the only reason you're here."

My eyebrows shot up. "A number of people? Like who?" I'd assumed Tessa and Dionysus had given Athena a nudge, but that was all.

She rolled her eyes and started ticking off names on her fingers. "My lovesick brother, for one, not to mention Chiron, who gave you a *glowing* recommendation, Tessa and Nathaniel, so then of *course* Athena vouched for you, and even Apollo admitted you had the right 'spirit' for a job like this. Zeus grumbled about it, but he grumbles about everything these days."

Shocking, I thought. The fact that even Apollo thought I'd be good at this job was most surprising, though.

"Well, I'll do my best not to let you down, Aphrodite. I promise."

She pressed her lips together and shook her head. "They better be right about you, Mary Miller, or I will *not* be happy."

With that, she took me home.

~

"HEY THERE, MARE BEAR."

I jolted upright, my heart pounding and my breaths coming in short gasps.

"Save the head for last . . ."

My breathing picked up as I scrambled to remember where I was. Pain pricked at my wrists, and I felt the press of cold stone all around me, a knife brushing against my ear—

"No, no no no." As panic set in, I pressed my thumb into the palm of my other hand, letting my nail dig into the skin.

"Not there," I murmured, digging my nail harder into my flesh. "You're here, you're home."

I opened my eyes wide and forced myself to take in my surroundings as my heart thundered in my ears. The moonlight filtering in through the window near my bed was full and bright. It wasn't squeezing through a small hole in the ceiling of a prison cell. The curtains were open, and I could see stars with a few wispy clouds floating by.

There were no witches chained to the wall across from me.

My breathing began to ease up.

"Not there," I whispered again, focusing my attention on the big, bright moon, and sucking in air through my nose and letting it out through my mouth. "I'm in my bed, I'm not there."

My breathing steadied, and I let my arms come to rest in my lap. I watched as the nail marks in my palms faded, the only physical reminder of my nightmare vanishing just like that.

I hadn't had a nightmare like that in a good month. I thought about my time being imprisoned in that cell all the time, but I'd come to terms with it. I'd talked it out over and over, with Dionysus and Tessa and even Chiron, who was a phenomenal listener and an even better counselor.

But now and then, when my brain was at rest, Chaos crept in and took over.

Chiron had taught me coping techniques to center myself in reality after bad dreams, like digging my thumb into my palm, and they worked for the most part. He'd always said things like, *"The minds of immortals heal more easily than humans. They must, in order for us to cope for the rest of existence. But even though we might be able to move on from trauma like this more quickly, moving on is still a difficult journey."*

Wise old centaur, that one.

Glancing down, I realized I was rubbing at my wrists, the phantom pinch of the godsbane-infused cuffs that had chained me to the wall still lingering in my mind. They never cut deep enough to scar, and Apollo's healing skills were impeccable, so fortunately, I wasn't left with any physical reminders of my kidnapping. The memory of them was still pretty sharp, though.

After I'd been returned to Olympus, I'd talked a lot to Tessa about the time she'd been tortured by Menoetius, her sadistic and now very dead older brother. It was painful to hear, but more helpful than speaking to Dionysus. He just wanted me to feel better, and while he made it simpler to ease back into the world, he couldn't help me cope. Tessa was stronger than any person should have to be, and she helped me keep from succumbing to my own pain a lot because she'd been doing the same for a long time. She didn't let what Menoetius had done to her define her, and I intended to follow in her footsteps.

I eased myself up on shaky legs and made my way out to the kitchen for some water.

I looked at the clock on the stove. Three on the dot. I considered calling Dionysus to come hang out, but that was a habit I didn't want to fall back into. So, I poured myself a glass of water and pulled out my textbooks, which I'd barely looked at since I bought them.

Forcing myself to shut down all thoughts unrelated to adult responsibilities, I dove into schoolwork, which was a surprisingly good distraction from my racing thoughts. I read through the first chapter of my chem book, outlined a short paper for lit, and I started picking through some research for a bio presentation Calla and I had in three weeks. It was nearly six by the time I finished, and with the sky starting to lighten, there was no way I was going to be able to fall back asleep.

It would be another hour before the coffee shop opened downstairs, so I set my own coffee maker brewing and turned on the TV. I didn't have class 'til that afternoon, so hopefully, I could get a nap in before then. But right now, it just wasn't happening.

I dragged my comforter off my bed and brought it out to the living room, then curled up on the couch with a cup of coffee and the TV remote. As I flipped through all the shows that had shown up on the streaming services Olympus subscribed to—for human interaction purposes, only, of course—I found myself mentally cataloging all the shows I thought Dionysus would like so we could watch them together later.

But cataloging them to watch later didn't help me find something now, so I clicked on the next teen drama I found and started the first episode.

I knew there wasn't anything wrong with making a list of things I wanted to watch with Dionysus. It was stupid that I was even spending this much time thinking about it.

What nagged at my mind was the fact that I was basing basic decisions, like what to watch on TV, around him.

I liked him. A lot. A shit ton, even. But I couldn't start making every little decision with him in mind.

With a huff, I snuggled in deeper and forced myself to focus on my show and my coffee.

15

MARY

The next week flew by in a blur of classes, work, and planning for my first visit to the Aidens' house. Before I knew it, my first full week of college was done, ushering in Rush week. I considered feigning interest in other sororities, but by the time the craziness of Rush actually arrived, I didn't care to waste the energy pretending. So, I focused all my attention on getting in good with the Iotas and figuring out how I was going to get Calla to take me on as her Little.

By Wednesday, two of the three Rush parties had come and gone. The sisters put on skits, sang songs, told stories of all the good times at Iota Sig, and explained what it took to be considered a good sister. They wanted to know all about my extracurriculars, hobbies, and my various "philanthropic goals" for the upcoming year. And, surprisingly, I learned a bit more about Calla's mom, Missa, which was good. If I wanted to get close to Stewart or had any hopes of exploring the Aidens' house, I needed to get into Missa's good graces, and that meant knocking it out of the park with the sorority sisters.

Fortunately, I wouldn't have to wait long to meet her. I thought the best opportunity to meet the Aidens would be at next month's party, but plans changed during Rush. The bid ceremony, to which only the rushees who were getting formal invitations to pledge would be invited, would be Saturday at the Aidens' house. In the week leading up to Rush, I'd done painful amounts of research on how to get in good with the active members. I didn't expect to *not* make it in, but I also didn't want to rely on my legacy status and Willow liking me for getting in.

On Thursday, I found myself desperate for a reprieve from the nonstop sorority gushing I'd been exposed to the last few days. I understand why it was necessary, but the whole "this is why you pick us" thing was getting tiring. As I walked to get coffee with Kristy and Calla, it seemed like Calla had her own set of Iota annoyances.

"It's so stupid," Calla whined after bio. She'd been complaining about her mom a lot this past week. "My mom literally thinks her word matters when it comes to choosing pledges. I just don't get it."

Kristy shrugged. "I don't know. She *was* a member, way back when. She might have some good insight."

Calla wrinkled her nose and looked at me. "Mary agrees with me, don't you?"

I bit my lip and winced. She had a habit of doing this—putting me in a position where she was all but forcing me to agree with her. "I mean, I get why she'd want to be involved. It was her house and you're her daughter, and she probably wants to make sure the people you guys pick are worthy of carrying on Iota Sig's legacy, you know? And besides, she isn't *actually* choosing the pledges. The girls will already have their bids by the time they get to your house, right?"

She huffed out a breath, blowing her hair off her face. "I guess."

"And look at it this way," I added. "Having the third party at the house of the university president is an amazing way to sell its exclusivity. The sorority house is amazing, but it'll be really easy to see how they'll stand up to pressure when they're given face time with your dad. You'll know right off the bat who needs work if they're going to make it as a pledge." I shrugged. "If any of them aren't going to be able to manage things like that, you'll want to weed them out early."

"Excellent point, Mary," Kristy said with a nod.

"Hmm." Calla looked back and forth between us. "I suppose you two may have a point. Sycophants are *so* draining, right? Especially when they don't have the spine to back it up."

"So draining," I agreed.

"Absolutely," Kristy added. She clapped her gloved hands together. "So, Bid Day. Mary, you know what to do, right? Willow went over it all?"

I nodded. "Yep. She gave me the run-down. Wait for my official bid to come through my email by six, then head to Calla's house by seven." I smiled at them both. "I'll absolutely not make a fool of myself, I promise."

Calla gave me a sidelong look. "You better not. If you make of fool of yourself, you'll make a fool of me *and* Willow, which she will *not* be happy about."

"Geez, Calla, chill," Kristy muttered.

"Well, it's the truth!"

"I'll be fine, I promise," I told her. We'd been over this at least five times since my meeting with Willow, and it was seriously starting to get on my nerves. I was absolutely certain I wouldn't make an idiot of myself, mainly because I needed to get closer to Stewart. If I screwed up, that would likely be shot to shit and I'd be bleaching toilets in Antarctica or wherever Athena thought most appropriate for punishment.

Dionysus had already walked me through the Rush and pledge processes in painful detail and gave me a lot of ideas about making a good impression after I got my bid. Still, with the amount of questioning I kept getting, I was starting to wonder whether people thought I was capable of functioning in mixed company.

"Okay. So, outfits," Calla said. "What are you *not* going to wear?"

"Nothing too fancy, and no red or gold," I said with a sigh. "If I show up wearing Iota Sig's colors before being *given* my colors, I'll look like a twat."

Kristy snorted.

"Exactly," Calla said. "You don't need to get dressed up, and it's fucking freezing, so leggings or cute jeans with those amazing riding boots you have will work. Most sororities give T-shirts on bid day, but we do cardigans, so wear something neutral on top."

I frowned. "Why cardigans?"

"It sets us apart, for one," Kristy said.

"And they're more versatile," Calla added. "During the pledge period, you'll be required to always wear your colors. A cardigan is something that makes that a little easier to do."

"That's . . . convenient," I said. I was already imagining a nightmarish amount of red and gold getting added to my wardrobe, so hopefully the cardigan was somewhat understated.

"Well, we take care of our own, Mary," Calla said, her face serious. "That's one of the most important parts of being an Iota sister. Loyalty to each other is paramount."

"Sounds like a great family," I said. I couldn't help but feel a little weirded out by the obsession these girls seemed to have to loyalty, though.

"And for the pinning ceremony next weekend?" Calla asked.

"Oh!" I slid my phone from my coat pocket and brought up the selfie I'd taken wearing my ceremony dress. "I totally forgot to show you. It came in the other day."

Calla narrowed her eyes and took the phone, then used her fingers to zoom in to look at the white minidress I'd spent an obscene amount of money on. It was pretty basic, with these pretty, soft ruffles on the arms that gave it a girlier look, but it was fitted through my stomach and thighs, so it showed off my figure.

After a moment, she nodded her approval. "It looks great. Good work, Mary."

"Thanks. As soon as my shoes get here, I'll take a pic of the full outfit for you."

Her eyes bugged out. "You don't have *shoes*?"

I laughed. "Relax. I ordered them. They'll be here later today."

"What if they don't fit?" Kristy asked, her eyes wide.

"Or pinch?" Calla added. "Mary!"

I arched a brow. "Have *you* ever come across a pair of Badgleys that pinched? Because I haven't."

Both relaxed a little at that.

"I suppose not," Calla said.

"I wanted to grab some accessories, though. Are you guys up for shopping?"

"Definitely," Calla replied. "Retail therapy sounds great, even if pickings are slim around here."

"And I've been dying for *actual* sushi," Kristy said, rolling her eyes. "The sushi counter at the supermarket just doesn't cut it."

I wrinkled my nose at that. "When should we go? We're getting a little down to the wire," I said sheepishly.

Calla shrugged. "Let's go today. None of us have any evening classes."

"Sounds like a plan," I said with a grin.

We talked a bit more over coffee before heading to lit, where Dionysus put us in groups of four to work on an assignment. Because he was either a sadist or literally wanted me to die a slow, painful death, he put me in a group with three of the most irritating students in the room.

Dick.

By the time class was over and I'd sent more than a few scathing insults Dionysus's way, I was ready to be done with classes for the week.

'*Want me to bring over barbecue?*' he asked as I left the room.

'*Tomorrow,*' I replied. '*I'm going shopping with Calla and Kristy. And only if you bring that prosecco we had in Trieste last fall, too.*'

'*Your wish is my command.*'

'*Then, I also wish to have beignets for dessert.*'

'*You're killing me.*'

'*Hey, if I could teleport, I'd totally do it myself.*'

'*Lies. Have fun.*'

⁓

ONE THING I wasn't overly crazy about was the lack of shopping options in Upstate New York. There were a ton of small specialty shops right in town, but nothing in the way of high-end designers. There were decent outlets about an hour to the south, though, so as soon as we left, Calla, Kristy, and I set out in Calla's car to go find accessories for my pinning ceremony dress. I could've ordered everything online, but the idea of actually browsing through displays was nice. I'd been so hemmed in lately, wandering through shops would be a nice change. Even though I totally could've gone by myself, I figured asking for Calla's input would endear me to her a little more.

The sun was blinding and the forecast called for no snow, so we planned to shop for a couple of hours then grab dinner at one of the nearby restaurants. When we parked, Calla immediately headed for the Michael Kors outlet, bypassing half a dozen others on her way.

"I need a new purse," she said as we walked inside. The heat was blasting, so I took off my coat and looped it over my purse. Kristy immediately made a beeline for the shoe section, while Calla made for the purses and I wandered toward a display of smaller bags.

"Mary, come look at these!" Kristy called a few minutes later.

I glanced up from the display of wristlets I'd been eyeing and saw her holding up a pair of white stilettos.

"Ohh, those are gorgeous!" I set down the magenta wristlet I'd been holding and walked over to her.

"They'd go great with your dress," she said as Calla came up.

"She's totally right," Calla agreed.

I wrinkled my nose. "They would, but I already have shoes, remember?"

Calla shrugged. "You can never have too many, as far as I'm concerned."

The shoes *were* pretty gorgeous. They were closed-toe suede, with straps that wrapped around the ankle and a four-inch heel with silver rivets running down the back.

If I was being honest, they were much more my style than the other pair I'd bought. I flicked my eyes up to the twenty-percent-off sign that hung above the display and shrugged.

"Sure, why not?"

Once we were loaded down with bags, we made our way to some

of the other shops. I didn't go all out like I had on my first shopping spree, but considering who I was shopping with, I couldn't *not* buy anything. Athena would totally understand. She'd have to.

Five stores and three hours later, we were majorly weighed down and starving, so we went to a hibachi just down the street to get dinner. Even though it was kind of a hike from Lake Placid, Calla said it was a pretty popular place for SLU students to go. So, neither she nor Kristy were surprised to find a handful of the Kappa O brothers seated at the bar.

"Yoooo! Calla!" Tristan called, holding up a tall, thin beer glass in greeting. Shep and Milo sat on either side of him, and I assumed the other guys with them were also members.

Calla waved, and we made our way through the crowded restaurant to the bar.

Shep sent one of the other guys over to tell the hostess to add three more to their party, then turned to me and grinned.

"So, what are you drinking?"

I shrugged. "Surprise me."

He laughed. "Brave girl." He got Calla's and Kristy's orders, then put in the order with the bartender. "Did you buy out the stores or what?"

"Not even close," Calla said, rolling her eyes. "We seriously need to take a trip into the city. I can't stand the shopping up here."

"New York is almost five hours away," Kristy pointed out.

"But the shopping is worth it."

I gave a smile and shrugged. "Can't disagree with that."

Kristy wrinkled her nose. "Yeah . . . I suppose."

Just then, the hostess called us over and led us to one of the wide, flat-top grills surrounded by a dozen stools. We took up ten of them, our purses and coats taking up the other two.

"So, what's good here?" I asked as we settled in.

Calla was poring over her own menu. "I usually get the filet and scallops," she said. "And the volcano roll."

My expression must've given away exactly how I felt about eel and cream cheese in my sushi, because Shep laughed.

"Not my thing, either." He turned his menu toward me. "Go for the crunchy California roll. It's way better."

When the waitress came over to get our orders a few minutes later, I'd settled on the filet and lobster from the grill and decided to go with Shep's suggestion for the sushi. Then, I racked my brain to come up with some sort of conversation topic, but Calla saved me by asking Shep about Rush week.

"How many new pledges did you guys get this year?" she asked, taking a sip of her mojito.

"Twenty-six," he replied.

She frowned and cocked her head to the side. "Mary, do you recall how many Iota pledges are coming in?"

I smirked at her faux forgetfulness. "Was it twenty-four?"

"Hmm, no. I think it was twenty . . . seven?"

"Oh! You forgot about Marcie, the quiet one." I grinned at Shep. "So, twenty-eight."

He shook his head. "Dammit. Okay. You girls win."

I gave them each an expectant look. "What's the prize?"

Calla shrugged. "Bragging rights, mainly. And we get to pick the first task for Kappa's pledges."

My eyes widened. "That sounds dangerous. Is that normal for sororities and frats?"

"Definitely not typical," Shep said. "But we like to do our own thing now and then."

"Sometimes, it's fun to step outside the box," I agreed.

We all talked for a while over drinks, then dinner. I limited myself to two Japanese microbrews and nursed them throughout appetizers and dinner. I'd made the decision to limit any alcohol intake until I managed to figure out how to use my water power to distill my drinks so I could avoid getting drunk. It was proving to be more difficult than I thought, but there was no way I was going to get away with fake drinking at parties with this crowd, so I would have to figure something out. It was easy enough to play it off while I was eating, but at a party, where getting trashed was sort of a collective goal, it just wouldn't work. My immortality processed most alcohol pretty quickly, but I didn't want to risk even a slight buzz while I was working.

The waitress came back around the see if we wanted dessert, and I was about to pass when Shep leaned over. "They have the best fried banana with green tea ice cream, but there's no way I can finish it all myself. Split it with me?"

My eyebrows shot up in surprise, then I smiled. "Sure! I was actually just wishing I had room for something else."

He beamed at me. "Great."

Calla cleared her throat. "Mare, come to the bathroom with me?"

Uh-oh.

She and Kristy stood from the table, and I excused myself and followed them, terrified I'd just made some major faux pas. I didn't think Calla had her eye on Shep, but the last thing I wanted was for her to think I was trying to horn in on her territory.

When we got into the black-and-white-tiled room, Calla spun around and locked the door. "Shep just asked to split dessert with you?" she asked.

I frowned. "Yes . . ."

She and Kristy exchanged a look.

"Okay, Mary, this is big," Kristy said, meeting my eyes. "You snagged the attention of the *president* of our brother frat. You need to capitalize on that ASAP."

"But you need to be very fucking careful," Calla said, pointing her finger at me. "This is a big godsdamned deal, so you absolutely can*not* screw this up."

"Guys, he just asked me to share a dessert with him, not stick his pin on me. Geez."

Calla rolled her eyes, as if I was literally the dumbest thing on the planet. "Ugh! Whatever. Think what you want. What we're saying is, having his attention is great. Girls would kill to get time with him. But whatever you do," she plowed ahead when I opened my mouth to speak, "do *not* be obnoxious about it."

"Otherwise, people will totally think you got a quick bid because of him," Kristy added.

"But I don't *know* him," I pointed out. "I've talked to him twice before now, and once doesn't count because I was buying books. I don't even know his last name."

"It's Stuyvesant," Calla said with a huff. "Just . . . don't fuck it up. It'll be a stain on the entire sorority if you do."

Overdramatic much?

I gave her my best reassuring smile. "I promise I'll be good. And not obnoxious."

"If he asks you for your number, give it to him."

"Obviously." Hopefully she didn't see my brief hesitation before I answered.

"So, you like him?" Kristy asked.

I shrugged. "I mean, I don't dislike him. He seems . . . nice."

Her shoulders sagged with relief. "Okay." She glanced at Calla, who nodded. "Great."

"Great?" I asked.

"It would just look bad if an Iota shot down a Kappa, you know?" Kristy said.

"Especially the President," Calla added.

"You'd want me to date him even if I didn't like him?"

Calla's eyes widened. "Gods, no! It just works out better if you *do*, you know, because then there isn't the awkwardness of him liking you but you not liking him."

I relaxed a little. "Oh. Yeah. That makes sense. But, still, I think you guys are reading too much into this. He didn't want to stuff himself with ice cream. I really don't think it's that deep."

"Maybe," Calla said. "But I doubt it."

I sighed. "Let's go back to the table. They're gonna wonder what's keeping us."

We walked back to our table, and the whole walk there, I couldn't help but wonder if this job had just gotten a shit ton more complicated than I'd anticipated.

16

MARY

The rest of dinner was pretty uneventful. I split the fried banana thing with Shep, and, as Calla and Kristy predicted, he'd asked for my number, with the promise of grabbing coffee together soon.

The twinge of guilt I felt at giving him my number nagged me the whole way home. Even though Dionysus and I weren't together, it still felt like I was doing something wrong by entertaining the idea of going on a coffee date with another guy. Even if it would just be for appearances and information-gathering purposes only, it still felt weird. I knew, without question, I'd feel hurt if the shoe was on the other foot.

But the job was the job, and Athena and Aphrodite would probably kill me if I shot down the president of Kappa O, so Dionysus would just have to deal.

The next day, Dionysus and I had dinner plans. Kristy and Calla had invited me to do something with them, but I'd blown him off three times since we'd been in Lake Placid, and I'd promised him I wouldn't bail again. So, he teleported to this little town in India he'd visited years ago and picked up food, then came back to my apartment.

As we dug into the Tandoori chicken, I told him about my shopping trip and dinner with Calla and the others.

His entire mood shifted in the tiniest way when I told him we'd run into the Kappa guys at the restaurant, and when I told him Shep had asked for my number, his jaw clenched. I'd tried to word it so it didn't seem like I was receptive of Shep's advances, but at the same time, a small, petty part of me wanted to make Dionysus a little jealous.

"So yeah," I said, getting up to grab a glass of water from the kitchen, "I might meet him for coffee at some point, see what I can get out of him, as far as Aiden dirt." I purposely avoided looking back at his reaction as I reached into the cabinet for two glasses. "I really think there's something up with their sorority-fraternity relationship, too. I get the whole brother-sister thing, but when Calla heard Shep ask me to split dessert, it was almost like she was desperate for me to not screw it up." I set the glasses on the island and sat back down. "It was kind of bizarre."

He frowned. "You shared dessert with him?"

I gave him a look. "I caught the interest of the president of Iota Sig's brother frat. So, yes, when he asked me to split dessert, I did. What was I going to do, say no?"

He looked thoughtful for a moment before shoveling a piece of chicken in his mouth. He chewed, swallowed, then shrugged. "No, I guess not." He grinned, his weird mood seeming to vanish. "I have to say, the way you switch personas is pretty impressive."

"It's surprisingly easy," I admitted. "I'm not sure what that says about me."

"That you're good at your job, and Athena made the right choice in picking you," he said as he started clearing dishes.

"You mean when she listened to you, Tessa, Nate, Chiron, and fucking *Apollo*, of all people before picking me?" I asked with a grin.

"Well, yes, that too. But, at the end of the day, it was her call."

As he started loading up the dishwasher, I picked up my glass of water and took a sip. I'd been thinking a lot about what a big job this was for someone like me, so new to immortal life. I'd always been confident since my powers had been awakened, cocky, even, but I never actually pictured myself on an assignment. Ischyra were stationed all over the planet, some working at training facilities, others in some of the most war-torn areas in the world. The job could be cushy or very, very hard. I honestly didn't know where I expected to end up, but it certainly wasn't here, fulfilling my one human desire of going to college. The fact that I had people in my life who cared enough about me to push for me to get this assignment kind of gave me the warm fuzzies in a way I hadn't felt in a long time.

"So, I've been meaning to ask," Dionysus said, closing the dishwasher. "Do you think there's any chance Willow has some secret power she's hiding? It'd make sense, since she's the president."

"If she does, she's cloaking really well. Ever since Aphrodite taught me how to 'feel' deific power, it's kind of hard to *not* notice it, you know?"

He frowned. "Well, don't make any assumptions yet. Your power is fully cloaked, so it could be just as easy for someone else's to be."

I narrowed my eyes, a little annoyed he assumed *I* was assuming. "I'm not an idiot, Dionysus. I won't let my guard down."

"I didn't say you were an idiot," he said.

"No, but you implied I was making assumptions that no one with half a brain would make." I touched my necklace. "I'm well aware of how easy it is to hide an immortal's magic."

"I'm sure you are, but—"

'Hey, I'm coming in.'

"Shit!" I slapped a hand to my forehead as my front door opened and Tessa walked in. "I totally forgot about girls' night." Tessa and I had planned it weeks ago, but with everything going on, it had completely slipped my mind.

Clearly aggravated, Dionysus cast a look at Tessa, then went about cleaning up takeout boxes on the counter.

She gave me a questioning look, and I just shook my head, not really caring to get into our discussion while Dionysus was still there.

"Aren't you meeting Nate and Hermes?" Tessa asked him.

Dionysus faced her and frowned, then rubbed a hand across his forehead. "Yeah. I guess I forgot too."

I almost felt bad, knowing how much that small burst of negative energy from our spat would've put a damper on his power. Maybe I'd gotten a little too defensive, but I seriously couldn't deal with him taking on a mother-hen role and hovering over my shoulder. I already felt like he was on the verge of doing that, but he needed to know I was fine doing this job on my own.

He sent me a quick look. *'I'll check in later?'*

'Sounds good.' I tried to give him a reassuring smile just so he knew I wasn't truly angry, but once he got gloomy, it was hard to get him to perk back up. Hopefully, his brothers would be able to do that for him.

17

DIONYSUS

I teleported to the deck on the roof of my house on Olympus and found Nathaniel and Hermes waiting for me. Hermes had raided my wine cellar, and Nathaniel had helped himself to a two-hundred-year-old bottle of scotch that had been sitting in my liquor cabinet for, well, two hundred years, waiting for a special occasion to be drank.

I snatched the bottle out of his hand before he could open it.

"That's for a special occasion," I snapped.

His eyebrows shot up, and his lips twitched in amusement. "Is that so?"

"There are a dozen other bottles of scotch in there," I told him. "Go find one of those."

Hermes snorted as he pulled the cork from one of the bottles of wine he'd swiped, then handed it to Nathaniel. "Someone's grumpy," he said, going to work opening the second bottle.

I dropped down in one of the lounge chairs and kicked my shoes off. "Fuck off."

"Something wrong?" Nathaniel asked.

"No."

I could practically feel him and Hermes exchange a look.

"You know I can read your mind with no problem," Nathaniel said. As if to demonstrate, he poked at my mental walls to show me just how easily he could peek inside. He never would—it was far beneath him to do something like that—but he wasn't above continuing to poke just to annoy me into talking.

"I'd kick your ass and you know it."

"I could sic Tessa on you. She's far less scrupulous than me."

I arched a brow. "Tessa would never do that, either, and you know it."

He shrugged and Hermes laughed, then handed me a bottle of wine.

"I think your problems can be summed up in two words: Mary Miller."

"Mary and I are . . . fine." I took a swig of wine, letting the sweet flavor swirl over my tongue.

"What happened, then?" Nathaniel asked, frowning.

I felt my face twisting into a scowl, but I forced it back and tried to find something to focus on that wasn't the little fight that had knocked my mood down about ten pegs. With a sigh, I ran through the conversation Mary and I had just had about that stupid prick Shep.

"You're a fucking idiot if you don't see how into you she is," Hermes said once I was done. "That tool's the last thing you need to worry about."

Nathaniel lifted the bottle in his hand in agreement.

"Maybe." I tried to picture it, hoping I could take some positive energy from just the thought of being with her. "She's been pretty busy so—"

"Doing her *job,*" Hermes said. "She's allowed to have a social life too. I think even Athena would agree to that."

"She does have a social life," I replied. "She's with Calla Aiden or one of her cronies daily."

"That's a good thing, right?" Nathaniel asked. "She's getting the job done. That bodes well for her future prospects."

"Which we all knew would never be an issue," Hermes added.

I lifted the bottle to my lips again, this time taking down nearly half its contents.

Nathaniel snorted. "I haven't seen you this worked up over a woman in centuries."

Just then, I heard steps on the spiral staircase that wound down into the house. A moment later, Apollo appeared.

"Oh." Hermes said. "By the way, Apollo's coming over."

"Wonderful."

"Hello to you, too," Apollo said with a wry grin.

"D's grumbly because Mary's spending a lot of time with the fraternity brothers on campus," Hermes explained. He leaned forward and lowered his voice to a stage whisper. "One of them asked for her number."

Apollo rolled his eyes and accepted a bottle of wine from Nathaniel. "You mean to tell me an attractive woman has other men in her life who might be interested in her? How shocking."

I gritted my teeth. "I thought you were turning over a new leaf, Apollo. Trying to be *less* of a miserable ass, not more."

"I don't recall making that promise," he replied. "And I *did* slip a compliment in there, in case you didn't notice. That should count for something."

"Calling her attractive isn't a compliment; it's a fact."

He made a small, noncommittal sound and shrugged. "So, how much progress is she making, anyway?"

"A lot, actually. She got in good with Calla Aiden right away, and she seems to have a good grip on how to feel for deific power." I sighed. "And yeah, the president of Kappa O has his eye on her. Which, considering the context, I guess you could say is a good thing." I went on to detail the rest of her progress and how she'd managed to land where she had with both Iota Sig and Kappa O.

"So, you're telling me," Hermes said as he set aside his empty bottle and uncorked another, "she got in with the Aiden girl on day one, risked giving her a concussion to do so, endeared herself enough to the Kappas that the damn president asked for her number, came up with the idea to map out the houses on her own, found the legacy angle, and is on her way to getting pinned with the Iotas?" He raised his eyebrows. "Am I missing anything?"

I glanced at Nathaniel, who was smirking, then Apollo, who looked at least somewhat impressed. It wasn't entirely lost on me that my brothers had gotten me to talk about Mary as a way to boost my mood, which, between that and Hermes's increasing inebriation, was working.

"No, I think that about covers it," I grumbled.

Hermes leaned back in the chaise and spread his hands, nearly upending his bottle in the process. "Admit it, D. Your girl's badass."

I couldn't help but smile at that one.

18

MARY

After Dionysus left, Tessa and I settled in on the sofa with a bottle of wine. We hadn't had any one-on-one time in months, so it was nice to finally get to hang out with my best friend without Nate and his brothers lurking in the background.

"So, how's sorority life?" Tessa asked as we sat.

I shrugged. "Not as bad as I thought, actually."

Tessa looked at me in surprise. "Seriously?"

"Yeah. It's weird. I was prepared for all these rules and bitchy girls and I-don't-know-what, and I guess there's some of that, but for the most part, the girls seem pretty nice. Normal, if that's even a thing."

She nodded slowly and sipped her wine. "Interesting. Have you figured out how you're going to get in with Stewart?"

"Yeah. I'm working on that. There's a coffee shop on campus that he's apparently nuts over, so I'm gonna try to get a job there." I rolled my eyes. "One of my duties as an Iota Sig."

Tessa bit her lip and smiled. "For some reason, I don't picture you taking to the role of barista all that well."

I shrugged. "How hard can it be? Steam some milk, grind some beans. I'll find some videos online so I can back up the job history on my resume."

"Yeah, I think it'll be a little more complicated than that," she replied.

I laughed. "Obviously. I'll study up before I go in and apply. I'm guessing they'll make me demonstrate my skills or whatever." I tapped a finger to my chin and eyed the semi-spacious kitchen counter. "Do you think Athena would kill me if I bought a cappuccino machine? It'd be for research purposes, obviously."

Tessa laughed. "Obviously. And no, I don't think she would. You need to know how to make a mean drink if you're going to leave a solid impression on him."

"Exactly." I shifted in my seat and tucked my legs under me. "So, how's the non-honeymoon going?"

"Kind of awesome, actually," Tessa said, mimicking my position. "Iceland was awesome, but I kind of want to go somewhere warm, so we're hitting the Maldives next. We're getting one of those fancy little huts that are on pilings over the ocean. I hear the diving is amazing."

"That sounds like fun," I said, smiling. "Maybe once I'm done here, I'll get to go someplace that's actually warm."

"We should definitely take a girls' trip," she agreed. "Maybe we can even get Yana to come."

"Oh, that would be so fun!"

"And after *that*, we should take another trip, just the four of us," she added.

I gave her a look. "I'm guessing numbers three and four would be Nate and Dionysus?"

"It would," she said with a nod.

I was quiet for a minute as I thought about that. It *would* be a lot of fun to go on a trip with Tessa and Nate. We'd had so much fun traveling around the past year, so there was no doubt we'd travel well together anywhere.

"So, I have a question," I said. "It's kind of weird and something I've been pondering for a while now."

"Pondering?" Tessa smirked. "This sounds ominous."

"So, one of the things that's been making me question this whole thing with Dionysus is . . . well, the age thing." While it wasn't my number one reason for second-guessing the wisdom of a relationship with him, it was up there. There was never a time where he actually seemed like he'd been around for three millennia, but the truth was, he had been.

Tessa hesitated a moment, as if she was trying to formulate her response before finally answering.

"Here's my take. And I can tell you it's pretty much the typical response you'll get from immortals. Once you're immortal, that kind of thing just . . . well, stops being a thing. Look at my relationships. I was born almost a thousand years before Nate, and Hades was nearly that much older than me. And if you really look at mine and Nate's relationship, I've only *technically* been alive, in a sense, for about eight hundred years. He's been living and breathing for more than three thousand."

I considered that for a moment. "Huh. I hadn't really considered that since you guys are so . . ."

"Old?" She smirked. "You will be, too, someday. The thing about gods, all immortals, really, is that we sort of . . . live our lives in a string of lifetimes, if that makes sense?" She wrinkled her nose when she saw the confusion on my face. "Basically, we're born, we grow up, and that's it. We hit a point where we stop aging. It's not like it is for humans, where they have to cram as much as possible into the blink of time they have on Earth before they die. There's always more time for us and there are seriously endless possibilities."

I sighed and leaned back against the arm of the sofa, twirling my wine glass gently in my lap, watching as the wine swirled back and forth.

"Look at it this way," she said. "Yeah, Dionysus has been around awhile, but do you really think he's the same person now that he was a hundred years ago? A thousand? We'll—" she gestured between the two of us "—be learning how the world works until the end of time, Mare. In a hundred years, he won't know any more about the time we're living in than you. He'll know more about the past, sure. And fine, he's had way more experience as far as relationships go, and if he were a manipulative dick, I'd be worried. But you know that's not the case. Dionysus . . . he just likes to . . ."

"Exist?" I'd seen it multiple times since last summer, each time we went somewhere new. He'd seen so much of the world, but each time we visited a city or landmark or national park, it was like he was seeing it for the first time. He wanted to absorb it all, as if he didn't have all the time in the world to examine every square inch of the planet.

I'm pretty sure the goofy smile on his face when we visited the Grand Canyon was the first time I realized I cared significantly more for him than I'd realized.

Tessa refilled her glass and topped off mine.

"The good thing about forever is that there's plenty of time to get things right and even more time to move on with your life if you get things wrong. Look at me and Hades. Not ideal, as far as relationships go, but he was a single point in time for me, a chapter in my life that I don't regret. I won't hit old age fretting about wasting away my prime on something that didn't last because I won't *hit* old age and my prime is, well, forever."

"And your hate sex with Hades has what to do with my non-relationship with Dionysus, exactly?"

"My *point,* jackass, is that you shouldn't wait until a certain point in time to start truly experiencing immortality. Hades was one experience, one that I dove into headfirst because, despite who he was or the difference in age, I wanted to. I had no reason not to. If I'd said 'I haven't been immortal long enough for this to be considered appropriate,' I would've missed out on so much. Because, despite what you may think, it wasn't just hate sex," she said with a wry smile. "For either of us. And I can honestly say if I had turned him down, I would've regretted it for the rest of my life. We didn't last and that's okay. He was one chapter in my life, but I knew I would have others chapters if we didn't work out. Nate's mine." She shrugged and sipped her wine. "You should put aside your concerns and consider—really consider—letting Dionysus be yours."

"I know you're not wrong," I said after a moment. "About the age thing. I get what you're saying. I guess there's just other stuff. Like, what if he's drawn to me because he thinks I'm still broken?"

Tessa gave me an incredulous look. "Mary, even when you *were* 'broken,' that wasn't what drew him to you. You guys hit it off before everything happened. I saw it, Nate saw it. Maybe you didn't, but it was definitely there."

I frowned as I thought back to the times he and I had goofed off before I'd been kidnapped, back when I was just a recruit and we would all get together at Nate's and hang out.

"You know," she said. "Atlas thought it was weird how comfortable you were with us." She smiled when I gave her a confused look. "He heard you laughing one night at Nate's. We were inside talking, and you guys were on the lawn. I don't know what Dionysus did, but he made you laugh so damn loud."

I arched a brow. "And your twin thought that was odd?"

"Yes, he thought it was odd that a fresh recruit was so comfortable around a bunch of gods. But I think that just goes to show how easy it's been for you and Dionysus this whole time. Yeah, maybe your trauma drew him in for a time, but that wasn't what drew him to you in the first place. And it's definitely not what's kept him around."

"I guess." I took a sip of my wine, then stared down into the glass. "Ugh. This is so *not* like me!"

She laughed. "I know! So, I don't know what the issue is. You've never second-guessed yourself when it came to guys before. No need to start now."

"I know. I just really don't want to end up making things awkward if it doesn't work out . . . *but* I hear what you're saying. We have eternity. So, yeah." I nodded. "I think it's time to stop being stupid."

She grinned and clinked her glass to mine. "That's my girl."

19

DIONYSUS

By the time I got back to Mary's apartment after work the next day, I was still pissed off.

I was jealous of a human.

A *human*.

Shepard Stuyvesant was officially on my last nerve, and I just couldn't shake it. My night with my brothers had helped, at least somewhat, but Shep ... yeah, he needed to go.

The worst part was, I didn't know why he bothered me so much. He hadn't done anything wrong. Shit, he hadn't even put a move on Mary. He'd asked for her number, as any sane guy would once they got to know her. I knew *she* wasn't interested in him, so I needed to let it go, at least for now.

But he *would* make a move. And that's what bugged me. He absolutely, without a doubt, would make a move sooner rather than later. I knew guys like him. I'd been around them for ages.

And damn it if my confidence didn't waver a little at the thought of her possibly accepting his advances.

Nope.

I stopped that thought cold. Mary was smart. Fucking brilliant. And he was a total tool. Mary didn't do tools. There was no way she'd go for a guy like him. She might fake a little attraction to get information, but she wouldn't actually take it any further.

Some stupid voice in my head told me it would be very easy to solve this problem right now. All I had to do was walk through the door in front of me and tell her how I felt.

I could do that. Maybe.

Letting out a breath, I turned the knob to Mary's apartment and let myself in. I smiled when I found her in front of her computer at the island, brow furrowed as she typed furiously.

When she heard me come in, she glanced up and smiled. "Dinner?"

"Yup." I tapped one of the bags. "Come on, let's eat."

Mary stretched her arms over her head and cracked her neck, and I couldn't resist poking her stomach when her shirt rode up. When she scowled and went to smack my chest, I caught her hand.

"So, I'm sorry about last night," I said, lacing my fingers through hers. "I know it came off like I was questioning your decision-making skills, but I wasn't. I know how capable you are, Mary."

She narrowed her eyes. "I suppose I can accept your apology." She inclined her head toward the bag. "Is that remorse food?"

I grinned. "I brought you beignets," I sing-songed, picking up one of the bags. "They're still warm."

Her eyes widened briefly, then she snatched the bag out of my hand before I could react.

"Hey!" I moved to grab it back, but she took a quick step back. "You have to share!"

"Oh?" She gave me a look of mock surprise, even though she knew damn well the beignets from Café Du Monde were my favorite. "Do I? I was under the impression these fell under the heading of 'penance.'" Opening the bag, she pulled out one of the pieces of sugary fried dough, not caring a lick that powdered sugar was drifting to the floor, and took a huge bite. "Oh my gods, these are so good," she mumbled around a mouthful.

I took a step forward and held out my hand for the bag. "Share, Mary."

She sucked the sugar off her thumb with a pop, and I just about died. "Nope."

I took another step closer, not quite sure what I planned to do once I touched her. "Mary . . ."

Smirking, she took another bite.

Seconds later, she was pinned under me on the couch, and I was holding the bag in the air above us.

"Jerk!" she exclaimed, laughing as she pushed against my chest. "You got sugar everywhere! Let me up!" There was sugar all over her lips and clinging to her eyelashes. It took every ounce of my willpower not to lick it all up right then.

"Not until you've agreed I've paid my penance," I said quietly.

"And give up instant access to all this amazing food? No way."

"I will literally lick your face if you don't agree."

I felt her heart give a heavy thud against my chest, and I could tell she was a little unnerved at how hot that actually sounded. "What —why?"

I leaned closer. "Because it's covered with sugar, for one, and because it would make you *so* mad."

"Oh?" She gave me a *you wouldn't dare* look. "How do you know?"

I arched a brow teasingly. "Are you saying you want me to lick your face?"

Her mouth opened, then fell closed as her cheeks flamed pink. "No!"

She was lying. She was one-hundred-percent lying through her teeth.

Yep. I was going for it.

"So, then, you'll agree I've paid my dues?" I asked, leaning a little closer.

"Definitely not."

"Okay . . . you asked for it." I ran my eyes over her face, taking in every beautiful inch. "Hmm . . . Where to start . . ."

"Don't you dare!" she squealed, struggling pointlessly against me, laughing the whole time. "Dionysus!" she let out breathless laugh. "You're such an idiot."

"Forehead, maybe?"

She squealed again when my lips touched her forehead. It wasn't a lick so much as a soft kiss, a testing move that I hoped wouldn't bite me in the ass.

When she didn't pull away, I gave her a slow smile.

"Hmm, it looks like you have some here, too," I said, doing the same movement to her temple. My voice had gone raspy, and I knew I was doing a shit job at hiding any kind of intention.

"I can get a napkin, you know," she said, although the annoyance she tried to work into her tone fell flat. Her body had completely relaxed against mine, and when I leaned back to look at her, a look came into her eyes that was almost . . . expectant.

"But this is mutually beneficial," I said. "I get sugar, and you don't have to waste a napkin. Oops." I touched my lips to her cheek. "Missed a spot."

Any fight she had left dwindled along with mine. I could tell by her stillness that this was teetering into completely new territory neither of us knew what to do with.

She gave me another look when I leaned back again, and I hoped she couldn't feel how fast my heart was beating. "Anywhere else, or can we get back to dinner?"

I touched a finger to her lower lip, steeling myself for what I was pretty sure I was about to do. "There's some right here. I'm a little afraid you'll bite me if I try for it, though."

When she didn't respond right away, I lowered my head, hesitating a fraction of a second before brushing my tongue lightly over her lip. I moved slowly, wanting to savor every second and give her the chance to take the reins.

She froze, her heart thundering against my chest. Her fingers curled around my arms, and for a second, I thought she might follow through.

I'd taken us to the edge. Everything in her eyes and body language said she wanted to press on, but I could still sense hesitation. As if she'd read my mind, her fingers loosened and she let her hands relax.

So, I made the decision for her and pulled back.

I smiled lazily. "Have you learned your lesson?"

Her breath whooshed out. "I'm not really sure, honestly. You brought them for me, so I don't really think that means I'm required to share," she said with a smirk. "But . . . I suppose I can be persuaded."

Her face was still so close; close enough that if she just leaned up a little . . .

I touched my forehead to hers and sighed. "I'll hold you to that," I murmured. "Now come on," I said, standing and pulling her with me. "The food's getting cold, and I didn't run across the literal globe for you just to eat lukewarm pulled pork." I turned her to face the kitchen and put my hands on her hips, then guided her forward.

I could practically hear her rolling her eyes. "Yeah, yeah. Wouldn't want to offend your sensitive taste buds."

And with that, we settled in to eat while we binged some new crime drama one of the other professors had told me about. Between the food and the show, there was almost enough of a distraction to keep me from thinking about how close I'd come to actually showing her how I felt.

About how I'd bitched out once again.

But that small hesitation I felt on her end . . . that's what stilled me. That's what kept me from truly putting my lips on hers.

Because if there was any hesitation, I didn't want it. She needed to be certain of me, of my intentions, and of my feelings for her. If there was anything inside her that made her second-guess anything, I wanted to quiet that voice first.

I needed to. It was the only way I could be sure she didn't think I was drawn to her because she was still healing or because of some insatiable need to make her happy.

And yet, that was the thing. I *did* want to make her happy. In every godsdamned sense of the word. I wanted her to be happy and fulfilled. And I wanted to experience that with her. Not because I thrived on the contentment of others. But because it was her.

I should've just fucking kissed her.

20

MARY

Desperately needing something big to distract me from my almost-kiss with Dionysus the night before, I spent the bulk of Saturday afternoon getting ready for the Bid Day party at the Aidens' house. I absolutely could not let my romantic life affect how I did this job, and not only because I didn't want to end up cleaning up mouse shit in East Bumblefuck.

But why didn't he just follow through?

That thought nagged at me all day, and the only thing I could come up with was that he felt that half-breath of hesitation I'd had when it seemed like he might finally go for it.

Which pissed me off, because that hesitation hadn't been because I didn't want him to kiss me. Quite the opposite, actually.

It was the thought of what would've immediately followed. I hadn't shaved *anything* in days, and while I was quite certain he'd had his share of unshaven romps back in the day, that just wasn't how I did things.

Stupid? Yes. But did it cause me to freeze for a nanosecond when I thought of him running his hands up my stubbly legs? Also, yes. Honestly, if he hadn't been a god, he probably wouldn't have even noticed.

So, I forced all thoughts of my stupidity and Dionysus and almost-kisses out of my head as I riffled through my Nordstrom haul. After considering the options for a few moments, I pulled out black, high-waisted leggings and a dark gray blousey-shirt thing that was painfully outside my fashion comfort zone. It wasn't red or gold, it was cute, and it would go with the Iota cardigan. So, it worked.

To avoid getting anything on my shirt, I started doing my makeup in just my pants and bra. I'd just finished contouring and had picked up a pot of navy eye shadow when a movement in the mirror caught my eye. I slid my eyes to the side and saw Dionysus standing behind me, very clearly staring at my lack of shirt. I knew I should've been at least a *little* embarrassed, but, well, modesty had never been my strong suit, and I kind of wanted to nudge open that door we'd cracked last night.

I couldn't help but smile when he saw I'd caught him looking. "Can I help you?"

He recovered quickly and leaned against the doorjamb, his lips tilted into a grin that made me want to either smack him or kiss him. "You look indecent."

"Yeah, I figured I'd go balls-out with Stewart tonight." I refocused my attention on my mascara and tried to ignore the way I could still feel him looking at me. "Hypnotize him with my womanly wiles and get him to spill all his secrets."

"I don't know how he could possibly resist," he said as he came into the bathroom and stood behind me, his face curious. "Not that I'm complaining, but can I ask why you're doing your makeup topless?"

He was so close, I could feel the heat coming off of him, and a bit of my irritation at his lack of follow-through from the day before ignited.

"There was an incident involving mascara and one of Tessa's cashmere sweaters a few years back that ended badly." I closed the tube and set it back on the counter, then turned to face him. When he didn't step back, I met his eyes. "What's up?"

He shrugged and slid his hands into his pockets. "Just checking in to see if you needed any help tonight."

"I don't think so." Stepping past him, I lifted my shirt off the hanger I'd hung on the shower rod and slipped it over my head, careful not to smear my makeup. "Thanks, though."

Once my shirt was in place, I began the arduous process of straightening my hair, something I'd barely done over the last eight months because it was a complete pain in the ass. It curled easily enough, but it was thick and had that stupid half-wave that took a good half hour to fully smooth out.

"Why not just wear your hair as is?" Dionysus asked as I started separating my hair into sections. He sat down on the edge of the tub and watched as I dragged the straightener through my hair. "I like that little wave thing you have going on."

"I thought about it, but pretty much all of the other girls straightened their hair for the last two parties." I shrugged. "It might be dumb, but I need to blend in, so if that means mimicking some of their habits, that's what I'll do."

"Kinda hard for you not to stand out," he said with a smirk.

I checked the clock on my phone once I was done and saw that I had exactly ten minutes before my official bid was supposed to come through. Even though Calla seemed certain I would get one, I couldn't help but be a little nervous that maybe all my work so far had been for nothing.

"Come on," Dionysus said. "I can tell you're nervous. Come on, I'll make that tea you like."

I nodded. "Yeah, okay."

We made our way out to the kitchen, where he pulled out a mug and a tea bag, then flicked on the electric kettle. "Do you want to go over the plan one more time?"

"I don't know that there's much to go over," I said. "My main goal tonight is to meet Stewart and Missa, not make a fool of myself in the process, and try to map out at least a little of their house."

"All right. And if anything goes sideways?"

"I'll call you," I said. I'd pushed against that one a bit when he first suggested it, but the more I thought about it, the more I saw reason in having someone ready to back me up at a moment's notice.

"I'm not going anywhere tonight, so I'll be there right away if you need me."

I smiled. "Thanks. As much as I'd rather tell you to back off and let me do this on my own, I see the logic. So, thank you."

He laughed. "Anytime."

We went over a few more things, like what I'd talk to Stewart about if I met him and how I'd assess Missa and the sisters. I was about halfway through my tea when my phone dinged. I picked it up and opened my email app, quickly scanning the message that had just come in.

"Good news?" Dionysus asked.

I looked up at him and grinned. "I'm in."

I'D SEEN the outside of the Aidens' house with Aphrodite, but that was from the fence, which was a few hundred yards from the house nestled into the mountain at the end of the long, winding drive. The monstrosity that loomed in front of me as I drove up the cobblestones was castle-like in size. A fresh layer of snow on the roof gave the whole property an ever more picture-perfect appearance.

Must be nice to be a demigod with coercive powers, I thought as I imagined how on earth Stewart's stock dividends and salary had afforded so much. Even as president of the university, he wouldn't make nearly enough to afford something this extravagant. So, my money was definitely on him using his "powers of persuasion" to get a good deal.

I parked in the circular drive behind Willow's Range Rover, and when I caught a glimpse of Calla's Porsche and a fiery red Aston Martin in the garage, I was super thankful Athena had gotten me a higher-end vehicle.

As I locked it, I felt around for that "hum" Aphrodite had shown me. It was faint, but I could feel it. It buzzed a bit stronger than when we'd been back by the fence, which presumably meant whichever deific object or objects were sending out their radio waves were or had been inside the house. For now, I was working with one of two possibilities—the sash and apple were inside, but cloaked, or they'd been there and had been removed entirely and their magic was just fading. Either way, if I could pinpoint a location for the energy I was feeling, it could go a long way in narrowing down where they might be.

So, I pulled out my phone, opened the route-tracker, and set it running, then walked up the marble steps and rang the bell.

The door opened a few seconds later by a tall, willowy brunette with skin the color of ocher, who I recognized from her pictures as Missa Aiden. Despite the fact that her daughter was nearly twenty-one, Missa barely looked a day past thirty. Whether it was good genes or magic, I didn't know, but it was pretty clear why it had been so easy for her to seduce a married man in order to steal Aphrodite's sash from Hera.

"Hi!" I gave her my brightest smile. "I'm Mary Jameson. I'm here for the Iota Sig party." I held up my phone. "My bid came through just a little while ago."

Her pretty face broke into a smile. "Ah, yes! You're the last to arrive, and we were just about to get started." She stepped back and gestured for me to come inside. "Come, let's get you out of the cold. Martha will take your coat," she said, gesturing to a petite blonde who'd just come down the wide, curved staircase and into the cavernous foyer.

All of the girls who'd arrived before me were gathered with the Iota sisters in the kitchen, which was easily twice the size of my apartment. The center island had a huge spread of food laid out, and the long, shiny dinner table sat under a picture window that would show a perfect view of the mountains behind the house during the day. Some of the sisters were seated around the table with a few of the rushees, nibbling at food from small plates. The rest were all mingling around the island, eating food and talking animatedly.

Standing next to Calla was a tall man with a smile that showed off two rows of shiny teeth and black hair that was combed to the side. It had that neat, gelled look that always made men look so put together. The strangest thing about him, though, was that he seemed . . . jovial. It was odd. I could totally see the politician in him —too-big smile, crinkly eyes, persuasive hand movements—but it also seemed like his interest in the rushee he was talking to was genuine.

"Mary!" Calla called when she spotted me, waving me over.

I grinned and made my way toward her. I tried not to look at Stewart, but I could feel his eyes following me as I approached.

"Daddy, this is Mary Jameson," Calla said as I gave him the same bright smile I'd given Missa. "She's new in town. Her grandmother was an Iota at Penn State."

Stewart's eyebrows went up as he shook my hand, his grip firm and confident. "A legacy! We don't get many of you up in this neck of the woods, believe it or not." He flashed those pearly whites. "This isn't exactly an area where students are eager to move."

I laughed. "Luckily, I don't mind the cold." I looked around the kitchen. "You home is beautiful. Thanks so much for having us."

"Don't mention it," Stewart said. "Missa and I adore meeting the new girls and getting to know what Calla's up to. And it's a great excuse to entertain," he added with a laugh.

"Well, it's certainly a great house for it." I shifted my full attention to him. "So, I hear you're running for Congress, Mr. Aiden. Congratulations!"

Calla rolled her eyes. "Ugh, don't get him started. You'll be here all day hearing about the local water supply and the quality of back roads.

Stewart gave her shoulder an affectionate squeeze. "She's not wrong. And thank you, Mary. Are you registered to vote in our district?"

"Nope, I'm still a PA girl. I'll be sure to tell everyone I meet to send their votes your way, though," I said with a grin.

He chuckled. "Well, you seem like the type of girl who can be pretty persuasive, so I appreciate that greatly."

Calla gave my arm a tug. "Come on, Mary. Let's get some food and sit. My mom's gonna start her spiel in just a minute."

"Which is also my cue to depart," Stewart said, finishing off the mug of coffee he'd been drinking. "You ladies have fun!" he called as we walked off.

"Bye, Daddy!" Calla said, then pulled me toward the food and dictated what I should put on my plate.

Missa came in a few minutes later and clapped her hands. "All right, ladies! Let's get started!"

Once all the rushees and sisters had settled around the table, Calla and Willow took their places at Missa's side.

"Welcome, everyone," Missa said, flashing a smile. "I'm so happy to meet the future sisters of Iota Sigma Xi! I was an Iota back in college and it was truly—" she laid a hand on her chest and smiled softly "—*truly*, one of the most precious times in my life. The relationships you build with one another will last a lifetime."

"I'd like to thank everyone here who has chosen to become part of the Iota family," Willow added, beaming. "It's so exciting to watch our sorority grow and change each year, and I can just tell by looking at all of your gorgeous faces that this is going to be a *great* semester."

"But first," Calla said, holding up a finger, her face all business. "If anyone is feeling *at all* conflicted about the bid you just received, feel free to see yourself out right now. We have no room for wishy-washy sisters in our house."

I arched a brow at her bluntness, but when I looked around, no one else seemed fazed by it.

"Great!" Calla motioned toward Kristy, who was standing to the side with another sister in front of two tall stacks of white gift boxes. "Now, it's time for your cardigans!"

I waited as Willow, Calla, and Missa handed the boxes out to the new recruits. When I opened mine, I breathed a small sigh of relief. It wasn't nearly as garish as I'd expected—just solid white with red trim around the hem, gold buttons, and the Iota Sig letters emblazoned on one side. Definitely not something I would normally wear, but as far as forced attire went, it wasn't too bad.

"I think we've gotten to know you all a bit this past week," Willow said as we shrugged into our cardigans. "So, let's move on to the next step—the pinning ceremony. This signals the start of your pledge period, which will last six weeks."

"The ceremony will be next Saturday at seven PM," Calla said. "As you all know, pledges are required to wear white. Do *not* deviate from this in the slightest. Shoes, any accessories, right down to your hair tie, *must be white.*"

"You'll meet us at the steps to the oldest building on campus," Willow continued, "and you will *tell no one.* Is that clear?"

As she spoke the words, the hair on the back of my neck prickled, like someone had just blown cold air down the back of my shirt. I almost ignored it, then remembered I was, one, sitting in the presence of a witch who was, two, married to a demigod, so I figured it might be worth noting.

As everyone else called out their yeses, I reached out to Dionysus.

'You there?'

'What's up?' Dionysus replied.

Keeping one eye on Calla and Willow's speech, I showed him the memory. *'Is that what I think it was?'*

'Definitely felt like an interdiction to me,' he confirmed.

Shit.

Interdictions were godly gag orders that prevented a person from talking about something. In this case, we were promising not to tell anyone where we were supposed to meet the Iota sisters before pledge. Which seemed kind of stupid, but obviously had some sort of significance.

'Did you agree?' he asked.

'I don't think so. I mean, I just nodded, but I wasn't actually looking at Willow when she said it. And I'm talking to you and just showed you the memory, so maybe that wasn't enough? And how would she have been able to do that, anyway?'

'It would've been Missa, most likely. I don't sense anything deific in Willow. And Missa wouldn't be strong enough to put an interdiction on an

Ischyra, but she'd be plenty strong enough to put one on a bunch of humans. Just be very careful going forward.'

'K. I'll talk to you more later. Gotta go.'

I cut the connection and refocused on Willow.

"The first thing you'll do at your pinning ceremony is take your pledge," she said. "You'll take another prior to your first pledge task."

One of the girls raised her hands. "What kind of pledge?"

"You'll pledge your loyalty and faithfulness to the sorority, swear to uphold our ideals, among other things," Willow said. Her smile was smooth. "Nothing crazy, don't worry."

I flicked a glance at Missa, whose shrewd eyes were running over the group of pledges. Something told me the tasks would be intense if she had anything to do with planning them.

Nothing crazy, my ass.

Calla grinned. "Okay, then! Now, let's talk about what it really means to be an Iota sister." She looked at her mother, indicating it was her turn to speak.

Missa looked around the room, taking in the girls in front of her with a wistful smile. "When I rushed nearly twenty-five years ago, the number one characteristic my president required of a sister was loyalty. There is no room for disloyalty in a sorority, especially one as special as yours. Each decision you make throughout your time as a sister should be with your house's best interest at heart. Things like sloppy drunkenness, blowing off classes, ending up in a boy's room, maintaining anything less than a B average, and slacking on things like volunteer work will all shed a poor light on your house." She sniffed. "In my day, those things led to immediate suspension, although things have relaxed a bit since then."

This time, a few of the girls exchanged wary looks.

I was actually kind of surprised "ending up in a boy's room" made the list, considering the obsession these girls seemed to have with pairing off with the Kappas. I'd half expect that kind of activity to be encouraged, at least to some extent.

"The other thing you need to start thinking about is who you'd like to be your big sister," Willow said. "There's no guarantee you'll be matched with your first choice, obviously, but if you choose a sister you feel truly compatible with, it's likely she'll feel the same. Since tonight is just a way of getting to know one another, this will be a good opportunity for you to explore the possibilities."

"Some of you may already have someone in mind," Missa added. "But there are more sisters than pledges, so make sure you consider who else might be a good fit."

Willow spread her hands with a smile. "So, last chance. Does anyone *not* want to be an Iota Sig?"

"No!" was the resounding response.

Willow clapped her hands. "Okay, then! Let's toast!" She raised a glass of champagne, and I noticed other glasses had been placed in front of or handed to everyone else in the room. I tilted it up, mimicking her motion, and took a small sip, suddenly feeling a bit wary about imbibing anything at the moment.

As everyone shuffled around to find seats at the massive dining room table, I walked over to Missa.

"Mrs. Aiden? Would you mind telling me where the bathroom is?"

Missa smiled. "Please, dear, call me Missa. We're all about to be family soon, aren't we?" Her eyes flicked down to my necklace, and she touched a finger to the charm. "My, isn't that lovely! It looks just like a real apple, doesn't it?"

I smiled and hoped she couldn't feel Hecate's magic somehow. "It was my grandmother's. She left it for me when she died."

Missa gave an exaggerated smile of sympathy. "Aren't family heirlooms just the most precious things?"

"They sure are."

"Come, I'll show you where the powder room is." She gestured toward the door on the opposite side of the kitchen from where we'd entered. "It's a bit of a walk, so it's easier if I just take you."

She wasn't exaggerating when she said the bathroom was a "bit of a walk." She led me through one hall, then another, then a third, until finally, she stopped outside a pretty white door. "Here you are! Do you think you can make your way back on your own?"

"Absolutely," I told her. I glanced down the hall in the direction we came. "I've got a great sense of direction."

"Lovely!"

With that, she turned and walked back to the party, and I went in the bathroom and shut the door.

Shaking my head at the sheer size of the "powder room," I took care of my business, then checked my phone to make sure the app was tracking everything correctly. It was, but I took a quick screenshot of what I had so far and sent it to myself, anyway, just in case my phone died or got lost or was zapped by lasers from Missa's eyes.

I turned right when I left the powder room, then stopped, frowned, and turned left. I hadn't seen any cameras, but that didn't mean there weren't any, so I figured it made more sense to actually *look* lost than just say I was. I also made a note to find out what kind of security the house had, both human and magical.

I tried not to wander too far from where I was supposed to be, because I could only play it off so much. So, I took four wrong turns down hallways that looked mildly promising, casually looking for cameras along the way before turning back in the other direction and going back to the kitchen. I tried to gauge the strength of the hum as I went, but it stayed more or less the same; still stronger than outside, but it got slightly stronger as I moved away from the bathroom toward the rear of the house. I had a feeling I'd barely scratched the surface of how much square footage this house had, but it was a start.

"Mary!" Kristy exclaimed when I walked back in. "We were just about to send out a search party!"

"Yeah, I guess my sense of direction isn't as good as I thought. Your house is huge, Calla."

She smiled smugly as I sat down across from her, then poured me a glass of champagne and slid it across the table for me. "Well, Daddy works hard."

"I can see that." I thanked her for the bubbly, then slid my plate closer and started picking at the fancy hors d'oeuvres I'd piled on.

The conversation from then on was pretty mundane. Majors, minors, hometowns, interests, extracurriculars, and so on were the main topics, with many of us finding sisters who we had a lot in common with. I tried to listen to Calla talk about herself before giving my own information, which was easy because it seemed to be a favorite pastime of hers. I didn't lay it on too thick, but just enough that I thought she might see how compatible we'd be when I put her on my list of who I wanted as my Big.

I was kind of hoping I'd get a chance to see where the bedrooms were, or any of the non-visitor areas of the house, but short of spilling something on myself and asking Calla for a new shirt, which I seriously considered, I couldn't see any way to discreetly achieve that.

So, I drank exactly one glass of expensive champagne, ate my fill of the food, and got to know the others. A few hours later, I said my goodbyes and was on my way home.

It was . . . fun.

As I drove back to my apartment, I couldn't help but wonder again what it would be like if this was actually my life. I'd only been at South Lake for a few weeks, but so far, college was exactly what I'd expected. It was exactly what I'd wanted.

And now I had it. It was enough to make me want to drag this assignment out as long as possible, even though I knew it wasn't worth suffering Athena's or Aphrodite's wrath. But I was damn sure I'd push for another assignment just like it if I could.

I'd barely walked in the door when Dionysus came in, clad in Scooby-Doo flannel pajama pants and a white T-shirt.

I gave him a look, trying to ignore how his shirt stretched across his chest in a way that should be illegal. "Were you that bored that you were waiting for me to get home?"

He shrugged and dropped onto the sofa. "Yes. I'm also interested to see what you learned."

Exhausted, I tugged off my boots and sat down next to him.

"Not much, really. I was able to map out some of the house, but that place is freaking huge." I shook my head, then leaned forward, picked up my laptop, and set my phone on the arm of the couch before bringing up the tracking app.

I pulled the satellite image of the Aidens' house up on the

computer and compared it to what was on my phone. Based on what I was seeing, I'd gotten a stretch of the eastern wing of the house, but it was hardly a dent.

"Pitiful," I muttered.

"Better than nothing," Dionysus said. "You'll go back again soon, I'm sure. Did you feel the apple's or sash's presence?"

"A little. It was stronger inside than out, and it seemed a little stronger when I was around here," I said, pointing to a section on the map. "I'm not sure what's behind any of the doors I walked past, except what looked like a maybe an office."

"Both are good places to hide deific objects, but if they were there—"

"I would've felt more of a pull," I said with a nod. "Exactly. So maybe they were there or were moved, or are still there and are cloaked somehow."

"My money's on the latter. Did you meet Stewart?"

"Yep. He looks exactly like a politician, but he seems really nice." I frowned. "Which, I guess, is also typical of a politician."

He laughed. "True, but you're a good judge of character. If he was slimy, you'd know."

"Yeah, I guess. But that begs the question—if he's *not* slimy and is actually a nice guy, are we sure he's the bad guy? I mean, I only talked to him for about two minutes, so I can't say I necessarily got a good read on him. It was enough to give me pause, though."

"It's definitely possible he's not the enemy here, so I think it's worth keeping in mind. So, store that away in your think bank," he said, tapping my forehead, "and save it for later." He closed my laptop and plucked my phone out of my hand, then set them both on the table. "Now, you've been working all night. Watch TV with me."

"K. Let me go get changed first." I flicked his leg. "What's with Scooby, anyway?"

He grinned. "The seventies were an amazing era for cartoons."

I shook my head and laughed. "You're such a child, I swear."

"And yet you love me, regardless."

"Fortunately for you," I said. "I'll be right back."

We stayed up for a few hours watching TV and talking. The whole time, I kept thinking how much nicer it would be if this wasn't just a friendship, and despite the way I felt so at ease tucked under his arm and the flirting that had clearly been intensifying lately, I still knew there were plenty of reasons a relationship wouldn't be a great idea. Even though I kept finding myself reflecting on my conversation with Tessa, those maybes still nagged at me.

My job was a huge concern, mainly. That was my number one. I couldn't screw this up. Not just because I was fearful of Athena's wrath. I wanted to do well for myself, too. It wasn't uncommon for people to think my general attitude about life meant I didn't take things seriously, to the point where they were surprised when they saw how smart I actually was. That alone was reason enough to put all my focus into this. I hadn't been Zeus's first choice—I'd been recommended by people he and Athena trusted and respected, so I needed to prove that I was worthy of those recommendations.

I also didn't think my friendship with Dionysus could survive if we started something up and it didn't work out. It was painful to think about him *not* being in my life, or being in my life as my best friend's brother-in-law, but separate from me.

But as I snuggled closer to him and pulled the blanket we were sharing tighter around me, I was pretty sure it might actually be worth the risk.

21

MARY

The next week flew by, and before I knew it, the day of my pin ceremony had arrived.

Dionysus was out early that morning doing something for Athena, but he promised he'd see me that night. I was a little disappointed I wouldn't be able to spend the day with him, because I really could've used a distraction. As each day had passed, I'd thought more and more about our almost-kiss and why it hadn't been an actual kiss.

You should consider letting Dionysus be yours.

I wanted him to be. Or, I was pretty sure I did. But his lack of follow-through made me think he still had doubts. Not because he wasn't attracted to me—I'd seen the way he looked at me when he thought I wasn't looking, and it was pretty damn obvious what his stance was on my appearance.

He wasn't a looks guy, though. He was the type to go for the whole package, but if part of that package included the best friend of someone who was engaged to his brother, I could see why he'd be hesitant.

But I was beginning to think it was all bullshit. Made-up excuses that were preventing both of us from actually acknowledging that there was something there.

I guess stubbornness might've also played a part, because I'd be damned before I made the first move.

Calla offered to come over and hang out with me while I got ready, which surprised me a little, but it also made me happy. If she was with me, that meant she wasn't with any of the other pledges, so that upped my chances of landing her as my Big. She wasn't going to stay long, because all pledges were required to drive themselves to the meeting place, but it'd at least give me someone to talk to. A distraction from the things I was dwelling on that were very much *not* happening.

When Calla arrived, she had a bottle of wine—white, of course— that she uncorked and poured into two glasses.

"Liquid courage," she said, setting a glass on the bathroom counter next to my makeup bag. "You'll do great tonight, I know it, but it can still be a little nerve-racking."

"Thanks." I sifted through my eyeshadow. "I'm nervous, but I'm super excited, too." I grinned at her in the mirror as I swiped a brush across the navy-blue shadow I'd picked. "And you don't have anything to worry about. I know you stuck your neck out, vouching for me when you didn't even know me, but I promise I won't let you down."

"I'm a good judge of character, Mary. I wouldn't have spoken for you if I didn't think you were the real deal."

Focusing my attention on my eye makeup, I considered that for a moment. There had been something pricking at my mind since I'd met Calla, and I was pretty sure that was it. She'd brought me into her circle very quickly, more quickly than I would've ever expected, but I'd chalked it up to her being a good judge of character. But now, listening to her actually say it out loud made me wonder if she hadn't gotten any powers from her dad, after all.

"That means a lot, Cal, really," I told her.

"Well, my dad liked you, so that kind of cemented it," she admitted. "He's even better at gauging people than me, and he told me he thought you'd be a great fit for Iota Sig. It's crazy. He can seriously sum a person up after interacting with them for thirty seconds. Some weird gift he has."

Carefully, I moved onto my eyeliner and swiped a thick winged line above my lashes. Combined with the navy shadow, it made the shades of green and gold in my eyes really pop.

"He seemed like a great guy." I paused. "Your mom, too. She seems super nice."

"I guess. She's too pushy, which I'm sure you saw, but my dad just kind of . . . gets it, if that makes sense?" She flipped her dark hair over her shoulder. "Plus, he's a self-made man. My mom never once tried to be anything other than a trophy wife. She just . . . does whatever he wants," she said with a dismissive wave of her hand.

I nearly dropped the makeup brush I'd just picked up, but I forced myself to focus on my makeup. I knew she wasn't crazy about her mom, but I hadn't expected her to speak with such disdain about her.

"I guess it's normal to be closer to one parent than the other," I said. "It's great you have your dad."

She frowned. "What about your parents, anyway? You never talk about them."

"There's not much to say, really. My mom died when I was two, so I never knew her, and my dad bailed when I was five." I pressed my lips together and tried to look like I was forcing back big emotions. "My grandmother is the one who raised me, but she died about two years ago. Now it's just me and my aunt."

It was a carefully crafted lie that Athena and I had taken great pains to perfect. I hadn't been super crazy about saying I had no parents, mainly because I didn't know how it would be taken by the Iotas, who seemed pretty particular about their sisters breeding. If my "mom" was still alive, her presence as another "legacy" would quite possibly be expected at some point, which obviously wasn't possible.

So, dead mom and shitty dad, it was. It honestly wasn't much of a stretch from my actual birth parents, the ones who'd dumped me at an emergency room door and never looked back. If they hadn't, I wouldn't be where I was now, just like all the other Ischyra, and I'd had amazing guardians who'd cared for me like I was their own. Still, it still hadn't been a terribly easy thing to accept.

Calla's sympathetic look hinted at a surprisingly soft side. "That's a total bummer. I always bitch about my mom, but I couldn't imagine her not being there."

Uncapping my liner, I moved on to carefully lining my lips. "It's definitely not something I'd wish on anyone."

She leaned forward, resting her forearms on her knees, her glass of wine dangling between her fingers. "So, I'm going to give you a little sneak peek of what you'll be facing the next couple of weeks."

Interesting. If I didn't know better, I'd think she was trying to cheer me up.

"You really don't have to do that if it goes against the rules or anything."

"More of an unspoken rule, so it's fine." She flashed a grin. "So, most of what you'll be doing will be simple—a promise of loyalty, getting a job or finding volunteer work, that kind of thing. But there are two things that pledges tend to have trouble with."

"That sounds ominous." With a frown, I set my lipstick back in my purse and turned to face her, leaning my butt against the edge of the sink.

"Of course. I just want to make sure you're ready for anything, that's all."

"So, what are these troublesome things you'll be having me do?"

"The first isn't so bad, depending on your personality. It'll be something super embarrassing and will happen in front of a *lot* of people. Like, easily a few dozen."

Lovely. "Can you give me an example?"

"Well, last year we had the pledges do wrestling in a pool of Jell-O."

I laughed. "That doesn't sound too bad, actually. Messy, but tolerable."

"Yeah, you don't really seem the type to get bothered by something like that. The other thing, though . . . well, the, uh, legalities of it are a bit of a gray area."

My eyes widened. That could definitely be problematic. If I got busted doing something illegal and the human police got involved, that would mean the Ischyra would get involved, meaning *Athena* would get involved, which I just couldn't deal with.

"What kind of gray area?"

"So, this year it will actually have something to do with my dad. Well, the president's mansion to be exact." She bit her lip. "Stealing something."

"Calla, that's not a fucking gray area!" I slapped my hand over my mouth. "Oh my gods, I'm so sorry."

After holding my stare for a painfully long moment, her face relaxed into a smile. "No worries. And it's not as bad as it seems. Technically, the house is the university's, but as my family are the current residents, I can give you entry." She pointed a manicured finger at me. "But I'll *only* give entry to the first person who gets there. Everyone else will have to find their own way in without getting caught."

"Okay . . ." Her logic was spotty, at best, but I didn't consider it wise to push it, considering my outburst. "What are we supposed to be stealing, anyway?"

"I'm actually not sure. As of right now, Willow is the only person who knows."

It seemed strange that Willow wouldn't even tell Calla what she was planning on hiding in her own house. My mind was racing over the kinds of things we could be put up to stealing, from something as mundane as a measuring cup to something as valuable as . . . well, I guess I didn't want to think about how absolutely fucking *insane* it would be for the thing we had to steal to be a deific object, but stranger things have happened. So, I stored that away in my think bank, along with my suspicions about Stewart, for later.

"Some things are only the business of Iota Sig's president," she continued. "Since I'm VP, Willow will bring me in on the day of, but I'll be the only other one who knows." She gestured toward my room, indicating it was time to get dressed, then got up and walked across the hall.

When we got in, she plopped down on the bed and I stepped into the closet to dress.

"I like you, Mary," Calla said, her tone telling me there was a "but" coming. "You seem like a great girl, which is the only reason I'm helping you out. But don't make me regret it."

I smiled. There was the Calla I knew. "You just gave me insider info that will help me get into Iota Sig. The last thing I'm gonna do is screw that up."

She laughed. "That's what I like to hear."

CALLA LEFT NOT long after I got dressed, about a half hour before I had to head out, leaving me to finish up my hair in silence. I opted for curls mainly because they made my cheekbones look great, but also because snow was in the forecast, and a little moisture frizz on curly hair was easier to conceal than if I straightened it. And, stupid as it might've been, I knew Dionysus liked it better that way.

Yep, I'd say Tessa's words had hit their mark.

I threw on a white cashmere coat I'd bought for exactly this occasion and locked up behind me, then made my way down the stairs, doing my best not to get a heel caught between the boards as I went. The last thing I needed was to bust my ass while I was wearing all white.

When I got to my car, I let it warm up for a few minutes. I always thought being immortal would make things like frigid temperatures not bother me anymore, but as it turns out, not having to worry about hypothermia killing me didn't take away the epic fucking discomfort brought on by subzero temps.

Twenty minutes later, I'd parked in the lot near the registrar's building, the oldest building on campus, and had joined the rest of the pledges at the base of the steps. I was surprised to find that the pledges for Kappa O, of whom I only recognized two or three, were waiting alongside the ones for Iota Sig.

I hadn't really gotten to know many of the girls on a personal level, but I recognized them all by name. When I walked up, I approached a girl named Lynn.

"Hey, what are the guys doing here?" I whispered.

She let her eyes scan over the groups of Kappa pledges. "I don't know. It's weird. Sororities and frats don't do ceremonies like this together. It's basically unheard of."

I eyed the Kappa pledges warily. It wouldn't be the first time I questioned how closely Iota and Kappa followed the letter of Greek law, but I kept that to myself.

Something was just . . . weird about it all.

"Could it just be that they're starting in the same spot?" I asked. "There's no way we'll be doing the ceremonies together, right?"

"I don't think so. I wouldn't be surprised if we all ended up in the same place after, though, which is still kind of weird."

"Huh. I wonder why."

She shrugged. "Not sure. It's kind of cool they have such a close relationship, though."

"Yep," I murmured. "Super cool."

About ten minutes later, four vans pulled up and hooded figures, who were absolutely Shep and Willow, hopped out. The hoods were solid black, a material so dark it almost looked like a black hole where their bodies should be. Both held two handfuls of long white satin sashes each, which I could only assume were blindfolds.

"Good evening, pledges," Shep said in a low monotone. "The path to our destination this evening is of utmost secrecy. Though our ceremonies will be separate, the connections between our houses are of such a nature that we have always felt your time with us should begin together."

"Let's get right into it," Willow said, stepping forward and not bothering with the same theatrics as her counterpart. She held out a hand, brandishing the sashes. "Each of you will take one of these and blindfold yourself. Iota pledges will get into these vans—" she indicated to the ones on her left "—and Kappa pledges will get into the others."

One by one, the pledges for both houses stepped forward to take their blindfolds. I almost made a comment about the houses being far kinkier than I expected, but I held back, since I figured Willow wasn't past kicking me out before I got pinned.

After getting our blindfolds, we climbed into the van to tie them on. The fabric was slippery, so getting a good knot behind my head was kind of tough, but I managed to get it securely enough in place that no light snuck in around the edges.

We waited in silence for a few minutes, then the van turned on and we were off.

I'm not gonna lie; it was kind of weird how cloak-and-dagger this all was. I knew Greek houses could have some odd traditions, but this seemed excessive. Then again, I really wouldn't have known any better.

My uneasiness still led me to try to count turns as we went in case I needed to send out an SOS to Dionysus. I realized pretty quickly that doing that wasn't nearly as easy as they made it look on TV, because I lost track after the fifth turn, and I cursed myself for not turning on the tracking app on my phone before I left home. I made a mental note—which was apparently all I did these days—to set it to track any time I went out with anyone from the sorority or fraternity.

A bit more time passed, maybe twenty minutes or so, before the van slowed to a stop and I heard the sound of two doors slamming shut, telling me there was a driver and a passenger in the front. I had no clue who would've been driving, but my guess was Calla. A moment later, the side door slid open and we were blasted with cold air.

"Out," Willow ordered.

A couple of pledges stumbled a bit as they stepped out, unable to see the step because of the blindfolds. Once we were all out and standing on what felt like a sidewalk, we waited in silence. I had no idea what was happening and was just about to start worrying when I felt two hands on my shoulders. Whoever it was turned me around roughly, stopping me when I was facing the direction opposite the way I'd been.

The person stepped aside, and a few moments later, Willow barked, "Walk!"

We walked forward, following the sound of her voice as our high heels clattered along a sidewalk. I had to stop myself from snapping at whoever was behind me because she kept running into me. I could practically feel her messing up my new shoes, which was totally not cool.

"Stairway going down!"

You've got to be fucking kidding me.

Going down a stairway blindfolded for someone like me, an immortal with damn strong senses, was a piece of cake. But for a typical human? Even if there was a handrail, it seemed destined to result in a sprained ankle or two, maybe a broken bone.

Sure enough, about ten seconds later, I heard the scrape of a shoe on stone followed by a cry and several loud thuds. I expected Willow to tell us to stop, but the line kept moving.

I reached out once I was through the door to touch the wall so I could keep track of where I was going and nearly recoiled when I felt the cold stone. Almost simultaneously, the door slammed shut behind us, loud and echoing.

Images of another stone room flashed through my head and pain lashed at my wrists, setting my heart racing.

"Hey there, Mare Bear."

Minding my balance, I pressed my thumb into my palm.

"Save the head—"

No! I slammed up a mental wall, blocking the memory out.

Absolutely not. Absolutely fucking not.

I focused on my breathing, trying to keep it as quiet as I could, then started counting.

One, two, three, four . . .

In through the nose, out through the mouth.

I'd gotten to sixty by the time we finally reached the bottom of the stairs and came to a stop. Thankfully, my breathing was a bit steadier, but I was struggling to put the echoes of those voices out of my head.

Suck it up, Mary.

Another door slammed shut behind us, drawing my focus to the task at hand. I was surprised at how quiet everyone was. I expected whispers, but the room was silent as a tomb.

A moment later, I felt hands touch the back of my head and untie the blindfold. I blinked against the sudden light, dim to human eyes but pretty vibrant to my sharpened sense of sight. A round firepit sat in the floor in the center of the room filled with a crackling fire, and torches were bolted to the walls every ten feet or so. Since the room wasn't filled with smoke, I assumed the fire must be gas-fueled, which was far less cool than wood-burning, considering the circumstances.

The room itself was pretty big, so I assumed it was some kind of basement. Maybe a bunker. Although I didn't know how many fallout shelters one might be able to find in the immediate vicinity of a college in Upstate New York.

As I scanned the stone walls, taking in every aspect of them I could, I noticed a door cut into the stone on the opposite side of the room, as far from the pledges as you could get. It blended in pretty seamlessly to the surrounding wall, but it looked to be the only exit aside from the one we'd just come through.

After taking in my surroundings, I finally turned my attention back to the sisters running the ceremony who'd just taken the blindfold off the last pledge. Willow and Calla stood side by side on the opposite side of the firepit, each taking us in with shrewd eyes.

"Welcome, pledges," Willow intoned. "Congratulations on making it this far. In just a few minutes, you'll cross over into the sisterhood of Iota Sigma Xi. This is your last chance. If you go through with this ceremony, you'll be an Iota for life."

The level of drama she was putting out nearly had me rolling my eyes.

Unsurprisingly, no one spoke up, so Willow continued talking.

"Good," she said with a firm nod. "Now, let's begin. Repeat after me. Today I commit to joining the sisterhood of Iota Sigma Xi." After we repeated it back, she continued, pausing between each sentence. "I will do all in my power to uphold the laws and legacies of this institution. I come today of my own free will to pledge my loyalty to my sisters. I will unselfishly give my energy and time to carry out my obligations to maintain this house's integrity. I solemnly promise to share my duties with my sisters unflinchingly."

After each repeated sentence, I waited for the telltale push of an interdiction, but it never came.

Odd.

Willow picked up a large pewter jug and poured a dark liquid into a matching goblet. Once it was filled to the brim, she handed it off to Calla, who took a sip.

"Now, to seal your oath, you'll speak the words, 'From now until eternity, an Iota I will be.'"

I pursed my lips. The other promises I could get behind, but that one seemed a bit excessive.

Silently, Calla passed the goblet to the first pledge, and it went down the line.

As each person took their sip, they repeated the final pledge. When the goblet finally made its way to me, I tried not to grimace at the amount of spit that was now on the cup from the fifteen people who'd sipped it before me.

As I said the words and took my sip, I braced myself for the interdiction I assumed was coming. Sure enough, as soon as the wine touched my lips, I felt the spell press against my mind. My teeth ground together as I pushed back against the spell, nudging it out of my mind, which was, according to Dionysus, only possible when an interdiction isn't consensual. Even then, it could be impossible if you weren't strong enough. It was hard and made me break into a bit of a sweat, but I was pretty sure I managed to keep it from taking hold.

Quickly, I reached out to Dionysus.

'Hey, can I test out whether I was able to stop that interdiction from latching on?'

'Go for it.'

I repeated the words of the pledge and shared the entire memory of the ceremony. I was surprised that they came so freely. Even though I'd been able to stop the interdiction, I kind of thought there might be some part of it that might've stuck.

'You're sure that's all of it?' Dionysus asked.

I ran back over Willow's words.

'Yep. But let me try one more thing.' I brought up the memory of the ceremonial words again and sent it to him. *'Can you tell if anything's missing?'*

'Doesn't seem like it. I don't feel any blank spots. Want me to run it by Nathaniel?

'Yeah, thanks. I'll check in later.' If anyone would be able to notice blank spots in a memory, it would be Nate.

I closed the connection, then refocused my attention on the pledges. The goblet had made its way to the last one, and the amount of backwash she was probably drinking made me gag a little.

As soon as she handed the empty goblet back to Calla, Willow clapped her hands and a few overhead lights came on, illuminating the whole room. The masks and robes came off, revealing the sisters of Iota Sig.

"Okay!" Willow grinned at all of us. "Time to party!"

22

MARY

Willow led the way toward the door I'd seen on the other side of the room, then opened it, revealing a perfectly normal wooden staircase. When no one was looking, I slipped my phone from my wristlet and switched on the tracking app.

When I reached the top of the steps, I found myself in the wallpapered hallway of Iota Sig. I followed the rest of the pledges into the living room, where the sisters had situated themselves on the side of the room near the windows.

"Congratulations, ladies!" Willow's words were met with applause from the sisters. "You are *officially* Iota Sigma Xi pledges. The next two months are going to be such a blast! But . . . before we get going with our little party, let's chat for a bit, K?"

Calla stepped forward. "Now that you're officially pledges, we need to go over what your duties will be. First thing's first, though. You must keep up a good image. What does that mean?" Her eyes skimmed over the group of pledges, seeming to assess each of us in a single look. "That means you always wear your colors and pin, and you *always* dress nicely—no PJs to class. If you're worried about not having enough red and gold in your wardrobe, we have a website where you can buy pretty much any style of clothing you want that bears our colors. If you're caught without your colors or not looking your best, you'll be punished. Is that clear?"

A girl named Lindsey standing a few feet away cleared her throat and raised her hand. "What, um, what will our punishment be?"

"That'll be up to your Big," Willow replied. "As your guide, your image directly reflects *hers*. So, it'll be on her to decide just how grievous your actions are."

Based on Lindsey's nervous expression, I got the sudden impression she was second-guessing her choice to join a sorority.

"Appearance aside," Willow continued, "there are other things you'll be responsible for." She held up a hand and started ticking off items on her fingers. "There will be mandatory study groups here or in the library three times a week. Each week, you will have a sorority knowledge test. This will test you on the alpha class, sorority traditions, and the Greek alphabet, among other things. Volunteer work on campus is mandatory, as well. We don't care what you do as long as it benefits the university or community in some way. Last, you'll have a number of pledge tasks that will be required over the next few weeks. The rules and circumstances of those tasks will be disclosed at a later date."

Calla smiled. "We'll meet soon regarding the first pledge task, but don't stress! As long as you do your job as a pledge, you'll be completely fine."

"Now, I know some of you have an idea of who you want for your Big and vice versa," Willow said, "but tonight, I'd like you to take a bit more time getting to know the sisters of Iota Sig. We're a family now, and it's important we know all there is to know about one another." She made a shooing motion with her hands. "Go on and get to know each other. We'll be heading over to the Kappa O house in a couple of hours."

As she dismissed us, the other pledges started wandering toward the sisters and introducing themselves.

"Mary!"

I glanced over and smiled when I saw Calla making her way over.

"Hey! Nice speech."

"Too scary?"

"Only mildly. So, I guess I need to go shopping?"

"Definitely." She gestured toward the door that led to the foyer. "Come on, a few of the sisters took some of the pledges into the sitting room across the hall."

I frowned, but followed her. "What for?"

"Just to chat," she said over her shoulder.

When we got into the sitting room, I saw there were about a half dozen sisters there, each talking to pledges. Calla sat down on one of those weird armless sofas and patted the spot next to her.

"What's up?" Gods, I hoped I hadn't committed some major faux pas. Or worse, that she somehow knew I was tracking my own movements through the house.

"Not a thing." With a smug smile, she reached under the sofa and pulled out a big white bag, then dropped it in my lap. I caught it just before it fell to the floor. "Here."

Curious, I peeked inside, shifting aside the mix of red and gold tissue paper until I found the gift. Eyes wide, I pulled out the most gorgeous red leather purse I'd ever seen. Carved in gold on the bottom corner were the sorority letters.

"Holy shit, Calla, it's gorgeous!"

She grinned. "I know, right?"

Still stunned, I turned the purse around and continued examining it. "What's the occasion?"

"I assumed you would submit your request for me to be your Big," she said with a shrug. "As a legacy and VP, I get dibs on whoever I want, and since you're the only legacy in this pledge class, well, I'm claiming you. It's standard practice for a sister to give a pledge a gift when she accepts her as a Little."

I nearly laughed at how blatantly self-serving she was being, but I couldn't help but respect her honesty.

"Well, you're right, but I thought we had to wait to request?"

"Eh. Like I said, I have dibs."

"Then, thank you." A bit enamored, I turned the purse over in my hands, admiring every inch of it. "It's awesome."

"Great! We'll sit down and dig through the Iota Sig website later this week and pick out a few things for you to wear. In the meantime, you have your cardigan, and I can lend you a few things, if you want."

"That'd be awesome," I said, feeling a little relieved. I'd bought a ton of clothes when Athena had handed me this job, but red and gold had never really been favorites of mine.

Not for the first time, I couldn't help but feel guilty for how badly I was deceiving Calla. Granted, I didn't know for sure she wasn't aware of what her mom and dad were up to, but between all she'd divulged before the pin ceremony and now this, well, she didn't seem all that bad.

For the next hour, we talked about pledge tasks, the kinds of things we would be expected to know, the timeline of the pledge period, and the best way to find a life/school/sorority balance so I wouldn't get burned out. A lot went into being a sorority sister, which I knew going in, but I guess I hadn't realized just how much it was going to consume my life.

By the time we headed across the street to Kappa O, it was nearly ten and I was honestly already feeling a little burned out. The amount of information that had just been poured into my head was exhausting.

Loud laughter and even louder music met us when we walked in, and it was clear the party had started long before we got there.

When Willow opened the door to let us all in, music that was far louder than it needed to be poured out.

"Yoooo, fresh meat!" one of the Kappas shouted when he saw us. His announcement was followed by hoots and hollers from the guys around him.

"Say hello to your new sisters, boys!" Willow called.

One of the guys let out a loud whistle, and a few of the others congratulated us. I couldn't help but smile at how genuinely welcoming everyone seemed. Almost like they really were a family or something.

"Come on." Kristy inclined her head toward the dining room,

which was where I'd seen a bar set up the first time I visited. "Let's go get a drink."

We followed Calla into the dining room, where Tristan and Milo greeted us from behind the bar when we walked in.

"Ladies!" Milo shouted, drawing more loud whoops from a few of the other guys in the room. "What'll it be, Miss Mary?"

I grinned at his obvious inebriation. "Surprise me."

"Brave girl," Tristan said with a laugh. "So, how'd it go?" he asked Calla.

"Perfect as always," she said, preening a little. "Willow's probably looking for you."

"I'll catch up with her eventually." He pulled a bottle of tequila from a shelf under the bar and started pouring a row of shots. Once he was done, he slid three forward toward me, Calla, and Kristy, then he and Milo picked up the others.

"To new recruits." Tristan held up his glass. "And a great year!"

I nearly groaned. I'd finally figured out how to distill alcohol so I could avoid getting drunk, but there was no way I'd be able to do it in front of everyone.

I guess this'll be my one drink of the night.

Wrinkling my nose, I took up the glass, tapped it against the others, and downed the liquor.

Kristy laughed at my expression. "Tequila not one of your favorites?"

"No, the opposite. I love it. It just tends to not love me back."

Milo flicked the top off of a bottle of beer and handed it to me. "That more your style?"

I gave him a relieved smile and tilted the bottle toward him in thanks. "It is. Thanks."

"Oh, ew," Calla muttered when her eyes caught sight of something over my shoulder. Kristy sighed and rolled her eyes.

"What is it?" I asked.

"Don't look!" she hissed, grabbing my arm when I turned my head. "It's Jared from bio. He's so . . . ugh."

"And he likes to follow Calla around like a little puppy at parties,"

Kristy added, watching over my shoulder with more disdain than I thought possible for her.

"I'll be your date," Milo said with a wink.

Calla gave him a disparaging look, then took my arm and Kristy's. "Come on, let's go find Willow."

The living room was packed to the brim, so Calla kept her grip on us as we wove through the crowd.

"So, what's your deal with Jared?" I asked her. She and Jared only ever interacted in bio when it was necessary, which was really only once a week when we did a lab. Other than that, he hadn't tried to start up much of a conversation with her since our first day.

"He's a total loser," Kristy said.

"Total loser," Calla agreed. "We grew up in the same town, graduated high school together, and he was a complete nobody back home, mainly because he has the personality of a raw potato."

I laughed. "He doesn't seem so bad in class."

"He's fine there, I guess," she said with a shrug. She gestured around the room. "It's once he's someplace like this that he gets kind of obnoxious. Like he has to let everyone know he's here or something. He thinks he's better than everybody because he got into Kappa O."

"Is that hard?" I asked.

"It's a feat," Kristy admitted. "You either have to be a legacy, a genius, or kick ass in some other way in order to get in."

"Which is he?"

Calla rolled her eyes. "He's fucking brilliant *and* a legacy, so they snapped him up. I get it, but he's just . . . I don't know. Annoying, I guess."

"Huh. That sucks." There really wasn't anything else to say. Between what Kristy said about him following her around and what she said about his personality, it seemed like he was just a guy who finally got hit with a dose of popularity. They knew him better than I did, though, so saying that probably wouldn't make much of a difference.

We found Willow on the far side of the living room talking with Shep, who stood behind another bar.

"Ladies," he said with a nod as we walked up. "Congrats on your pin, Mary."

Remembering my promise to Calla to "show attraction," I gave him a small smile. "Thanks."

He gestured toward my beer. "Need a refill?"

"Not yet, but thanks."

"Hey, Mary!" Willow pulled me into a quick hug, then gave me an expectant look. "So, are you loving it?"

"I am." I didn't bother pointing out I'd only been a pledge for a half hour. Something told me her words were a test, even if they came off completely innocent. "I'm so excited to dive in, really."

"Great!" She pointed a finger at me. "And don't forget your promise. Have fun tonight, but no sloppiness, understand?"

I nodded. "One-hundred-percent. I won't let you down."

"Good." Satisfied, she picked up her drink from the bar. "Now, I'm gonna go find Tristan. I'll catch up with you girls later." With a wink, she sauntered off.

"They're a thing," Calla said, nodding toward Tristan, who Willow seemed to have aimed her sights on. "For the last year. Not serious, but serious enough that we all know not to even attempt getting near him."

"Good to know."

"So, you stressed out yet?" Shep asked.

I laughed. "Nah. Willow's a bit intense, but I like her a lot. I'm excited to get started."

"That's great. And don't worry about Willow. She just takes her job seriously."

"As she should," Calla said.

I'd just opened my mouth to respond when I saw her eyes widen. Assuming Jared had shown up again, I laughed. "He stalking you or something?"

"What? No! Mary, our *professor* is here!" she hissed, then grabbed my arm when I went to turn my head.

"What? Why?"

Confusion flashed across her face. "I didn't tell you?"

"Tell me what?"

"He's like, a hardcore legacy. Or was, I guess, since he's obviously not in college anymore."

"So, what's the big?" I took a sip of my beer, needing to steady myself a bit. If Dionysus's story was that he was a legacy of Kappa O, that would definitely make his presence at their pinning understandable. Sort of.

Maybe.

"He's a direct descendant of the alpha class," Kristy explained. "Of the founder, himself."

"I totally forgot he was coming," Calla said. She frowned. "Ew, and he's got a girl with him." She rolled her eyes and muttered something about being glad she didn't go after him if that was his type. I barely heard her, though, because all I was thinking was that Dionysus was here with someone else.

"Just be cool, though, ok?" Calla said, cutting off my thoughts. "Don't act like he's a professor, but also, don't make us look bad. And if he shows even the least bit of interest in you, lean into it."

"Calla!" I hissed, hoping Shep couldn't hear me. "You can't keep telling me to pretend to like guys who show interest in me!"

To her credit, it looked like she knew how cringeworthy that sounded. "You're right. I'm sorry. That's totally shitty of me to even ask. I just don't want Iota Sig to look bad. And I'm not telling you to like, whore yourself out or anything—"

"Sounds like it to me."

Her mouth snapped shut, and I realized I might've just pushed it a little too far.

"Sorry," I said with a huff. "I didn't mean to snap, but it just seemed weird, that's all."

Her expression softened a little. "No, I get it. Just . . . if you have to shut him down, be nice about it."

I arched a brow. "And if he shows interest in *you*?"

She flicked another glance over my shoulder. "Like I said, if that's the kind of girl he considers his type, I want nothing to do with him."

"Joe!" Shep shouted with a grin as he pulled out a glass and started pouring whiskey. "Glad you could make it! Who's your friend?"

Dionysus reached past me and Calla and shook Shep's hand. "Glad to be here." He put his hand on the shoulder of the girl he'd brought, and I nearly cringed. "This is my cousin, Erin."

Eris, clad in her typical black leather jacket, her hair streaked in vibrant shades of red, grinned and snapped her gum. A gold necklace glinted at her neck, concealing her identity as a goddess. Her bright red dress perfectly matched her hair and looked fabulous with her knee-high black boots. What would've looked like a Halloween costume on me looked killer on her.

"Hey!" She held out her hand to shake Shep's. "How's it going?"

This was not going to be good.

23

DIONYSUS

Admittedly, bringing Eris to a frat party where she could easily overdose on discord may not have been the best idea. And yeah, her appearance—sort of grunge-meets-motorcycle-gang—definitely stood out. A lot. But she'd promised to be on her best behavior, and I wanted the company.

'Are you insane?!' Mary asked.

'Only on Saturdays.' Grinning, I took the glass Shep offered.

"So, how long are you in town, Erin?" he asked.

"As long as Joe lets me stay." Her smile turned demure. "I'm absolutely dying to put my snowboard to good use."

"Well, I'm happy to point you toward the best runs," Shep replied smoothly.

Something in me loosened a little at the clear interest he was showing in my sister, although that could've just been her general pull as a goddess. Empathic gods had a way of drawing people in like that. It was likely he'd go right back to hitting on Mary once Eris was out of his eyeline.

Turning toward Calla and Mary, I tipped back my drink in greeting. "Ladies. Which one's the new pledge?"

Calla snorted, the offense clear on her face.

"I was just pinned tonight," Mary said, touching the small pin on her dress.

Fuck me, that dress. As I took a sip of my drink, I tried hard to swallow down the very ill-timed urges that were hitting me.

"She's officially my Little," Calla said, giving Mary a hip-bump. "Luckiest girl on campus, this one."

"Oh? Why's that?"

Her eyes widened incredulously. "My father? Stewart *Aiden*?"

"Like, the president?"

'You're being an ass,' Mary said.

"Ohh!" I nodded. "Right. You're his daughter. I'm sorry, it must've slipped my mind."

"I'm super lucky," Mary gushed. "I'm so excited to have Calla as a role model while I'm going through the pledge process."

"We're both legacies," Calla explained. "We have to stick together, you know?"

"Oh, I completely agree," I replied. "I always took another legacy as my protege."

Calla loosened up a little at that, letting go of the offense I'd caused. It had been completely intentional, but I certainly didn't want to make Mary's night more miserable if Calla started a major bitch session about me.

After we talked for a few minutes, Calla excused herself to go talk to Willow and some guy, leaving me and Eris with Mary and Shep. Eris had Shep completely on her hook, leaving me free to focus on Mary, who looked absolutely fucking destructive in her little white dress. I had her halfway undressed in my mind when she finally spoke, drawing my eyes to her face. Her smirk told me she'd totally caught me checking her out.

"So, how's it going, Joe? Do you like being a professor?"

Leaning a hip against the bar to try and keep the evidence of my attraction out of sight, I shrugged. "I do. I'm still getting used to the cold, but I've always liked teaching."

She nodded. "Where did you teach before South Lake?"

"I was an adjunct at a few places out west. I'm not a fan of staying in any one place too long."

'Because people would notice pretty damn quick that you weren't aging?' she asked, arching a brow.

"What about you?" I asked. "I know you're in my lit class, but is that your major?"

"Nope. Bio." She took a slow sip of her beer, bringing attention to the deep red she'd painted her lips.

Killing me. The girl was absolutely killing me, and the way she was acting, she absolutely knew it. There was something bizarre, and oddly hot, about pretending we didn't know each other. Like we were just two people contemplating whether there was an attraction and if we should explore it.

"I thought about majoring in a science," I said. "After failing chem for the third time, I gave up on that dream and went for the liberal arts."

"Yeah, it's not for everyone," she replied. "Some brains just aren't wired for formulas and numbers."

'Are you calling me dumb?'

'Are you *calling you dumb?'*

"So, you're one of Joey's students?" Eris asked, sidling up beside me. Annoyed, I glanced at the bar and saw Shep busy mixing a drink for the Kappa VP.

Mary smirked. "Yep. Probably his best one, to be honest."

Eris looked over at the bar. Seeing Shep was sufficiently occupied, she rolled her eyes and lowered her voice. "So, if you two are done eye-fucking, do you care to tell me what you plan to do to get that apple back?"

"There's no way you're getting that *or* the sash before Aphrodite," I told her. "And I know that's the only reason you're visiting, by the way."

"Come onnnn," she groaned. "You guys never let me have any fun."

"The last time you had fun with that apple, you started a war," Mary pointed out.

"Unintentionally! And I've totally learned my lesson!"

"Don't you have someone to torture?" I needed her gone.

"I'm tired of torturing. I'm in more of a havoc-wreaking mood." Tapping a finger on her chin, she started scanning the people around us, obviously looking for someone to bother.

Mary huffed. "Is there a point to you two being here?"

"I was in the area and wanted to see my baby brother." Eris shrugged. "D invited me to party with him because that's what he does, and I wanted an update from someone *other* than my daddy-pleasing sister."

"I'm so shocked you don't have more friends," I muttered.

"Whatever. I think I see two lovebirds in need of an argument." She tossed back the rest of her drink, then looked between me and Mary with a smirk. "You kids have fun."

Then, blessedly, she wiggled her fingers goodbye and sauntered off across the room.

"So, how do you plan on not getting loopy?" I asked Mary, tilting my drink toward hers. Immortals typically needed a lot of alcohol to get drunk because of how quickly it metabolized, but it was still possible to get a solid buzz going.

"I figured out how to separate the water from the alcohol," she said.

My eyebrows flew up. She said it as easily as if she were talking about fixing a bowl of cereal.

"You . . . distill the beer? In the bottle?" I frowned. "But you need heat for that."

"No, I need to make steam, which is no different than using my power to make ice. I steam off the alcohol, or as much of it as I can, then I'm basically left with just water."

"Wow." I didn't have to fake how impressed I was. "That's pretty amazing. Doesn't it get hot, though?"

"I won't do it while it's in my hand, obviously. I'll either go to the bathroom or set it down and block it from view." She gestured around the room. "I haven't had a chance to do it yet, but Calla's going to notice soon if I don't get another drink."

"I need to see this," I said.

"Now?" Her hazel eyes went wide. "I think it would be kind of obvious if we slipped into the bathroom together."

With a slow smile, I leaned in close. "I have it on good authority there's a bathroom upstairs outside of Shep's room that we can use."

Something flashed across her face, so subtly she probably didn't even realize she did it. There was no question whether she'd picked up on how the drunken debauchery surrounding us had all but annihilated my inhibitions.

"I'll meet you there," she said. After sending a quick wave to Calla, who was standing about ten feet away with a few of the other sisters, she headed out of the room.

'Careful with that one, D,' Eris said. *'Don't let her blow your cover. Or hers.'*

'No one's blowing anything,' I muttered.

'She can blow whatever the fuck she wants, just not here.'

'You're so crass.'

'As if you weren't thinking the exact same thing.'

I hadn't been, but it was kind of hard not to now.

'Be good,' I told her. *'I mean it.'*

I set my empty glass on the bar and made my way out of the room in the direction of the stairs.

On a normal day, I would've taken the time to actually admire how nice the house was. Victorians had always been my favorite, and this one had a lot of character and was surprisingly well-maintained.

Today wasn't a normal day, though.

24

MARY

When Dionysus stepped into the bathroom, he had that slightly glazed-over look he always got when he was surround by people partying. It wasn't a drunk look, but more of a giddy or even semi-euphoric look that kind of made me want to hug him. The bathroom was just big enough to house the bathtub, sink, and toilet, so once he'd closed his six-six frame into the small space, there was barely enough room for both of us.

I leaned against the counter and folded my arms, putting a little bit of space between us. There was no way I was going to be able to focus with him so close.

"So, are you going to tell me what you're doing here?" I asked.

"I need to normalize my presence with the frat in case you need backup," he replied, leaning against the opposite wall. "I thought Athena told you?"

"Nope." I couldn't decide whether to be annoyed or not, but it wasn't worth stressing about right then. I held up my beer. "You wanna see this or what?"

"Absolutely." He gestured with his hand for me to continue. "Let's see it."

It was impossible not to smile at how excited he looked to watch me use my power. It almost made me blush, which was mortifying all on its own, so I turned my back to him and set my beer on the counter.

"How does this work, exactly?" Dionysus asked.

I could feel his heat against my back, so close that if I leaned back just a bit . . .

"I just need to get the water molecules moving fast enough to make steam. It takes a few minutes sometimes, depending on how strong the drink is. I figure I'll try to stick to beer since it's pretty low in alcohol content."

"Makes sense." His eyes found mine in the mirror in front of us, and there was something there, something in his eyes that looked almost like . . . intent.

Shifting my attention to the bottle, I focused my energy on the liquid inside. After a few seconds, a small trickle of steam started to rise from the opening and steadily began increasing.

Stepping closer, Dionysus touched my hip lightly as he leaned forward to look over my shoulder. On instinct, I almost told him he could stand next to me or even just look in the mirror to see better, but I really, *really* didn't want to. So instead, I forced my body to relax and continued on with my task.

"That's pretty impressive," he said after a few more seconds.

"Yeah, I was pretty proud of myself when I figured it out, I'm not gonna lie."

My smile faltered a little when I saw the way he was watching me —me, not the bottle of steaming beer in front of me. His eyes, full of intensity, stayed locked on mine, and I felt his hand slide forward on my hip just a fraction.

Fuck it, I thought, and slowly, I turned to face him. Surprise flashed in his eyes at the sudden movement, but then a slow smile spread across his face and he put a hand on the sink on either side of me.

I tilted my face up and peered at him, refusing to look away. Up until him, I'd never had a problem being forward with a guy, with letting a guy know I was completely into him. But Dionysus was different. *I* was different. This past year had changed me in more ways than one, but I couldn't let the shitty things that had happened in my life dictate how I moved forward.

There was a question in his eyes that I answered by putting a tentative hand on either side of his waist.

Knock, knock, knock.

I jumped and Dionysus' head whipped toward the door.

"Mary, you in there?" Shep's voice called from the other side. "Calla saw you come up. You okay?"

"Shit," I muttered as the spell shattered. "Yeah, I'll be right out!"

I met Dionysus' eyes, which were boring into me. "I'll see you downstairs," he said quietly.

And with that, he vanished.

Shakily, I exhaled a deep breath, then turned to the sink and let the cold water run. I splashed some on my wrists and neck to cool off the heat that had risen in me.

When I opened the door, Shep was standing there, looking worried.

"Sorry," I said sheepishly. "There was a line downstairs and, well, you know."

"No problem," he said with a smile. "I definitely get it. You ready to head back down?"

"Yup. Let's go."

Trying my damnedest to force my moment with Dionysus out of my mind so I could dissect it later, I followed Shep down the stairs and back to the party.

25

DIONYSUS

'*We need to leave. Now.*'

Eris's aggravation at my abrupt command was nearly palpable. I'd just gotten back to the living room and saw her talking to the couple she'd mentioned earlier. She looked like she was flirting with them both, which would only prove disastrous if they made it to a bedroom.

'*I'm busy.*'

'*Get over it. Let's go.*'

'*Fine,*' she replied with a sigh.

I watched as she gave the guy one last sultry smile and brushed her fingers against his chest. She tossed a wink at the girl, then walked toward me. Almost instantly, the girlfriend smacked the boyfriend's chest and they started arguing.

Her smile shifted to a glower as she strode across the room, then stopped and folded her arms when she reached me.

"You told me I'd get to feed tonight," she snapped.

"Take a good whiff, then, because you definitely worked your magic with those two." I glanced over my shoulder. "And I'm pretty sure a fight's about to break out in the kitchen."

Her eyes brightened at that. "Perfect!" She looped her arm

through mine and started leading me in the direction of the steadily rising voices in the kitchen. "There's a back door we can take."

As soon as we were in the backyard, we teleported to my apartment and went inside.

"What's got your knickers in a twist?" Eris asked as she flopped down on the couch.

I pulled a bottle of wine off the rack on the counter and proceeded to uncork it and pour two glasses. Nathaniel was her favorite—he was all of our sisters' favorite, the prick—but she and I had this low-effort friendship that I always appreciated. Even when she was being a raging bitch.

"Ah, I love the smell of angry and in love."

"I literally hate you."

"Oh, stop." She mimed crossing her heart. "I'll take off my bitch hat, okay?"

I sighed as I sat down in the chair across from her.

"You're acting lovesick," she commented.

"I'm not lovesick."

Her expression told me just how little she believed that. "I've been watching you two for months, D. When Mary first got brought back, yeah, I just thought it was your incessant need to fix broken shit. But it's clear as fucking crystal she's not broken, and you're still clinging to her like a toddler with a teddy bear."

"I know she's not broken," I muttered. I sounded petulant, but I didn't care. I was hitting my low for the night and needed to just ride it out.

Eris didn't get the message, though, because she plowed on ahead.

"And it's also been equally obvious that you're pissed as hell she went off with that stupid Neanderthal—"

"There's no evidence Neanderthals were stupid—"

"Fucking whatever. It's obvious it pissed you off."

"She didn't 'go off with him,'" I told her.

"He knocked on the door looking for her and she didn't come after you. Same difference."

"And?" I gave her an expectant look. "She's here to do a job, which means getting close to the important people in the sorority *and* the fraternity."

Based on my sister's silence, I could tell she was trying to figure out which angle to come at. As far as sisters went, Eris was actually pretty great, relatively speaking. So, when she promised to do something like take off her bitch hat, she usually meant it.

But she also knew me, and poking at me was something she knew would force me to talk.

"Athena said she had dinner with him," she finally said. "And that he asked for her number."

I rolled my eyes. "Did Athena also mention there were ten people at that 'dinner' and that they all ran into each other at the restaurant? It's not like it was a date."

"She also said he asked her to get coffee."

"Try again. Mary already told me she was thinking about taking him up on it." I rubbed my forehead and slumped back in my seat. The image of Mary standing in front of the bathroom sink, staring up at me, had seared itself into my brain. I couldn't shake the way it felt to put my hand on her hip and for her to put her hands on my waist. We'd touched before, obviously, but never in such an intentionally intimate way.

But then that godsdamn Neanderthal had to show up.

"Keep it up, kiddo, and I won't be pissed you made me leave the party early," Eris said with a smirk.

Realizing I'd let my anger get the best of me—likely due to her presence—I took a sip of my wine and pushed the thoughts of Mary out of my head.

"So, what are you going to do?" Eris asked.

That was the question of the century, one I had absolutely no answer for.

"I don't know."

26

MARY

To say I was pissed at Shep for interrupting me and Dionysus was the understatement of the year. Any hopes I had of potentially revisiting our moment in the bathroom vanished when I got back to my apartment at nearly three in the morning and his lights were off.

I thought about waking him up but decided it'd be better to hash things out in the light of day.

If anything, I wasn't entirely sure what the heck I was going to say. A small part of me wondered if I'd been overthinking it.

But the second the thought formed, I knew it was bullshit.

So, I'd talk to him in the morning.

After putting on my pajamas and dragging myself to bed, I expected to fall asleep pretty quickly. Apparently, near-kisses in the bathroom were all I needed to stay wide awake most of the night. By the time I finally fell asleep, it was nearly six, and I'd officially gone through every potential scenario for how I would approach the situation when I woke up.

My phone dinged with a text at eight AM, dragging me out of a deep sleep. I ignored it and let my eyes fall shut. I'd just started to doze when it went off again.

Then again.

At the fifth ding, I grabbed it off the nightstand with so much force, it yanked the whole charger from the wall.

"What the fuck," I muttered as I unlocked my phone to read the messages.

Calla: *Come over.*

Calla: *Hellooooooo*

Calla: *We need to shop.*

Calla: *You don't have enough red and gold.*

Calla: *Helllllloooooooooooo, little sis. You need to answer me NOW before I come drag your ass out of bed. That's a direct order from your vp.*

I groaned, then as soon as I saw the three little dots telling me she was writing another message, I typed a quick "be over in a bit," then dropped the phone on the bed beside me.

Five hours. I'd been home for all of five hours, part of Iota Sig for barely twelve, and I was already being shorted sleep.

'Breakfast?'

I winced when I heard Dionysus's voice in my head.

'Can't,' I said with a sigh. *'I really want to, but Calla's already on my ass about shopping for red and gold today.'*

'Ouch. Bummer. Have fun. I'm meeting Hermes in Cape Town this afternoon, but I'll be back Monday morning.'

'K. Have fun. I'll check in later?'

'Sounds good.'

Now I was annoyed and pissed off. I didn't care all that much about shopping with Calla, especially since I assumed it would mainly be online, but I needed to talk to Dionysus about our almost-kiss last night. Because it was, without question, an almost-kiss.

But I also needed to shove down my aggravation at Calla now before I actually took it out on her.

Another ding had me checking my phone again.

Calla: *Hurry. We're having breakfast with the girls at nine.*

Shaking my head, I threw back the covers and got out of bed.

There was no way Calla didn't know last night we were going to breakfast today. So, I could only assume this was going to be life in the coming weeks. Calla says *jump* with no advance warning, I say *how high*.

If I didn't get a killer assignment after I was done here, I might have to pull a Nate and flee Olympus.

I snorted and shook my head at the thought.

Like that could ever happen.

MY FIRST FULL day as an Iota Sig consisted of sitting at the sorority house poring over a sorority clothing website with Calla. By the time we were done, I'd put a big dent in the budget Athena had so graciously given me for sorority wear "and nothing else." Calla insisted on two-day shipping so I would have everything as soon as possible.

Not having anything aside from a cardigan and purse didn't stop Calla from picking out my outfit for class the next day, though. Which was how I ended up walking into class Monday wearing a red button-down under my Iota cardigan and a red and gold knotted headband Calla lent me. The giant red purse she'd given me was on my shoulder. It was bigger than what I'd normally use, but I kind of loved it.

It was the most non-me outfit I'd ever worn, but the double take Dionysus did when he saw my outfit made it worth it.

'That's some outfit.'

'Zip it.'

He hadn't checked in since the previous morning because he was off doing whatever with Hermes in wherever. It was kind of annoying but a bit of a relief at the same time. I was torn between wanting to pick up where we'd semi-left off and kind of glad we'd gotten two days to reconsider what had almost happened.

Deep down, I wanted it to happen. Logically, though, if we were going to have our first kiss, it was probably best that it hadn't happened in a frat house bathroom. No, something told me it needed to be when we had more time.

Class was entirely uneventful, but I had a much harder time than usual not staring at Dionysus's ass. Plus, it seemed like he was very intentionally avoiding looking in my direction.

A few minutes before class was over, he started handing back papers that we'd turned in the week before. Once he was done, he called for me and another student to stay behind.

"What did you do?" Calla hissed as she packed up her bag.

"Nothing!" I hissed.

"Then why does he need to see you? You didn't like, do anything with him Saturday night, did you?" Her eyes went wide. "I told you to let him down easy! Or—Shit, Mary, you didn't—"

"Nothing happened, Calla, I swear!" I closed my bag and lifted it onto my shoulder. "He probably just needs to talk about the C I got on this paper." I held up my folded assignment that I'd gotten an A on.

She shook her head. "He's right to talk to you, then. You need to keep your grades up. B-plus average at all times."

"I know, I know. I was super distracted last week. It won't happen again, I promise."

"Okay. I'll talk to you later, then."

I waited outside Dionysus's office while he talked the other student for a few minutes about the grade he'd received on the paper. Once they were done, the student left and I went inside.

He shut the door behind me, then slid his hands in his pockets and turned to face me. "So," he said. "Did you have fun Saturday?"

Was he seriously making small talk?

"Yep. Becoming a sorority girl is the pinnacle of my existence. Didn't you know?"

His lips twitched. "That's not what I'm talking about."

I knew he'd been pissed I hadn't come after him after getting rid of Shep. There was no way he wouldn't have been.

"You mean hanging out with those frat guys?" I shrugged and set my bag down on the chair in front of his desk. "Shep's a great beer pong partner."

"Is that so?"

His teeth dug into his bottom lip as his eyes ran across my face.

"It is."

"I happen to know someone much more experienced. He practically invented the game, actually."

Slowly, he moved toward me again, backing me into the wall.

"Oh?" He absolutely had to hear my heart pounding. "Who might that be?"

Placing a hand on the wall on either side of my head, he brought his forehead to rest against mine.

My heart went from pounding to galloping leaps.

"What is it?" I whispered.

He closed his eyes and sighed, then opened them and looked at me.

"I wanted to kiss you the other night, and that fucking idiot ruined it."

Finally.

"And now?"

"Now . . . I think I'd like a do-over."

I swallowed hard and tried not to let him see how much that excited me. "What's stopping you?"

Something shifted in his eyes, and a smile turned up the corner of his mouth. Then, as if he wanted to absolutely torture me, he leaned down slowly and kissed me.

My fingers curled into his shirt as his body pressed against mine, pinning me to the wall.

He trailed his hands down my arms, then gripped me by the hips and lifted me off my feet. I wrapped my legs around his waist, sucking in a breath at the hardness between his legs.

"You know," he murmured against my lips. "There's something about this cardigan that really does it for me."

I didn't have a chance to respond before he brought me over to his desk and sat me down. His mouth became more fevered against mine, and I tightened my legs around him, drawing him closer. He ground against me, and I couldn't hold back the small sigh that escaped at the friction.

He dragged his hands up my sides, then to my shoulders, where he shoved the stupid cardigan down my arms. It snagged on my wrist, but I gave it a quick shake and flung it to the ground. Then, gently, he laid me back on the desk.

Some small part of my brain screamed at me about how utterly insane this was. I was getting stripped down by a god who was also technically my teacher on his desk in the middle of the day.

Any concerns that may have been brought on by that evaporated when his mouth crashed to mine again and he started unbuttoning my shirt.

Yep. We were doing this.

"Fuck, Mary," he murmured when he caught the first glimpse of my red bra.

Knock, knock, knock.

We both froze, my hands tangled in his hair and his fingers hovering over the fourth button on my shirt.

"Again? Are you fucking kidding me?" he whispered.

"Professor D? It's Calla Aiden."

This chick was getting so good at ruining everything. I was starting to think it was deliberate.

"You've got to be kidding me," I muttered, shoving Dionysus back so I could fix myself.

"Yeah," he breathed. He ran his fingers through his hair, straightening the mess I'd made of it, and walked toward the door. I laid my cardigan on top of my bag and sat down in one of the chairs in front of his desk as he opened the door.

Calla stepped in, smiling.

"Sorry, I hope I'm not interrupting." She beamed at me. "My father was hoping I could meet him for lunch and he asked me to bring Mary. So, if you're all done here, I'm going to steal her away."

"Yes, of course. We were just finishing up." He lifted his brows at me. "Unless you have any further questions?"

Only about a million, I thought.

Gods, I hoped my lips weren't as red as they felt. "Nope. I think we're all good. I'll make sure to correct those mistakes on the next paper."

"You do that. Have a nice afternoon, ladies."

I tried not to let my aggravation show as I put my cardigan and jacket back on. Calla's timing was the absolute fucking worst, but she had no way of knowing that.

So, I forced a grin. "Let's go."

When Dionysus had shut the door behind us and we started walking down the hall, I turned to Calla. "Are we really meeting your dad for lunch?" As much as I would've loved that, it didn't make a damn bit of sense.

"Of course not, silly! He just had that 'we need to talk about your grade' look. What kind of Big Sister would I be if I didn't rescue you from that?"

A very good one.

"Thanks for the save," I replied, forcing myself to sound grateful. "I really appreciate it.

"What did he want, anyway? Was it really about your grade, or did you offend him or something on Saturday?"

I shrugged. "He just mentioned a few things to do differently for the next paper."

Calla tapped a finger against her chin. "Hmm. I wonder if he actually does have a thing for you."

"Highly unlikely."

"It's okay, you know," she pressed. "I mean, if you have a thing or whatever."

"I'm not going after my professor, Cal."

"Eh. He's only here for a while, and he's only a few years older than you. It's not like he's going to be your teacher forever."

"He's only a few years older," nearly had me giggling, but I kept it in. I also found it odd that Calla continuously seemed so perfectly at ease with a student sleeping with a professor. Obviously, I knew it happened, but I'd never known of anyone who was so fine with it that she basically lumped him in to whatever dating pool she seemed to be building for me.

Linking her arm through mine, Calla led me through the building. "Did you shuttle or drive this morning?"

"Shuttle."

"Awesome." She grinned. "Let's go."

AFTER WE LEFT CAMPUS, Calla and I made our way over to the Iota Sig house for a pledge meeting. From what I could tell, we would be having these meetings a couple of times a week, which was already annoying the shit out of me.

Once all of the pledges and I were settled in the living room, Willow stood in front of the fireplace and smiled, clasping her hands in front of her hips. Calla was next to her, eyeing all of us shrewdly.

"So, ladies," Willow said. "This starts your first week as an Iota pledge. As we've discussed before, your duties as pledges will involve a number of responsibilities, including tests and various tasks."

As Willow spoke, Calla picked up a stack of papers from the mantel and started to hand them out.

"These contain information on all of the current Iota Sigma Xi sisters, members of the alpha class, and other notable sisters, along with house rules," Willow continued. "You're expected to study these and memorize them, front to back. You'll be tested on this information over the course of the next two weeks."

"These tests will be in the form of written exams and pop quizzes," Calla said as she moved around the room.

"Which means," Willow said, "you should be prepared at all times for one of your sisters to test you. There'll be a written test at the end of next week, but starting Sunday, you should be ready for anything."

"Next week will also be your first task," Calla added as she returned to Willow's side. "It'll be a simple one, just a campus cleanup, but it will have certain rules you need to follow. That will happen on Wednesday."

"You'll also be expected to memorize all of the letters of the Greek alphabet," Willow said. "It may seem silly, but you're living the Greek life now, so get used to it."

Thank the gods Chris and Alan had made me recite my alpha, beta, gammas daily since I was five.

Willow looked around the room expectantly. "Now, does anyone have any questions?"

When no one said anything, she grinned. "Okay, then, let's take a quick tour! Once we're done, we'll have a little study session so you can get a head start on what you need to know."

The rest of the pledges and I stood to follow Willow and Calla out of the room for a tour of the entire house. After double-checking my phone to make sure the tracking app was running, I kept toward the back of the group so I could observe without distractions.

The rest of the house was just as gorgeous as the few rooms I'd already seen. Intricate Victorian features, built-in shelves and cabinets and wallpaper and furniture that fit the style of the house perfectly. If it hadn't been done so well, I would've thought it was borderline tacky. As it was, the designer had done a damn good job at keeping to the original style while also adapting it to house twenty-plus women.

It was kind of weird. As we moved through the house, Willow and Calla pointing out the different rooms and areas and showing us the living quarters, I almost wished I was one of the girls who lived in the house. The thought of sharing bathrooms with that many people was truly atrocious, but at the same time, the sense of belonging was tempting. It was a similar feeling to what I'd experienced on Olympus when I was living with all the other Ischyra, but I didn't realize how much I'd enjoyed it until it was taken away.

Once the tour was over and pledges asked their follow-up questions, we spread out in the comfier section of the basement—an entirely separate room from the stone dungeon, filled with over-stuffed chairs, a massive sectional sofa, and plush carpet—and started studying up on all things Iota Sig.

I'm pretty sure I absorbed about a third of what I read because my mind kept wandering back to Dionysus. Memories of him laying me out on the desk, touching me the way I'd wanted him to touch me for months, kept flashing through my mind.

I kept wondering what it meant. Obviously, I knew it meant he'd finally decided to buck up, but what I didn't know is what that meant for us.

Greek letters and pictures of old Iota Sig members blurred together on paper as I thought back on my conversation with Tessa.

Did he want a relationship? Did I want a relationship? Could a relationship between us even work?

Those questions made it pretty damn impossible to focus on things like Willow's career aspirations and the members of the alpha class.

But, no matter how badly I wanted to go straight back to Dionysus's office and finish whatever it was we started, I knew it would have to wait. I wasn't getting out of this house any time soon.

I'd just started reading over the list of majors for the most current members when Calla sat down on the floor next to me. I looked up and saw that a few other sisters had arrived and were checking in with other pledges.

"This fucking blows, right?" she asked with a grin.

"Everything's blurry," I muttered, rubbing my eyes.

"Just another hour." She bit her lip and looked around the room, then leaned closer. "So, don't tell anyone this, but I think Shep's going to ask you to the mixer in a few weeks."

It was a real struggle to keep the "fuck no" expression off my face as I smiled. "Yeah? Why do you think that?"

She snorted a laugh. "Because I'm Calla Aiden, and I know absolutely everything that goes down between our houses? Milo asked me to go with him," she said, shaking her head at my dubious look. "Tristan is asking Kristy. Milo told me Shep wants to triple."

"What, is he nervous to ask or something? That doesn't really make sense." If anyone would be confident enough to ask out, well, anyone, it would be the president of a prestigious fraternity. Considering the type of guy Shep was, I thought it was pretty weird he would wait to ask me, considering it was entirely possible someone else would.

Then again, Shep could also be the kind of guy who assumed I'd drop whichever poor sap I was going with if he asked me. It didn't seem like he was that into himself, but I didn't know him well enough to say for sure.

Calla rolled her eyes. "No, dummy. Milo said Shep mentioned it the other day, but I guess he hasn't gotten around to asking yet."

"Should I say yes?" I asked.

Nonchalantly, Calla examined her nails. "I mean, it's totally up to you, of course. But the more matches between houses, the better."

"Why?" My suspicions about Iota Sig and Kappa having some gross breeding program were growing by the day, at this point.

"Just good for appearances, that's all. And partnerships are really good for morale too. Gives a bigger sense of community and family, you know?"

"K. I'll think about it. I don't see why not, though," I added, so she wouldn't think I was being weird.

We talked for a few more minutes about upcoming events, but I couldn't keep myself from dwelling on how weird it was that these girls seemed way too obsessed with having relationships with the Kappa O boys. Something was off there, but I just couldn't figure out what.

27

MARY

I hadn't heard from Dionysus since leaving his office earlier, and I wasn't quite sure how to take that. The logical part of my brain told me he was giving me space while I was out with Calla, so I wouldn't get distracted from doing my job. The stupidly emotional part, that seemed to enjoy flicking at my frontal lobe, kept telling me he hadn't checked in because he regretted kissing me.

Luckily for me, I was about sick and tired of the stupidly emotional part of my brain that had become an epic pain in my ass recently.

By the time I got back to my apartment later, I had shoved every aspect of sororities and fraternities and classes and what-ifs from my mind. I may have been wary of addressing my feelings with Dionysus before, but well, he rang that damn bell, and I wasn't about to ignore it.

So, I'd put my stuff down, then march over to his apartment and tell him exactly what I thought about our kiss.

Fortunately, he saved me the trip.

I couldn't help but smile when I saw him sitting on the couch when I walked in.

"Hey," I said as I dropped my bag by the door.

"Hi." His eyes seemed . . . curious. "How was your day?"

I shrugged and toed off my shoes. His eyes followed every movement as I walked toward him, and the mix of desire and hesitance I saw there made me even more certain of where this was going.

"It was fine." Butterflies rioted in my stomach, but I ignored them. *Now or never, Mary.*

He tilted his face up toward me when I stopped in front of him, then he smiled. "Do you think we should talk?"

"Nope." Then, before I could second-guess myself, I leaned down and kissed him.

His lips curved against mine as he ran his hands up the back of my thighs. With a quick tug, he pulled me down so I was straddling his hips. Then, he drew back for just a moment to look at me.

"Are you sure you don't want to talk first?"

"Shut up."

With a laugh, he flipped me around so I was on my back, and he was using his hips to pin mine down.

His kisses started out slow, lazy, even, but gradually started to increase in intensity until I wrapped my legs around his waist and pulled him flush against me. He let out a groan, then slipped his hands up the back of my shirt. He made to tug it over my head, then growled in annoyance.

"Fucking buttons," he muttered.

For a second, I thought he was going to tear the damn thing open, but instead, he started unbuttoning it, one button at a time.

"The buttons aren't so bad," I murmured as his lips found their way to my neck. Slowly, he continued to open my shirt, dragging his lips across every bit of revealed skin until finally, it was completely open. He gripped my waist and shifted to his knees, then helped me shrug out of my top and cardigan.

His eyes went dark with lust as he laid me back down.

I bit my lip, loving the thrill that went through me as his eyes ran over my stomach and chest. Seeing me in a bra wasn't a new thing, but it had never been in a situation like this.

As he kissed me, all I could imagine was how his lips would feel on other parts of me.

He brought his mouth back to mine, this time more feverishly than before as he let his hands roam across my body. When he reached behind me and unhooked my bra, the reality of what was about to happen sank in.

And I was *so* fucking happy about it.

With a quick movement, he had my bra on the floor.

"I've been waiting too damn long to touch you. Way too fucking long." Slowly, he lowered his mouth to my breast, flicking his tongue across the sensitive skin. I arched my back at the quick burst of electricity that zipped through my body.

"It's your own fault." Gods, I could barely form words.

With a small "mm-hmm," he shifted his attention to the other side. Slowly, in the most torturous way possible, he started to work me over.

"Holy fuck," I gasped. His tongue was doing something absolutely amazing, and I started to think I wasn't even going to make it to the bedroom. I ran my fingers through his hair, arching my back toward him.

He let out a small laugh, his breath warm as it danced across my skin. "Nope." He leaned back, then kissed me again. "Not here."

Swiftly, before I could protest, he lifted me off the couch and teleported us to my bedroom.

Giving me no time to adjust to the change in scenery, he laid me down on my unmade bed. His eyes were filled with heat and that hazy look he got whenever he started to absorb positive emotions. Clearly, he was getting a big dose right now.

"You . . . are fucking beautiful," he breathed, leaning down to kiss my chest.

"You're not so bad yourself," I whispered.

He flashed me a grin, then flicked open the button on my jeans. I lifted my butt in the air as he wiggled them down my hips, then he tossed them aside, leaving me in just my underwear.

When his expression shifted into pure lust, I was very, very thankful I'd decided to match my bra and panties, because the red lace definitely seemed to be doing it for him.

"It's a shame these have to go." His teeth dug into his bottom lip as he dragged my panties down my hips.

When he stripped away the last remaining scrap of fabric separating us, I thought how weird it was that I didn't feel the least bit self-conscious. But then, I never did with him. I'd never once felt like I had to pose or present myself in a certain way.

So, yeah. I was good with this.

He shucked off his shirt and tossed it aside. I moved to undo his zipper, but he had his pants off before I could sit up. Seconds later, he was on top of me again, lying between my legs with barely any space separating us from the point of no return.

Every inch of his skin pressed against me, and I was absolutely *loving* it.

He propped himself up on his elbows and brushed his lips over mine. "You're beautiful."

This time, when he kissed me, it was soft and slow, full of more emotion than the others. He drew one of my legs up around his waist, then slowly slid inside me.

I arched against him at the feel of him filling me, touching every sensitive spot I'd explored with my own hands and a few I never knew existed.

"Shit," he hissed as his body stilled, his forehead resting against mine. "Fuck, Mary."

I smiled, shamelessly loving the effect this had on him.

I wrapped my other leg around his waist and lifted my hips, drawing him further inside.

Then, I put my lips to his ear.

"I want you to fuck me, Dionysus. Right godsdamn now."

With a growl, his mouth came crashing down on mine as he thrust his hips, driving in deeper.

Yep, he'd wanted this as badly as I had.

My orgasm started to build, my breaths coming in quick pants as he kissed my neck and ran a hand down my side. He gripped my hips and tilted me upward, and the small movement brought me right to the edge.

Instantly, he slowed his movements to a torturous pace, smirking in the most infuriating way. "Not yet, Mary."

I wanted to tell him he didn't have a say in that, but as the first flutters began, words suddenly became impossible.

The mischievous, sleepy smile he wore told me he was enjoying driving me crazy.

That smile did me in.

My back arched and my nails dug into his skin as I came, the feelings crashing into me like a tidal wave.

I was pretty sure I went blind.

That was all he needed, because when I tightened around him, he let out a heavy groan as he came right along with me.

28

DIONYSUS

O ne of the biggest perks of being an immortal—immortality aside—was not having to stop what you're doing to eat.

The second biggest perk was a quick recovery time.

I lost track of how many times Mary and I made love that night, but by the time we finally took a break to rest, the sky was starting to lighten.

When I woke up, the first thing I saw was those gorgeous hazel eyes staring back at me. My lips curved into a smile, and Mary gave me that infuriating smirk of hers.

"Took you long enough," she said.

Before I could dredge up a comeback, she was on top of me.

Grinning lazily, I gripped her hips as she guided herself over me. The second I felt her warmth wrap around me, I groaned. If I had any less self-control, I would've fucking exploded.

She must've been able to tell, because she tucked a strand of hair behind her ear and leaned down. "Not yet," she teased.

Not helpful, I wanted to say.

As she started to move on top of me, my mind began to clear and I was able to focus on the only thing that mattered—her.

Gods, I'd stay here with her forever if I could.

When I felt my impending orgasm, I tightened my hold on her hips and rolled on top of her. I repositioned myself inside of her, then drew one of her legs over my shoulder, slowly sliding in deeper as I watched her eyes flutter closed.

"I'm literally going to kill you," she breathed.

"Never," I whispered, then slid the rest of the way inside her, drawing a soft cry from her lips.

I ran my hands up her sides, grinning when her back arched and she let out a breathy moan.

Gods, I'd been waiting for this for so long.

Slowly, she began to writhe against me, making it pretty damn hard not to give in and just fuck her silly.

I met the roll of her hips with my own thrusts, increasing in speed until I could barely stand it. Seconds later, she came hard. Clenching my jaw, I forced myself to hold out until she was done, then let myself go alongside her.

A few minutes later, after we'd both caught our breath, I turned to her and smiled. "We don't have class today," I said.

She grinned. "You can have me as much as you want until noon." Glancing at her phone, she huffed. "I have to go *study*."

"Ah, the life of a sorority girl. Gotta keep those grades up." I was really looking forward to when this job was done and she didn't have to run at Calla Aiden's beck and call.

She rolled her eyes. "As if I need these stupid study sessions."

"It's all about appearances, doll. Don't worry. It won't last forever."

"Gods, I fucking hope not. I'll be back for dinner, though, if you wanna grab wings from that place in PA."

"Consider it done." I kissed her forehead, then got up and picked up my clothes that were scattered on the floor and started pulling them on.

"I'll go get coffee and cookies," I told her. "Feel free to stay exactly as you are."

She laughed, and that smile . . . that godsdamned fucking smile. It would be the end of me.

Even though I thought I already knew—no, I *did* already know—
Eris was right.

I fucking loved this girl.

~

'Ew. I can practically feel you glowing.'

I chuckled when I heard Eris's disgusted voice as I made my way
down the stairs to the coffee shop.

'Jealous?'

'Gods, no. You know hate sex is more my thing.'

'Gross. TMI.'

'Whatever. Any word on my apple?'

'Even if there was, you'd be the last person I'd tell.'

I loved my sister, but I wouldn't put it past her to try and start
another family brawl if she got her hands on that apple again.

'You wound me, baby brother.'

'So, is there a reason for this early morning call?'

*'I'm the goddess of discord, and your stupid mushy love shit just hit me
like a truck.'*

'Benefits of being my blood.' Empaths who were closely related often
shared a stronger connection with each other than with other
siblings. It was rare, but when I got hit with a massive dose of happiness, sometimes Eris felt it. We weren't really sure why, but all I knew
was that it pissed her off. I was better at brushing off whatever bits of
her power hit me, but she had no patience for it.

'Benefits,' she scoffed.

'Just because you like to be miserable—'

'I don't like to be miserable. I like other people to be miserable.'

I rolled my eyes and opened the shop door.

'Goodbye, Eris.'

She sent me an image of her flipping me off, then I broke the
connection.

29

MARY

Finally crossing that line with Dionysus seemed to have jump-started something between us, because I barely made it out of bed with enough time to shower before going to the Iota Sig house. It didn't help that he insisted on joining me in the shower, but I wasn't about to complain.

As much as I knew I needed to focus on my studying once I got to the sorority house, it just wasn't happening. For five hours, I sat around with the other girls doing work for our classes and pop-quizzing each other on Iota trivia. Most of it went by in a blur, because I could barely drag my thoughts away from all the delicious things Dionysus had done to me in the last twelve hours.

I was in the middle of a particularly fond memory involving his tongue when fingers snapped in front of my face.

"Yoo-hoo," Calla said. "Earth to Mary!"

"Shit, I'm sorry," I said sheepishly. "I, um, didn't sleep well last night, so I'm still kind of tired."

She frowned. "Well, get over it. You need to focus."

"Yeah. Sorry about that." I looked down at the packet of Iota info I was studying and held it up. "Quiz me?"

Calla rolled her eyes and snatched the booklet out of my hand. "That's literally what I just asked you when you were zoned out."

"Right." I cleared my throat and sat up straighter on the sofa. "Okay, I'm ready."

She arched a brow. "President of the alpha class?"

"Serina Billings, U Penn."

"Her major?"

"English lit."

"Graduation year?"

Shit.

"Um . . . 1762."

"And what is the significance of that?"

"It means Iota Sig is the oldest sorority still in existence today."

With a sharp nod, Calla went to the next card. "Good. Now, let's move on to the current class."

For the next twenty minutes, we went over every current member, their majors, and their intended careers. Thankfully, immortality kept my brain sharp, but good gods, this shit was dull.

By the time Willow let us call it a day at six, with the friendly reminder that we were expected to spend at least two hours a day in the Iota house, I all but booked it out of there.

Dionysus, bless him, was waiting with buffalo wings, cheese fries, and a growler of chocolate porter when I got home.

"Ugh, thank the gods." With a groan, I let my bag drop to the floor next to the door, then kicked off my boots and went to the island to assault the cheese fries that were still steaming.

Dionysus leaned against the island. "Rough day?"

I wrinkled my nose. "No, just long and boring."

He came around the island and took my hips. "Then I guess it's a good thing I'm here to show you a good time."

I laughed, nearly choking on the scorching fry in my mouth. "Shit, that might be the worst line I've ever heard."

"Funny," he murmured. He tilted my chin toward his and gave me a soft kiss. "Almost as bad as kissing a girl with cheese-fry breath."

I smirked. "No, I definitely think your pickup lines are worse."

He sat down on a stool and drew me closer, so I was standing between his thighs. "So, when do you have to go back? Are they doing daily meetings?"

I sighed. "Two hours a day, minimum. It just seems so extreme."

He shrugged. "It's more than what I would've expected but not outside the realm of normal."

"Whatever." I pulled back and sat on the stool next to him, then pulled a container of wings toward me. "Thanks for dinner. I've been thinking about these all day."

He smiled. "So, does this mean my penance is over?"

I laughed. "Like you're not benefiting at all. You love this food just as much as I do."

His smiled widened. "Well, if it's not penance, I think a thank you is in order."

I set down the wing I'd just bitten into and turned toward him. "Yeah? What'd you have in mind?"

He touched my chin and smirked. "A few things, actually."

And just like that, my appetite was gone.

AFTER A FEW ROUNDS WITH DIONYSUS, I slept solidly until about two o'clock, but then Iapetus's voice in my head startled me awake.

"Save the head for last."

My heart thundered in my chest as I tried to push the memory back. Wincing, I pushed my thumb into my palm, centering myself, trying very hard not to jostle the bed.

"Not there," I murmured, focusing my eyes on the window. "I'm home, I'm in my bed."

Slowly, my heart settled. After a few moments, my mind had cleared enough for me to ease back down to the pillow.

Exhaling, I glanced down at Dionysus, who was passed out beside me. He hadn't so much as flinched, so he either didn't get hit with emotions when he was sleeping, or the dream hadn't lasted long enough for my feelings to reach him. Either way, I was glad he hadn't woken up.

I needed to deal with my shit in my own way. Even though my nightmares had become more annoying than terrifying, he would still worry. He'd hover and mother-hen me, and that just wasn't what I needed.

After taking a few calming breaths, I laid back down and rolled to my side. I closed my eyes and tried to fall back asleep, but each time I started to doze, images of stone cells and the vivid blue of my magic had my eyes flying open.

Briefly, I contemplated waking Dionysus up so he could distract me with his body, but decided against it. He'd know right away that something was wrong.

Quietly, I slipped out of bed and tugged on my PJ pants and long-sleeved T-shirt, then went out to the kitchen to make a cup of herbal tea. It was a bedtime blend that Tessa had brought from one of her last trips to England, and it was almost always a surefire way to knock me out.

Once the tea was done, I sat down on the couch with the Iota materials and started reading them over. Even if I didn't absorb anything, the combination of Iota history and the tea would at least make me drowsy enough to fall back asleep.

I'd finished my cup of tea and had started on a second when Dionysus came out of my room, bleary-eyed.

"What's wrong?"

I looked up from my reading and smiled. "Couldn't sleep."

He glanced at the clock. "It's almost four. Come back to bed." He smirked. "I'll make it worth your while."

"Oh?" With a grin, I set my mug down on the coffee table and watched as he approached. "I suppose you might be able to entice me."

"'Might be,' hmm?" With a grin, he plucked the textbook out of my hands and put it on the table next to the mug, then knelt at the other end of the couch. Then, before I had time to react, he grabbed my ankles and tugged, pulling me from a sitting position to flat on my back.

He held my eyes as he settled himself on top of me. "Or maybe we could stay right here," he murmured.

My eyes fluttered closed when he dragged one hand down my side and slowly slid up my shirt.

"Right here is good," I said quietly, silently kicking myself for not waking him up earlier. *This* was exactly what I needed.

He laughed quietly. "I think you mean right *here*."

One thumb brushed over my breast, and I hissed out a breath at the burst of pleasure.

"Yep," I said, trying to control the tremor the feeling put in my voice. "There's good, too."

"And here . . ."

He started kissing my neck, slowly making his way toward my shoulder. He dragged his tongue up the length of my throat, then started kissing his way down my chest. When he got to the hem of my shirt, he slid it all the way and tugged it over my head. Each touch, each kiss on my chest and stomach sent tremors through my body. I didn't know if it was his power or his skill that was making such simple touches feel so amazing, but I didn't really care.

He lifted his head and grinned. "Do you think I could get you off like this?"

I let out a shuddering breath. "Probably, but I might kill you if you try."

With deliberate slowness, he slid one hand under the waistband of my shorts. "Like this, then?"

Trying to speak coherently wasn't happening, so I just nodded and closed my eyes, letting my head fall back onto the pillow as he slowly, almost painfully, started to work me over.

Yeah, I could *definitely* get used to this.

30

MARY

The next few days consisted of going to class, then heading right to the Iota Sig house for mandatory study sessions. The study sessions were getting really freaking tiring, especially because they were cutting into things I'd much rather be doing.

I was totally all for keeping my grades up and busting my ass to maintain the house's image, but I didn't need the sisters hanging over my shoulder constantly, making sure I was doing what I was supposed to do.

It was part of the job, though, which I had to remind myself of about a dozen times a day. I was here to do a job, not make lifelong friends. This assignment would be done and over with eventually, and I'd move on to wherever Athena sent me next. It wouldn't be the last time I'd get a job that had aspects I didn't like. And honestly, as far as inconveniences go, being required to study with a bunch of girls who liked to order takeout on the daily was pretty minor in the grand scheme. It just sucked, because all I wanted to do was curl up with Dionysus and relax at the end of the day.

Soon. I'd be able to do that soon.

On Thursday, Tessa forced herself into my schedule for twenty minutes so I could give her all the sordid details about everything that had happened with Dionysus.

"I can't believe he finally made a move," she said, pulling her knees to her chest on the couch.

"I guess he got tired of Shep poking around," I said with a shrug. "Whatever. I'm just glad he did."

"Me too. Nate told me he's been waiting for it to happen, that he and Hermes have been on his case, but he's a guy, so you know how it goes."

I rolled my eyes. "I sure do."

"So, about Shep," she began. "What's the deal with him? Do you think he's involved with the Aidens at all?"

"I honestly don't know. Sometimes, I get a weird vibe from him, but it might just be because he's close with Calla. She's way too obsessed with pairings between Iotas and Kappas."

She frowned. "That's weird. Why do you think that is?"

"I think it's really just for appearances. Solidarity or whatever." I honestly hadn't come up with any other logical explanation, although something told me these girls weren't entirely logical.

"That makes sense, I suppose. What's Dionysus think?"

"That I need to be careful," I said, not bothering to hide my mild annoyance. "As if that isn't supremely obvious."

"He just cares about you," she replied. "A lot."

"I know, and I care about him too. But sometimes he's just very . . . hover-y."

"Well, that's part of the package. You have to accept that if you guys are going to be together." Now it was her turn to be show some annoyance. "He's an empath, Mare. He can't just shut off his feelings. Feelings that he feels much more deeply than most."

"I know, I know."

There was no mistaking her dubious look, but she didn't press. "So, when's you next party?"

"Saturday. A mixer at the Aidens' house. Missa is legit obsessed," I added, shaking my head. "I guarantee she tried to get the pledge ceremony there."

"That's pretty weird." Tessa frowned. "Any thoughts on where you'll look for the apple and sash?"

"I want to try to get into the basement and Stewart's office. I'm hoping it'll be easy enough to sneak off, since everyone from both houses will be there."

"Well, be careful." Concern flashed across her face. "I know you said Stewart seems like an okay guy, but . . ."

"I'm not going to let my guard down, trust me. I still think Missa's the bigger threat, but we'll see." I picked up my glass of wine and took a sip. "Tell me what's up with you. Have you left Iceland yet?"

She shook her head. "Nope. I haven't seen the volcanoes yet. I want to bake bread in volcano dirt first."

"I don't know what that means, but it sounds horrible."

She laughed. "No, it's actually pretty neat. You put the ingredients in a can, bury it, and the next day, boom. Bread."

"And why do you want to do this, exactly?"

She shrugged. "Why not? It's a cool thing, and I have all the time in the world to do cool things. I don't have to rush or pick and choose. So, I want to make volcano bread."

"Well, bring some back here. I'm officially intrigued."

She grinned. "Will do."

31

MARY

The next night, Athena and Aphrodite came by to talk about what they wanted me to accomplish at the Aidens' house. Despite having made fast friends with Calla and getting in good with Willow, I could tell they both expected me to have more to offer by now. Which was annoying, considering I was also expected to keep my grades up and get a job in order to stay in the damn sorority.

It was also annoying because *I* hoped to have more to give them by now.

Since the mixer was at the Aidens' house, we ended up going over what I knew of its layout.

"We're thinking Stewart's office is here, correct?" Athena asked, tapping a finger at a spot on the map I'd drawn up.

I nodded. "Yeah. I felt that pull just a little bit stronger there. I only got a glance through the crack in the door, but I saw a desk and bookshelves, so I'm assuming an office or library of some sort. I'm working on the best way to get in there."

"Okay." Athena's brow puckered into a small frown. "Have you managed to get a date?"

I flicked a glance at Dionysus, who was keeping his face dangerously neutral, before smiling at Athena. "Not yet, but Calla thinks Shep is going to ask me, so I guess we'll see."

Aphrodite slid a curious look at her brother, but I didn't want to draw any attention to his reaction by looking at him.

"Good," Athena said with a nod. "That's good."

"You know, this whole 'faking an attraction' thing is starting to feel kind of gross," I commented.

"Is it?" Aphrodite smirked.

I met her dark eyes. "Yes. It is."

"Well, it's part of the job," she said. "You can take it or leave it, but leaving it means a much less interesting assignment, I promise."

"I wasn't asking for a different assignment," I said, forcing calm into my voice. "But if this guy tries to get me in bed or whatever, it's not happening. I draw the line at trading sex for information."

Dionysus coughed to cover a laugh.

Aphrodite's answering look was borderline pitying. "One of these centuries, you'll see that offering up your body to get information is hardly the worst thing in the world."

No shit, I thought.

"It's moot, anyway. I don't think Stewart or Missa know Shep well enough to give him unfettered access to their house."

"Maybe," Athena said. "That's what you need to find out. At the very least, being on Shep's arm gives you more clout with Calla, who *does* have unfettered access."

There was no argument for that because she was absolutely right.

"Eris thinks we should be there," Dionysus said. "Just in case."

Before I could point out the ridiculousness of that idea, Athena was nodding. "That's not a bad idea, actually."

"Are you serious?" I asked. "I don't need babysitters."

"They're not babysitters," Athena replied calmly. "They're backup."

"If Dionysus hadn't decided to come here, I would've been doing this on my own," I pointed out. I *really* didn't want those two hovering while I tried to work. It had been damn near impossible to keep a straight face at the last party Dionysus and Eris were at with me. Now that we'd actually slept together, there was no way I could pretend to fake attraction to another guy with Dionysus right there.

"I would've sent backup for something like this," Athena said.

"Why didn't you send any the last time I went to the Aidens'?" I asked.

"Because you weren't there to search for anything other than confirmation the apple and sash were or are on the property," Athena said patiently.

"You're actually going to be snooping now, hon," Aphrodite added. "The last thing you want is a demigod or witch catching you off guard."

"Better me and Eris than . . . anyone else, honestly." Dionysus almost looked a little hurt that I was protesting so much. "We'll stay in the background, I promise."

"He's right," Athena agreed. "You're lucky Dionysus is here and Eris is feeling so . . . helpful."

I smirked. "Helpful?"

Athena rolled her eyes in a very uncharacteristic gesture, and I had to bite my tongue to keep from smiling. It was hilarious how much Eris's presence pissed her off, but there was no way she'd ever let me live it down if I called her out on it.

"Fine." I pointed a finger at Dionysus. "But let me do my job, okay?"

"I wouldn't dream of interfering."

THE NEXT DAY was my first day working at the café on campus. I'd submitted my application the week before and the manager, Carol, got back to me within a few hours to discuss when I'd start.

I'd worked at a coffee shop back in Renville for a few months in the summer going into junior year, but it seemed kind of pointless to continue since building job skills wasn't exactly something I needed to worry about. I learned enough about making cappuccinos watching videos online, and I'd worked a register before, but I wasn't going to bank on anything.

When Carol pulled out the list of specialty coffee drinks and started running through the recipes with me, I was glad I hadn't assumed this job would be easy.

"It's really not so hard," she said. "All of the lattes and caps have the same base. You just have to remember what flavors and extras go in them."

Frowning, I looked over the list. "Will I be allowed to reference this?"

"Definitely! It took me months to memorize them all. Don't worry, though. Most of those you'll hardly ever have to make. The ones at the top are the most popular." She picked up a frothing pitcher from beside the cappuccino machine and held it out. "Wanna give one a shot?"

"Sure." Taking the pitcher from her, I added some low-fat milk. "Just a basic cap?"

"Yup."

I went about grinding the beans, brewing the espresso, and frothing the milk until it was nice and fluffy. Then, I poured it on top of the espresso and handed it to Carol.

She took a sip, then narrowed her eyes and took another. Finally, she nodded. "You've got the basics. That's good."

Good. If she was happy with a simple cappuccino, I'd be fine to handle everything else. Which was nice, considering I seriously didn't want this job exhausting me.

The next couple of hours dragged by pretty slowly, so I spent most of my time reading the recipes for drinks so I wouldn't have to fuss with them later. There was a little rush around ten, just before the mid-morning classes started.

Around eleven, Shep showed up.

Calla had texted me that morning to tell me she'd told Shep I'd started working at the café and to expect him to pay me a visit. Whether she orchestrated it or just knew he'd take the bait, I wasn't sure, but I wasn't at all surprised to see him.

He caught my eye when he walked in, then grinned and made his way up to the counter.

Carol eyed him warily, but stayed off to the side so I could take his order.

"How's the first day going?" he asked.

"I haven't messed up any orders yet, so I can't complain. What can I get you?"

He narrowed his eyes and looked up at the menu. "I'm torn between going easy on you or picking the most annoying drink on the menu."

I rolled my eyes and picked up a medium cup. "How about I just make you a mocha latte and call it a day?"

He put a hand to his chest and sighed. "It's like you can read my mind."

When I started making his coffee, he shifted his attention to Carol. "Any chance I can steal her for a break?"

"Sure. She's due." She lifted her brows when I glanced over at her from the cap machine. "Fifteen minutes, okay?"

I gave her a thumbs up. "Sounds great."

"Coffee's free for employees," she said pointedly.

Taking the hint, I grabbed a cup and filled it to the brim, then followed Shep toward a table in the center of the room. I preferred sitting against the wall, but it was obvious he had a purpose, so I wasn't going to deter him from it. No matter how much I wanted to.

Once we'd settled in our seats, I waited for him to speak, trying not to look like I knew exactly why he was here.

"So," he started. "We have a mixer next weekend."

I nodded and took a sip of my coffee. "That, we do."

"I was wondering if you were going with anyone?" He looked hopeful, but I also knew he was damn sure no one else had asked me.

"Nope. Not yet."

His grin widened. "Great. You should come with me."

Slowly, I took another sip of my coffee and tried to balance my expression between coy and amused. "Should I?"

He smirked, and the confidence I would've expected from the president of Kappa O emerged. "You definitely should."

I pursed my lips and pretended to consider it. "I suppose it's not the worst idea."

He laughed. "No, I don't think it is."

"Then sure, I'd love to go with you."

"Awesome. I'll pick you up at seven?"

My stomach did a weird icky flip at his excitement. "Sounds good."

"Sheppard!"

Shep and I both glanced over at the sound of his name, and my eyes widened slightly when I saw Stewart and Missa Aiden approaching us. Stewart was smiling, while Missa was looking back and forth between us like she couldn't figure out where she knew me from.

"Mr. Aiden!" Shep said, smiling. "How are you?"

"Oh, doing all right," Stewart said. He held up a cup of coffee. "Just stopping for my mid-morning cup."

I glanced at the clock above the exit and made a mental note of the time. 10:30.

"Do you two remember Mary?" Shep asked. "She's an Iota pledge."

"Of course!" Missa beamed at me. "We met at your bid acceptance, isn't that right?"

"It is," I said with a nod. "It was so nice of you to let us have the ceremony in your home."

"Missa gets just as much enjoyment out of those things as you girls do, trust me." Stewart looked at Shep expectantly. "So, what are you kids up to?"

Shep flashed me a grin. "Well, we were just talking about the mixer next week. Mary's going to be my date."

"Atta boy," Stewart said, patting Shep on the shoulder, then nodding at me. "You've got yourself a good one here, Mary."

I gave him a tight smile. "We'll see about that, won't we?"

We made small talk with the Aidens for another minute or two before they said their goodbyes. Stewart gave Shep a quick wink as they left.

"What was that all about?" I asked, frowning after them. "The wink?"

Shep took a sip of his neglected coffee. "He was a Kappa back in the day, and when he took the job as president, he made it a point to get to know me and our VP. He's a cool guy."

I wrinkled my nose. "He doesn't seem . . . politician-y to you?"

Shep laughed. "Oh, totally. But not in the snake-oil salesman kind of way. He's just good at getting things done." He gestured toward the café. "This place is case in point. You wouldn't believe how shitty the coffee was last year."

"True," I said with a nod. "I've heard he's really successful."

"Without a doubt." Shep almost looked bashful. "To be honest, he's kind of a role model. He just puts his mind to things and gets them done. I want that kind of energy."

"Don't we all," I murmured. A flash of movement drew my eye toward the door, and I saw a petite girl with a pixie cut walking toward us. Before I could register my confusion, Eris's voice sounded in my head.

'It's me. Hecate loaned me a glamour charm. Call me Candy.'

I bit back a groan.

'Candy?! Seriously?'

"Mary!" she squealed. "There you are!"

Shep frowned and glanced toward her, then gave me a questioning look. "Friend of yours?"

"Yep," I muttered. "Hi, Candy. Fancy meeting you here."

Without bothering to wait for an invite, Eris dragged a chair from a nearby table and slid it next to mine. "Who's this?" She cracked her gum and grinned at Shep. "New boy toy?"

Shep cleared his throat, then held out his hand. "Shep. And you are?"

Eris put on her best doe-eyed look as she shook his hand. "Mary, you didn't tell him your favorite cousin is in town?"

Great. Another lie I'd have to keep up with. "Shep, this is my cousin Candy. Candy, Shep. He's the president of Kappa O. Why are you here?"

"I just needed a cup of coffee, so I figured I'd see if my baby cousin was working. I guess I got lucky," Eris said with a sly look at him. "Now I get to meet the new guy, too."

His brow rose in amusement, and I felt my cheeks go red.

"Shoot, I have to run." Shep said as he checked his phone. He stood and picked up his coffee. "It was good talking to you, Mary. We'll catch up soon?"

I'd bet all the gold on Olympus he was full of shit, but it didn't seem nice to call him out. Heck, I'd bail if I could. "Definitely."

With one last perplexed look toward Eris, he left.

As soon as he was out of earshot, Eris snorted. "That guy looks like he irons his boxers almost as often as his polos. And hasn't anyone told him pink polos are so turn-of-the-century?"

"Is it ever possible for you to, I don't know, *not* be a raging bitch?"

She ruffled my hair. "Aw. Did I insult your wittle boyfwend?"

"I have to get back to work," I told her, swatting her hand away. "My fifteen minutes are up." Technically I still had five, but she didn't need to know that.

"So, does my brother know you're going to the mixer with Pink Polo?" she asked, following me as I made my way back up to the counter.

Gods, she was annoying. She knew damn well what Dionysus did and didn't know about my job, so the only reason she would be asking would be to irritate me.

"Why are you really here, Eris?" I asked.

"Just curious how the search is going. That's all."

That was obviously bullshit, but whatever. "Did Athena send you to watch me?"

Eris's answering cackle was answer enough.

"Dionysus, then?" Just the thought aggravated me. I expected Athena to micromanage the crap out of me, but Dionysus seemed like he was on my side. Most of the time, anyway.

But the more likely scenario was that Eris just wanted to get her hands on the apple and/or sash first, just so she could piss off Hera and Athena.

"Why are you so convinced someone sent me here? Maybe I'm just . . . invested in your progress."

Again with the bullshit.

"Mary?"

Grateful, I looked toward Carol. "Break time over?"

She glanced at Eris, then me. "Yep. If you need another minute to say goodbye to your friend—"

"Nope." I picked up my apron off the counter and started to tie it on. "We're all good. She was just leaving."

Without another look at Eris, I went back to work.

32

DIONYSUS

I loved my sister.

But sometimes I really, *really,* hated her.

For example, when Eris felt the need to stop by my office to tell me about her visit with Mary and Shep in the café. As she told me about what a great job Mary was doing of "infiltrating every aspect of the Iota Sig and Kappa O houses," I started to see red.

Which was exactly what she wanted, of course. She just couldn't help stirring up trouble.

After she left, I couldn't stop stewing over the idea of Mary and Shep together. Yes, logically, I knew why she was going to the mixer with him. We'd talked about it on multiple occasions.

Still, knowing it was actually in the works, that plans had been made?

That fucking sucked.

'Why are you letting her get to you?'

I shouldn't have been surprised Nathaniel picked up on my shitty mood.

'You mean Eris? I'm not letting her get to me. She was exceptionally bitchy today and a little too much leaked in. I can't help it.'

'In other words, you let her get to you?'

Asshole.

'Go home and talk to Mary,' he suggested. *'I guarantee this is eating at her just as much as you.'*

'Yeah. Maybe.'

He laughed. *'Moroseness doesn't suit you, brother. Put Eris out of your mind. She doesn't belong there.'*

'Tell her that.'

'Listen, do you remember when we had to go to that club in Iceland with Tessa? And she had to pretend to be some ditz so she could get the drop on that Telchine?'

'Yeah. What's your point?' It had been Tessa's biggest show of badassery to date, so it wasn't something I'd forget any time soon. She'd wiped out nearly every Telchine in existence without breaking a sweat.

'My point is that every single one of us has to pretend we're someone we're not all the damn time. Sometimes, it's pretending to be douchebags at a bar hitting on girls; other times, it's going on a date with someone we don't have any interest in.'

'Doesn't mean I have to like it.'

'She's undercover, D. You don't have to like it, but that's the job. Unless you want her to be stuck training recruits or doing bureaucratic bullshit, she's going to be doing things that require her to be someone she isn't.'

The thought of Mary doing anything bureaucratic was laughable, and I would never insist she take a job that wouldn't fulfill her.

But this whole being in love thing, because that's absolutely what this was, was something I hadn't felt in centuries.

'Just go home and do something, I don't know, couple-ish,' he said.

'I am,' I replied. *'I just need to get my head straight first.'*

'Don't stress too much about that. I guarantee her head isn't straight right now, either.'

Instantly, realization set in. *'She talked to Tessa, didn't she?'*

There was a long pause, then, *'It's possible Tessa may have . . . divulged a bit of information after her last conversation with Mary.'*

Something eased inside of me at that. If Nathaniel was getting involved, that meant Mary must be more bothered about all of this than I'd thought.

I sighed. *'Okay. Thanks.'*

'No problem. Now, you've spent enough time stressing over a girl. Tell me how the job's going.'

Thankful for the shift in topic, I smiled. *'It's good. I like teaching again. I needed a break from counseling.'*

'When does Zeus want you back in Germany?'

'Don't know, don't care.'

'Finally taking a page from my book?'

'It's becoming increasingly more obvious how beneficial being away from Olympus will be for me,' I admitted. *'So, yeah, it seems like I might be following in my baby brother's footsteps.'*

'Where will you go?'

'Not sure.' I thought about the kinds of places Mary would enjoy, far away from the frigid winters of the Northeast. *'Someplace warm, most likely.'*

He chuckled. *'Somehow, that doesn't surprise me. Let me know if you need me to help run interference with Zeus. He'll be a pain about this.'*

I sighed. *'Yeah. I know. Thanks.'*

'Now, go talk to your girl.'

And *that* brought a stupid smile to my face.

My girl. Mary was finally my girl.

I LEFT WORK a few hours later after finishing up some grading and taking some time to reread the assigned readings for the following week. It was close to sunset by the time I finally settled in behind the wheel of the Audi I'd convinced Athena to budget for me.

Even though it was just for appearances, having a nice car was one of the best parts about pretending to be human.

Mary was already in her pajamas when I walked in the door.

"Hey." She set down the textbook that was open in her lap and smiled. "How was your day?"

"Boring," I said, giving her a quick kiss. "You? How was your first shift?"

She gave me a pointed look. "I know Eris already talked to you."

I shrugged, then sat on the couch and pulled her down next to me. "She did, but I wasn't talking about your duplicitous intentions with poor Shep. How was the work part of it?"

She wrinkled her nose. "It was okay, I guess. I worked at a coffee-house a couple of summers ago, so I remembered the basics. But Stewart popped by when I was talking to Shep, so that was a bonus."

That was interesting. "Yeah? How'd that go?"

"Okay, I guess. He seems so nice. Definitely a politician, but I barely get that slimy politician vibe from him at all. Missa seems kind of iffy, though. She seems way too into sorority relations."

"How so?"

"It's hard to explain," Mary said. "Calla and the other higher-up Iota's all have this weird thing about maintaining good relationships with the Kappa boys. When Shep showed interest in me, Calla all but told me to lean into it. She did the same thing when you came over to talk at the party. She told me if you showed interest, not to brush you off."

I arched a brow. "What do you think it is?"

An adorable look of consternation formed on her brow. "I don't know. Like, I get wanting the houses to pair up and all, but the way they're like sharks in the water when the possibility of a relationship comes up is just ... odd."

"So, do we think this means the fraternity and sorority are involved in this business with Aphrodite's sash and apple?"

"Maybe? But what would that have to do with them wanting—" She made a face. "Do you think Stewart wants to like, I don't know, use the members for some kind of weird breeding experiment? And the apple and the sash are a means to getting that to happen?" She scrubbed a hand over her face. "Gods, I can't believe I just said that out loud. Feel free to shoot me."

"Believe it or not, the idea of a demigod politician wanting to create an army of sycophants[isn't as crazy as you think."

"Yeah?"

She actually seemed surprised that I didn't write her idea off as completely crazy.

"Yeah. I'm not sure my sisters will go for it, but I don't think it's out of the realm of possibility. Do you think Calla's involved at all?"

"Doubtful. Her mom drives her nuts, and I honestly see Iota as a stepping stone for her. She definitely drank the Kool-Aid, no question, but she doesn't seem the type to concoct and carry out some nefarious plan like that. And I'm honestly not convinced she knows what her parents are." She held up a hand when I opened my mouth to speak. "But I haven't completely written off the idea, so yes, I'm still remaining suspicious of everyone."

"Including Shep?"

She narrowed her eyes. "Is that jealousy I hear?"

"Possibly. You should probably tend to my wounded ego."

"If you must know, yes, I'm considering every person in both houses worthy of a good side-eye." She sniffed primly. "I mean, I know I'm awesome and all, but even I'll admit it's a little questionable that the president of Kappa O took such as interest in me so quickly."

"Calla did," I pointed out.

"Different," Mary replied. "I nearly caused her bodily harm in my attempts to ingrain myself into her life. There was no escaping me."

"True. Now." I gripped her by the hips and pulled her onto my lap. "About my wounded ego . . ."

She grinned. "I might be able to help with that."

33

MARY

That Wednesday, I had the glorious pleasure of helping the Iota girls with the semesterly campus cleanup. Despite the five inches of snow on the ground, Willow insisted that it was "our duty as Iotas to keep our campus tidy."

So, that's how I found myself in the bitter cold with a trash-picker-stick thing, walking around campus with Calla and Kristy, who I'd not-so-subtly teamed up with.

I had to remind myself about a dozen times that I was immortal, the cold wouldn't kill me, and this was all for a good cause.

But damn the gods, it was fucking cold. And the "specific rules" Willow had mentioned previously consisted of filling up *exactly* twenty pounds in one bag.

Willow also mentioned she would be checking to make sure we didn't put any rocks or other non-trash items to inflate our bags' weight.

"Let's just get this over with ASAP," Calla grumbled. "Fill the damn bag, and let's get going."

"Sounds like a plan." I looked around, trying to figure out where the heck we'd find a lot of litter. "Where should we head first? Any particularly messy spots we can fill our bag up quick?"

We'd met up with the other sisters in front of the student center, but most of the others had gone off their separate ways to start filling up their bags. Kristy, Calla, and I had decided to team up, although I wasn't sure it was really the best idea.

"Probably over by the Comm building," Kristy said. "It was super windy last night, and I always see a ton of trash getting blown around over there when it's windy out."

"Nice," I said, impressed with her logic. "Let's do it."

"Yes, *please*," Calla groaned, tugging on her beanie.

We made our way across campus to the Comm building, a U-shaped structure that, sure enough, seemed to act like a veritable trash collector in the wind. Unfortunately, Kristy wasn't the only one who was in on that fact. Five other sisters had already beat us there.

"Ugh," Kristy said. "Well, that blows."

Annoyed, I scoped out the surrounding area. When I caught sight of the president's mansion a bit further down campus, I jerked my chin toward it and hoped I wasn't pressing my luck.

"What about the mansion? Should we check that out? It doesn't seem like the kind of place many people would look for trash."

Calla eyed it appraisingly. "Maybe. Daddy never really stays there, unless he has a reason to be on campus late. I think the groundskeepers are there pretty often, though."

"It's worth a shot," Kristy said before I could try to press. "I doubt anyone else is heading that way. It's kind of off the beaten."

"Fine," Calla said. "I guess it can't hurt."

"So, what are we wearing for the mixer?" Kristy asked as we headed down the path toward the mansion.

"I'm going for the classic little red dress," Calla said, tugging her beanie down over her ears. It had gone bitter cold overnight, which I was so not into.

Kristy eyed her dubiously. "How little?"

"*Tastefully* little."

I couldn't help but smile. "I'm sure it'll look great."

"What about you, Mare?" Kristy smiled. "You always have the cutest outfits."

"Thanks. I got the best dress for the mixer. It's red, though," I said, wincing as I look at Calla.

Annoyance filled her features, then she gestured toward my phone. "Let me see."

I pulled up the picture of the dress Tessa was bringing me from Italy and showed it to her. It was a deep ruby with gold stitching along the top and sides. There was literally no way I was going to let Calla give me shit for it.

"Ohh, that's gorgeous!" Calla gushed, her earlier annoyance evaporating. "Kris, look at this!"

Kristy peered over Calla's shoulder. "Wow, Mary, that's beautiful. Where's it from?"

"A friend of mine was in Italy a few weeks ago and saw it. She sent me a picture and I told her to grab it for me. Some boutique in Rome, I think?"

Calla nodded appreciatively. "Well, it looks nothing like mine, so you're all good. There'll be a lot of girls wearing red, but it'd look weird if my Little was wearing the same dress as me."

"Definitely," I agreed.

Once again, I was hit with this weird twinge of guilt. Calla had her quirks, certainly, and I still wasn't entirely convinced she wasn't evil. But Kristy, Willow, and the rest of the girls were genuinely fun to be around. I kind of hated that I was lying to everyone.

But then I thought back to what Tessa said about living forever. Long after Calla, Kristy, and the rest of the Iotas I knew were gone, I'd still be here. This wouldn't be the first time I'd have to let people into my life who wouldn't or couldn't be there permanently. Mortal lives were fleeting and, well, getting attached to them would just make for a lonely existence.

Since that thought was making my mood plummet, I shifted my focus back to Calla and Kristy, who were going on about the gold stilettos Calla would wear to the mixer.

The president's mansion was an old stone building that I assumed had been there since the university was built. It wasn't a mansion so much as it was a really large, fancy house.

Compared to the Aidens' house, there was no question which was nicer.

"It's really pretty," I commented. "How come you guys didn't want to live here?"

Calla shrugged and looked up at the house as we approached. "It's nice enough, but it's so old and drafty. Plus, Daddy has so many valuable art pieces he likes to display, but there's not enough room for them here."

"I didn't know he was into art," I said, taking the opening. "What kind does he collect?"

"Ancient artifacts, mainly."

Calla's expression told me ancient artifacts weren't remotely interesting, so I filed it away so I could come up with a way to talk to Stewart at the mixer.

Fortunately, Kristy gave me an idea.

"You know what he has that's pretty cool?" Kristy asked.

"What?"

"A first translation of *The Odyssey*."

I raised my eyebrows. "Seriously? That's impressive." I paused. "That was one of my favorite books in high school."

Silently, I begged Calla to take the bait. She looked too interested in scanning for trash, though.

"You should ask Mr. Aiden to show you," Kristy suggested. "I saw it when I was there a few months ago. He has some other old books, but that was the only one I recognized."

"I'm sure he'd be happy to show you," Calla said. She jerked her chin down a side path. "Let's check down there."

Kristy sighed as we ventured down the path. "It doesn't look like there's much here, but there's some over by those trees," she said, pointing toward a little copse of trees behind the house.

Sure enough, when we reached the backyard, we saw a bunch of trash had blown through the night before.

"Geez, it must've been windy last night," Calla muttered. "They're usually good about keeping this place clean."

We got to work straightening up, but since there were three of us, we barely put a dent in the bags we were supposed to fill. It took us all of ten minutes to pick up the trash, so I scrambled to try and figure out how to get into the house.

As we headed back toward the path to the main part of campus, I settled for an old favorite.

Focusing my power on the path in front of us, I melted some of the snow, then froze it into ice just as Calla stepped on it. She slipped, and it was only because Kristy was next to her that she didn't completely bust her ass in the snow.

As it was, when Kristy pulled her upright, one leg of her jeans was damp with melted snow.

"God damn it!" Calla started batting at her jeans. "Now I'm gonna be fucking freezing."

"Are you okay?" I asked.

"Yeah," Calla muttered. "Come on, let's go inside so I can dry this off."

She dug into her coat pocket and pulled out her keys, then flipped through until she found the one she was looking for. As she let us in the back door, I took a deep breath. My focus *had* to be on sensing any godly objects. It was highly unlikely that I'd find anything there, but considering I couldn't exactly go wandering around the Aidens' house snooping just yet, it was worth a shot.

The house was borderline chilly, presumably because no one was actually living in it. Part of me had hoped Stewart might be around so I could chat him up, maybe get a little info, but no such luck.

Still, there was no mistaking the press of magic that greeted me when I stepped through the door. It wasn't Aphrodite's magic—it was different somehow. Hopefully Dionysus would be able to tell me what it meant.

Calla led us through the kitchen, a huge dining room, and into a hall, where a wide staircase rose upward. Across from the dining room was a dark-paneled living room with fancy leather furniture and a gorgeous fireplace.

Coming from inside the room was the hard, unmistakable tingle of deific magic. Aphrodite's, specifically.

Shit.

"I can't believe your parents don't want to live here," Kristy commented, stepping toward the living room. "It's so nice."

"It really is," I agreed, looking around the room.

"I guess," Calla replied airily. "Our house is bigger, though." She stopped at the foot of the stairs. "I'm gonna see if my mom left any clothes here so I can get out of these pants. Go on and sit down."

"Hey, Cal, where's the bathroom?" I asked.

"Third door on the left," she called as she walked upstairs.

As Kristy went into the living room to sit down, I made my way down the hall toward the bathroom, desperately needing a game plan. I stupidly hadn't taken the time to plan out what I'd do if I actually came across something.

'You there?'

A few seconds later, I got Dionysus's reply.

'Always. What's up?'

I smiled a little. *'I'm in the Aidens' house on campus and totally feel that godly magic tingle. I'm not sure if I'm going to be able to do much snooping, though, because I'm here with Calla and Kristy. Wanna come back with me later?'*

'Mary, are you asking me to break and enter with you?'

I rolled my eyes at his teasing tone. *'Sure. Let's go with that.'*

'Then yes, I'd love to do a little B and E. Let me know once you get home and we'll figure out a game plan.'

Footsteps sounded from down the hall, much heavier than I would've expected from Calla and Kristy, so I flushed the toilet and turned on the water.

'I gotta go. I'll check in in a bit.'

'Be careful. Have fun.'

'Will do.'

When I opened the door, I nearly collided Stewart Aiden.

"Mr. Aiden!" I exclaimed, casting a furtive glance down the hall for Calla. "So nice to see you."

Surprise flashed across his face, then he frowned. "Hi, Mary. Might I ask why you're in my house?"

My eyes widened. "Oh! Um, Calla and Kristy are here somewhere. Calla slipped and—"

"Daddy!" Calla came bounding down the stairs. "What are you doing here?"

"Campus security called." He folded his arms and gave her a total "dad" look. "Apparently they saw three girls snooping around the property, and they were concerned someone was trying to break in."

"At least they're not sitting around with their thumbs up their asses." Calla held up the jeans in her hand. "I slipped outside and got my jeans wet, so I needed to change."

"I see. Well, I suppose that's understandable." His eyes flickered with . . . something as Kristy stepped out of the living room.

"Hi, Mr. Aiden." She smiled. "Sorry to burst in on you."

His eyes flicked toward the living room again, so quickly I almost missed it. "No worries, Kristy." He looked back at Calla. "In the future, just shoot me a text, please? I was in the middle of a meeting."

I frowned, but didn't bother pointing out he could've just sent security over.

"No problem, Daddy." Calla shrugged into her jacket. "We're heading back out now, so we'll be out of your hair." Her eyes widened. "Oh! Mary was wondering if she could see that old ratty copy of *The Odyssey* you have at home."

Stewart gave me a curious look. "You don't seem the type to like the classics, Mary."

Unsure whether I should take that as an insult, I smiled. "I love mythology, and Homer's stories are what got me into it."

His expression turning appreciative. "Very nice. Well, I'm happy to share it, then. When you come by for the mixer, remind me and I'll let you flip through." He grinned. "Carefully, of course."

"Absolutely," I said with a nod. "And thank you. That's so generous."

He waved his hand dismissively. "What's the sense in having these things if I keep them to myself?"

I laughed. "I like that mindset."

"Well, you girls enjoy the rest of your day," Stewart said,

squeezing Calla's shoulder. "And Calla, please, just let me know if you need to get in here. I'll let security know, so they don't waste their time or mine."

Surprisingly, Calla looked a bit sheepish. "I promise."

Kristy and I said our goodbyes, then followed Calla out.

When we got outside, Kristy exhaled a breath. "He's not pissed, is he?"

"No," Calla said. "I think there's a lot of stuff in there that belongs to the university that's pretty valuable. Campus artifacts or whatever. He gets kind of fussy about having too many people around."

"So, where should we head next?" I asked, holding up my bag. "We're only half full."

"It looks like it might rain," Calla said, frowning up at the sky.

Kristy sighed. "Dumpster dive?"

My eyes widened. "Seriously?"

Calla laughed and exchanged a look with Kristy. "Well, as our pledge... yep, dumpster dive."

My mouth dropped open. There was no possible way she actually expected me to dive into a fucking dumpster.

Kristy giggled. "Don't worry, Mary. We'll go to the one behind the library. That's mostly boxes and bottles."

"You guys are serious?"

Calla put a solemn hand on my shoulder. "Listen, Mary. We like you, but you're still a pledge. All the others will be doing way worse, trust me. And ... we'll give you a boost."

I narrowed my eyes, seriously contemplating causing a cloudburst right over her head. Instead, I took a deep breath. She was right. This could be worse. Much worse.

"Fine." I huffed. "Let's go."

34

DIONYSUS

"So, hang on." I set down the birch beer I'd brought from a pizza place in New Jersey. "You're telling me you went *dumpster diving* to get trash for your campus cleanup?"

I was trying so, so hard not to laugh, but the image of Mary digging through a dumpster was making it pretty damn hard to keep it together.

"I seriously wanted to die," she said. "I mean, what the fuck? I guess this is their version of hazing or whatever. It kind of caught me off guard since Calla and Kristy have been so nice."

"Yeah, that's usually how it goes. Sometimes frats and sororities can be a lot worse to pledges, though, so this wasn't too bad."

"Did you miss the part where I literally went dumpster diving?"

I wrinkled my nose. "Did you shower when you got home?"

She scowled. "I hate you."

"Liar."

"Whatever. Back to the more important things. How are we getting into the president's house? We need to find out what was making the god buzz."

I arched a brow. "God buzz?

"It's a buzz coming from a godly thing. So yeah. God buzz."

With a sigh, I picked up my pizza and took a bite. I didn't doubt that she'd felt something godly in the house. She was no idiot, and she'd shown me the memory. There was definitely something there.

"Well, I can't teleport in," I said. "So, we'll have to do it the old-fashioned way."

She brightened at that. "Lock picking?"

"Lock picking."

UNSURPRISINGLY, Mary was quite skilled at using her water powers to pick locks. Within minutes of teleporting to the President's mansion's lawn, she'd worked the lock open, using ice to work the mechanism free. According to her, she'd mastered the skill when she was bored on the Ishcyra compound in Jackson. While she took care of the lock, I walked around the house to check for security cameras. We'd both donned dark pants and hoodies, and our immortal powers were still concealed by Hecate's charms, but I still wanted to cover all my bases.

"So, where are we going?" I asked once we were standing in the kitchen.

She gestured toward a room across from us. "It's in there, whatever it is."

Quietly, we made our way across the hall and into the living room. It was decorated exactly as you'd expect a hundred-year-old college president mansion to be. Dark wood furniture, massive Oriental rug, heavy drapes at the windows, and a wall lined with floor-to-ceiling bookshelves.

"I feel it," I murmured. It wasn't strong, but it was strong enough that it made me think whatever it was was still there.

"Good." Mary put her hands on her hips and looked around. "Now we just need to find it."

Carefully, we started making our way around the room. While Mary started going through cabinets and drawers, I started in on the bookshelf. Although a secret compartment wasn't out of the question, it almost seemed too easy.

An hour later, we were still empty-handed.

"It's like it's coming from all around," she complained, flopping down on the couch. "Do you feel the buzz stronger one place?"

"No, so I'm guessing the cloaking spell is more of a dampener." Frowning, I turned in a slow circle, opening myself up to the power emanating toward us. Then, like I was in a damn movie, the floorboard under me squeaked.

I froze, then looked at Mary.

"No fucking way," she whispered, jumping from her seat.

Hastily, I pulled back the corner of the carpet.

Nothing.

With a small huff, she leaned back on her heels. "Well, that's annoying."

"We need to check the rest of the floor," I said, refusing to get discouraged. *Something* was in the room with us. It was just a matter of figuring out what it was.

So, we went back to work. After about a half hour, I heard a knocking sound, then Mary snapped her fingers.

"I found something!" she hissed.

When I reached her side, she rapped her knuckles over a section of wood that was only about a foot long. Compared to the rest of the six-foot planks, it definitely looked suspicious. When she knocked on it, it made a hollow *thunk*.

"Could just be shitty subflooring," I pointed out. "Is there a latch?"

"I think so. Feel this." She ran her finger along the seam between two boards, then moved aside so I could do the same.

"That feels like metal," I agreed. "A hinge?"

"Definitely." Pulling her phone from her pocket, she turned on the flashlight to the lowest setting. When she shined it over the ends of the board, we could clearly see metal gleaming at either end.

"Can you do that thing where you freeze the metal and it breaks?" I asked.

She considered it for a moment, then shook her head. "No, I don't want to leave any obvious evidence we were here." Frowning, she looked around. "This looks like a room that would have a letter opener."

I stood and made my way over to a desk in the corner. It was one of those old, ornate pieces that looked like it absolutely belonged in an old house. And, sure enough, in a pen cup beside a fountain pen stood a shiny silver letter opener. I grabbed it, then brought it back to Mary.

Carefully, she slid the tip of the blade between the two boards. Her top teeth dug into her bottom lip as she focused on not marking the wood.

"You look cute when you're concentrating," I whispered.

She flicked me a look and a smile, then went back to work. A few seconds later, there was a quiet click, and the board shifted up. Almost immediately, the feeling of deific power intensified.

Eyes wide, Mary looked at me. "You feel that?"

I sure did. "Be careful."

Slowly, she lifted the board and set it gently on the floor next to her. Using the light on her phone, she peered inside. I leaned forward and followed her gaze.

"Thank the fucking gods," she groaned. Reaching in, she picked up an object and pulled it out.

It was a gleaming gold apple.

I let out a sigh of relief. Thank the fucking gods was right.

WE DIDN'T FIND the sash at the mansion, so we put the board back and set everything to rights. Once we teleported back to Mary's apartment, I put out a call to Athena.

Within seconds, she was walking into the apartment.

"Where did you find it?" she demanded.

Mary, who was holding the apple, staring at it in wonder, glanced up. "Under a floorboard. The sash wasn't there, though."

Athena's dumbstruck expression was nearly comical. "Under a floorboard *where?*"

"The president mansion on campus," I replied. "Mary felt its power earlier, so we went back to check it out."

With a frown, Athena took the apple when Mary offered it to her. "I need to get this back to Olympus. Any thoughts on the sash?"

The damn thing was hard not to stare at. It was gold, but it had an odd sheen to it, like its magic took physical form. It glittered in the overhead lights as Athena turned it in her hands.

Mary shook her head. "This was the only thing we could find there that held any type of godly power. My guess is the sash is at the Aidens' house."

Athena nodded slowly. "And the mixer for that is this weekend?"

"It is," Mary confirmed.

Athena sent me the briefest glance before addressing Mary. "Mary, it's crucial that you access every part of that house you can. Stewart's office, in particular, but any other areas where he might keep his personal effects."

Mary reached the same conclusion I did almost instantly.

"Are you telling me to weasel my way into his bedroom?" Mary asked incredulously.

Athena instantly backpedaled when she saw the outrage on my face. "No, I'm not suggesting you do anything you're uncomfortable with. All I'm saying is you should try to find a way into all potential rooms that could house the sash." She rolled her eyes at Mary's dubious look. "It would be a very easy feat to allow anyone who stumbled across you in, say, Stewart's office, to believe you were finding a place for a rendezvous with your *date*, not Stewart, himself."

"I suppose that's not unreasonable," Mary said slowly. "But I'm absolutely not going to give Shep any mixed signals."

"And if we find it while we're there?" I asked, trying to keep the dirty look from my face.

"Call me immediately," Athena responded. "Stewart will be dealt with once we have both items back where they belong."

She looked back down at the apple and smiled. With a nod, she looked at Mary. "Good work, Mary. Hera and Aphrodite will both be thrilled, as will my father. I hate to admit how impressed I am."

Mary gave her a rueful smile. "I'm very, very used to that sentiment. Trust me."

35

MARY

Basking in our success didn't last long. As soon as Athena had the apple, Dionysus and I started planning how I'd get into Stewart's office to look for the sash. The simplest solution was to sneak in during the mixer, which was the plan we went with. Shep had invited him to the mixer, so he'd be there for backup if I needed him.

By the time Saturday arrived, I was ready to find the damn sash and be done with this whole charade. I didn't doubt that I'd have fun at the mixer, even if I didn't find the sash. Whatever else they might be, Calla and the rest were a pretty fun crew to spend time with.

I just hated the thought of having to fake any interest in Shep. I'd done a decent enough job of being semi-flirty at the café, enough that he'd texted me a few times just to send funny videos and say hi, but it just all made me feel so . . . ick.

Dionysus hadn't really said much about my "date" with Shep, but I could tell it was bugging him. Normally, he'd be all about helping me get ready and planning out how to handle myself. Not this time, though.

Aside from working out how I'd sneak off to Stewart's office, he didn't offer any help, so I just picked out my outfit and went over everything I'd need to do with Athena, who stopped by to check in twice before the mixer. Calla texted me no less than three times to check how my dress, hair, makeup, and shoes looked. Once I sent her a mirror selfie of the finished product, she sent me five thumbs up emojis.

Calla: *Shep is gonna FREAK, Mary, that's so hot.*

That icky feeling invaded my stomach again.

Mary: *Thanks. I kind of love it.*

Gods, I really hoped he didn't freak. The last thing I needed was him thinking my outfit was meant to be anything other than a nod to Iota Sig.

Shep came by and picked me up at seven so we could go to dinner before the mixer started. I seriously considered saying I would just meet him at the Aidens' house, but on the off chance he had any kind of information I could use to get closer to Stewart, I needed to spend as much one-on-one time with Shep as possible.

Plus, a restaurant was a nice, neutral place where we could talk without being interrupted by frat brothers or sorority sisters who wanted us to . . . whatever.

So, we ended up at a restaurant down on the lake that had small plates and drinks. Once we sat down, he suggested we split a bunch of apps instead of ordering big meals.

My kind of guy.

After ordering our food, the waiter brought our drinks over— beer for Shep, club soda for me—and he flashed me a smile.

"So, Mary Jameson. Tell me about yourself."

I groaned. "Don't you know that's the worst question to ever exist ever?"

"True, but I still want to know about you." He leaned forward and rested his elbows on the table. "What do you like to do when you're not winning the hearts of sorority sisters?"

I shrugged and picked up a piece of bread and started breaking off small pieces. Realizing that might look like a nervous habit— which it totally wasn't—I popped a piece in my mouth and put on a thoughtful expression.

"Well, I do enjoy the occasional binge of trashy reality tv," I said. "And archery. Although I don't get much of that up here."

His eyebrows winged up. "Yeah? You don't strike me as the archery type. Compound or recurve?"

"Recurve," I said, semi-surprised he knew the difference. "You a fan?"

"My dad is. I used to hunt with him as a kid, but I never really took to the sport."

"Are you any good?" I asked, somewhat teasing.

"I can hold my own. There's an archery lane a few towns over, if you want a demonstration."

I paused for a second and examined the opportunity he'd given me. Another chance to get to know him, more time to ask questions without seeming suspicious, and something that would get both Calla and Athena off my back.

Plus, I really missed my damn bow.

"Sure!" I smiled brightly. "Tell me when."

He leaned back, nodding at the waiter as he started setting plates down in front of us. "Next weekend?"

"Sounds like a plan," I said, pulling a small plate toward me.

Dionysus wasn't going to like it. I knew that for certain. But, again, I had a job to do and he knew it, even if I *did* have the icks about taking another date with Shep. The sooner I wrapped things up here, the better. He'd understand that.

Hopefully.

The rest of dinner was nice. Shep actually was a cool guy that I could totally see myself being friends with. There wasn't a flicker of attraction anywhere in my body, though. Not that I expected there to be. It certainly made it easier to not feel shitty about deceiving him like I was.

After we wrapped up dessert, we got into Shep's car and drove to the Aidens' house.

"Damn," he commented when we rolled into the drive and saw it packed to the brim with cars. "Looks like we're the last ones here."

I flashed a smile as I unclipped my seatbelt. "Better to be fashion-ably late than too early, right?"

He laughed. "Absolutely."

After we deposited our coats with the housekeeper, I took a look around. The Aidens' house had gone from standard mansion luxury to a red and gold monstrosity that left no question who this party was for.

The kitchen and dining rooms looked like a true event venue. The dining room table had been removed entirely, leaving just a big, empty space that worked perfectly as a dance floor. A DJ was set up in one corner, pumping out music as guests danced.

Waiters walked around with trays of hors d'oeuvres and flutes of champagne. About half the people there were dancing, while others were hanging around the edges of the room chatting at high-top tables.

"Come on, I see Calla," Shep said when he saw her, Willow, and the guys over by the dining room entryway.

Before I could respond, he took my hand and started to lead me toward our small group of friends.

When we were about halfway across the room, I spotted Dionysus engrossed in conversation with two Kappa O brothers, Eris at his side, looking far more proper than I'd ever thought possible in a black shift dress.

A flash of annoyance went through me. I understood why he was there, of course. We'd talked about it extensively. I was starting to become annoyed at Eris's constant insistence on sticking around. I knew she wasn't just trying to be helpful, and her incessant need to draw on negative energy made it a lot harder to do my job.

"Hey, guys!" Calla's greeting when we reached them drew my attention away from Eris and Dionysus. "It's about time! What took you so long?"

The mischievous look in her eyes told me she had plenty of thoughts on what took us so long, which kind of made my stomach turn.

"Dinner," I told her, needing to squash her assumption immediately.

"It ended up taking longer than we thought," Shep added.

If I didn't know better, I could've sworn Calla looked disappointed that something as mundane as dinner made us late.

"I'll grab you guys drinks," Shep said. "Mary?"

"Beer me, please," I said, smiling.

Calla waited until he was out of earshot, then looped her arm through mine and led me to a nearby high-top table. "So, how was your date?"

"It was nice. The food there is delicious."

"Isn't it?" She sighed and looked around the room. "My mom kind of outdid herself this time, don't you think?"

"Definitely," I agreed.

Just then, Shep appeared with our drinks.

"Thanks," I said as I took the bottle of beer from him. "I'm gonna run to the bathroom real quick. I'll be right back."

"We'll be here," Shep replied, to which Calla smirked.

Seeing Stewart and Missa were sufficiently occupied with their guests, I made my way toward the bathroom I'd used the last time I was here. As I walked, I tried to map out where I should try to go. I'd set up the running app when we got out of the car, but I double checked to make sure it was still open. It was, so I stuck it back in my clutch and considered my options.

Since Stewart was very clearly away from his office, and I didn't see Missa leaving his side, I needed to try and seize the moment. I had no interest in trying to worm my way into bedrooms, at least not on my first search. So, when I got to the bathroom, I went in for a few minutes to keep up the ruse in case anyone had followed me.

After I left the room, I headed straight toward the study. It was the only place I'd felt any significant pull of power, so it seemed the best place to start. Glancing at my phone, I saw I'd already been gone four minutes, so I'd have to hustle.

When I reached his office, I gingerly pushed open the door. It wasn't locked, which I took as a bad sign. If there was something as valuable as a deific object in here, the door would've been locked.

Then again, he'd hidden the apple under a damn floorboard, so his secrecy skills seemed questionable, at best.

As I stepped inside, the pull of magic increased slightly, which had me second-guessing my assumption about the door.

Moving quickly, I strode toward his desk. I had all of three minutes to do a quick search before my absence would officially be deemed weird. So, I started opening and closing doors, looking for anything suspicious.

Most held the standard stacks of paper, pens, and junk. There was nothing that indicated a godly object was lying around.

With a frown, I did a slow circle and looked around the room. There was no way I could start checking floorboards. I was about to head out when the door started to open. Frantically, I ran to hide behind the desk, then froze when I saw Eris walk in.

"Shit, you scared me!" I exclaimed.

"Sorry. I figured you'd need an alibi so people don't think it's weird you've been gone for ten minutes. We'll walk back in together, talking like total besties, then anyone who gives a shit will assume we got caught up talking."

"Oh." I exhaled. "Yeah, that makes sense."

"So, what do you have?" With a frown, Eris looked around the room. "They were definitely in here. I can't tell if they're gone or just hidden really well."

"I'm going with the latter," I told her, frowning. It didn't seem like she knew I'd found the apple. Which, knowing Athena, wasn't surprising.

She nodded slowly. "Okay, we have to be quick. Get searching."

We set about searching through the office. Although I was tempted to use my immortal speed to quicken the process, I figured I was more likely to miss something that way.

"Here!" Eris hissed from in front of a massive painting of Stewart and Missa behind the desk.

"Does he seriously have a hiding spot behind the painting?" I asked. "That's so . . . cliché." Almost as cliché as a loose floorboard, but I kept that to myself.

"No, idiot. There's a false compartment on this shelf," she replied, pointing to a spot on the wide shelf beneath the painting. It was a thick, floating shelf about four inches tall.

I checked the time. "One minute," I said as I rushed to her side.

Eris was already running her fingers along the underside of the shelf, looking for a release. A few seconds later, there was a quiet *click*, then a small panel opened from the bottom.

As if on cue, Eris's head shot up.

"Shit, someone's coming." She grimaced as she looked back at the shelf. "Okay, we'll just come back later."

"Whatever, just close it and let's go!" I hissed.

She snapped the compartment shut, then, just as the knob on the door turned, she put her hand on my arm and teleported us out of the room.

36

DIONYSUS

M ary and Eris were taking too long to get back from Stewart's office. I was just about to go find them when Shep sauntered over to say hi.

"So, did they have parties like this back in your day?" he asked.

I laughed. "Not quite as high-class, but close. Where's your date?"

He took a sip of his beer and looked around. "Off to the restroom. I'm guessing she ran into one of the other girls along the way."

"Yeah, they'll do that," I said with a nod. Then, as if he knew I was planning on excusing myself, Stewart Aiden came over.

"Joe!" He shook my hand. "So glad you could make it. How's our lovely town treating you?"

"Couldn't be better," I replied. It was a struggle to keep my focus on him when all I wanted to do was go find where my sister and Mary were. "A bit colder than I remember."

He laughed. "Yes, well, it'll be spring soon enough. Sheppard, where's your date?"

"Bathroom," Shep replied. "Actually, there she is, now. It looks like she ran into Joe's cousin."

As he said it, I saw Mary and Eris enter the room, giggling.

"Guess you were right," I told him. "So, how's the campaign going, Mr. Aiden?"

"Stewart, please. And it's going well." He took a small sip of his drink. "We're polling well, considering how recently I started my bid."

Keeping one eye on Mary as she and Eris walked over, I shifted most of my attention to him. "Yes, I heard you announced your campaign late. Was it hard to decide whether to run?"

He smiled, but it looked almost like a grimace. "I was a bit torn, but my Missa talked me into it. She's quite supportive, that one."

"Persistent, too," Shep said with a laugh.

"Who's persistent?" Mary asked, coming to a stop beside him.

"My lovely wife," Stewart said. "We were just talking about my campaign. How are you, Mary?"

She gave him her brightest smile, one that had probably won over plenty of guys in the past. "I'm well. Your home looks amazing."

He chuckled. "Yes, Missa has quite an eye for decor. She could've had a career as an event planner, if she'd wanted."

"Where is the missus, anyway?" Eris asked.

"I believe she went to go check on things in the kitchen," Stewart said, his smile a bit too smooth for my liking. His eyes flicked over Mary and Eris with something akin to suspicion in them, but . . . not.

'More like nearly catching us in the act in his office,' Eris said. *'We need to get back in that room.'*

Ignoring her, I kept my focus on Stewart. Demigods could communicate telepathically just like gods, and the charms we wore to cloak our power worked best if we were limiting said power in his presence.

"So, Shep, did you know your Mary has an interest in Greek mythology?" Stewart asked, shifting the subject away from his wife.

With a small smile, Shep looked down at Mary. "Is that so?"

Her eyes darted between Stewart and Shep, but fortunately, she didn't send a look my way. "I do," she said.

"My Calla told her about my George Chapman translation of the *Odyssey*," Stewart explained. "Mary, I believe I promised you a peek at it?"

"Oh!" Her eyes went wide. "Yes, but I wouldn't want to ask you to step away—"

"It's no bother." He gestured toward the hall she and Eris had just come through. "It's in the library."

Shit. There was no way I'd be able to worm my way into that room, and I wanted to stick around in case Missa came back.

"Mind if I tag along?" Shep asked. "I'd love to see it."

There was a brief flash of hesitation on Stewart's face, so quick that Shep's human eyes wouldn't have caught it.

Then, Stewart nodded. "Of course, Sheppard. As a lit major, I'm sure you'll find it quite interesting."

As expected, he didn't offer an invite for me or Eris.

Once the three of them walked off, Eris spun to face me.

"There's something in the study," she hissed. "We almost found it, but someone opened the door."

"What was it?"

"I don't know." Frustrated, she tapped her fingers on her lips. "It was strong, whatever it was. Not as strong as two deific objects, but there was something giving off deific energy. I suppose there might be something in the library too."

"Well, there's no way we're getting in that room with them," I said with a sigh. "It'll be painfully obvious we're being nosy."

"True," she agreed. "Let's just hope your girl stays on her toes. We need to get back in the study."

Mary staying on her toes was the least of my worries. With Missa unaccounted for, I had no idea what she would be walking into, and I had zero trust in Shep. Sure, he seemed like an okay enough guy, but there were too many variables. If he was on the up-and-up, he'd have no chance defending Mary if Stewart or Missa tried something. If he wasn't, then she'd be completely on her own.

Needing reassurance, I reached out to her.

'You good?'

'I am. I think we're almost at the library. Just stay in the house in case I need you to teleport in.'

'Will do.'

"Tell her to let you in her head when she gets in," Eris suggested. "Two pairs of eyes are better than one, and she sure as shit won't let me do it."

"Good call," I said.

'Is it okay for me to watch through your eyes while you're in there?' I asked.

I could practically feel her hesitation, but then she opened up her mind completely.

'Definitely not your worst idea,' she admitted. *'But I'm claiming victory if we find anything.'*

Eris and I continued to pretend to talk while we waited for Mary to get into Stewart's library. Once she was in, I focused more on what Mary was seeing as Eris subtly monitored the room. Right now, everyone was enjoying the party. It was like any other high-class mixer I'd been to in the past, so I didn't expect anything nefarious to happen. Still, having my sister there to act as backup wasn't the worst thing.

"Why don't you go find somebody to hit on?" I suggested. "It's going to look weird if we're just standing here, not talking."

Eris nodded. "True. Go find a room to camp out in, and call me if you need me."

Once she walked off, I made my way toward the hall that Stewart had led Shep and Mary down. It led in the opposite direction of where Mary and Eris had come from when they were in his study, so it seemed the library was in a different area of the house. I wasn't entirely sure where, but I assumed it took up a fair portion of the eastern wing.

'Down the hall until you can't go any farther, turn left, you'll see a big fancy door,' Mary said.

'Thanks.'

Keeping my ears peeled along the way, I heard sounds from a couple of rooms that sounded like couples had gone off in search of a bit of privacy. Finally, I found a room that was relatively close to the turnoff for the library and was completely empty. Stepping inside, I shut the door and flicked the lock. The room looked like a guest suit of some sort, with a bed and en suite bathroom. It was smaller than I would've expected, so I assumed it was likely a servant's room or something. Sure enough, a uniform that matched the housekeeper's hung on the back of the closet door.

Good. The housekeeper was thoroughly occupied, so I wouldn't have to worry about her coming in.

I sat down on the bed and started focusing on what was happening with Mary.

37

MARY

Thankfully, Missa wasn't in Stewart's library when we reached it. I didn't know where she'd gone off to, but I assumed she was the one who'd almost walked in on me and Eris. I also had no interest in being stuck in a room with her and Stewart so far from the rest of the party. Yes, Dionysus and Eris could be there within a heartbeat, but I preferred to walk out on my own two feet without any type of scene.

When we stepped into the library, I felt the unmistakable press of magic. The second he flicked on the light, I saw why.

Nearly every inch of wall space was occupied by a piece of artwork or a glass case displaying a book or artifact. More glass cases stood on pedestals around the room, and the bookshelves were filled to the brim with books that looked long past their prime. Dark leather sofas and chairs encircled a gleaming wood coffee table in the center of the room, inviting anyone who entered to sink in. If I was more of a book nerd or history buff, I would've been in heaven.

"Welcome," Stewart said, gesturing for us to come inside. "It's a bit of a mess, still, but we've gotten almost everything unpacked."

As I took a few more steps inside, I was hit with the pressure of deific power. It felt like it was coming from all over, just like the rest of the house, only more intense. Far more intense than what Eris and I had felt in the study.

'You feel that?' I asked Dionysus.

'Yep. Something's in there, for sure.'

"You've got quite a collection," Shep commented. His English major eyes had gone wide with awe.

Stewart chuckled. "Thank you, Sheppard. It's taken quite some time to curate the collection, but I'm quite proud of it, if I do say so myself."

Trying not to look suspicious, I wandered over to a wall that separated two floor-to-ceiling bookshelves. A large painting that I immediately recognized as a Monet hung beneath a light. "This is beautiful."

"You like Monet?" Stewart asked.

"I had a book when I was a kid about a little girl who went to see his paintings in Paris," I said. "I've always wanted to see one in person."

"That one was a gift from a generous campaign donor," he replied. "One who's hoping to have a few laws changed in regards to how stolen art is handled."

"Are the current laws insufficient?" Shep asked, coming to stand on my other side.

"They can always be better," Stewart replied. "Here, the book is just back here."

Shep and I followed him toward a standing metal case near the back of the room, nestled in a recessed section of the wall between a bookshelf and a rear door. Above the case, some type of gold armor hung in a shadow box. I'd hoped the pulsing godly energy I felt throughout the room would change as we moved, but it felt like we were just sitting in a cloud of it with no apparent source.

"Ah," Stewart said when he saw where I was looking. "The baldric of Heracles. A relic from the Trojan years. It took us about fifteen years to track that one down." His expression turned almost reverent as he examined the gold baldric that was inscribed with animals and gory scenes of battle. "There's never been another piece like it."

"It's . . . impressive," I replied. As far as I knew, all the relics from the Trojan era were in storage in Zeus's palace, but clearly some things hadn't made it back to Olympus.

"Now, for the book." Stewart stepped up to the case and tapped the glass. "The George Chapman translation of the *Odyssey*, dated to the mid-seventeenth century. It's been passed down in my family for several hundred years."

Shep gave the book a curious look. "I'm surprised it's held together for so long."

"Yes, well, we Aidens always take good care of our artifacts." Sliding his hands in his pockets, he gave me a nod. "Go on, take a look. It's rare I find someone else with an interest in the classics."

I nearly cringed, considering my "interest in the classics" essentially began and ended with the *Odyssey*. Still, I stepped up to the case and slid my hands in the gloves attached to the front pane of glass. The book lay spread open on a small stand covered with smooth, white velvet. A faded red ribbon acted as a bookmark between the pages.

Gently, I touched the old paper, surprised at how sturdy it felt. Idly, I wondered if he'd had someone work a protection spell on it to keep it from rotting.

As I skimmed over Chapman's seventeenth century flowery prose, I was immensely happy the version I'd read was more recent.

"A bit of a mouthful, isn't it?"

I glanced up and saw Stewart looking at me expectantly. "I'm sorry?"

"The writing. It's a bit . . . much."

"Oh!" I laughed. "Yes, I was just thinking how happy I am that I read a more modern version."

Shep peered over my shoulder, getting a bit too close for comfort. "It's impressive. Have you ever read through the entire thing?"

As they spoke, I reached out to Dionysus.

'See anything unseemly?'

'Not really, although I'm interested to find out when Hebe handed over

Heracles's baldric. My sister was never one to give away things with such sentimental value, even if he has been dead for a thousand years.'

'*Are we sure she gave it away?*' Hebe was Dionysus's half-sister and the daughter of Hera and Zeus. By all accounts, she'd been Heracles's lover way back when.

'*No, but it's possible. I'll check in with Athena.*' He paused. '*Who knows? Maybe that'll be your next assignment. Retrieve the stolen baldric of Heracles.*'

'*Stop. Stop it right now. I will not become Olympus' very own Indiana Jones.*'

'*But you're so good at it.*'

Shifting my focus away from Dionysus, I gently turned the page in front of me. I expected Stewart to caution me, but when I glanced up to see his reaction, he was staring intently at my hands.

Weird.

"Thanks so much for letting me see this, Mr. Aiden," I said as I slid my hands from the gloves. "I've seen artifacts before, but I've never gotten to handle them."

"Yes, of course. As I said, I enjoy sharing these things. Please, feel free to look around." His tight smile turned sheepish. "It's a bit of a dream of mine to own a museum, but for now, this is what I have."

Own a museum? Sheesh. How much money did this guy actually have?

I left Shep and Stewart to chat as I meandered around the room. I kept one ear on their conversation, but they'd fallen into a conversation about French translations of Shakespeare's works.

As I walked through the room admiring Stewart's collection, I opened myself up as wide as possible to the power flowing through the room. But, even with Dionysus's help, I couldn't pinpoint a source. It was just . . . everywhere.

I refused to let myself get discouraged, though. There was something here—something bigger than whatever Eris and I had come across in the study. I just needed more time to figure out what it was.

38

MARY

After we left the library, we headed back to the mixer for awhile, but I couldn't keep my focus on anything but Stewart's library. So, after about an hour, I feigned a stomach ache and hopped an Uber home. It probably wasn't the best idea, but I was more likely to draw suspicion if I was distracted than if I wasn't feeling well.

I stayed up most of the night trying to puzzle out what could've been in Stewart's library and where. Considering how many things he had in there, it wasn't surprising to feel some deific energy floating around. Heracles's baldric certainly would've had some power coming off it, but not nearly as much as I felt.

No, there was something bigger in there. Whether or not it was the sash, I had no clue.

The next morning, I slipped out of bed before Dionysus got up, with a desperate need for coffee. I'd just started loading up the machine when the door open. I nearly winced when I saw Athena walk in.

"Oh, hey." Glancing toward my bedroom, I silently told Dionysus to stay put.

"I came to see how things went last night." A little frown marred her forehead. "Since I hadn't heard from you."

"Oh. It went great, actually. I was just about to check in. Eris and I found a hidden shelf in Stewart's office that was giving off some energy, but Stewart's library seems to be a hot spot. I think I'll spend today trying to figure out how I can get back in there without getting caught.

"All right, that's good—" Her jaw clenched, and she huffed out a sigh as footsteps sounded behind me. "Oh, for the gods' sakes."

Turning, I glared at Dionysus, who'd just walked out of my room in nothing but the pajama pants he'd taken thirty seconds to get from his apartment last night.

I sent him a furious look. '*I told you to stay.*'

"I didn't want to," he murmured, touching a hand to my back and kissing the top of my head. "Morning, dear sister."

Athena met his eyes and sucked in a slow breath through her nose. "*This* is why you insisted on coming here? So you could chase after a *girl*?"

I frowned as insult bloomed inside me.

"No!" he exclaimed. "Well, yes. I just—"

"*Came here for a godsdamned girl!*"

I lifted my eyebrows and took a few steps away from the arguing siblings and tried not be aggravated at how harsh her words were. "Yeah, this girl is just going to, uh, let you guys do your thing."

Athena shot me a venomous look. "Oh, no you don't, Mary Miller. We're hashing this out right-fucking-now, because, so help me, if your libidos mess up this mission—"

"I think you're overreacting a bit," Dionysus said.

"—I will tell our father!"

Shit.

Dionysus smirked. "Are you threatening to tattle, Athena? That's a bit beneath you, don't you think?"

Her slim brows shot up, and she pointed at her brother. "Do you know how much of a hassle it was to get Father to agree to you coming here? How much of my time it took to convince him you'd be more useful here than in Germany? The web of *bullshit* I had to spin? You said you wanted to apologize, Dionysus, make things up to your *friend*." She gestured vaguely toward the two of us. "This is not how 'making things up to friends' works!"

My face went hot.

Dionysus grinned. "Well, technically—"

I clamped a hand over his mouth before he could finish his retort, then smiled at Athena.

"It's fine, Athena, really. You've got nothing to worry about." Athena never got worked up like this, and if she wasn't so terrifying, it might've actually been funny. Slowly, I let my hand drop from Dionysus's face. *'Keep your mouth shut, okay?'*

"'Nothing to worry about,'" Athena muttered. "Do you know how angry Aphrodite will be when she hears you two have been shagging when you're supposed to be finding her—"

"Please don't say it," I begged.

"—*girdle?*"

"Considering her profession, I think Aphrodite would be perfectly fine with our extracurriculars." Dionysus was clearly enjoying this far too much. "Especially considering we already found her apple."

"Oh? Perhaps we should ask her, then, hmm?"

Dionysus rolled his eyes. "She's not going to care, Athena."

Before I could comment, Athena glanced at the door. A moment later, Aphrodite, in all of her tall, dark-haired beauty, walked in, looking less-than pleased.

"There better be a good reason I'm here, Athena. I was sleeping." Frowning, she eyed me and Dionysus, then sniffed. "It smells like sex in here. Lots of it."

"Oh, for fuck's sake," I muttered, covering my face with my hands. When I looked up, Aphrodite was staring at me through narrowed eyes.

Aphrodite's eyes traveled up, then down my body, taking in my messy ponytail, long-sleeved sleep shirt, and plaid pajama pants. Clenching my teeth, I tried to hold back any sign of unease.

After a few seconds, she shrugged and looked at her brother. "I suppose she's better than the ones you normally go for."

Dionysus gave my shoulder a squeeze. "Why don't you go grab some coffee from downstairs," he murmured. "I'll get rid of them."

Athena snorted. "Not likely. Go on, Mary. We need to talk to our brother alone, anyway."

"Gladly," I muttered. Shaking my head, I turned and walked back to my bedroom, all the while annoyed at the turn things had taken.

I had no clue what Athena was going to do with this new information, so I was a bit surprised she hadn't considered it sooner. I guess when it came to romantic stuff, she wasn't exactly a pro, considering she'd been a soldier her entire existence. Based on her tone and the hissed whispers coming from the living room, it was clear she was pissed.

The thing was, I didn't really get why she was so pissed. Yeah, Dionysus and me having a relationship could cause a concern due to the distraction factor, but she knew her brother well enough to know he wouldn't let that happen. I guess she didn't know me well enough to know I wouldn't let it happen, either. Still, her response was a bit much, considering she was normally so coolheaded.

"Anyone want anything?" I asked when I walked back into the living room after getting dressed. The room had gone silent at my appearance.

"Double espresso," Dionysus said, still looking mildly pissed off. Which, for him, was significant. Whatever the deal was between the two of them, it didn't seem like us being together was the catalyst.

"Got it." I shrugged into my jacket and shoved my furry boots on. "I'll be back."

Athena continued to meet Dionysus's glare with one of her own. When I looked at Aphrodite, I saw she wore an amused expression, one that was a bit calculating, but she didn't look nearly as pissed as Athena seemed to have thought she'd be.

Whatever.

I left, then made my way down the loud wooden stairs to the

coffee shop. Needing to give myself a few minutes of space, I went for a large mocha cap instead of my regular coffee with sugar.

A few minutes later, armed with our coffee, I headed back to my hopefully empty apartment. My immortal hearing picked up the sound of continued arguing halfway up the stairs, although I couldn't quite make out what they were saying. I stepped carefully, hoping they wouldn't hear me. Athena was clearly on a tear.

"Have you even told her Zeus wants you reassigned at the end of the semester? What if she hasn't finished here? What are you going to do then? Do you think Zeus is going to let you two Bonnie-and-Clyde your way around the world for the next thousand years?"

"Bonnie and Clyde were criminals, Athena. Be reasonable."

"Oh, that's not the point and you know it! Don't you remember how busy you get on assignments? You forget about everyone but the people right in front of you!"

"People I'm helping, Athena! And as much as you don't want to hear it—"

"He's done with that," Aphrodite cut in. "Isn't that right?"

There was a moment of silence, then I heard a sigh.

"It doesn't change anything," Athena said. "Does she know Zeus's plans to send you back to—"

Rolling my eyes, I opened the door and walked in.

Athena cut off mid-sentence when she saw me, and Dionysus looked absolutely furious.

I arched a brow at them and set the coffee on the island, curious just how honest they'd be with me. "Who's sending who where?"

With a huff, Athena sent a pointed look at her brother.

"My father wants me to go back to Germany when we're done here," Dionysus said through gritted teeth.

My heart gave a heavy thump, but I forced myself to keep a neutral face. "And?"

"And if he doesn't listen to Zeus—"

"He'll do what, Athena?" Dionysus folded his arms and stared at her expectantly. "What will the almighty do if I refuse?"

That set off a whole new round of arguing that I didn't particularly care to be a party to, so I checked out and retreated to my bedroom to enjoy my coffee alone.

Zeus wanting to send Dionysus back to Germany wasn't surprising. Dionysus was good at his job and Zeus knew that. Not to mention, he'd up and left pretty quickly. I wasn't sure who they got to fill in for him, but I imagined it wasn't anyone nearly as effective. There'd never been a question in my mind as to whether he'd go back to work, but it sucked to think about. I was just finding it really hard to believe Dionysus would actually refuse an order from Zeus. Even Nate, rebel that he was, still followed orders. Sort of.

Plus, Dionysus liked working at colleges. He enjoyed the parties, the counseling, and the human interaction. So, why wouldn't he want to go back to that? I mean, really, what was he getting here other than time with me?

Which, yes, was great and I knew he felt it was worth it. If he didn't think being with me was worthwhile, he wouldn't have asked Athena to rearrange his life to be here.

I just hadn't really thought much about what came next. We were together. There was no question about that. But I was also fresh out of my training year. Rules for me were still different than they were for older generations, and didn't compare to those for the gods. I couldn't opt out of being in the field or on duty. The only reason Dionysus could was because his dad was the ruler. Regardless, just because he could refuse didn't mean he would. Dionysus was a fun guy who didn't have a rebellious bone in his body. Yeah, he got himself transferred here, but Athena and Zeus had both been clear that would be temporary.

Sure, Nate got away with refusing Zeus. But Nate was the youngest and Hera's favorite. She'd give him whatever he wanted, even if it was just to piss Zeus off. She didn't have that same loyalty to Dionysus because, well, he wasn't hers.

My phone dinged with a text on my nightstand. With a sigh, I picked it up, wincing when I saw Shep's name.

Shep: *Feeling better?*

Biting my lip, I said the first thing that came to mind.

Me: *Hey! I was going to call you in a little bit. I think I got food poisoning or something. I've been feeling icky since last night.*

Shep: *Oh, shit, I'm sorry to hear that! Do you need anything? I'm pretty good at nursing people back to health :-)*

Me: *Lol. No, I'd rather wait a bit before you see me like that.*

Shep: *No worries. I get it. You heading to Iota for studying tomorrow?*

Me: *Yup. Be there around noon.*

Shep: *Stop by after? I'll cook you dinner.*

My stomach did another one of those weird flips. I was almost hoping me bailing the night before would've thrown up red flags for him that I was a total flake or something. But no, Mr. Nice President didn't seem to care one bit.

Me: *Sounds good! I'll text you when I'm done.*

The door opened. I looked up, expecting Dionysus. Instead, Aphrodite came in, her dark eyes instantly scrutinizing me.

"Talking to your boyfriend?"

I glanced down at my phone, then at her. "I'm talking to Shep, if that's what you're asking."

There was no mistaking the look of suspicion she wore. "You've been sleeping with my brother."

Unsure of her point, I set my phone down and faced her fully. "I have."

"But you're still texting that frat boy."

"I have a job to do. You know that."

Narrowing her eyes, she considered me for a moment, then held out her hand. "Let me see your phone."

Although it infuriated me to do so, I handed it to her. The look of surprise on her face was borderline hilarious. But, well, I had nothing to hide and I had zero patience for this shit.

"I get that you're protective of your brother, Aphrodite, but you can trust me." Annoyed, I watched as she started scrolling through my messages. "And I thought you wanted me to—"

"Of course, I didn't want you to," she snapped, handing me my phone back. "That was a test."

Good fucking grief. "So, did I pass? Because I can assure you, there's nothing going on with me and Shep."

"Clearly." She frowned. "Why aren't you out there arguing in my brother's defense?"

"Seriously? You think I'm getting between Athena and literally anyone?"

"My sister isn't as scary as you seem to think she is."

"Maybe not, but I don't feel like getting reamed out because she disapproves of my sex life, and Dionysus is a big boy."

Aphrodite sat down on the edge of my bed, crossing one leg over the other. "Fair enough. My sister doesn't really 'get' relationships."

Silence hung between us for a moment that bordered on awkward.

"I care about him, Aphrodite. You really don't have anything to worry about."

She looked at me, her expression curious. "And if he told you that you were just a fling? An accomplishment?"

The thought made my stomach turn, but I shoved it away. "I think I know him better than that."

"Oh?" She smirked. "You've known him for what, nine months?"

I gave her a curious look. "Are you trying to tell me your baby brother is so much of an asshole that he'd form a friendship and fake falling for me, have Athena rearrange his life, and risk pissing off Zeus just to screw me?"

She narrowed her eyes. "Fair enough. Do you love him?"

Considering he and I hadn't actually had that talk yet, I was a little hesitant to respond, but it was kind of hard to keep quiet around the goddess of love. "Yes, Aphrodite, I love him."

"Good. That's good." Then, her demeanor shifted entirely and her expression turned warm. "You'll be good for him, Mary, truly."

"Really?"

"I saw it the first time I saw you together." She brushed a strand of hair from her eyes. "In his mind, when he showed me memories of your idiotic trip to Disney World. He's in it for the long haul with you. Don't fuck it up."

As she said that, Dionysus walked in. If possible, he looked even angrier than he had a few minutes ago.

"Get out," he snapped at Aphrodite.

My eyebrows shot up at the bite to his tone.

Aphrodite smirked. "Big sister got your panties in a bunch?"

"I will literally throw you out," he said. "Take Athena and leave."

With a heavy sigh, Aphrodite stood. "Dionysus, you know I don't do reassurance, but I'll make an exception in your case." She looked down at me, then back at him. "You two will be fine. Father will get over it. Hera knows a bond when she sees one, so you won't have to worry about that."

"Awesome." Dionysus held the door open and gestured for her to leave. "Goodbye."

Once she was gone, he sat down next to me and huffed.

"So?" I asked.

"So, nothing," he muttered. "Zeus can kiss my ass."

"Can he?"

He flopped back on the bed, letting his long legs dangle over the edge as he glared up at the ceiling. "He wants me to go back to Germany." He turned his head to look at me. "I'm not going. Just so we're clear."

That was good to hear, but at the same time, a bit concerning. "Why?"

"Why do you think? I'm going where you go. Period."

His expression made it impossible to tell whether he actually meant it, or if he was just being stubborn. There was about a fifty-fifty chance of either.

"You're gonna make him angry," I pointed out. "Am I—"

"Don't you dare ask me if you're worth it," he said, looking up at me. "You know you are."

"To you, maybe." I gestured toward the living room. "But not to Athena. Not to Zeus. They'll probably ship me to the most miserable place on the planet to keep you from tagging along."

"They both know me well enough to know I really wouldn't give a shit about living conditions in your case."

For someone so smart and insightful, I couldn't understand how he wasn't seeing the bigger issue here.

"Right, but *I* don't want to get shipped to the most miserable place on earth. So, it'd be helpful if you just . . . proceed carefully. I really don't want to be on Zeus's bad side."

His eyes ran over my face with a look that bordered on frustration. "Considering the fact that you landed here before your training year was up should tell you that no one would let Zeus waste your talent because he was angry with my life choices. Plenty of his children bail on Olympus. Look at Nathaniel. I'm no different."

I tried to think about that as logically as I could. Yes, it made sense. Clearly, I had plenty of people to vouch for me, so I probably could get assigned pretty much anywhere I wanted.

Yet, all of that smacked of special treatment, which I absolutely did not want.

"I'd just like to get any future assignments based on merit, not who I'm sleeping with. That's hardly fair to the other recruits who've worked harder than me for years."

"You know that wouldn't be the case," he said. "The fact that you would even think that—"

"Is logical," I finished. "We know it's not true, the handful of people who know us know it isn't true, but you can be damn sure the other Ischyra—"

"Since when do you care what other people think of you?"

I gritted my teeth. "You've been at this a lot longer than me, Dionysus."

"So, what, then?" Annoyance rose in his voice. "You bounce around for a few centuries to convince the other Ischyra you're good at your job, then we can settle down? In case you missed the memo, literally everyone who knows who you are knows exactly what you did to Chaos. Your name is made."

"I shot a few arrows," I snapped. "Into the back of someone who was one of my closest friends for years. Excuse me for not basking in the kick-ass reputation that came from that."

He pressed his fingers to his eyes and huffed out a breath, then let his hands fall to his lap. "You're right. That's not fair. I'm sorry."

Seeing his anger rising again, I slid closer and took one of his hands. "Look, I'm not saying you're wrong about my reputation. I'd just like my reputation to be based off more than the worst moment of my life."

Wrapping his fingers around mine, he touched his lips to my knuckles. "It won't be, Mary."

I smiled, but it was hard not to let him see just how little his words did to reassure me.

39

DIONYSUS

As much as I'd hoped to be reassuring, I knew Mary didn't buy anything I was telling her. I meant every word and knew without a doubt that her reputation was hers and hers alone.

But I also knew that she still had nightmares that she didn't want to talk about. That she worried more than she let on about what would happen if she failed this mission. And that she very, very clearly didn't want me taking on any of her concerns. So, I wouldn't push it.

I was dead set on sticking with her no matter where she went next, but I also understood why she thought us being together would be a bad look.

Despite that, I couldn't help but be upset that she thought I didn't understand her concerns. I appreciated her worries about favoritism, but she'd have to get over that. Even if I wasn't in the picture, Tessa was her best friend. Mary didn't need me to get her special assignments when her best friend was a titaness engaged to Hera's favorite son.

Unfortunately, we had bigger issues to focus on than romantic ones. While I would've loved nothing more than to go away and work out the details, she had a job to do. Mary had gotten some good intel when she was in Stewart's library, narrowing down whatever was letting off godly magic to that room. So, now, our goal was to figure out how to get her back in there.

The day after Athena showed up, Mary went to Iota for a study session, then to the Kappa house for dinner with Shep. Desperately needing a distraction from her having another dinner date, I told her I was going to see if I could glean anything from the research she'd done, which was significant. Between typed documents, spreadsheets, articles, and social media activity, I felt like I knew the Aidens inside and out.

I wanted to plop Athena down in front of Mary's computer so she could see exactly how hard Mary had been working this whole time.

As I read over her notes on all of the Aidens, a few questions kept repeating in my mind.

First, did Calla Aiden know what her parents were? Mary and I had pondered that one quite a bit. She certainly benefited from it, but based on the information we had, she hadn't shown any indication she knew she was the daughter of a demigod and witch. And if she did know, would it matter?

Second, who was in charge? Based on what Mary had gathered, Missa and Stewart both seemed to carry equal weight in their machinations. Missa had tricked Hera into handing over the sash, but Stewart was the one who benefited the most from having it. Sure, Missa got the fancy house and status, but ultimately, Stewart got the power. There was no question he would win his bid for Congress, putting him in a direct position to affect change in the legal system. The problem was, we had no clear picture of the kind of person he was, meaning that change could be highly detrimental.

I'd talked to him for a while at the mixer after Mary left, and it seemed like he had every intention of bringing forward legislation for popular issues if he won. He'd also done a lot to revamp South Lake's campus and had started dipping his toes into local issues, including funding a repaving of Main Street and handing over a huge donation to committees involved in funding local projects. At the same time, I'd never known a politician not to run on hot-button issues.

Even so, I was an excellent judge of character, and he didn't strike me as disingenuous. My assessment lined up with Mary's—he seemed like a politician, but also, not.

Which begged the final question—if Stewart wasn't a bad guy, what was he doing with the sash and apple? He'd gotten all he wanted before he came into their possession, so why would he need them now?

Another thing I struggled with was the fact that he'd hidden Aphrodite's apple under a floorboard in the president's mansion. It just didn't make any sense. An apple that molded itself to the whims of its owner should be kept under every lock and key imaginable, yet he'd hidden it with the skill of an amateur thief.

Something wasn't adding up.

Frustrated, I reached out to Nathaniel.

'Over-under on Zeus letting you come interrogate Stewart Aiden so Mary and I can wrap up this damn job?'

'You really want me to answer that?'

Annoyed, I drummed my fingers on the counter. Nathaniel's interrogation skills were unmatched, but he rarely used them. Picking through someone's mind wasn't something he relished, even with the worst criminals. Considering we didn't know how duplicitous Stewart was, even if Zeus allowed Nathaniel to jump in, it was unlikely my brother would agree to it.

'What do you have so far?'

'Mary has a ton of intel on this guy, but something isn't sitting right, and I can't figure out what it is.'

'You mean where he hid the apple?'

'Yeah.' It might not have been the most important detail, but it had been weighing on me most. *'For a demigod with powers like his who's clearly comfortable using those powers, it just seemed so . . . irresponsible.'*

'So, take a step back. Does he seem like an irresponsible guy, or is it more likely there's something else going on?'

'Like what?'

'*Were there any other protective measures in place where you found it?*'

I thought back to the room where we'd found the apple. It had been pulsing with godly magic, but I'd assumed that was only because of the apple's presence. Mary had felt protective magic as soon as she stepped through the door of Stewart's library, so it would stand to reason the same would've happened at the mansion.

'*It's possible there was magical protection,*' I allowed. '*Neither of us have been back into the mansion, so I don't know if there was anything lingering when we left. There weren't any physical measures that we saw, and neither of us felt anything when we walked in.*'

'*That's where I'd start, then. Get back in there and see if there's any protective magic hanging around. It makes sense you wouldn't have noticed it when you were there, considering the apple is so powerful.*'

'*Protecting against who, though? That's where I'm struggling.*'

'*No clue. You're on the ground, so you'd have a better idea than I would. My guess is someone close to him, though.*'

'*Like his daughter?*' Even if Calla didn't know what her dad was, the golden apple of discord wasn't an obscure relic. Anyone who paid attention to history growing up knew what it was and what it could do.

'*That would be my guess, but you and Mary would know best.*'

'*I suppose that could explain the shitty hiding spot. She never goes to the house on campus, so she might not be bothered to look there.*' Even as I said it, though, I knew it still didn't sit right.

Just then, the door opened and Mary walked in. When she saw me at the island with her research spread out in front of me, she paused. "Bored?"

I cut off with my brother, then stood and stretched. "Sort of. There's been a lot nagging at me since we were at the mixer, and I wanted to give your research another look."

After dropping her bag by the door, she came over and sat down at the island. "What have you got?"

"Questions." I slid my notes toward her. "You recorded a ton of info on the Aidens, so I wanted to look at it from an outside perspective."

"You've been helping me with this the whole time," she pointed out as she skimmed over what I'd written.

"In chunks. I wanted to look at it all as a whole story." I laid out all the questions I had and what I'd talked over with Nathaniel. Once I finished, she sat back in her chair and stared down at all the research contemplatively.

"The apple bit has been irking me too," she finally said. "A house where no one lives with no security in place other than campus security? I agree that we have to be missing something. I'm positive Stewart is the one who hid it, just based on the look on his face when he saw us near the living room."

"Or maybe he knows it's there and can't get to it?"

"I thought about that, but I'd expect him to be able to figure out a way in, considering his powers."

"True." So, back to square one, then. "Okay, so what about the sash? That's a major question mark right now."

"There was something in the study giving off power, and the library was filled with it," Mary replied. "It has to be in one of those places. I just don't know how to get back in there. The house doesn't have any physical security that I can see, which means it probably has magical booby traps in place." With a huff, she ran her hand through her hair. "On a positive note, I'm pretty sure I know how to get back into the president's mansion."

"Oh?" That *was* good news. "How?"

"Our next pledge task is a scavenger hunt on campus," she explained. "Based on what Calla told me, it's going to end at the mansion. We'll be required to 'retrieve' something. Any bets on what that might be?"

"The apple," I murmured. "So, someone in Iota Sig knows it's there."

"Exactly my thoughts," she agreed. "It's going to be a bit of a   ·
problem when we show up and there's nothing there."

"Yeah, I can see that being a problem. We need to get a fake, then."

Her expression turned dubious. "Okay, but I'm pretty sure a demigod and his witch wife will know immediately it's not real."

"True, but the second they indicate they know it's a fake, it'll be clear they were knowingly in possession of Olympic property."

"And Athena and the Ischyra will step in," she finished. "Athena needs to be on standby, then. Watching through my eyes, the whole nine. Even if they don't suspect me as having taken it, they won't be happy."

"Exactly. So, when is this going down?"

"Friday. We have to meet at the student center and we'll get our instructions from there. They were pretty vague about everything today. The only reason I know it's ending at the mansion is because Calla told me, but I'm assuming other Bigs have told their Littles. Maybe not all of them, but I can't imagine Calla's the only one magnanimous enough to help her charge."

"Okay, then, work on the assumption they all know," I replied. "Don't even worry about figuring out who does and doesn't. Just assume the worst—"

"And hope for the best." She smiled. "Trust me, that's been my mantra since I got here."

40

MARY

For the rest of the week, Dionysus and I planned out the best way for me to get to the president's mansion before any of the other pledges. Between my immortal speed and him helping me out if I had to figure out puzzles or riddles, I didn't antici- pate any problems. Having a plan B and C in place didn't hurt, though.

I found out on Thursday that the Kappa pledges were running their own scavenger hunt, too.

"Theirs is different than ours, though," Calla explained. The pledges and sisters had all gathered at the Iota house for a study session, but it had turned into a Q and A of sorts after about an hour.

"How?" Lindsey asked.

"They won't be ending at the same place, for one," Calla replied. "And they won't have the same requirements along the way."

"And that's all we're going to say on the matter," Willow added. We'd been at it for a solid half hour, so I didn't really blame her for putting a stop to the questions. "We'll tell you everything else you need to know tomorrow."

Not wanting to draw any attention to myself, I went back to studying bio. Dr. Trebauer had turned out to be a pretty cool professor, despite his hard-ass demeanor on day one. He was challenging, though, so I needed to stay on my toes to keep up that B average.

As I went over my text, though, my mind kept drifting toward the significance of this scavenger hunt with the pledges. I'd said since day one the relationship between the Kappas and Iotas was weird. The fact that we were doing yet another important task with them further convinced me of that.

Then it hit me.

'You there?'

Dionysus's reply came almost immediately.

'Yep, what's up?'

'We need to get into the Aidens' house ASAP. I think the Kappas might be going after the sash while we're going after the apple.' It was the only thing that made sense. The Kappas and Iotas were too close not to have similar goals, and I had no doubts the houses saw the benefit to possessing two deific objects.

'That would require a ton of cooperation,' Dionysus replied. *'I don't see two houses full of members agreeing on that. How would the Kappas even know?'*

'Calla is Stewart's daughter. If she wants either of those things, she could've convinced Willow and Shep to use her family's property as the endpoints. All she'd have to do is say she hid items at each place, and no one would be the wiser. I'm pretty sure the only reason she told me about the task ahead of time is because she thinks her influence as my Big will ensure I give the apple to her, not Willow.'

As much as I hated to admit it, the idea of Calla being the bad guy here really rankled. There was no question she was entitled, bratty, and a host of other things, but the thought of her being just as two-faced as, well, me, bothered me. At the same time, I'd gone into this knowing there was a possibility she was in on this whole thing, so it shouldn't have come as a surprise.

'Valid. Let's loop Athena in when you get home, though. She might be able to help with a game plan.'

My initial reaction was to balk at asking Athena for help, but I bit my tongue. As a goddess of war, Athena's planning skills were untouchable. If anyone was going to put in their two cents about our breaking and entering plans, it was her.

'See if she can come by tonight. I'll get out of here as early as possible.' Refocusing my attention on the rest of the room, I saw they'd abandoned Q and A for the most part, so it didn't seem like I'd missed anything. So, I cut off with Dionysus and went back to studying.

~

ATHENA WAS in my apartment when I got home, her face stern as she looked over my research and whatever notes Dionysus had taken in the last couple of days.

"Good, you're here," she said, not bothering to greet me. "Let's get started."

Dionysus shook his head at my questioning look.

'She's still irritated with both of us, but she'll get over it.'

Shaking my head, I walked to the island, where the two of them had spread everything out.

"I've been looking over your maps," Athena began, picking up a printed sheet that showed a partial map of the eastern wing of the Aidens'. "You weren't able to get more of the western half of the Aidens' home?"

"No, there was never an opportunity. The only time I had a reason to be there was when Stewart took us to the library, but that was a pretty straight shot."

"All right, then we need to overlay your maps with the satellite images. I want to know every possible escape route."

"The library had a veranda," I said. "There were three sets of French doors leading outside on the east wall. That was the closest exit I could see."

Pursing her lips pensively, Athena drummed her fingers against the countertop. "I don't think going in alone would be wise," she said after a moment. "Based on your reports, the library is filled to the brim, and the study is on the other side of the house. Checking both without the ability to teleport would be too time consuming, and you need to be in and out as quickly as possible."

"Fair enough." As much as I wanted to prove myself, I could also acknowledge when team work was the best tool for getting the job done. "The sooner we can wrap this up, the better."

"Agreed. However, depending on how things go tonight, you might need to complete tomorrow's task, just to avoid suspicion."

"Why?"

She set down the papers she'd been skimming, her face serious. "Because the best way to ensure this arrest is done efficiently is by catching our culprit in the act or committing a crime. Ideally, you'll be found out tonight and we can take Stewart and any other parties in right away."

"But if that doesn't happen," Dionysus continued, "you'll need to go tomorrow to find out who's most interested in obtaining both objects."

"Okay, then." I gestured toward the map in Athena's hands. "So, what's the plan?"

"Tonight, Dionysus will teleport you outside the Aidens' library. We didn't detect any form of magical protection getting onto the property, so that shouldn't be an issue."

"What about the protection that was on the room, itself?" It had been pretty unmistakable, after all.

"We have two theories for that," she began. "Since you've already been in the room, it's likely the spell will recognize you, so to speak, so it won't alert anyone of your presence or react when you enter."

Although I wanted to acknowledge what a stretch that was, I kept my mouth shut. "And the second theory?"

The two siblings exchanged a quick glance. "The second theory is that the magic will register your essence, but since you were in the room so recently, it won't be immediately evident you were the intruder."

"That's a lot of assumptions," I replied. "Could we, I don't know, find out what kind of protective magic is on the room before I go in?"

"I've tried," Athena said. "Hecate wasn't able to get enough from the memory you sent, so we're hoping the fact that you already entered the room will work to your advantage."

The fact that Hecate couldn't recognize the magic was troubling, but I hadn't exactly given her much to go on. The room was full of magic, and I'd been more focused on looking for the sash.

She inclined her head at Dionysus. "For various reasons, my brother won't be able to accompany you. The magic certainly won't recognize him, for one. Second, an elder breaking into anyone's home would be a PR nightmare we don't need to deal with. An Ischyra is one thing—you are, after all, essentially Olympic law enforcement. Sending an elder in would be akin to sending in the human president to do the job of an FBI agent."

"As long as I have backup, I'll be fine." Sliding my laptop forward, I pulled up the aerial view of the Aidens' house on the navigation app. "Now, let's figure out how the heck I'm getting inside."

41

MARY

A few hours later, under cover of darkness, Dionysus teleported me to the southernmost door of the Aidens' library veranda. Several tall pines bordered the south wall, giving me a lot of cover to sneak inside. We'd agreed he would sit in his car down the street, pretending to wait for someone so he could keep an eye out for anyone who might be out and about. Athena was on standby at Olympus with a handful of the palace guard just in case things went sideways. They were the most highly skilled Ischyra in Olympus's employ and were only ever brought off the mountain when high-profile criminals needed to be taken in.

Unfortunately, since Zeus wanted the Elders on the sidelines, that left me on my own for the time being.

We'd assessed the Aidens' outdoor security and found it to be thorough, but basic. I was able to avoid motion detectors easily enough, and I used my powers to freeze open the locks and depress the trigger switches on the door. Getting in was easy. The magic that permeated the room was where the real challenge lay. I wasn't a god, but even I could feel the mixing threads of magic weaving protections across the objects in the room. So, I would have to tread lightly when I found what I was looking for.

The only light in the library was from the half-moon that filtered in through the windows and doors. It didn't offer much, but my above-average eyesight did well enough as I navigated the moon-washed space.

Gnawing my lip, I looked around the room.

Think, Mary. What was Stewart most interested in?

The only things we'd discussed in any detail were the Monet, the baldric, and *The Odyssey*. Everything else, he'd kind of glossed over or not mentioned at all. So, I started with those.

Heracles's baldric was, unsurprisingly, putting off a shit ton of power. He'd been a demigod, a son of Zeus, after all. As I stood in front of its case, I closed my eyes and focused only on the power coming off of it. It took a minute, but I was finally able to differentiate the feel of its magic from the rest of the magic in the room. Despite being powerful, it was otherwise unremarkable.

Next, I focused on *The Odyssey*. I couldn't get that expression he wore when he looked at the book out of my mind. Unfortunately, I didn't feel anything coming off the book. After getting the same frustrating results from the painting, I started to make my way around the room, feeling for stronger pulls of magic. I found a few other objects, mainly trinkets that didn't have a lot of magic on their own, but combined, packed a punch.

Finally, I'd whittled down the multiple threads of power to a single one that had the unmistakable feel of Aphrodite's magic. Unfortunately, although it pulsed all around me, I still couldn't pinpoint a source.

'Any bright ideas?' Dionysus, Athena, and Aphrodite were each waiting on standby in case I needed guidance. *'It's nearly one, and I don't want to be here till dawn.'*

'*What was Stewart most interested in when you were there?*' Athena asked.

'*The book, but that's because we came in here specifically to see it.*'

'*And the magic you felt in the study—was it stronger than what you feel now?*'

'*Weaker. It was definitely Aphrodite's magic, but not nearly as strong as it is here.*'

A moment later, Aphrodite chimed in. '*He'd probably already moved it, then. You still would've felt the power, but if he took it from a hiding place in the study and moved it to the library, that would explain why the magic felt stronger throughout the room.*'

'*I'd say that's the most likely scenario,*' Athena replied.

'*Go to the book,*' Dionysus said. '*I want to see something.*'

Gently, I picked my way around the display cases and furniture to the pedestal displaying the *Odyssey*.

'*What passage is there?*'

'*It's not a passage, it's a damn wall of text. What are you looking for, specifically?*'

'*Is it the first page?*'

'*Yes.*'

'*Of which book?*'

Glancing at the top of the page, I noted the number. '*Book twelve.*'

Silence.

Frowning, I skimmed over the text. My seventeenth century English wasn't exactly stellar, but I'd read the story enough to understand it.

'*This is about Odysseus' journey home,*' I said. '*Circe tells him what he'll encounter, right?*'

'*Yeah.*' Dionysus' voice sounded resigned. '*Read the Argument at the top. Where does it say he'd end up first?*'

Quickly, I read the small chunk of text that was absent from my modern translation at home. As I read each line, my heart sank.

Sirens. The first hurdle Odysseus would face was the Sirens.

We'd ended the war with the Sirens firmly on our side. Tessa and Scylla had lifted their curse, and the Sirens were now free to move about as they pleased. Of course, that was after they'd spent months helping Chaos in his pursuits. Even so, there was no real reason to think they'd flipped on us again.

'*Okay, so what does this mean? Do you think Stewart was trying to* send me a message or something?' It definitely would've explained the pointed look, although not necessarily the reasoning behind it.

'It might not mean anything,' Athena said. 'Let me reach out to a few people and see if anyone's heard about rogue Sirens roaming around.'

'My money's on a coincidence,' Aphrodite said, sounding bored. 'Book twelve in the Odyssey is smack in the middle. It makes sense that's what it would be open to.'

'Well, while you all puzzle that out, I'm going to keep looking for the sash.' Too many voices trying to troubleshoot was just going to get irritating. If there was a Siren involved, we'd deal with it. We'd done it before; we'd do it again.

Shoving the mental conversation to the back of my mind, I started wandering the room again, examining each item. There had to be a thread I could latch on to that would lead me to the sash. It was just a matter of finding it . . .

A few moments later, I felt it. Aphrodite's magic pulsed toward me from across the room. Turning away from the Rembrandt I'd been examining, I looked toward the magic's source, homing in on a small glass case sitting on a wooden table. Quickly, I made my way across the room, suddenly desperate to leave.

Inside lay a small gold coin. It was completely unremarkable, which was why I'd barely registered it on my first few loops around the room. It looked thin, too thin to be actual currency, even considering its age. A nine-headed serpent was stamped in the center, the Hydra that swam the Acheron River in the Underworld. It didn't gleam like you might expect a gold coin to, though. Instead, it looked tarnished and worn.

'Guys, I think I found something,' I said, hesitant to touch the case for risk of setting off some invisible alarm. Something told me this was protected far more than the apple.

'What is it?' Athena asked.

'A gold coin. But it's giving off a ton of Aphrodite's magic.'

'Let me see,' Aphrodite demanded.

Opening my mind a bit further, I let her see through my eyes.

'That's one of Charon's coins,' Athena said. 'Aphrodite, why is your power coming from one of Charon's coins?'

'Because it's sewn onto my sash, you fools.'

I winced at the bite in Aphrodite's voice, but I didn't really blame her. The coin was sitting on a bed of red satin interwoven with threads of gold. Even in the dim moonlight, its colors were clear as day. A single hole had been drilled through the coin, and it was sewn to the girdle with golden string.

'Okay, well, that's unfortunate,' Dionysus said. 'Charon's coins are meant for safe passage to the Underworld. If you touch it—'

'It's a trip straight downstairs,' I finished with a sigh. Charon's coins were closely guarded and given only to those who were worthy. They were intended for the dead, though, not the living, making it the perfect object to guard a deific object. Getting teleported to the Underworld wasn't a death sentence, but it would be a humongous waste of time.

'Can you find some scissors?' Athena asked. 'Perhaps you can cut the string?'

Aphrodite snorted impatiently. 'Just grab the damn thing and take care not to touch the coin. Gods, this is amateur work.'

I bit back the retort that she could've disobeyed Daddy and just done this herself, but I held my tongue. It was hard not to latch onto her impatience, but something was holding me back from doing exactly as she suggested. True, the sash had been shrouded in more protection than the apple. Between the magic at the door and the other deific power drawing out the sash's own magic, it was obvious whoever put the sash here wanted it to be in easy reach but also concealed. I had no doubt lesser immortals and humans probably saw a pretty backdrop for a stunning artifact. Creatures who were the descendants of the descendants of gods, like, for example, the newest generation of Sirens, simply weren't able to feel out magic the way I could.

The apple had been easy. Perhaps too easy. Maybe that was because Stewart hadn't had a chance to put proper protections around it, or maybe he was just stupid. Either way, considering the sash was on display in a magic-soaked room, it was all but guaranteed it would be booby-trapped straight to the Underworld.

'Okay, so I'm not touching this thing,' I finally said. *'I think it makes more sense to wait until tomorrow, let someone else open it, and get it then.'*

I expected arguing. Instead, I felt all their hesitation.

'I think that's wise,' Aphrodite finally replied, her tone full of aggravation. *'If you get caught now, which you undoubtedly will, we'll be back to the drawing board.'*

Ignoring her dig at my inability to not get caught, I stepped away from the case. Then, as stealthily as I'd entered, I slipped out the veranda door and quietly closed it.

As if on cue, a light flicked on in the library not two seconds later.

42

DIONYSUS

To say we were disappointed that Mary left the Aidens' without the sash was an understatement. Aphrodite was pissed, of course. Athena was aggravated because she'd pulled palace guards and was therefore required to report back to Zeus. His irritation filtered through my sister to me, which was completely undeserved, but also understandable.

The next morning, Aphrodite and Athena showed up at Mary's to lay out a detailed plan for that night's Iota task. Since we knew Mary would be going after the apple on campus, we needed to figure out the best way to get her to the mansion first, then to the Aidens' house immediately after. I didn't know how long it would take one of the Kappas to figure out their clues and get to the sash, but I could only assume at least one of them had someone helping them just as much as Calla was helping Mary.

That was, of course, if our guesses about the Kappas being involved were accurate. We all agreed that was still a big "if," regardless of how logical it might have been.

"With so many unknowns, I think we need to play a lot of this by ear," Athena said. "The Iotas are meeting at the student center at seven, so it'll be nearly full dark by then. Calla hasn't provided any indication of what the scavenger hunt will consist of, correct? You'll need to answer riddles, but that's all you have so far?"

"Yup," Mary said. "All I know is that the final stage is stealing something from the mansion. Logic puzzles aren't my thing, so if I'm going to get to the mansion first, I'll need help."

There was no doubt in my mind she'd be able to manage whatever the riddles were on her own, but I didn't bother saying so.

"We'll have backup stationed around campus," Athena told Mary, pointing out a few spots on the campus map she'd brought up on Mary's computer screen. "This way, you won't have to call for help—you'll have others watching your back."

"Who?" Mary asked, seeming surprised.

"A few Ischyra. As I said, we'd like to avoid Elders getting involved, but Zeus was willing to release a few well-seasoned Ischyra from their posts temporarily to be on standby."

"I guess I can't complain about that," Mary replied. "Any chance one of you could go stake out the Iota house and read Willow's mind, maybe find out what the riddles will be?"

Athena smiled, for once, not looking annoyed. "Trust me, if that was an option, we would. Unfortunately, Zeus wants this mission to be as god-free as possible. He's already chastised Eris for showing up, even in disguise, and the only reason he's tolerating Dionysus being here is because he trusts him to not involve himself."

Mary's expression at that was nearly comical.

We spent the next few hours going over every variation of the night's events we could concoct. By the time Mary had to start getting ready to head to campus, we had plans in place for all possible scenarios, even the most obscure.

Just after six, Athena and Aphrodite left, leaving me and Mary alone in her apartment.

"Is it crazy that I'm nervous?" she asked. "I've felt so confident up until now, even last night, breaking into the Aidens' house."

"You're facing a lot of unknowns tonight," I said, pulling her down on the couch next to me. "I'd be more concerned if you didn't feel uneasy, to be honest."

She gave me a rueful smile. "Thanks. That helps."

"You don't need my help." Taking her chin in my hands, I gave her a soft kiss. "You don't need anyone's help."

Her lips curved against mine when she laughed, but she kissed me back. Then, not breaking the kiss, she shifted so she was straddling my lap. We were running short on time, otherwise I would've taken the opportunity to take her to bed for the rest of the night. As it was, we'd barely have time for a quickie.

"You're going to make yourself late," I murmured.

With one last, lingering kiss, she pulled back, then, smirking, used her thumb to wipe her lip gloss off my mouth. "We can pick up later, then." She hesitated a moment, her teeth digging into her bottom lip.

"What is it?" I asked.

She took a deep breath, then rested her hands on my shoulders and stared into my eyes. "Before I go tonight, I just wanted to tell you that . . . I love you. And I think you already know that, or at least, I hope you do, but I wanted to say it—"

Elation at her words swelled inside me, and I knew it had left a dopey smile on my face. "Mary, I love you too. I just wish you'd let me say it first."

"Yeah, well, I got impatient," she said with a shrug as she stood.

Standing, I leaned down and kissed her again, not caring that I ended up with glittery pink lip gloss all over my lips again.

"I'll make it up to you when you get home," I told her.

"Sounds like a plan."

A SHORT WHILE LATER, I was waiting not-so-patiently for Mary's pledge task to start. The Iotas and Kappas all met in front of the student center, but Mary was focused entirely on Willow's instructions, so neither of us caught much of what the Kappa's were told to do.

"You'll have five stops along the way to your goal," Willow

explained. "At each stop, you'll need to collect something. When you reach the final destination, you'll present each of these things to the sister who awaits you. If you don't have these things or you go to the wrong place, you'll have to return to the start. Any questions?" After the murmured collective "no," Willow gave a curt nod. "All right, then. Your first clue is . . . what can you put in a barrel to make it weigh less?"

'A hole,' I said immediately.

'Duh. I had that question in Mindquest in eighth grade.'

'Well pardon me, then.'

'But what does it mean? It's a simple answer, yeah, but where do I go?'

That was where this scavenger hunt would get interesting. Deceptively simple riddles would lead to incredibly vague instructions on each destination.

'Well, you're on campus. What could a hole relate to?'

'Hole in one, watering hole, hole in the wall, hole in the ground . . .'

I tried to skim over her memories of being on campus as well as my own. 'They're installing new landscaping in front of the comm building. I think they just dug a hole for a fountain. Maybe start there?'

'Better than nothing.'

As the rest of the pledges puzzled out their clue or scattered, Mary headed straight toward the communications building. She detoured a few times to make sure no one was behind her, but by the time she got there, one of the other pledges was already poking around.

'I see it.' Without hesitation, Mary darted toward the shallow impression in the dirt. Two dozen paper-wrapped packages were piled up in the bottom. Grabbing one of the packages, she ignored the other pledge and took off down a path to open it in private. She tore open the package and revealed an index cared with a short riddle. A small, wooden bear was taped to it.

'I left my campsite and hiked three miles south, then east, then north, at which time I returned to my campsite and found a bear eating my food. What color was the bear? Shit, I know this one.'

'White,' I said. 'The only place you could do that is at the North Pole—'

'And all they have there are polar bears,' she finished. '*SLU's mascot is a polar bear. They're all over the place. Signs, statues, the whole nine.*'

I thought for a moment about the most likely spots Willow would send them. '*My guess is the statue at the student center, the locker room in the gym where they keep the mascot, or that one trash can in Stevenson that's shaped like a polar bear.*'

She groaned, but started heading in the direction of the student center. After thirty minutes of searching and troubleshooting, she finally ended up finding her next clue under a trash can in the cafeteria—a unicorn on a string.

We worked through the next few clues until she'd found the final three items, the last of which very clearly directed her toward the president's mansion. As she made her way across campus to the mansion, her steps quickened. It seemed like she'd been getting to each spot before other pledges, but there was no guarantee.

Excitement washed through her and into me, but I couldn't help but tamp down my own matching emotions. She was almost done, but the last few stages of this plan were going to be tricky, especially if she was going to get to the Aidens' house. I kept my thoughts to myself, though, as she made her way down the path toward the mansion.

The mansion had just come into view when Mary felt a thump on her head. Panic struck, both hers and mine, as everything went black and I was kicked from her mind.

43

MARY

The only thing that kept me from panicking as I woke was the brightly lit room I was in. The fear I'd felt the last time I'd been kidnapped, when I'd woken up in a stone room steeped in magic that dampened my powers, was absent. Instead, as my eyes fluttered open in the Aidens' library, I felt my powers fully awake in my mind. The curtains were drawn tight, preventing any outside light from coming through. Despite my magic's obvious presence, I couldn't help the trickle of fear that filtered through me as my mind began to clear.

Immediately, I reached out for Dionysus. When I got no response, I tried Tessa, Nate, Athena, Eris, all of them.

Something was blocking my ability to call out.

Memories of chains on my wrists and cold stone at my back invaded my thoughts, making it impossible to focus on the things in front of me.

Details. I needed to focus on details.

"Save the head for last..."

My breaths started to come quicker, but with my hands bound, it was nearly impossible to press my thumb to my palm, one of the few tricks that worked to center me.

But I wasn't there. I wasn't in that stone room in Louisiana. I wasn't chained to a wall. My magic was awake and ready to be weaponized. Just because I couldn't reach anyone didn't mean they wouldn't find me.

"*...heal between amputations...*"

"Is she awake?"

Startled, I jerked my head toward the voice that had just spoken. The sudden sound yanked me from my memories and the dark place I was spiraling to.

When I took in an unconscious Stewart Aiden chained to a chair next to me, the fear I felt shifted toward confusion. But the sight in front of me was even more confusing than the demigod beside me.

All visions of chains and stone walls and vicious titans evaporated as I took in Kristy standing next to Jared from freaking bio, of all people.

Where the fuck did he come from?

Missa stood behind them, leaning causally against the wall, presumably the reason I couldn't call out to anyone mentally.

"Oh, hey, guys." My mind was still a bit fuzzy, but things were coming into focus. I had no clue how I'd gotten to the Aidens' library, but I knew teleportation had to have been involved. If someone had tossed me in a car, one of the Ischyra on campus would've been on us in a heartbeat. "Some party."

Gently, I tugged the binds on my wrists. Tight, but just basic rope. Easy enough to break through...which meant they probably didn't know I was an immortal.

"Good luck with that," Jared said with a snort when he saw me tugging at my bonds. "My dad was a firefighter. My knots are unbreakable."

Gods, what a douche.

The bravado that I'd desperately missed when I'd been kidnapped was awake and itching to piss somebody off, but I needed to play dumb human as long as possible. "Sooo, what's the plan?" I looked pointedly at the still-unconscious Stewart. "And what'd he do?"

Missa stepped forward, causing the other two to step aside. Jared looked uneasy, but Kristy wore a look of annoyance at Missa's proximity.

"Let's skip the banter." Missa leaned down and put her hands on the arms of the chair I was tied to. "You took something of mine. I'd like it back."

A little dash of crazy danced in her dark eyes, far more than I would've expected in a witch who always seemed so put together.

I gave her a look of fake remorse. "Ya know, if I knew what you were talking about, I'd consider it."

Her eyes flashed, and I knew in that instant she was going to hit me. There was no way—

Crack!

The backhand across the face wasn't a surprise, but damn, it hurt. I tasted blood, which said a lot about her strength, considering she was half human.

Scowling, I spit the blood on the carpet. "That was uncalled for. Geez."

A huff sounded from behind Missa. Kristy, clearly irritated.

"Move," Kristy demanded.

Eyes narrowed in fury, Missa obeyed.

Interesting. I kept my face stony, but a whole new brand of weird was emerging that I wasn't quite sure what to make of. Kristy had honestly been the last person I suspected of anything nefarious. Helpful, nice, basically the complete opposite of Calla. Although, considering the events of the past year, all of that probably should've made her my prime suspect.

"Where's the apple, Mary?" Kristy's eyes bored into mine, almost like she was trying to lure me into telling her the truth. "And the girdle?"

I blinked innocently. "Apple? And why would I have your underwear?" Something pressed against my mind, and a flash of hope flowed through me. There were very few people who could push against a mind-blocking spell, and I knew most of them.

Teeth bared, Kristy leaned in closer. A scent wafted off of her, one

I'd noticed before but had never really put a finger on. It reminded me of a body spray I wore in middle school.

"You took the apple from the mansion." Again, she sent me that imploring look, only this time, her words sounded...musical. "You took the apple and somehow, you found the girdle. Stewart tried to hide them from us, but we know you snuck in there and took them. Where are they?"

In that moment, I wanted to answer. I wanted to tell her the apple was long gone, safe and sound on Olympus, and that the sash was barely ten feet away from her, guarded by a coin that would suck her straight to Hades' front door if she touched it.

Unbidden, the memory of beaches filled my mind. Soft sand and cool water...gentle ocean breezes.

Ocean Breezes.

That had been the name of my body spray. Ocean fucking breezes.

Shit.

Jerking my eyes away from Kristy's, I started reciting the Greek alphabet, forcing myself not to succumb the melodic voice of the Siren in front of me. This was bad. This was really, really bad.

Ischyra had a lot of immunities and natural protections against immortal enemies. Sirens weren't strong enough to ensnare and incapacitate us like they would a human, but they could still put us in enough of a haze that we'd easily divulge state secrets, especially when they were mere inches away.

A snarl rumbled in her throat, and surprise registered on Jared and Missa's faces.

Right. A human wouldn't be able to shut out a Siren like that. Their surprise made me even more confident they had no clue who or what I was, which would definitely work in my favor.

Kristy gripped my chin, forcing my face toward hers. Strength-wise, we were pretty evenly matched. Still, if I wanted to continue playing the human act, I couldn't let on that I had powers.

Again, I felt someone pushing against my mental walls, trying to break through.

Yes, yes, please come through.

Kristy leaned closer. I focused on the whites of her eyes, the small red veins that were barely visible. I just needed it to look like I was entranced. I could do that.

"Let's try this again," she hissed. "Where is the apple?"

On Olympus.

I swallowed back my instinctual response and tried to keep my voice mellow. "I don't know."

"And the girdle?"

Behind you. It's right behind you.

It took all my strength not to let my eyes stray toward the case that held the sash. "I don't know."

Something shifted in her expression, and I could tell she wasn't convinced. A chair scraped, followed by a grunt.

Kristy closed her eyes and exhaled. "Missa, please deal with your husband."

"What's going on?" Stewart's panicked voice sounded slurred, like he'd been drugged when they'd knocked him out.

"Shh, sweetheart," Missa cooed, going to his side. "We're almost done here. Then, we can go."

"What?" Panicked eyes met mine as he tried to jerk against the chains he'd been tethered with. "Mary? What on Earth—"

"Hey, Mr. Aiden." I needed to get out of here ASAP. "How's it going?"

"Kristy, just knock him out again," Jared hissed. "We need to get out of here."

"One of them knows where they are," Kristy snapped, rounding on him. "I'm not leaving here until I have the girdle and the apple."

"Someone is going to realize we took her, and he's a *demigod*, Kristy. You think Olympus won't be banging the door down? They're probably already here!" He jerked his head toward Stewart. "Get going on him. Mary doesn't know anything."

Ok, I thought. *This is good. Focus on each other.*

"Do *not* tell me what to do, you human rat. You're here for one reason and one reason only. Now, go keep an eye out for Calla and *shut your mouth.*" Her final words rang with authority, and Jared's eyes immediately glazed over. Silently, he nodded, then walked to the door and left the room.

"Missa, what is this about?" Despite Stewart's words, there wasn't enough panic in his voice to make me believe he didn't know what was going on. Clearly he'd hidden the apple and sash from his wife, but I couldn't tell if he knew what was up with Kristy or Jared. Not that *I* knew what was going on with Jared, but I honestly didn't care to deal with a human hanger-on.

"We just need the apple and girdle, darling." Missa's voice dripped with honey.

Stewart's eyes darted toward me, then Kristy, before he looked back at his wife and shook his head. "No, Missa. Not like this. Those things corrupt—we don't *need*—"

"We absolutely *need*," Kristy snarled. "You're a demigod, but you're too weak-minded to see their importance."

"No, that's not true!" Stewart shook his head, then looked at Missa imploringly. "She's a Siren, Missa. Don't let her do this to you. We already have everything we could possibly want."

Shocked, Missa stared at her husband, then laughed. "Stewart, she didn't need to convince me of anything. Do you *know* what we'd be able to do with the apple and girdle? We could take over Olympus, finish the job Chaos started. The apple alone is enough to set both sides against each other again..."

"And the girdle will give us the compliance we need to maintain power," Kristy finished.

I barely suppressed my eye roll. The constant need for dominance with these creatures was beyond exhausting.

"But for now," Kristy continued, "I'm more interested in why this one—" she kicked the leg of my chair, nearly sending it toppling, "isn't answering my questions honestly."

I blinked up at her innocently. "But I am."

"You pledged loyalty to your sisters at your pledge ceremony, yet I feel lies bleeding off of you. You're resisting my powers, yet you shouldn't be able to. Which means..." Pursing her lips, she studied

me, her gaze finally settling on my necklace. After half a breath, her
eyes widened a fraction. "You're not who you say you are."

"What are you talking about?" Missa snapped.

Wordlessly, Kristy grabbed my necklace and tore it from my neck.
"Ow!" I cried.

A moment later, Missa gasped, and Stewart let out a startled
breath as my powers were suddenly broadcast to everyone in the
room.

"It all makes sense now." Kristy took a step back, letting my necklace fall to the carpet. "A filthy Ischyra, sent from Olympus to fetch
the apple and girdle." She clicked her tongue. "I should've expected
this."

My mind raced as I tried to figure out the best way to spin this in
my favor. There was literally no way I could convince her she was
wrong—my power would be clearly visible to her, Missa, and Stewart
now that Hecate's charm was gone.

"She was here this whole time?" Missa looked frantically between
Kristy and Stewart. "On whose orders?"

"Mine."

There was a thump at the door, Jared's unconsciousness body
slumping to the floor, and Eris walked in.

"Eris!" Startled, Kristy jumped back. Missa looked absolutely
ashen, and I didn't know whether to be relieved or irritated. Eris was
just as likely to want to help as she was to want to make matters
worse.

It was kind of nice seeing how scared Kristy and Missa seemed to
be of Eris. I mean, it was understandable. She was fucking terrifying
when it came to anyone on her bad side.

"You two think I didn't know you were after my things?" she
asked, nudging Jared aside with her foot. Her next words were
directed at me. *'Don't worry—I didn't kill him.'*

"We weren't—"

"I only wanted to keep them safe!" Stewart shouted, cutting Kristy
off as he struggled to stand. "I swear!"

"Sit down," Eris snapped. "I literally don't give a single shit about you, Stewie." Her ire shifted toward the witch and Siren as she pointed a long, thin blade in their direction. "These two are the ones I'm after."

Inwardly, I groaned. Eris could *not* end up with the sash. I'd never hear the end of it from Athena, and Eris would be absolutely insufferable. Not to mention, a goddess of discord with a coercion-soaked weapon was horrible for more reasons than I could count.

"Unchain him," Eris snapped, her head turning slightly in my direction.

With a sigh, I flexed my wrists and broke through my bonds. The phantom pain of chains flickered briefly, but I shoved it down as I stood and turned toward Stewart. Flicking a glance toward Eris, I crouched in front of him and attempted to reach out to him mentally, hoping the cloaking didn't block contact within the room.

'Mr. Aiden? Can you hear me?'

He gave a slight start. *'Yes, I can hear you.'*

'Listen very carefully. We cannot let Eris get that sash.' With an annoyed huff, I forced more of my power into the chains in an attempt to freeze them. Whatever spell they were infused with was a bitch and a half.

'What do you suggest we do?'

'You tell me. You're the one who tied one of Charon's coins to it.' Finally, a link started to thin. *'I'm not touching it, but we need to get the sash back to Olympus where it'll be safe.'*

'The coin will only transport itself and the person who touched it,' he said. *'Not the girdle. I ensured that would stay behind.'*

'Good thinking,' I muttered. I wondered who helped him manage that feat.

"Eris, we can work together on this," Kristy said. Eris had her backed against a wall, knife pointed at her throat. "We can all benefit. I know how much you'd love to take over—"

"You don't know anything about me," Eris said with a sneer. "You think I'd want the likes of *you*—" She gestured with the knife toward Missa and Kristy "running my family's mountain? Fat chance."

"The apple and girdle—"

"The apple," Eris cut off Kristy, "is tucked away safe on Olympus. You were too weak to get through Stewart's protection charms, but we weren't."

Stewart looked down at me, wide-eyed. *'Did you take the apple?'*

'Yep.' I continued focusing my ice on his chains. *'Under a floorboard, Stewart? Really?'*

'There was enough protection surrounding the house against witches and sirens...'

'Pro tip, Stewart. Never assume it ends with witches and sirens.' Finally, I got one side of his chains free, then went to work on the other. *'What's blocking communication out of this room?'*

'Probably the baldric,' he said. *'Missa purchased it for me, she said someone had woven protection spells into it. It's the only other thing in this room that would be powerful enough to affect either of us.'*

'It wasn't blocking anything when we were here the other night.' One more link and he'd be free.

'Then it must need to be activated to work,' he replied, flexing his free hand.

'We need to get you out of here.' The final link was about to give. *'Eris is pissed at them, but she'll be on you—'*

"You done with him yet?"

Startled, I peered up into Eris' eyes, then glanced over at Kristy and Missa. They seemed to be in some kind of heated argument, likely set off by Eris as a distraction. I was surprised she hadn't killed them, but knowing her, she'd want to draw it out, and clearly, they weren't her priority right now.

"Almost," I told her, going back to work.

"Good." The link broke, and Eris shoved me aside and jerked Stewart to his feet. "Come on, bud. You're gonna take a trip."

"Eris—"

"Shut up, Mary. I'm still pissed at you for not telling me you found the apple."

"Please," Stewart begged. "I was only trying to—"

"Help, we know," Eris said with a sigh. "Now's your chance to help some more. Go open the damn case."

"Eris, leave him alone and just call Athena," I hissed.

"I'll call my sister when I'm good and ready," she snapped. "I haven't laid hands on that girdle in centuries, so I'm having a look first."

With a heavy sigh, Stewart cast a wary glance at his wife and Kristy. "What will happen to them?"

Smirking, Eris stared at the two arguing women. "I haven't decided yet."

"All right." Stewart approached the case. "What do you want me to do?"

"You know exactly what to do," Eris said. "Touch the coin, get booted to the Underworld. We'll make sure you get back in one piece."

Something told me that was total bullshit, but I didn't press. Instead, I looked toward the windows.

"Where's everyone else?" I asked her.

"Outside," she replied, eyeing the sash hungrily as Stewart fumbled with a key. "I came back to check the study an hour ago, but the others can't get in."

"Why?" That would certainly explain why she was the only one to come for help, although I wasn't entirely convinced she was actually here *to* help.

"The baldric," Stewart said as he turned the key in the lock on the case. "That would be my guess. Its protective power likely extends outside this room if no other deities are able to get in."

"Yes, Hebe *would've* worked that kind of magic in," Eris said. "My sister loved her demigod a bit too much, if you ask me." Eyeing Heracles' baldric, she nodded. "We'll be taking that when we go, too, just so we're clear."

With a sigh, Stewart opened the case, and I shifted my attention to the baldric. If there was a way to turn the magic on, there must be a way to shut it off. But, since I didn't have enough time to screw around with riddles, I figured brute force was just as solid an option. Eris approached the case, her back to me. Silently, I formed a rock-solid mace of ice the size of a baseball in my hand. I'd prefer arrows but with no bow, they wouldn't do me much good. The spikes on the ball would do the trick.

Stewart caught my eye just as I lifted my arm to throw, his hand hesitating a fraction of a second over the coin. Eris noted his hesitation, turned her head, but by the time she reached out a hand to stop me, I'd launched the mace at the case holding the baldric. The glass shattered, and the spiked ball lodged itself in the ancient leather. Half a breath later, the spell evaporated and my head was filled with panicked voices.

44

DIONYSUS

The second I heard Mary's voice in my head, I slumped in relief. I'd been pacing outside the Aidens' house as Athena and Hecate tried to figure out a way past the protective magic that suddenly cloaked it. We'd tried to get Hebe to come break the spell on Heracles' baldric, but all we'd gotten was a curt, "Aphrodite can clean up her own messes, and I don't care what you do with the baldric" in response. Apparently a thousand years *had* been enough time for her to get over her dead lover, otherwise she would've been chomping at the bit to get it back.

'Get inside,' Mary demanded the second she felt my presence. *'Eris is about to send Stewart to the Underworld so she can get a few minutes alone with this damn sash.'*

"Athena!" I called.

"I heard! Let's go!"

Athena, Aphrodite, and I teleported to the library veranda, me praying that Eris wasn't choosing now to throw one of her tantrums. She was just as likely to hand the sash over as she was to vanish with it.

Bursting through the door, we were just in time to see Stewart Aiden vanish in a flash of light, and Eris pluck Aphrodite's girdle up from inside the case. Kristy and Missa were arguing, likely thanks to my sister, and there was a human slumped on the floor, unconscious.

Mary stood beside Eris, relief washing over her face when she saw us.

I rushed to her side, taking her face in my hands. "Are you alright?" She looked like she was in one piece, but I had to be sure.

"I am. I'm not sure about those two, though," she said, casting a look toward where Kristy and Missa were arguing. I was about to ask what they were doing when Aphrodite teleported to Eris' side, snatching her sash from her hands.

"Nice try, sis," she cooed.

Eris rolled her eyes, then laughed when she took in our expressions. "You guys really thought I wasn't going to hand it over. What little faith."

"Can you blame us?" Aphrodite snapped as she wrapped the sash around her midsection.

Athena jerked her chin toward Jared. "Go check on him," she told me. "I'm going to get Stewart."

She vanished, leaving me alone with my sisters, Mary, and the bickering witch and Siren.

I couldn't believe we'd missed a Siren hiding right in front of us. But then, I hadn't taken too much time to keep track of the Sirens after the war. They'd seemed happy and content once that they were able to go where they pleased, so I never thought any might want to pick up where Chaos left off.

"Come on, Aphrodite," Eris groaned. "Just let me—"

"No." Aphrodite's words rang with finality. "Absolutely not. Under no circumstances will you ever get your hands on my girdle."

Mary tilted forward, pressing her forehead against my chest, her shoulders shaking. For a moment, I thought she was crying, having reverted back to that dark place she'd been in.

Then, I realized she was laughing.

"What's so funny?" I asked.

"It's just...hearing Aphrodite tell Eris she'll never get her hands on her girdle..." A hysterical giggle escaped.

Smiling, I rubbed a hand down her back. "I'm happy to hear you can find the silver lining." Shifting my focus to my sisters, I asked, "What's our plan for those two?"

Eris cast a look of disgust toward Missa and Kristy, who looked to be nearly foaming at the mouth. "Let them keep going till they desiccate. That should be punishment enough."

Aphrodite eyed her consideringly. "Not your worst idea, I'll grant you. *Not* enough to let you borrow my girdle," she added when she saw Eris' wicked smile.

Mary giggled again. Yep. She was bordering on hysterical. I needed to get her out of there.

I sent out a call to the Ischyra who were standing by outside to come in and deal with Kristy and Missa. They'd be restrained and transported back to Olympus for questioning.

"Come on," I murmured. "They can finish up here."

"No, it's fine," she said, stepping back and rolling her shoulders. "I'm good. I want to make sure Stewart's alright." Frowning at the unconscious human, she added, "And Jared, I guess."

"Jared? The guy from bio? How'd he get wrapped up in all this?"

With a sigh, she made her way over to him. "My guess is Kristy tried to use him as a way into the mansion to get the apple." Opening her hand, she let water pool in her palm. "Clearly that didn't work, so she was using him as a lookout here." Crouching beside him, she tossed the water onto Jared's face, startling him awake.

"What the—" He jerked up, staring at his surroundings. "Where —where am I?"

"In trouble," Mary muttered. "Come on, get up."

Arguing sounded at the door, a female's voice shouting at one of the Ischyra who'd made their way inside.

"This is *my* house! You let me inside!"

I hurried toward the library door, opening it to find Calla Aiden staring down a female Ischyra who was blocking the door.

"Ms. Aiden, I cannot let you inside." The Ischyra sidestepped when Calla tried to duck around her. Willow stood behind her, pressed against the opposite wall.

"I've got it," Mary said, appearing beside me.

Eyes narrowed, Calla took in Mary's presence, then mine. "What the *fuck* is going on!"

"Go deal with the others," Mary murmured. "I'll talk to her."

When Mary went to take Calla's arm, Calla jerked away, scowling. "You better have a good reason for this!"

I exhaled, then shook my head. Telling someone you've deceived them was a common occurrence in Mary's line of work. She wouldn't always have to reveal her identity, and in most cases, she wouldn't. There was no getting around it this time, though, and in a way, that was good. She'd been struggling with the friendships she'd formed while she was at SLU, but part of me hoped she might be able to hang on to a friendship with Calla, since Calla's father was a demigod.

Still, Mary had deceived Calla, and Calla didn't seem the type to be overly forgiving, considering the circumstances.

I instructed one Ischyra to get the human out of there, then told the others who were filing in to start scouring the house for any other artifacts that needed to go back to Olympus. Then, I went back into the library to check on my sisters.

Eris was leaning against the now empty case that had held Aphrodite's girdle, sulking. Aphrodite was watching Kristy and Missa with interest, presumably trying to decide how long to leave them ranting at one another. Whatever argument Eris set off didn't have them screaming at each other yet, but it was a heated enough conversation that I could see it getting to that point.

"Where's your girl?" Eris asked.

"Dealing with Calla. Eris—"

"Stop, Dionysus. You know me better than that. I might be a bitch, but I wouldn't have taken that stupid thing for myself." Something akin to hurt flickered across her face. "And you know, it kind of pisses me off that you would think that."

"Eris, you started a damn *war* the last time you got your hands on the apple. What were any of us supposed to think when you showed up here tonight looking for the girdle and none of us could get inside?"

She shrugged, the movement jerky and petulant. "Maybe trusted that I was actually here to help, like I've said from the start."

"A little head's up would've been nice, then."

"Whatever. Aphrodite, you want me to shut that down?" The arguing was increasing in tempo and pitch.

"Yes, please. I'd like them questioned as soon as possible." Aphrodite watched as Ischyra began circling the room, examining each object Stewart had collected. They'd ultimately create a list of everything the Aidens had stored away in their home, then the Elders would decide what warranted returning to Olympus.

With a snap of her fingers, Eris silenced Kristy and Missa. "All right, you two. Time to go."

Four Ischyra materialized at their sides, taking their arms. "To the palace?" one asked.

"To the palace," Aphrodite confirmed. She and Eris placed a hand on the back of each female, then teleported them all back to the mountain.

Since I assumed Mary needed more time with Calla, I set to work helping the Ischyra catalog the items in the library.

45

MARY

When Calla, Willow, and I reached the kitchen, a steady stream of Ischyra were making their way through the house. I assumed they were going to find and return any deific items back to Olympus, although I wasn't sure how much they were going to find.

"You guys should sit down," I said. They both had every right to be angry with me, and I knew this was likely to be the first of many cases where I'd have to lie to people I liked. But still, it didn't change the fact that I didn't like doing it.

"What's going to happen to my parents?" Calla asked, ignoring my request.

"And who *are* you?" Willow added. "Clearly you've been lying to us this whole time."

Slowly, I sat down at the island. "Sit down, and I'll explain."

Warily, Willow sat down, but Calla was spitting mad and not about to cooperate. Seeing that she needed her space, I focused on Willow. As succinctly as possible, I explained my purpose—that I'd been sent to Lake Placid to monitor a situation and help return a few things to the Elders. I didn't explicitly state what Stewart and Missa were, just implied they'd had unfortunate dealings with Olympus that got them into some hot water. Missa was in more trouble than Stewart, but it was likely they'd both face consequences.

"Again, what's going to happen to my parents?" Calla demanded.

"That depends on them," I replied patiently. "They landed on the wrong side of the Elders. Considering your dad's motives weren't exactly nefarious, they might go easy on him. Your mom was plotting against the mountain, though."

Slowly, she sat down. "I didn't know, you know. About what they were doing."

"I figured as much."

"Are they—are they gods, or something?" Willow asked, her eyes darting to Calla, then me.

"I'm not at liberty to disclose any more details. I'm sorry." As I said it, I meant it. I was really, truly sorry that I couldn't provide either of them with any more information. "How did you two end up here, anyway?"

Calla huffed. "You were supposed to be the first one at the house. When you didn't show, I started calling your cell. It wasn't like you not to answer. Then Shep said he hadn't heard from any of the guys who were supposed to end up here, which was doubly weird, so we told him to stay on campus and we would come check things out." Shaking her head, she stared out the window. "I show up and the house is surrounded by Ischyra, and you're in here with—wait. That was Dionysus, wasn't it? At the door with you?"

"It was," I confirmed.

"I thought he looked familiar," she murmured. "I've seen pictures of the Elders, but they were really old. His hair was longer."

"So, what happens now?" Willow asked. "Will you stick around?"

"No, I'll get reassigned somewhere else."

Just then, Athena appeared in the doorway, a weary looking Stewart Aiden at her side.

"Daddy!" Calla leapt from her seat and ran to him, throwing her arms around his neck. Closing his eyes, he wrapped his arms around her, hugging her in a way that only a father would hug his daughter.

"I'm so sorry, Calla," he whispered.

"I'll give you a few minutes," Athena said. "Then we'll have to go."

Stepping aside, Athena leaned against a nearby wall, watching Stewart like a hawk.

'Is he done for?' I asked.

'No, I don't think so. He should've returned the objects to Olympus, but at the end of the day, he was trying to conceal them from those who would use them to harm us all. And, as Zeus' son, it's unlikely he'll see any prison time.'

'That's good. He doesn't seem like a bad guy.'

'No, he doesn't.'

"I should probably go..." Willow said, watching as Calla and Stewart said their tearful, and hopefully very temporary, goodbyes. "I don't think there's much more I can do. I can call a ride share or something."

"Willow, I'm really sorry about all this," I said. "I want you to know I really enjoyed my time with Iota Sig. I didn't think I would, but if circumstances had been, well, normal, you'd likely have me for life."

She smiled ruefully. "Then I wish circumstances had been different." She hesitated a moment, then opened her arms and hugged me.

Surprised, I hesitated, then returned the gesture.

"It was good to know you, Mary."

"You, too, Willow." I slumped back in my seat as she started to walk away, then remembered what I wanted to ask her. "Hey, Willow, can I ask you a question?"

Willow looked like back at me curiously. "What?"

"What's with the obsession you girls seem to have about the Iotas and Kappas pairing up?"

She rolled her eyes, then smiled. "Like we told you, pairings are good for morale. It promotes camaraderie. What, did you think we had some weird breeding program or something?"

"What?" I barely hid my surprise at how close she was to the truth. "It just seemed...odd."

"Well, it wasn't anything nefarious, so don't worry."

"Okay." There was one more thing I wanted to ask, but I almost felt wrong doing so. "And, um, would you mind telling Shep what happened? I don't think they'll let me go to him myself, but I don't like the idea of him thinking I just bailed."

"Of course." With one last farewell smile, she turned and left.

EPILOGUE
ONE MONTH LATER

The quiet ocean waves lapped gently under the boards beneath me, lulling me in and out of sleep as I lazed in a sun chair. A frozen margarita sat beside me, my water powers keeping it from melting in the hot Caribbean sun.

Footsteps sounded nearby, and a shadow covered my face. "Sleeping?"

I opened one eye and looked up at Dionysus, bare-chested wearing nothing but swim trunks. "Yes and no. What's up?"

He dropped down on the chair next to me and leaned back, pillowing his head on his hands. "I just talked to Athena."

"Really?" Dread pooled in my stomach as I steeled myself for the news of where she would send me next.

Once Stewart, Missa, and Kristy had been questioned, the Elders agreed Stewart could go back home under temporary house arrest. Missa and Kristy, unsurprisingly, had been tossed in the palace dungeons to await sentencing. Saia, the leader of the Sirens, completely renounced any affiliation with Kristy, exiling her entirely. As a half human witch, Missa had no real affiliations with anyone on Olympus who could speak for or against her. So, Zeus left it to Hecate to decide how to punish her. We were still waiting to hear exactly what their sentences would be, but it was clear there was no plan to go easy on either of them.

After Dionysus and I had submitted our final reports on the case, we each packed a bag and booked in to the Caribbean and rented one of those little huts over the water so we could soak up the tropics in peace. As the days went by, I started to get more nervous about how much time we would have before either of us got a new assignment.

"Yup. We're good to stay as long as we want."

"We're—what?" There was no way Athena or Zeus would let us stay away from Olympus indefinitely. I was too new and Dionysus was a damn Elder.

Turning his head, he smiled smugly and took my hand. "Apparently she delivered my message to Zeus about how unhappy I've been. At the risk of losing another son to Earthly temptations, Zeus has agreed to give us a sabbatical."

"Zeus...is giving us a vacation?"

"Hera might've gotten involved, as she tends to do." He let our joined hands hang between our chairs as I soaked in the good news.

"That's...amazing."

"Tessa and Nathaniel want us to meet them in Tuscany for a wine tour in two weeks, if you're interested."

"Um, *yeah*. That sounds amazing!" Tessa and I had been talking about doing a wine tour for ages.

Grinning, he kissed my knuckles. "They're looking at putting down some roots there, so we'll be able to go anytime."

"Anytime until Zeus decides it's time for us to go back to the mountain," I grumbled.

"Eh. I wouldn't worry about that. I was pretty clear that we'd be gone for a while, and a while for an immortal is a long time."

"Years?" I asked, not daring to hope.

"Decades, more like," he said with a grin.

Gods, that was music to my ears. A rush of relief washed through me, lifting the weight that had been on my shoulders for months. Suddenly, I felt free.

Biting my lip, I finally worked up the nerve to say what I'd been wanting to say for weeks. "I love you. You know that, right?"

Turning on his side, he touched my chin, his smile brilliant. "I love you, too, doll."

I stood up, then reached down and took his hand.

When he got to his feet, he leaned down and kissed me. "I want to show you the world, Mary."

"Then let's go see it."

THE END

Continue reading for a preview of The Valkyrie's Bond, book one in the Half-Blood Rising series...

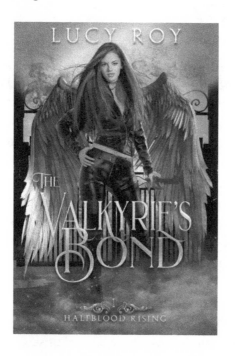

CHAPTER 1

Freya swooped over the docked ships in the Bay of Brystone, deftly slipping between towering masts and furled sails as she approached the darkened bulkhead before her. A shadow moved, a thing slithering up the slick wood toward the dimly lit street that ran along the harbor. As the stench of decay stung her nostrils, she let out a muttered curse and closed in.

It had been a slow night so far. Her aerial patrols had yielded little more than a few angry tavern-goers who needed only to sleep off their inebriation at the marshal station before finding their way home in the morning.

When the scent of a Jotnar draug hit her, she couldn't say she was disappointed that her night seemed to be picking up a bit. They always seemed to think coming into Lindorothian lands through the waterways was a surefire way to avoid being seen, yet the one and only reason Freya patrolled the bay was because of the incessant stupidity of the creatures who thought they could pull one over on her.

She slipped on a glamour to conceal her presence, circling wide before setting her feet down in an alleyway facing the bay, then darted toward the bulkhead. As the creature neared street-level, the cloying scent of death became stronger, mixing unpleasantly with the briny odor of low tide and causing Freya's nose to wrinkle.

Moments later, a set of clawed, bile-brown hands covered in pustules reached over the splintered wooden ledge, and a tall, black-haired draug appeared—a creature who'd managed to sneak from the northern lands of Jotunheim to hunt the citizens of Lindoroth.

If he was lucky enough to get past Freya, that was.

Cocking her hip against the stone building, Freya folded her arms across her chest, waiting until the creature found his footing on solid ground before announcing her presence. She forced back the desire to tug on the black vambraces protecting her forearms that itched thanks to the thin film of sweat that had formed underneath.

"Hello, there!" she said brightly, letting her glamour fall as she stepped forward, revealing broad, gray wings and sturdy armor made of thick, spelled leather.

The creature stopped, momentarily startled, then growled, low and guttural, when he took her in.

"You're a Valkyrie," he hissed, his gnarled hands clenching into fists at his sides.

"And you've got eyes," Freya replied dryly. She gestured toward the bay. "You know these waters are infested with kraken, don't you? They aren't so particular about what they eat, so you really should take more care when sneaking about."

"Kraken," he scoffed, the sound a mix between a growl and a hacking cough. His nostrils flared and the thick tendons in his neck trembled with the anticipation of a fight. "I thought your kind kept to the north these days. I'd be rewarded well if I brought you and those fancy feathers of yours back to Jotunheim."

Wrinkling her nose at the offensive odor that wafted toward her, she tightened the cord that fastened her long hair off her face and wordlessly curled her fingers in challenge.

The draug roared and lunged, his claws reaching for her neck. Just as he would've gotten his hands around her throat, Freya struck out, bringing the heel of her hand to his nose in a wet, satisfying *crunch* while the other fist found purchase in his gut. She spun, and the ridge of her wing sliced through the air and to his temple. Blood, black as pitch, spurted from his nostrils and ear as he roared in pain. Before he could regain his balance, she twisted his arm behind his back and pulled him hard against her chest. Plucking a single feather from her wing, she dragged the metallic, venomous tip across his neck, tearing his throat open from ear to ear, sending out a long arc of arterial spray. His gnarled hand flew up to grab her wrist, but he'd hardly gained purchase when he went slack against her. His entire body stiffened, and seconds later, he began foaming at the mouth as her venom made quick work of his insides.

Freya dropped the gurgling body to the ground, wincing as her feather regrew, the burn of venom filling the shaft. It was a sting she didn't think she'd ever get used to. Shaking it off, she wiped her hands, now reeking with blood, on her leather pants, scowling at the scrubbing she—or more preferably, her aunt—would have to do when she got home.

"Gloves, Freya," she muttered to herself. "Get yourself a damn pair of gloves."

With a huff, she hefted the draug's body over her shoulder and took to the skies once again, aiming this time for the wide, deep ravine that ran along the outskirts of Watoria, separating the small capital of Allanor from the dark expanse of evergreen forest that stretched for miles all around. The dark crevice worked well as a means of defense but was also the perfect dumping ground for pesky bodies that stunk to the heavens if burned.

Not wanting to waste time landing, Freya dropped the body into the black abyss, hovering above only long enough to hear the satis- fying *thunk* when it landed on the rocky floor before changing her direction back toward the city.

A moment later, her feet came down quietly on the roof of the local town hall, a three-story building that sat in a large public square in the center of town.

The square was a bustling area for shopping during the day, the small shops around it and down the sprawling side streets offering all manner of goods, from foods and freshly dyed fabrics, to talismans and potions imported from the other four realms of Lindoroth as well as the neighboring lands of Jotunheim and Dystone. Now, in the dead of night, it was silent, lit only by the few sparkling pixie lights that dotted the air along the stone sidewalks.

Crouching behind the building's wide brick chimney, Freya watched the street below, the building giving her the advantage of height without revealing her position. A few marshals, oblivious to her presence above them, ambled through the streets, no doubt keeping an eye out for mischief makers. The marshals were in charge of roaming the city streets, but it was Freya's job to climb and fly where no one else in Watoria would or could go.

Satisfied there were no immediate threats in the area, Freya scanned the city, assessing where she'd be most useful. The town-hall's rooftop was slick with rain, making any movement a bit cumbersome, so she waited, choosing her next location carefully. Settling on a brighter area toward the north, she took off toward the busy North Ward, a place rife with dancing, drinking, and debauchery. If she was going to find anything more to occupy her time tonight, it would be there.

For the next few hours, she flew low over the roofs, stopping here and there to avoid being seen by any ruffians or other such troublemakers in the darkened streets and alleyways. Despite the usefulness of a Valkyrie's wings, they were, in fact, wings, which were pretty damn hard to miss in the sky, often making the element of surprise difficult to maintain unless she wanted to drain her power by wearing an invisibility glamour for every patrol.

After depositing two more brawling drunkards at the marshal station, she landed on the clock tower of Watoria's secondary school —the school that had been her second home up until a few short months ago—and sat down on the edge, letting her legs dangle over the side. Leaning back on her hands, she looked around the city, watching as the last lights winked off in Watoria's late-night establishments.

She closed her eyes in contentment and tilted her face toward the night sky. *This* was her favorite time of night—when she was on patrol but also able to take just a few moments to enjoy the silence that cloaked this part of the city. Even her home in her own neighborhood in the South Ward, posh as it was, didn't hold the same level of tranquility she found sitting forty-feet above the rest of the world.

Casting her eyes toward the northern sky, she found the large grouping of stars that represented her namesake—Freyja, the goddess and progenitor of all Linds. The triangular shape was low to the horizon, telling her dawn would arrive in just a few hours. She pulled herself to a standing position and yawned, stretching her arms above her head as she took one last look around.

She saw nothing of import in the street, so she spread her wings, smiling to herself as the damp night wind rushed through her feathers. She shot forward, staying as low over the rooftops as was wise, for one final sweep over the city before returning to her quiet neighborhood.

Ana, her aunt and fellow Valkyrie, was waiting in the warm kitchen when she arrived wearing a green silk robe knotted tightly at the waist, a steaming cup of tea in front of her, her chin-length blond hair mussed from sleep. A flame, small and vibrant, floated inside a lantern in front of her, casting a soft glow over the room.

Freya paused at the sight when she stepped through the door.

Ana leaned back in her seat and arched a single, blonde brow as she walked in. "Busy night?"

With a sigh, Freya fully retracted her wings.

"Not so bad," she hedged as she kicked off her shoes and began to divest herself of her leathers, dropping her pants, shin guards, jacket, and vambraces until she was left in her underthings and a thigh-length beige tunic. She dropped down into one of the chairs with a huff, gladly accepting the cup of peppermint tea her aunt offered.

Ana gave her an expectant look. "Well?"

Freya took the tea and sipped before answering. "There was a draug," she said, setting the cup down. "I killed it. Aside from that, a few drunks got a bit rough with one another. They're sleeping it off at the marshal station." She jerked her chin toward her pile of leather. "One ripped a fastener off my jacket, the bastard."

"Then I suppose it's a good thing we've still got your mother's sewing kit. Go get changed," Ana said wearily, running a hand through her knotted hair. "Those clothes will start stinking if you've gotten any blood on them. I'll start them soaking. Once they're done, you can do the fastener repair." She held up a long finger. "And don't even think about asking me to do it, young lady. I told you ages ago you needed a new jacket."

Freya made a face, knowing there was no point in arguing. "Can I at least finish my tea first?" she complained.

"No. Now, go. Your tea will be here when you get back."

Grumbling, Freya made her way to the bathroom, stopping in her spacious bedroom to get a change of clothes on the way. She made a face in the mirror when she saw the messy state of her thick reddish-brown hair and the smudge of draug blood on the tip of one of her ears. Picking up a washrag, she scrubbed at it, wincing when she had to rub extra hard to get the blood off. After changing into a pair of soft silk pajamas, she pulled the tie out of her hair and ran her fingers through, then brushed out the tangles before wrapping it up into a high bun.

She cracked her neck, still a bit sore from carrying the weight of the draug across the city, and sighed.

Then, picking up her dirty shirt and underwear, she went back out to the kitchen to finish her tea.

Ana had just entered the kitchen when Freya returned. As Ana poured herself another cup of tea, Freya saw she wore a pursed expression.

"What is it?" Freya asked, sitting down and sliding her lukewarm tea toward her.

"I spoke with Nadya down the street, who heard from one of the marshals who heard from the commander. Aldridge is expected to send scouts out to gather up any remaining students who haven't yet arrived on campus." Turning, she took a slow sip of tea, her eyes narrowed at Freya over the rim. "Oddly enough, there seems to be just one who hasn't made her way there." When Freya merely stared back, Ana huffed out a sigh. "You were supposed to be on a ship four days ago! Now, Freya, I've been lenient with you, considering, but do you know how it looks—"

Freya rolled her eyes. "The first school term doesn't begin for five days, and I've already booked passage for tomorrow afternoon. Most of my things are packed. The only thing I'm missing out on is—"

"*Four* days, and you're missing out on getting to *know* people, reconnecting with people," her aunt lamented. "Gods above, Freya! Training at Aldridge is a gift most can only dream of and it's important you show your appreciation for it! I thought you'd be happy!"

Freya snorted and turned to gaze out the window. "I'm fairly certain my happiness is the last thing I need to worry about." She smirked at her aunt and circled her finger in the air. "You, on the other hand..."

"*I* will be returning to Iston, where I plan to live out my last few centuries happily with the rest of our kind. As honored as I was when your father chose me to raise you in his absence..." She sighed and smiled at her niece. "I'm eager to return home, just as you should be eager to dive into this new phase of your life."

"I'm going, aren't I? I have no intention of shirking my duties, Aunt Ana." And, as hard as it was for her to admit, she was excited to go back to Iladel, Lindoroth's capital, so she could finally learn and train under experienced professors. The physical training she'd received from the marshals and her aunt, her father's sister and a battle-tested Valkyrie, had been of the highest quality, but the education she would receive at Aldridge Academy, a small, elite university, would set her on another level.

"They won't change you as much as you fear," Ana said quietly. "If that's what's worrying you."

Freya was silent for a few moments, letting her mind wander over her future—one that had been laid out for her when she was just a child. Traveling several hundred miles to Iladel was something that had always loomed on her horizon, getting closer as each day, each *year* slipped past. It wasn't something she feared, but lack of fear did little to quell her anxiety of returning to a place and people she hadn't seen in years.

At the age of thirteen, her nineteenth year had seemed a million years away. Her mother, a general in the Allanorian army that helped protect the western lands of Lindoroth, had just been killed. Freya's father had decided she'd no longer be summering with the royal family, who were long-time family friends. After that, she was sent on her way. She'd trained and fought in Watoria, the capital of the realm of Allanor, earning herself a reputation with the local marshals at the age of sixteen as an ally worth having, while also ensuring she excelled in academics.

Her graduation from secondary school had come and gone three months' past, and since then, a clock had been ticking relentlessly in her mind, counting down the hours until she left her home for good. The obligations she'd made for herself here in Watoria would soon be replaced by those that had been set on her shoulders by others, that would recreate the female she'd grown into.

With a sigh, she drank down the dregs of her tea, wincing at the bitter taste of the leaves that had found their way through the infuser.

"It will be alright, Freya." Ana stared down at her own cup. "When you go... it will be alright."

"I know it will," Freya muttered.

CHAPTER 2

Freya was woken several hours later by rough shaking and her aunt hissing in my ear.

"Freya, wake up! There's been an attack!"

Freya bolted out of bed, her mind instantly alert as she lunged toward her armoire.

"Where?" She flung the wardrobe's doors open and pulled out a fresh pair of leathers and began tugging them on. "Was it draugs?"

"Yes, at Keranal's," Ana replied breathlessly.

Freya paused in the middle of fastening her jacket. "Draugs attacked a tavern? What in heavens for?"

Ana shook her head. "Not a clue, but the marshals are there now and there are at least a dozen patrons injured. Ashton just called for you. Do you need me to come?"

"No, stay here. If I need any backup, I'll send for you."

"Alright. Be safe, Freya."

Once her protective gear was secure, Freya stepped onto the front porch and let out her wings, leaping into flight and shooting toward the tavern she'd been dragging raucous drunks toward the marshals' wagon not three hours prior. She did a quick loop around the area to check the side streets for any movement before landing silently in front of the small building.

A marshal stood a few feet from the door, a male called Gideon, who she'd been friends with since she began working with them four years ago.

"What do you have?" she asked him.

He jumped at her sudden and silent appearance. "Freya! You startled me."

She flashed him a quick grin. "Apologies. My aunt said you called for me?"

He nodded gravely, then jerked his chin toward the door. "Ashton is just inside. I think he's waiting for you."

Nodding her thanks, Freya stepped through the doorway and cast her eyes around the darkened establishment. The smell of old ale mixed with death assaulted her nostrils as she stepped further inside, causing her face to scrunch. The stench was forgotten as she took in the scene before her, though. Ana's report had been accurate—there were about a dozen patrons bearing injuries of an attack. A few clutched their heads, no doubt thanks to hard blows, while others were pressing rags against seeping wounds.

"Ah, Freya." The warm voice of Ashton Carinald, one of Watoria's five senior marshals, reached her. She and Ashton had become friends not long after she moved to Watoria when she was thirteen. Three years her senior, he'd been the first to suggest she train with the marshals. Their friendship teetered on the edge of romantic at times, but considering her imminent departure from Watoria, she tried very hard to keep from giving him any type of false hope.

She frowned as he approached. "How long ago was this?"

He dragged a hand through his blond curls and blew out a breath as he gazed around them. "Maybe three hours ago, so far as we can tell."

"Three hours? How—" She huffed out a breath though her nose. "They were entranced?"

Ashton shook his head. "Poisoned. We found a vial of widow

venom on the ground outside and the doors were locked. They're only just waking up."

Frowning, she began to make her way around the room, examining the patrons as she went. She crouched down beside a witch with skin pale as chalk who was clutching her heart.

"May I see?" she asked gently.

The female nodded and pulled her hand away, revealing four vicious claw marks across her chest, the edges hard and blue.

"I didn't see much." Her lips trembled as she struggled to meet Freya's gaze. "I felt the hit, then it all went black."

"These are draug claw marks," Freya said, glancing up at Ashton briefly before continuing. "It may take a bit longer to heal, but give it a few hours and you should be good as new," she told the female with a smile.

The female returned her smile, and Freya gave her hand a squeeze before shifting position so she could get a better look at the male bear shifter slumped on the floor beside her.

She assessed the large gash across his neck and gave him a questioning look. He grimaced, then nodded and tilted his chin up.

Touching a finger to the male's jaw, she nodded. "These are draug marks as well. Slightly different, though. A bit more jagged than hers," she said, indicating toward the female. She winced and lightly touched the edge of the wound. "Have you tried shifting to heal yourself?"

The male nodded. "It was the first thing I did, but my strength still hasn't returned."

Freya gave him an encouraging smile. "Give it time. I know how painful draug venom is."

"A pack was seen roaming the outlands a few days ago," Ashton informed her. "They emptied the till and relieved all patrons of their valuables before leaving."

Freya gave a hum of annoyance and stood, wiping her hands on her pants as she turned to face him. "I killed one earlier. It was climbing over the bulkhead across from the fishery. He was alone, though."

"What did you do with the body?" Ashton asked sharply.

"I dumped him in the ravine." She cocked her head to the side, her lips quirking. "He made a nice *crunch* when he landed."

Ashton ran a hand over his face and shook his head. "Considering how strictly Caelora guards the Jotunheim border, don't you think it would have been wise to report that when it happened?"

Freya's eyes narrowed. "This isn't the first time Jotnar draugs have gotten into our lands. Caeloiran knights are strong, but until they agree to send more support to the coast, draugs and their ilk will continue to come in by sea. And as I said, I dealt with it."

"And you're certain he was alone?"

"Yes."

Ashton's brow lifted in question.

"Yes, Ash, I am certain he was alone," she said with a smirk. "They're defensive creatures. If he had others with him, they would've come after me. That and he was talking about dragging me back to Jotunheim in exchange for a handsome reward. It's unlikely he would've been willing to share such wealth."

Ashton chuckled darkly. "I would've paid to see that fight." He scanned the patrons around them. "Is there a chance this could be payback, then?"

Freya's eyes widened at his insinuation. "You think this is *my* fault?"

He shifted his stern gaze back to her, and a small muscle in his jaw twitched. "I think retaliatory attacks are something draugs are known for, *considering* their defensive nature."

Freya blew out a small breath to keep herself from delivering Senior Marshal Ashton Carinald a backhand worthy of his title.

"If that were the case," she said slowly, "they would've come after me and Aunt Ana, not a bunch of people I don't know."

"Maybe. Maybe not. Are you certain you killed it?"

"I stunned it and sliced its neck with my own feather. It's dead as a goddamn doornail."

Ashton's warm brown eyes ran over her face, then cast a glance toward the door where another officer had just entered and gestured for her to follow him outside.

When they stepped into the cool night air, his expression softened, and he brushed a thumb across her cheek. "You're right. I'm sorry. I didn't intend for it to seem as though I don't trust your judgement."

"Apology accepted." She grinned, then backed away when he tried to reach for her and pull her closer. "I'll do a few more sweeps around the city and let you know if I find our assailants. And, if it will ease that pretty mind of yours, I'll also confirm that the body I dropped earlier remained where I left it."

A smile tugged at the corner of his mouth, one that melted the bit of annoyance she'd allowed to creep in.

Once outside, she stormed away from the building, frustrated at the turn the night had taken. With a leap, she was airborne, banking hard to arc over the nearby buildings. She flew down dark alleys and streets, her wings pinned to her body, cutting through the air soundlessly. Keeping her eyes and ears peeled for any sort of disturbance, she did a thorough air patrol of the North Ward, moving next into the East Ward's marketplace, and, finally, the residential neighborhoods that dotted the Southern and Western Wards.

As she continued her sweep, her concerns seemed to be valid. A few drunks stumbling home, a couple fornicating behind the town hall, and a few vagabonds settling in for the night under a bridge were the only activity she saw. When she glided over the outermost neighborhoods, her worry grew. If the draugs had already fled the city, there was little chance they'd be caught.

When she'd covered the rest of the city, she turned eastward, aiming for the spot where the sun was beginning to lighten the sky. In the soft glow of dawn, the deep ravine appeared like a thick black line drawn in the ground around the city. Banking low, she eyed the surrounding area carefully. It was unlikely any draugs in the area would attempt to recover their fallen comrade, but it wasn't in Freya's nature to assume anything of those creatures, wretched as they were. The Jotnar were, on the whole, quite intelligent and not unlike the

Linds, although the lower strata of their society—draugs, huldra, and their ilk—couldn't make that same claim. They ran on instinct and greed, which was often more than enough to get them killed.

Rubbing her fingers together, she blew on them, forming a soft ball of glowing light that illuminated the air around her as she descended into the darkness. Coming to a silent stop, she held the light at shoulder-height and looked around.

The draug was just as she'd left him—dead, his body broken, the boulders he'd fallen on coated with blood and whatever muck had spilled when his flesh tore on contact with the sharp granite.

Annoyed that Ashton's words had caused her to question her own methods, Freya pulled a vial of accelerant from the pouch at her waist and cracked it open, pouring the contents over the thing's ruined body. She flicked the small light that still glowed in her hand downward, setting the corpse ablaze. After watching for a few moments as the green flames slowly turned the draug to ash, she took to the air for what she hoped would be the last time for the night. She'd check in with Ashton later in the morning, but for now, she wanted— needed—rest.

Freya landed quietly on the cobblestone street in front of her house, keeping her steps silent as she ascended the stairs toward the front door. She knew it would be of little use—if she knew her aunt, Ana had refused to go back to sleep until she knew Freya was home and safe in her own bed. At times, it annoyed Freya that her aunt had fallen so effortlessly into the role of mother after her own had died. But despite Ana's softer nature, she was nearly as good a fighter as Freya, having been subject to the same training regimen in her youth, centuries ago. Unlike Freya's father, though, Ana hadn't followed the same path most of their kind did, by entering the military or law enforcement field. Instead, she'd chosen medicine, acting first as a physician in the field for Lindoroth's royal army, then as a traveling physician in Watoria, a job that kept her aunt busy most days.

Freya turned the knob as quietly as she could, hoping in vain she could avoid the annoying screech that almost always sounded halfway through a full turn. Much to her dismay, the old mechanism squealed, sharply announcing her entry.

When she stepped through the foyer and into the kitchen, she came to a halt, her eyes widening, then narrowing to slits as she took in the scene before her.

Her aunt sat at the table, a look of resignation on her face, her hair rumpled as if she'd actually attempted to get back into bed. A fresh cup of steaming tea sat in front of her. Four males, slender and resplendent in their gold-adorned navy blue uniforms, stood at attention in the four corners of the room, the white epaulets and bronze shields pinned to their lapels identifying them as Iladel's palace knights. The crest of House Harridan, Lindoroth's ruling family, was carved into the metal—two large, golden lynx reared on their hind legs in mid-battle. Each guard wore a longsword at one hip and an onyx-handled dagger at the other.

Freya's nose twitched as she took in their scents, the sharp, earthy smell identifying them as wolf shifters, the type most commonly employed by the monarchy.

A fifth male, tall and foreboding, with dark brown hair shot through with streaks the color of cinnabar, stood beside Ana. His uniform was pitch black with mother-of-pearl buttons. The gold epaulets identified *him* as the commander of King Salazar's Royal Army. The corner of his mouth quirked up when Freya appeared, amusement at her surprise lighting his aged gray eyes.

Freya allowed herself three seconds to recover, then tilted her chin up and folded her arms across her chest. "Commander."

He inclined his head in greeting. "Freya."

"Are you here to drag me off?"

The commander set down the glass of water he'd been drinking and folded his arms, mimicking Freya's pose. "You should have been on a ship days ago."

She walked toward the stove and poured herself a cup of tea from the kettle that still sat there steaming. Ignoring the guard to her left, she busied her hands doctoring her tea with cream and a bit of honey before turning to face the commander again. Leaning against the stove, she crossed her legs at the ankle and took a slow sip of the steaming liquid. She held back a smug smile as the tension in the room thickened, refusing to acknowledge the dirty looks she was sure her aunt was sending her way.

"Is there a reason you couldn't wait until daylight to make this visit?" Freya asked. "It's been a busy night, as I'm sure you know."

"Ah, yes." The commander nodded knowingly, and she winced at the impending barb. "You killed a single draug that was sneaking onto a deserted street, if I'm not mistaken, while twelve of Watoria's citizens were being beaten and robbed less than a mile away." He strode forward, stopping a foot away from her, hands now clasped behind his back. The authority behind the gesture, the kind one had achieved after spending several centuries as a warrior, oozed from him, slapping Freya's own sense of confidence down in a single hit.

"Odd coincidence, isn't it?" he mused. "One draug keeping one of the city's strongest fighters occupied while his comrades attack elsewhere."

Freya ground her teeth together. Commander Balthana delighted in irritating others when they misstepped, and the pleasure he took in goading her, trying to get a rise out of her, was clear in his eyes.

"Yes, I suppose that would be an odd coincidence," Freya said slowly, cursing herself for not considering the possibility when she'd spoken with Ashton. "Although, organized crime has never been their strong suit."

"Quite true." He held up a finger. "But a good warrior knows that her biggest enemies are ignorance and assumption. You allow your assumptions of a creature's behavior to be dictated by what you think you know."

With a sigh, Freya straightened her shoulders. "If you're going to cart me off to Iladel, I'd like to at least get a few hours' sleep before I go. May I have that, at least?"

The commander clicked his tongue and shook his head. "Unfortunately, no. Your disdain for your obligations has caught the eye of those above me. I'm under orders to bring you—kicking and screaming, if necessary—to the capital *now*."

"But—"

He held up a hand at her protest. "No, you may not rest. The belongings you've already packed have been taken to the carriage and will be loaded onto the ship for Iladel shortly. What you *may* do is change out of those filthy clothes and be in the carriage out front in ten minutes. I have an army to lead, and chasing the king's wayward students is preventing me from doing my job." He ran his eyes over her hair and sighed. "And do something about that hair. It looks as though you've been rolling in mud."

She held his stare for several moments before giving him a small smile. "I'll be ready shortly. Feel free to let Ana go back to sleep," she added, glancing down at her aunt, who already appeared halfway there. "She's had a rough night as well."

Not waiting for permission, Ana stood.

"Safe travels, Officers," she said quietly. "Commander."

He nodded a farewell, then turned back to Freya once Ana left the room. "Ten minutes."

Pushing herself away from the stove, she brushed past him. "Make yourselves comfortable."

When she reached her room, she found her aunt perched on the edge of her bed, Freya's repaired jacket draped over the back of a chair.

"Thank you," Freya said softly, picking it up.

"I couldn't very well trust you to do it right, could I?" she mumbled. "Half-witch or not, using your magic to sew has never been your strong suit."

"Are you sure you don't want to come with me?" Freya asked, sitting down gently on the end of the bed. This was a conversation they'd had countless times, and though Freya knew the answer, she needed to ask one last time before she left. "I'm sure there are plenty of opportunities for healers in Iladel."

Ana smiled sleepily and shook her head. "No, my job here is done. I'll come visit when I can, though."

"I know," Freya said with a sigh. She flopped back on the bed and closed her eyes. "Gods above, why does he have to be so... tyrannical?"

"Centuries of experience being such? Best not to goad him, dear," Ana warned. "It's a long way to the capital from here, and the king and queen don't take kindly to their commander being harassed."

"Harassed," Freya scoffed. "If anyone's being harassed, it's the two of us." She gave Ana a small frown. "Shouldn't you be in bed?"

"I'll go to sleep once you're gone," Ana said, sitting up. "I don't think either of us intend for you to leave here without packing the rest of your things, so let me help."

Freya grinned. "You couldn't be more correct."

NEARLY AN HOUR LATER, after multiple rounds of Commander Balthana banging on Freya's locked and spelled bedroom door, she emerged with a knapsack slung over one shoulder packed with the few articles of clothing she hadn't had time to stuff in her trunks.

Ignoring Ana's exasperated look and the expression of pure annoyance Balthana wore, Freya strode down the front walk toward the first of two large, black carriages that waited at the street's edge. Each was pulled by a single black stallion and bore the royal crest on the door. She held her head high as she climbed inside, taking great care to kick her feet on the sill before sitting on the red-cushioned bench. Once settled, Ana stepped up to the door and reached inside, taking Freya's hands.

"Be good, Freya," she said, the warning clear in her tone. "It's been a long time since you've been in the capital and at court. Things change over the years."

Freya smiled. "Have you known me to be incapable of adapting?"

Ana gave her a pointed look, her eyes sliding to the left toward where the commander stood before responding. "Incapable and unwilling are two different things."

"I am fully willing to adapt to my imminent change in circumstances. I promise." She squeezed her aunt's hands for extra emphasis. "I'll get all my brattiness out before we've reached midway, don't worry," she teased.

"Please see that you do," Ana said wearily. "Salazar and Ordona are lovely monarchs, but even they have their limits."

Leaning out, Freya planted a kiss on Ana's cheek. "It will all be fine. Try not to worry. I'll send word when I get there. And, Aunt Ana? Travel safe."

"I will, dear. You do the same."

"Time to go," the commander said.

Smiling reluctantly, Ana stepped away from her. "You be good, Freya," she said in one last warning. "I'll see you at Winter Solstice."

Balthana pulled himself up inside the carriage and took a seat across from Freya.

With one last farewell, Ana waved and stepped back from the road.

Freya took one final look at the house she'd lived in for the last six years, surprised when she found herself struggling against a lump in her throat. Slowly, the carriage pulled away, the tall wheels rattling so loudly on the cobblestone Freya knew better than attempt to sleep on the short trip to the port.

"You'll be happy to know I received word from Officer Carinald," Balthana said. "They located a cadre of draugs in the forest less than an hour ago. The draugs have been destroyed, and the stolen goods are on their way back to their owners."

Freya let out a quiet breath, relieved to know she wasn't leaving the city behind with a mess for the marshals to clean up. "Thank you for the update. I appreciate it."

He gave her a curt nod.

Not wanting to dive into a full conversation just yet, she contented herself with resting her forehead against the cool glass, watching as the rows of familiar houses slipped past, drinking it all in one last time before she left Watoria behind for good.

CHAPTER 3

A short while later, Freya found herself settling into a first-class cabin on the ship leaving Watoria for the capital.

A small bed covered in lush velvet the color of new spring leaves caught her eye, contrasting with the carpeted floor in deep colors of autumn. With the white-paneled walls, gauzy curtains in shades of sunrise, and touches of gold in the fluffy bedding, the cabin seemed to encompass all five of Lindoroth's regions in one small space. The beauty of it made Freya feel a bit remorseful about her filthy shoes, so as soon as she sat down on the small bed, she tugged them off and changed them out for her spare boots, ignoring the commander's smug look as she wrapped her dirty boots in a tunic and shoved them into her bag.

Satisfied, she slid her bag under the bed and met his stare, jolting slightly when the ship let out a loud *creak* as it pulled away from the dock and into the Southern Canal, which would take them south through Saith and Edhil, the two southernmost realms of Lindoroth, then east to the capital realm of Iladel.

"Will I go straight to the academy when we arrive, or do you have any stops planned?" she asked.

"You'll be taken straight there," he told her. "Classes start in four days and you'll need to get settled in before then."

"And what about supplies? Clothes?" She gestured toward the simple nature of her outfit. "As much as I'm loathe to admit it, my current wardrobe isn't well-suited for the capital, considering. I'd planned to take one last trip to the markets before leaving this afternoon."

"All of those things will be provided to you. We'll arrive in Iladel in two days' time, so take the third to acquire your supplies and make a trip into Iladel this week to purchase some new clothes. Everything will be billed directly to the capital."

Her brows shot up in surprise. "That's a dangerously long leash to give a girl," she said, smiling. "What if I find a sudden taste for Errestian jewels? I hear Edhil's mines have been quite fruitful this year."

He gave her a dry look. "Your 'leash' consists of clothing, texts, and whatever other supplies the professors at Aldridge require of you. Your roommate will show you the best places to purchase what you need."

Freya wrinkled her nose in distaste. "So I'll have a roommate, then? Have you met her?"

He nodded. "Grevillea Calliwell. A cousin to Prince Aerilius and daughter of Orin Calliwell, the Governor of Edhil. Her mother is the queen's sister."

Freya gawked. "Grevil—good heavens, is that the name she goes by? Please tell me it's not!"

He gave her a warning look. "She goes by Lea. She's quite lovely."

Freya gave a noncommittal *hmm*, unsure if she was ready to trust the commander's version of 'lovely' just yet. It had been her experience that females who lived in the capital could be *lovely* in their own way, but that way typically involved a long look down pointed noses at anyone who wasn't a lifelong Iladelian.

"A schedule of upcoming events you'll be required to attend will also be made available, although some final adjustments are still being made."

Freya rubbed her fingers across her forehead as a small headache began to form behind her eyes. "What kind of events?"

"A few dinners, the annual commencement ball, and the Winter Solstice celebration, among others. I would recommend bringing Lea with you when you're choosing attire for those."

She narrowed her eyes. "Lea..." Freya couldn't bring herself to use the poor girl's proper name. "Should I expect her to act as my shadow, or will she simply be my roommate?"

"That is entirely dependent on you, although the hope is that you'll become friends."

"And is she aware of who I am?"

"She is."

"Lovely," Freya murmured.

He flicked a glance out the small porthole window, then tugged the heavy velvet curtains closed to block out the light. "We'll be on the water for some time. You might as well get some sleep. My cabin is just down the hall if you need anything."

THERE WAS a favorable wind behind them as they sailed, so the trip to the capital took just under three days, much of which Freya spent abovedeck talking with the crew, sunning her wings, and generally lazing about. The commander made appearances now and then, but for the most part he was off doing whatever it was he did. He was a curmudgeonly fellow on a good day, so Freya wasn't overly eager to bask in his company.

When she awoke on the third day to the steady sound of the sloshing water and the call of gulls, the sun appeared high in the sky, and the flowering fields of the southern realm of Edhil were drifting past outside the porthole beside her bed.

There was a knock at her door. Groggily, she rolled out of bed and opened it, then greeted the commander with a tired wave.

"It's nearly noon," he said by way of greeting. "You shouldn't have stayed out so late."

"The crew wanted to wish me well before the start of term," she muttered, ignoring his chastising tone as she flopped back down on the bed. "How much longer until we arrive?"

"About an hour and a half." He stepped aside as a servant set a pot of coffee and a paper-wrapped sandwich on the bedside table. "We passed through Saith and into Edhil about three hours ago. We're just outside Errest now, so pack up your things."

Once the commander and the servant left the room, she began to eat the sandwich, wincing a bit as the crusty bread scraped against her still-dry throat. The roasted chicken was juicy and flavorful, though, and by the time she was done, she felt more alert and less like she'd been up half the night with the crew members.

After packing up her belongs and tugging on a pair of soft linen pants and pale blue tunic, she went abovedeck and spent the rest of the time watching the lush scenery of Edhil slide past.

Her home realm of Allanor consisted largely of grasslands and evergreen-covered mountains dotted through with a few towns, with the largest city being Watoria, the realm's capital. But where Allanor was full of vivid golds, greens, and reds, the region of Edhil that drifted past now was filled with all color imaginable. Far to the south sat the Edhilian desert, a dry, hot expanse of land that spanned most of the southernmost portion of the continent. The waving grasses appeared greener, the trees taller, and even the sun's golden glow seemed to glitter a bit brighter.

The sun was well past its midpoint by the time the captain rang the bell signaling their arrival. As the crew began to prepare to dock, Freya got her first view of the capital, a sight she hadn't seen in nearly six years.

The bustling city spread out before her, rising to the foothills that led up to the craggy peaks of the Aldridge Mountains. Five hundred years earlier, the region had been a shared capital between humans and the Linds, a race of shifters and magic-wielders. When a chain of earthquakes shattered their lands and weakened the humans, the Jotnar, a race of witches and warlocks who lived to the north of Lindoroth, had attempted to take the human territories for their own, taking any opportunity to kill, capture, or enslave every human they could find. After nearly a decade at war, the Linds assisted in negotiating a treaty that allowed the humans safe passage to settle on the eastern continent of Dystone, while the Linds and Jotnar divided the western continent.

Freya cast her eyes upward as the ship slid into the port. From her vantage point, she could just make out the high, sharp turrets of the palace peeking over the lower part of the mountain far in the distance. When the crew dropped anchor and began throwing out ropes to tie down, her attention was drawn down to the busy port, where she saw gray-uniformed guards bearing the official seal of the capital swarming the area.

"Why are there so many guards?" she asked the commander beside her, lowering her voice to a whisper once they disembarked and stepped onto the aged wooden dock.

"Guard presence increased last week when students began arriving at Aldridge. Prince Aerilius will be attending Aldridge this year." Balthana gave her a curious frown. "How do you not know this?"

Freya's heart stuttered a bit and her words carried a sharp edge when she responded. "How would I?"

"Hmm. You received all of your correspondence from Aldridge, correct?"

"Yes, of course," Freya replied, hefting her duffel over her shoulder as he began to lead her up the dock toward the roadway.

The prince had been a good friend of Freya's in their youth—one of her closest—but time and distance had caused that friendship to wane, and now nearly six years had gone by since they'd last spoken. While she knew she'd see him soon enough, she was surprised to hear she'd see him every day.

"Well, had you taken the time to read it," he admonished, "you would've received news of the increased guard presence in the capital and on campus due to the attendance of the crown prince." He didn't bother looking back at her as they quickly navigated the busy port, his purposeful stride and black uniform parting the crowds like water. A long line had formed at the tall gates that led into the city, all passengers who'd just disembarked, each going through the process of stating their business before being allowed through.

Freya quickened her pace to keep up with him, ignoring the glares and grumbles of those queued up beside them. The commander stepped through a narrow door cut into the gate, giving a terse nod to the guards as he passed, then held it open for Freya to step through and onto the paved walkway.

"Why is he attending? That wasn't—surely he can acquire training of equal measure privately and without all the fuss?" Freya adjusted her bag on her shoulder. "It seems a bit unfair to the rest of the students, wouldn't you say? Having a prince on campus, attending classes?"

"Perhaps, although the same could be said for you, considering your background. The assumption, of course, is that he'll find a mate and choose his queen while he's there."

Freya snorted quietly. "A farce, if I ever heard one. Everyone knows the king and queen will choose his betrothed. Will he be living on campus?"

The commander gestured toward a black carriage trimmed in gold and bearing the royal crest waiting at the curb. "No, he'll continue to live at the palace. Come, let's get you settled in."

As was her habit, Freya took in her surroundings as she walked, letting her eyes drift about as she stepped toward the carriage. The city's tree-lined cobblestone thoroughfare stretched away from the station, the foot and carriage traffic neatly separated by a long, narrow flowerbed that bisected the road that stretched off into the distance. Looking skyward, Freya imagined the pale color of the stone would appear as a long, white ribbon from above, stretching from the port clear across the city before splintering off into the rolling hills beyond.

"You know," she commented, turning to face him as he sat down on the bench across from her, "it's quite unprecedented for the royal commander to be escorting one wayward student to school. Might I ask your reasoning?"

He gave her a stern look. "The king and queen don't take kindly to 'wayward students,' especially when an invitation to Aldridge has been handed to her *personally*. As the king, queen, and royal commander are aware of said student's propensity for flying off, they thought it best she have an escort."

"If said parties are so aware of my propensities, they should also know that I wouldn't shirk my duties simply to spite them."

"Certainly, but one can't blame them for being a bit overcautious."

Freya made a face but didn't argue. Her invitation to Aldridge had been written just after her fifth by the king himself when her status as a true halfblood—a Lind who inherited equal parts witch and shifter blood—became clear around her sixth birthday. In unions like those of Freya's parents, where one was a shifter and the other a witch or warlock, witch blood always won out. It was incredibly rare for a person to be both shifter and witch, but on the rare occasion a half-blood was born, they were prized, often coveted.

One morning when her father had taken her down to the training yard to learn with the children who were training to become squires, the king came down to check on the progress of the students. After watching Freya hit archery targets thirty yards away and fling knives made of magic alongside the prince and some of the best squires of the king's Guard, Salazar had insisted she attend once she came of age. Her parents and aunt had been proud, as had she, but her pride had faded years later, when her mother, a highly-respected witch who worked for the crown, was killed on a routine patrol of the northern border between Caelora and Jotunheim.

Ever since, her father had become distant, immersing himself in his work and checking in only once or twice a month to ensure both she, the marshals, and her teachers in Watoria were keeping up with her training, continuing to prepare her for life in the Capital. Her aunt Ana had ensured the sums of money left behind when Cina passed were used for housing, food, schooling, and anything else she might have needed.

"You know, I was under the impression you were eager to attend Aldridge," Balthana commented, breaking her from her reverie.

She looked at him. "I was just dragged from my home after patrolling and fighting all night, put on a boat for three days, and now I'm being taken to meet this new best friend that's being forced on me. It's not lack of eagerness that has me down, it's exhaustion and a strong desire to bathe."

"Fair enough." He nodded. "But I trust you'll keep your thoughts to yourself once you arrive. Get it out of your system now because Headmistress Dyren won't tolerate it."

"Your lack of faith in my ability to simper is appalling."

"No one expects you to *simper*, just to behave."

"So long as I get a few hours of sleep before I'm expected to present myself to anyone, I will be the picture of propriety," she said primly.

Exasperated, Balthana shook his head. "A lie, if I've ever heard one."

CHAPTER 4

They rode the rest of the way in silence, Freya occupying herself with watching the citizens of Iladel bustle about the city as their carriage rolled along the cobblestone streets. Iladel really was a beautiful place, and despite having been absent for six years, Freya felt a sense of home as they rolled past the people stepping in and out of shops and restaurants. It was nearly three times the size of Watoria and seemed to run at double the pace, but Freya had always enjoyed sinking into the capital's exuberance as a child. She and her mother had taken many trips into the city, wandering the busy streets and strolling past restaurants and taverns, dressmakers and tailors, florists, jewelers, and art galleries that burst with goods and wares from across the realms. As she and the commander traveled now, apartment buildings and homes rose above the din, and when she turned to look through the rear window, Freya could make out the tops of tall masts of ships docked in Iladel's port slipping off in the distance.

When they finally pulled down the shady road that led to Aldridge, Freya shifted in her seat to get a better glimpse of the tall, wooden gates that loomed ahead. Towering oak trees bordered the sprawling grounds of the university, and as unseen magic opened the gates to usher them inside, neatly-trimmed lawns rose away from the main road. A stone path that bisected the vibrant lawn led from the gates to the behemoth stone structure that housed the classrooms of the academy. Some students lounged about on the front lawn, while others walked along the paths in small groups chatting with one another.

She thought it would be rushed, more fitting to the capital, but instead it seemed... serene.

As Freya hopped down from the carriage, taking the footman's hand when he reached out to help, she inhaled deeply, taking in the scent of the woods, the pines and oaks that towered above, and the flower beds overflowing with blooms that waved gently in the breeze along the fence. The unfettered scent of nature was a far cry from the brine-and-soot smell of Watoria, and while she felt a bit homesick being so far from what she'd become accustomed to, she had to admit this wasn't the worst place to call home. Everything about it carried an air of serenity, something she was suddenly eager to explore in depth.

"I take it by your expression you aren't entirely disappointed to be here?" Balthana asked.

Keeping her eyes trained forward, she huffed. "I suppose circumstances could be worse," she admitted. "Although I've never once said I wouldn't like it here."

"Come, I'll take you to your dormitory."

Freya desperately wanted to get a lay of the land from above, but instead chose to follow the commander as he led her away from the carriage.

Despite her skills, her rarity and parentage often caused others to either avoid her entirely or attempt to slip into her good graces. She knew it was only a matter of time before her true identity was revealed, but for the time being, she just wanted to bask in her anonymity. A student eager to succeed, just like everyone else, as opposed to the daughter of one of the fiercest warriors and most gifted witches Lindoroth had ever seen.

Tightening the strap of her bag on her shoulder, she followed the commander through the wide gates and up the path toward the main building. Matching her stride to his, she eyed the busy campus warily.

"Shouldn't I check in somewhere?" she asked when he began to veer off the main path toward a cluster of four stone buildings nestled along the woods away from the academic building that had rose with grandiosity in front of them. Small turrets rose at all four corners of each, the windows tall and arched. If the buildings hadn't been so lovely, the silence and ivy snaking up the walls would've made them seem abandoned, Freya thought.

"That's already been taken care of," he replied. "You're to meet with Headmistress Dyren tomorrow morning to go over your course-work, schedule, and whatever else she feels needs discussing."

"What am I to do with myself for the rest of today, then?" she asked, annoyed. "You were in such a rush to get me here, after all."

"Meet your new roommate, get to know the campus, hopefully make some friends," he said, ascending the three marble steps that led to the glass dormitory entrance. "I'm quite sure those skills aren't beyond you."

Clenching her teeth, she sent him a stormy glare as she passed him and entered the building, where a wide, curved staircase greeted them. On the left, an archway opened into a quaint common area with overstuffed couches and a fireplace, and to the right, a second archway revealed a small study area, the walls lined with shelves of books from floor to ceiling. A fireplace was set in the far wall, and three long wooden tables sat in the center of the room, giving Freya a clear image of students hunched over texts and whispering softly. Both rooms were brightly sun-lit through the curtained windows that faced the busy grounds of campus, with gas-fueled lamps installed on the walls to chase away the gloom come nightfall.

As the door shut with a *thud* behind them, Freya noticed it was conspicuously quiet inside.

Freya peered into the other rooms. "Where is everyone?"

He started up the stairs, not looking back as he answered. "On their way to a gathering with the headmistress. I thought it best it not be made obvious I was the one settling you in."

Knowing better than to ask why he hadn't brought her there, Freya followed him up two flights of stairs to the top floor, pausing to look out the large window on the landing of the staircase. The building was laid out in a square with a large central courtyard that appeared to offer outdoor living space that could be enjoyed in Iladel's warmest months.

When they reached the hallway that contained her living quarters, he pulled a large brass key from his pocket and opened the door, then gestured for Freya to go in.

A short entryway led away from the door into a large room. Two wood-framed sleigh beds were pushed against the walls on either side, one already made up with a soft pink quilt and airy-looking pillows. A small stack of books sat on the nightstand beside it. Matching armoires were built into the walls on either side of the window seat that overlooked the campus grounds. The walls were a similar color to the exterior stone—a pale, unassuming gray—and the floors were made of deep brown hardwood that had been smoothed with age. A pale blue rug embroidered with a complex floral pattern covered most of the floor, which Freya hoped would keep some of the chill at bay once night fell. Despite the summer heat that still permeated the capital, nights in the mountains, even as low as the foothills, often turned chilly in the summer.

"Lea should be arriving a bit later," the commander said, hovering at the mouth of the entryway. "So go on and get yourself settled. And Freya?"

Turning to face him, she gave him a questioning look. "Hmm?"

"Be nice."

She feigned offense, pressing a hand to her heart and letting her mouth drop open in an O of shock. "What little you think of me!"

He gave her a chastising look, then left the room.

There was a slightly musty smell lingering in the air, no doubt a result of the building having been sealed up for several months while the academy was closed for the summer holiday. Moving to the window, she pushed the white sheers aside and slid up the sash, letting in a soft, warm breeze.

She dropped her bag onto the unclaimed bed, then groaned when she realized all of her belongings were still on their way from the port and likely wouldn't arrive for several hours. Cursing Balthana for his haste when they disembarked, she threw open the wardrobe on her side of the room and opened the drawers, breathing a sigh of relief when she found a small pile of white sheets and a blue quilt. They would do for the time being, although she was desperately wishing for the down quilt from her bed in Watoria.

After making her bed, Freya eyed her bag of belongings before looking back at the soft mattress. Seeing no choice between unpacking or sleeping, she kicked off her boots and flopped down on the bed, burying her face in the pillow.

~

"Do you think we should wake her?"

"I don't know!"

"Well, I wouldn't!"

"I don't think Valkyrie take kindly to being woken by strangers."

"They don't," Freya mumbled into her pillow. "And you've already done it so you might as well stop hissing over there." Rolling onto her back, she rubbed her eyes, then sat up, frowning as her mind tried to adjust to the dim light coming through the windows. It seemed she'd slept longer than she intended.

Running a hand through her hair and frowning when her fingers snagged in the tangled brown locks, she looked at the three people standing across the room. A dark-skinned, waifish female with wide, bright blue eyes—Grevillea, she assumed—stood between two males, biting her lip. She had curly, black-brown hair tied up in a chignon and wore a flowing blouse and pants set in pale blue and beige. The male to the girl's right had similar coloring and striking green eyes, with short black hair cut close to his scalp.

The second male, the one who stood to her left, had hair that was a vibrant shade of red, with pale skin and a smattering of freckles across a perfectly straight nose.

Freya inhaled a bit, taking in their scents. The female carried the sweet scent of a witch, but the two males smelled heavily of wolf.

"A witch and two wolves." She stood and gave them all an appraising look. "I'll assume you're Gr—"

"For the love of all that's holy, please do *not* finish that sentence," the girl said, holding up a hand and closing her eyes. "Call me Lea. My proper name was a cruel, drunken trick on my parents' part that I have yet to forgive them for. And yes, I'm a witch."

Freya's lips quirked up in a smile. "Lea it is, then." Angling her head, she addressed the two males. "I don't know who you are, though."

The one on Lea's right lifted a hand in greeting, his green eyes brightening as he smiled. "I'm Lazarus Cailen, Lea's cousin. You can call me Laz."

"Cailen, as in Governor Cailen of Caelora?" Freya asked.

"The very same," Laz confirmed. "Rischa Cailen is my father."

"And King Salazar's cousin, making you one of Aerelius' cousins, too." She arched a brow at the other male. "And you? Are you a governor's son and cousin to the prince, as well?"

"Nephew, actually, and no, there's no relation. I'm Collin Maddix. My uncle is Gunnar Maddix of Allanor," the auburn-haired male said.

"Ah!" Freya smiled. "Yes, I believe my grandfather named your uncle as his successor. I've only met him once, but Governor Maddix seems to be a good man. He's done well by Allanor since he was appointed." As was tradition in Lindoroth, each governor chose their own successor prior to retirement. Freya's grandfather, Governor Jora Enrieth, had retired fifteen years past, naming in his place Lord Gunnar Maddix to succeed him.

"Yes, he always spoke highly of Governor Enrieth and was quite saddened by his passing," Collin told her, tilting his head to the side and running those stunning blue eyes over her. "Don't mind me saying this, but you look different than I expected. More... plain."

Lea smacked his chest. "She doesn't look *plain*, you buffoon."

Collin's eyes widened. "No, I only meant—"

She gave Freya a smile, then stepped forward and held out her hand. "Ignore him, please. He doesn't get out much. They live in the dorm just next door," she said, gesturing toward the window where their building could be seen about twenty yards off.

Freya shook the outstretched hand as she eyed them all suspiciously. "Are you all to be my watchdogs, then?"

Lazarus and Collin exchanged a confused look.

Lea's eyes widened in surprise. "Heavens, no!" She clicked her tongue then made a sound of disgust. "Is that what Balthana told you? Oh, I'm going to wring his—" Cutting herself off, she took a deep breath. "No, Freya, none of us are going to be your 'watchdogs.' Commander Balthana simply wanted to ensure you roomed with someone well-suited to helping you reacclimate to life in the capital. As Aer's cousin, I am just that. These two just like to follow me around," she added, jerking her thumb over her shoulder. "They're easy enough to ignore, though."

Freya bit back a smirk. "Alright, then. I'll hold you to that." At that, her stomach rumbled, reminding her that all she'd had to eat was the sandwich the commander had given her hours earlier. "Well, now that we're such good friends and all, care to tell me where I can get something to eat?"

"The dining hall is open for a few more hours, and we were just about to head over for dinner," Lea said. "We were hoping you'd join us."

"That sounds great," Freya said, surprised at how easy her answering smile came.

"Alright, then!" Lea beamed at her. "Let's go!"

∿

"So, Freya, the most important thing to remember here is that Aldridge is full of cliques," Lea said quietly as the four traversed the grassy expanse of Aldridge's grounds toward the brightly lit stone building that housed dining hall. "Some are better than others, but it'd be in your best interest to cement your status as quickly as possible to avoid the wrong types trying to sink their claws in."

"The wrong types?" Freya eyed her dubiously, hoping her initial opinion of females in the capital wasn't about to be confirmed. "What does that mean?"

"Oh!" Lea covered her mouth with her hand when she realized how her words had been construed. "I don't mean—no, it's just that opportunism is rampant here. There are certain groups who are, to put it simply, cruel. Females, mainly, hoping to detract attention from others in the hopes of finding a mate." She rolled her eyes. "It will be especially awful this year, what with my cousin attending and all."

Freya sighed. "Well, I'm not here to find a mate, so they're in luck."

"They don't know that, though," Collin replied from beside her. "You're quite pretty, and considering your background and the fact that you're a halfblood..."

Lazarus snorted. "What my darling Collin is trying to say is, you will be, without question, competition. Or perceived competition. You won't be given time to prove otherwise before some of the more rabid females here make that determination."

Once again, Freya became suspicious. "How do I know you three aren't simply saying this to keep me close-by?"

Lea looped her arm through Freya's as they approached the outside stone patio of the dining hall, where the scent of deliciously cooking food from inside was wafting toward them. A dozen or so tables were scattered about, some crammed with students, others sitting empty.

"Again, you don't," Lea told her. "And nothing any of us say will convince you otherwise."

Freya looked at her, surprised. "So why should I trust your intentions?"

"Do you trust Commander Balthana?" Lea asked, arching a brow. "Do you trust his judgement?"

"Now and then."

"Then that's all you need for now." Lea paused as Lazarus opened the door for them. "The rest will come in time, Freya, but I do hope we can be friends."

Smiling, Freya followed the three of them into the dining hall, quietly and surprisingly finding herself hoping for the same thing.

Echoing voices buzzed throughout the large hall, far more than Freya had expected, despite the busy nature of campus earlier. Students sat at round tables, some perched on top, others in the benches around them, talking, laughing, and eating. There was a carefree air about the room, the sincerity of which Freya immediately questioned.

Lea tugged on Freya's arm and waved off the males. "Come, let's take a table while Laz and Collin get us some dinner."

Collin looked at Freya in question. "They've got most everything here, so is there anything you don't like?"

"Not in the least," Freya told him. "Feel free to surprise me."

As Lea led her toward the back of the room, Freya noticed two black-uniformed guards standing sentry along the wall. Her eyes were immediately drawn toward the table they were watching over, already knowing what, or who, she'd find there. There, holding court with a number of male and females, was Freya's old friend, the dark-haired Prince Aerelius of House Harridan. A striking female, blond with all the signs of a would-be royal, sat at his side, laughing with the small group that surrounded him. She looked the type to set her goal for a mate high.

There was no question who the female had set her sights on.

Despite not having seen Aerelius for six years, she immediately noticed the muted look of vexation on his face, one he wore when he was annoyed and trying not to show it.

Before Freya could glance away, Aerelius' dark eyes lifted and he sent a look of pure exasperation at Lea before his gaze slid to meet Freya's. His face took on a confused expression, then his lips tilted in a smirk, the same infuriating one she remembered from their youth. The one that somehow made his handsome face even more so.

"He's only here for dinner because the meeting with the head-mistress ran so long," Lea whispered, ignoring him and dragging

Freya's attention away from the prince's table. "I told the boys we wouldn't be sitting with him if the social leeches had descended before we got here, if that's what's got that look on your face. Unless you want to..."

"No, it's fine." Freya forced herself to focus on her roommate. "I'd rather get to know you three, if that's alright."

"Oh, I completely understand, trust me. And to be fair to my cousin, he can't stand the lot of them. He's just got to be polite, you know." They came to a stop at an empty table in front of a picture window that looked out over a large pond. "Maybe now that we have a Valkyrie witch to scare them all off, he won't have to worry about being bothered anymore."

Freya replied with a noncommittal hum as she took a seat across from Lea.

"Well, what can you tell me about this place I'll now call home?" she asked.

Lea puffed out a breath of air, blowing a few stray curls from her forehead. "Goodness, where to begin? Let's see... have you gotten your schedule yet?"

"No, I'm to meet with the headmistress tomorrow."

Lea nodded, narrowing her eyes as she bit her lip. "Well, there's only so much I can say without knowing who your professors will be, although those I've met already seem to be quite fair. As for the student body... I would keep to yourself for the most part, observe more than you interact for the first few days or even the week, otherwise you won't get a proper feel for the place."

"But above all, make sure you mark your place here," Lazarus said, setting two trays down and taking a seat beside her.

"Ideally in Combat," Collin said, putting a tray with a small bowl of soup, a piece of seeded bread, and a plate of fruit in front of Lea while setting another tray loaded with food down at his own place. "Otherwise, females like Myria—the shameless blonde fawning over the prince—will challenge you at the first opportunity they see."

"Yes, make it clear that you are *not* to be fucked with," Lea added sagely.

Freya nearly laughed at the way the curse sounded coming from the pretty girl's lips.

"But you just told me to observe more than interact," she pointed out, picking up her silverware and cutting into the roasted chicken Laz had just given her.

"Socially and in classes," Lea clarified. "I don't quite know what your social skills are like—"

"Lea!" Lazarus hissed.

"Well I don't!" Rolling her eyes, Lea looked at Freya. "You lived in the capital each summer, correct?"

Freya nodded. "Until I was thirteen, yes. Winter Solstice, too."

"Considering your parentage and the length of time you lived in the capital as a child," Lea continued, "I would assume you have some fairly-honed social graces and are highly intelligent. Therefore, you'll have a fair number of males attempting to court you."

All true, Freya thought, but her "fairly-honed social graces" told her not to confirm that.

"Well, I suppose we'll see how things go," Freya said. "I'm certainly not here to be courted."

Collin nodded slowly. "I'd suggest getting that information out there as soon as possible."

"Somehow I don't think that will be an issue," she muttered.

ABOUT THE AUTHOR

Lucy grew up "down the shore" in New Jersey, where her love of the mythological was born when her middle school English teacher introduced her to the Odyssey. After high school, she received Bachelor's degrees in Psychology and English Literature before continuing on to her Master's degree in Library and Information Science. In her spare time, Lucy loves to read, cook, and go hiking with her husband and two daughters. Chaos is her debut novel.

Stay up to date! Hop over to www.lucyroyauthor.com to sign up for Lucy's newsletter, follow her on social media, and read up on news and other bookish things!

ALSO BY LUCY ROY